In Pursuit of
Eliza Cynster

"I can't." Drawing back, still gripping the sill, Eliza raised her eyes to his. "Believe me, I'd like nothing more than to go with you, but I . . ." She reached out and grasped his forearm.

Looking at her hand, he saw it shake as she tightened her grip, just a fraction, but no more.

She released him on a sigh. Met his gaze as he lifted his eyes questioningly to hers. "That's the best I can do—the hardest I can grip anything at the moment. They gave me laudanum for the past three days and it still hasn't worn off. My legs are still shaky, and I can't hold onto anything. If I slip . . ."

A chill coursed down Jeremy's spine. If she slipped . . . he might not be able to catch and hold her and stop her from pitching over the roof's edge. She was tallish, admittedly slender, yet there was enough of her to make him question whether he would be strong enough to hold and save her. "All right." He nodded, keeping both gesture and tone calm and even. "It won't help our cause if either of us falls and breaks a limb, so we'll think of another way."

She blinked as if taken aback, but then nodded. "Yes. Good." She paused, then asked, "Do you have any suggestions?"

By Stephanie Laurens

Stephanie Laurens

In Pursuit of Eliza Cynster

AVON
An Imprint of HarperCollins*Publishers*

AVON BOOKS
An Imprint of HarperCollins*Publishers*
10 East 53rd Street
New York, New York 10022-5299

In Pursuit of
Eliza Cynster

The Cynster Family Tree

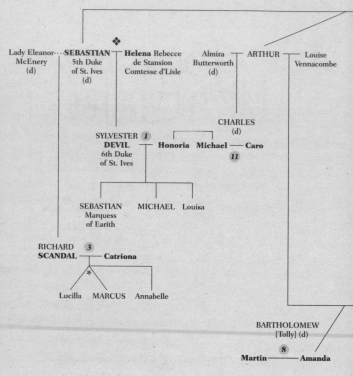

Lady Eleanor····McEnery (d) — **SEBASTIAN** 5th Duke of St. Ives (d) — **Helena** Rebecce de Stansion Comtesse d'Lisle

Almira Butterworth (d) — **ARTHUR** — Louise Vennacombe

CHARLES (d)

SYLVESTER **DEVIL** 1 6th Duke of St. Ives — **Honoria** Michael — **Caro** 11

SEBASTIAN Marquess of Earith   MICHAEL   Louisa

RICHARD **SCANDAL** 3 — **Catriona**

Lucilla   *MARCUS   Annabelle

BARTHOLOMEW [Tolly] (d)

Martin 8 — **Amanda**

MALE Cynsters in capitals   * denotes twins
CHILDREN BORN AFTER 1825 NOT SHOWN

THE CYNSTER NOVELS

1. Devil's Bride   *4.* A Rogue's Proposal   *7.* All About Passion
2. A Rake's Vow   *5.* A Secret Love   *8.* On a Wild Night
3. Scandal's Bride   *6.* All About Love   *9.* On a Wicked Dawn
     10. The Perfect Lover

❖ Cynster Special—The Promise in a Kiss

CBA#1—Casebook of Barnaby Adair #1—Where the Heart Leads

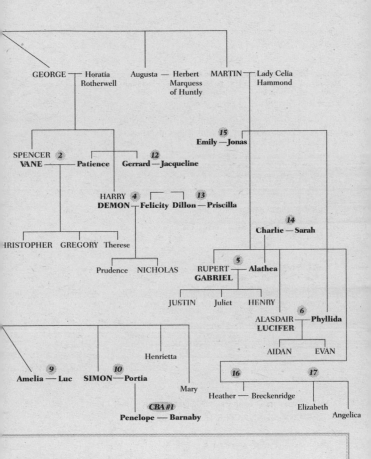

GEORGE — Horatia Rotherwell   Augusta — Herbert Marquess of Huntly   MARTIN — Lady Celia Hammond

15
Emily — Jonas

SPENCER **2**
VANE — Patience   **12**
Gerrard — Jacqueline

HARRY **4**
DEMON — Felicity   Dillon — Priscilla **13**

14
Charlie — Sarah

CHRISTOPHER   GREGORY   Therese

Prudence   NICHOLAS

RUPERT **5**
GABRIEL — **Alathea**

JUSTIN   Juliet   HENRY

ALASDAIR **6**
LUCIFER — **Phyllida**

AIDAN   EVAN

9
Amelia — Luc   SIMON — Portia **10**   Henrietta

Mary

CBA #1
Penelope — Barnaby

16
Heather — Breckenridge   **17**

Elizabeth   Angelica

Prologue

April, 1829
The Green Man Tavern
Auld Town, Edinburgh

As previously discussed, Mr. Scrope, my request is straightforward. I require you to kidnap Miss Eliza Cynster from London and deliver her to me here, in Edinburgh." McKinsey—he was still calling himself that; it was a perfectly good alias, after all—lounged in a booth at the rear of the dimly lit tavern, his gaze leveled on the man seated opposite. "You have had your two weeks to reconnoiter and consider. The only question remaining is whether you can deliver Eliza Cynster to me, unharmed and in good health, or not."

Scrope, dark-haired and dark-eyed, his face long, his features haughty, held his gaze. "After due consideration, I believe we can do business, sir."

"Indeed?" McKinsey lowered his gaze to where his fingers caressed the sides of an ale glass. What was he doing? He didn't trust Scrope as far as he could throw him, and yet here he was, dealing with the man.

His equivocation was genuine, although Scrope would doubtless see it as a ploy—that McKinsey assumed disbelief to keep his price down. In reality, McKinsey thought Scrope would succeed; that was why he was there, hiring a gentleman—Scrope actually was one—known among the wealthy, especially the aristocracy, as the man who could, for a fee, make inconvenient relatives disappear.

In blunt terms, Scrope was a kidnap and disposal specialist. The word about the clubs was that he never failed, which in part explained his exceedingly high price. A price McKinsey, for all his hesitancy, was prepared to pay—doubly over—to have Eliza Cynster delivered into his hands.

Raising his glass, he sipped, then looked at Scrope. "How do you propose to accomplish Miss Cynster's abduction?"

Scrope leaned forward, forearms on the table; folding his hands, he lowered his voice even though there was no one else near enough to hear. "As you predicted, in the wake of the recent failed attempt to kidnap Miss Heather Cynster, Eliza Cynster is being kept under strict and constant guard. Unhelpfully, that guard includes her brothers and cousins—over an entire week she did not once appear in public, even when traveling to and from private functions, without one or more of said gentlemen hovering close. The Cynster family is not relying on mere footmen to keep their young lady safe." Scrope paused, his dark eyes trying to read McKinsey's lighter ones. "To be candid, the only way to lay hands on Eliza Cynster will be to stage some form of ambush. Which, of course, will run the risk of injuring not only her guards. If force is our only option, I cannot guarantee Miss Cynster's safety, not until she's in my keeping."

"No." McKinsey's flat tone made the prohibition absolute. "No violence of any kind. Not toward the young lady, nor even her guards."

Scrope pulled a face and spread his hands. "If you forbid the use of force, then I can't see how the task can be accomplished."

McKinsey arched a brow. One nail slowly tapping the wooden table, he studied Scrope's passably elegant face. No emotion of any kind showed; Scrope's poker face was as good as McKinsey's own.

But his eyes . . .

The man was cold; there was no other word for it. Emotionless, detached, the sort of man who would do murder as easily as dropping his hat.

Unfortunately, fate had left McKinsey few options; he needed someone who could get the job done. Retreat wasn't an option, not now, not for him. But if he was going to unleash the man and send him after Eliza Cynster . . . slowly he straightened, then leaned his elbows on the table so his gaze was level with Scrope's. "I comprehend that this task—stealing Eliza Cynster away from under her powerful family's very noses, even more when said noses are already on guard—will, if completed successfully, elevate your reputation in your chosen field to something akin to a god. If the Cynsters can't protect against you, then who can?"

He'd done his own reconnoitering while Scrope had been in London assessing his chances of kidnapping Eliza Cynster. Scrope was considered to be at the top of his league, but more than one of the previous employers Scrope had cited as references had, when McKinsey, as his true self, had inquired, mentioned Scrope's overweening drive to excel. To succeed beyond question with assignments more cautious hirelings declined. Scrope, it seemed, had become addicted to the glory of pulling off the improbable. His former employers had viewed that as a positive; while agreeing in regard to getting a difficult job done, McKinsey could also see how Scrope's addiction could be used to further his own ends.

Scrope hadn't reacted to McKinsey's statement, but that he was trying so hard to keep his face impassive told its own story.

McKinsey let his lips curve understandingly. "Indeed. With this mission successfully completed, you'll be able to command even higher—quite astronomical—fees."

"My fees—"

McKinsey held up a hand. "I am not about to haggle over your already agreed fee. However"—still holding Scrope's gaze, he let his face harden, let his voice harden, too—"in return for telling you of the one way in which Eliza Cynster can be kidnapped, even in the teeth of her male relatives' protectiveness, without the use of force, I will require one thing."

Scrope hesitated. A full minute ticked by before quietly he asked, "What?"

McKinsey was wise enough not to smile in triumph. "That *we* will plan the action together, from the moment you move to kidnap Miss Cynster to the moment you hand her over to me."

Again Scrope spent a long moment in thought, but McKinsey wasn't at all surprised when eventually Scrope said, "Just to be perfectly clear, you want to dictate how I do this job."

"No. I want to be assured that you will do this job in a way that satisfies my requirements fully. I suggest that once I tell you how the abduction can be accomplished, you suggest how you wish to proceed through each stage. If I agree, you go ahead. If I don't, we discuss alternatives and settle on one that will satisfy us both." He was wagering that Scrope wouldn't be able to walk away from the prospect of being the man who successfully kidnapped a Cynster chit.

Scrope looked away, shifted, then met McKinsey's eyes again. "Very well. I agree." After an instant's pause—if Scrope had been a different man McKinsey would have shaken his hand to seal the deal, but, instead, he sat woodenly waiting—Scrope smoothly went on, "So where and how do I seize Eliza Cynster?"

McKinsey told him. Drawing a folded copy of the London *Gazette* from his coat pocket, he showed Scrope the relevant entry. Scrope hadn't known of the event and was unlikely to have appreciated the potential on his own. It wasn't hard, after that, to work out the details, first of the seizing, then of the journey back to Edinburgh.

Both agreed that the journey should be accomplished with all speed.

"As I will not be disposing of her but rather handing her on, I would prefer to place her into your hands as soon as possible."

"Agreed." McKinsey met Scrope's dark eyes. "No sense in courting danger for longer than you need to."

Scrope's lips pinched, but he said nothing.

"I will," McKinsey went on, "remain in town so as to be on hand to relieve you of Miss Cynster when you return."

Scrope nodded. "I'll send word to the same place through which we arranged this meeting."

McKinsey trapped and held Scrope's gaze. "One point bears repeating—under no circumstance whatever is any harm, of any description, to befall Eliza Cynster while she's in your care. I will accept that it might be necessary to sedate her to effect her silent removal from the house, but thereafter I'm sure it will not prove beyond your abilities, and that of your colleagues, to keep her calm and quiet throughout the journey without recourse to further drugs or unnecessary restraints. The story of fetching her home under her guardian's orders proved effective in controling Heather Cynster. It will work equally well with her sister."

"Very well—we'll use that." Scrope made a show of thinking back over their plan, then met McKinsey's eyes. "I believe, sir, that we have an agreement. By my calculation, we'll be back in Edinburgh with Miss Cynster and ready to hand her over by the fifth morning after seizing her."

"Indeed. By taking the route we discussed, you'll very likely avoid all opposition."

For the first time, Scrope smiled. "As you say."

McKinsey got to his feet.

Scrope did, too. He wasn't a small man, but McKinsey towered over him. Regardless, Scrope's features lit as he confidently stated, "Rest assured, you may rely on me and my colleagues—I am, indeed, as eager as you to see this job brought to a successful conclusion." Scrope's lips lifted as he joined McKinsey in turning toward the tavern door. "It will, as you so rightly noted, make my name."

"It will, as you so rightly noted, make my name."

Hands in his trouser pockets, his greatcoat open and hanging from his shoulders, the wind blowing in his face, the nobleman masquerading as McKinsey stood on a rocky outcrop not far from the walls of Holyrood Palace. Gazing northward toward his home, he replayed yet again Scrope's parting words. It wasn't the words themselves that concerned him—they'd been his own, after all—but Scrope's tone had resonated with an almost fanatical enthusiasm, a disturbingly deep relish.

The man was a damned sight too invested in vaingloriously furthering his reputation than McKinsey liked.

He would have preferred not to deal with a man of Scrope's ilk, but desperate situations made for desperate measures. If he didn't kidnap a Cynster sister and take her north to parade before his mother as "ruined," his mother wouldn't hand over the ceremonial goblet she'd filched and successfully hidden. If he couldn't produce said goblet on the first of July, he would lose his castle and his lands, and be forced to stand helplessly by while his people—his clan—were dispossessed and driven from their centuries-old holdings.

He would lose his heritage, and so would they.

He would lose everything—except for the two boys he'd promised to raise as his own. But they, and he, would lose their rightful place, the one place on earth they truly belonged.

Fate had left him no choice but to satisfy his mother's demands, insane though they might be.

Unfortunately, his first attempt had gone awry. Wanting to remain distanced from the kidnapping and simultaneously seeking to use no more force than necessary, he'd employed a pair of lesser but routinely successful villains known as Fletcher and Cobbins. The pair had kidnapped Heather Cynster and brought her north, but she'd escaped through the intervention of an English nobleman, one Timothy Danvers, Viscount Breckenridge. Breckenridge was now Heather Cynster's fiancé.

That failure had left McKinsey no choice but to engage Scrope to kidnap Eliza Cynster.

No matter how logically he justified that action, he still didn't like it; he remained restless, unsettled—highly uncomfortable with the deal he'd just struck. His prickling instincts were a constant, abrading irritation, as if he were wearing a hair shirt.

He'd felt no such qualms over hiring Fletcher and Cobbins; while capable of violence, the pair hadn't been the sort to contemplate murder, not readily. In contrast, Scrope's business normally involved murder. While in this instance murder wasn't on the agenda, that the man had a proven propensity for the act was anything but reassuring.

But McKinsey needed Eliza Cynster delivered into his hands in short order. With Fletcher and Cobbins, he'd stipulated any of the Cynster sisters—Heather, Eliza, or Angelica—yet by the time they'd seized Heather, he'd learned enough to realize his mistake. He'd been hugely relieved that it had been Heather they'd abducted; at twenty-five years old, on the shelf marriage-wise, she'd been all but tailor-made for the proposition he'd intended to lay before her.

Yet that hadn't come to be. Fate had intervened and Heather had escaped with Breckenridge. McKinsey hadn't been overly perturbed, knowing he had an alternative in Eliza; at twenty-four, she was almost as well-suited to his purpose as Heather. But if he didn't succeed in securing Eliza . . .

Angelica was the third and youngest of the sisters on the critical branch of the Cynster family tree. Theoretically, she could serve to fulfill his purpose, but she was only twenty-one. He had no wish to deal with a young lady of her age.

He could be patient when a situation required it, but he wasn't an inherently patient man. Inveigling a giddy, twenty-one-year-old haut ton princess to fall in with his wishes would require greater tact than he possessed.

And the alternative of forcing her to his will would require the exercise of a greater degree of coldhearted pressure than he suspected he could bring to bear. Not and live with himself thereafter.

So . . . Eliza Cynster it had to be, and for that he needed Scrope's talents and the man's drive to succeed.

He'd done all he could to ensure Eliza's safety and comfort, done all he could to ensure nothing went wrong. Yet . . .

Staring at the purple haze on the horizon, the mountains many miles beyond which his home—glen, loch, and castle—lay, he tried to tell himself he'd done all he could, that he could now, as he'd planned, return home—to his people, to the castle, to the boys—and return later, in time to be waiting when Scrope returned with Eliza Cynster.

Honor above all.

His family's motto, the words inscribed in stone over the castle's main doors and on all the major fireplaces.

Honor wouldn't let him ride away.

Honor kept pricking, a burr beneath his skin.

Now he'd unleashed Scrope on the Cynsters, now he'd shown Scrope exactly how to spirit Eliza out from under her family's watchful noses, now he'd set his plan in motion, honor insisted he ride guard.

That he follow Scrope and, surreptitiously, clandestinely, keep watch and ensure nothing went wrong.

Ensure Scrope didn't exceed his remit.

He stood looking out over the flatter lowlands to the highlands far away. Remained there, unmoving, his mind yearning for the peace, the intense silence, his senses questing for the scent of pine and fir, while the sun slowly westered and darkness closed in.

The shadows deepened. Eventually, he stirred. Straightening, hands still sunk in his pockets, he turned and climbed back to the street, then headed for his town house. Head down, his gaze on the cobbles, he composed a letter to his steward explaining he'd been delayed and would return in a few weeks. After that . . . he hoped and prayed he'd be able to ride home to the highlands with Eliza Cynster by his side.

Chapter One

St. Ives House
Grosvenor Square, London

J t's just not fair." Elizabeth Marguerite Cynster, Eliza to all, grumbled the complaint beneath her breath as she stood alone, cloaked in the shadows of a massive potted palm by the wall of her eldest cousin's ballroom. Tonight, the magnificent ducal ballroom was glittering and glowing, playing host to the crème de la crème of the ton, bedecked in their finest satins and silks, bejeweled and beringed, all swept up in a near-rapturous outpouring of happiness and unbridled delight.

As there were few among the ton likely to decline an invitation to waltz at an event hosted by Honoria, Duchess of St. Ives, and her powerful husband, Devil Cynster, the huge room was packed.

The light from the sparkling chandeliers sheened over elaborately coiffed curls and winked and blinked from the hearts of countless diamonds. Gowns in a range of brilliant hues swirled as the ladies danced, creating a shifting sea of vibrant plumage contrasting with the regulation black-and-white of their partners. Laughter and conversation blanketed the scene. A riot of perfumes filled the air. In the background a small orchestra strove to deliver one of the most popular waltzes.

Eliza watched as her elder sister, Heather, circled the

dance floor in the arms of her handsome husband-to-be, ex-foremost rake of the ton, Timothy Danvers, Viscount Breckenridge. Even if the ball had not been thrown expressly to celebrate their betrothal, to formally announce it to the ton and the polite world, the besotted look in Breckenridge's eyes every time his gaze rested on Heather was more than enough to tell the tale. The ex-darling of the ton's ladies was now Heather's sworn protector and slave.

And Heather was his. The joy in her face, that lit her eyes, declared that to the world.

Despite Eliza's own less-than-happy state, much of it a direct outcome of the events leading to Heather's engagement, Eliza was sincerely, to her soul, happy for her sister.

They'd both spent years—literally *years*—searching for their respective heroes among the ton, through the drawing rooms and ballrooms in which young ladies such as they were expected to confine themselves in hunting for suitable, eligible partis. Yet neither Heather, Eliza, nor Angelica, their younger sister, had had any luck in locating the gentlemen fated to be their heroes. They had, logically, concluded that said heroes, the gentlemen for them, were not to be found within their prescribed orbit, so they had, also logically, decided to extend their search into those areas where the more elusive, yet still suitable and eligible, male members of the ton congregated.

That strategy had worked for their eldest female cousin, Amanda, and, employed with a different twist, for her twin sister, Amelia, as well.

And, albeit in a most unexpected way, the same approach had worked for Heather, too.

Clearly for Cynster females, success in finding their own true hero lay in boldly stepping beyond their accustomed circles.

Which was precisely what Eliza was set on doing, *except* that, through the adventure that had befallen Heather within minutes of her taking her first step into that racier world—

namely being kidnapped, rescued by Breckenridge, and then escaping in his company—a plot to target "the Cynster sisters" had been exposed.

Whether the targets were limited to Heather, Eliza, and Angelica, or included their younger cousins, Henrietta and Mary, no one knew.

No one understood the motive behind the threat, not even what was eventually intended beyond kidnapping the victim and possibly taking her to Scotland. As for who was behind it, no one had any real clue, but the upshot was that Eliza and the other three "Cynster sisters" as yet unbetrothed had been placed under constant guard. She hadn't been able to set toe outside her parents' house without one of her brothers, or if not them, one of her cousins—every bit as bad—appearing at her elbow.

And looming.

For her, taking even half a step outside the restrictive circles of the upper echelons of the ton was now impossible. If she tried, a large, male, brotherly or cousinly hand would close about her elbow and yank her unceremoniously back.

Such behavior on their part was, she had to admit, understandable, but . . . "For how long?" Their protective cordon had been in place for three weeks and showed no signs of relaxing. "I'm already twenty-four. If I don't find my hero this year, next year I'll be on the shelf."

Muttering to herself wasn't a habit, but the evening was drawing to a close and, as usual at such ton events, nothing had come of it for her. Which was why she was hugging the wall in the screening shadows of the huge palm; she was worn out with smiling and pretending she had any interest whatever in the very proper young gentlemen who, through the night, had vied for her attention.

As a well-dowered, well-bred, well brought-up Cynster young lady she'd never been short of would-be Romeos. Sadly, she'd never felt the slightest inclination to play Juliet to any of them. Like Angelica, Eliza was convinced she would recognize her hero, if not in the instant she laid eyes on him—Angelica's theory—then at least once she'd spent a few hours in his company.

Heather, in contrast, had always been uncertain over recognizing her hero—but then she'd known Breckenridge, not well but more than by sight, for many years, and until their adventure she hadn't realized he was the one for her. Heather had mentioned that their cousin by marriage, Catriona, who, being an earthly representative of the deity known in parts of Scotland as "The Lady," tended to "know" things, had suggested that Heather needed to "see" her hero clearly, which had proved very much to be the case.

Catriona had given Heather a necklace and pendant designed to assist a young lady in finding her true love—her hero; Catriona had said the necklace was supposed to be passed from Heather, to Eliza, to Angelica, then to Henrietta and Mary, before ultimately returning to Scotland, to Catriona's daughter, Lucilla.

Raising one hand, Eliza touched the fine chain interspersed with small amethyst beads that circled her neck; the rose quartz pendant depending from it was hidden in the valley between her breasts. The chain lay concealed beneath the delicate lace of the fashionable fichu and collar that filled the scooped neckline of her gold silk gown.

The chain was now hers, so where was the hero it was supposed to help her recognize?

Obviously not here. No gentleman with hero-potential had miraculously appeared. Not that she had expected one to, not here in the very heart of the upper echelons of tonnish society. Nevertheless, disappointment and dragging dejection bloomed.

Through finding her hero, Heather had—entirely unintentionally, but nevertheless effectively—stymied Eliza. Her hero did not exist within tonnish circles, but she could no longer step outside to hunt him down.

"What the devil am I to do?"

A footman drifting around the outskirts of the ballroom with a silver salver balanced on one hand heard her and turned to peer into the shadows. Eliza barely glanced at him, but seeing her, his features relaxed and he stepped forward.

"Miss Eliza." Relief in his voice, the footman bowed and offered the salver. "A gentleman asked that this be delivered to you, miss. A good half hour ago, it must be now. We couldn't find you in the crowd."

Wondering which tedious gentleman was now sending her notes, Eliza reached for the folded parchment resting on the salver. "Thank you, Cameron."

The footman was from her parents' household, seconded to the St. Ives' household to assist with the massive ball. "Who was it, do you know?"

"No, miss. It wasn't handed to me but to one of the others. They passed it on."

"Thank you." Eliza nodded a dismissal.

With a brief bow, Cameron withdrew.

With no great expectations, Eliza unfolded the note. The writing was bold, a series of brash, black strokes on the white paper.

Very masculine in style.

Tipping the sheet to catch the light, Eliza read:

Meet me in the back parlor, if you dare. No, we're not acquainted. I haven't signed this note because my name will mean nothing to you. We haven't been introduced, and there is no grande dame present who would be likely to oblige me. However, the fact I am here, attending this ball, speaks well enough to my antecedents and my social standing. And I know where the back parlor is.

I believe it is time we met face-to-face, if nothing else to discover if there is any further degree of association we might feel inclined to broach.

*As I started this note, so I will end it: Meet me in the
back parlor, if you dare.
I'll be waiting.*

Eliza couldn't help but smile. How . . . impertinent. How
daring. To send her such a note in her cousin's house, under
the very noses of the grandes dames and all her family.

Yet whoever he was, he was patently there, in the house,
and if he knew where the back parlor was . . .

She read the note again, debating, but there was no reason
she could see why she shouldn't slip away to the back parlor
and discover who it was who had dared send such a note.

Stepping out from her hiding place, she slipped swiftly, as
unobtrusively as she could, around the still crowded room.
She felt certain the note-writer was correct—she didn't
know him; they'd never met. She didn't know any gentleman who would have thought to send such an outrageous
summons to a private tryst inside St. Ives House.

Excitement, anticipation, surged. Perhaps this was it—the
moment when her hero would appear before her.

Stepping through a minor door, she walked quickly down a
corridor, then turned down another, then another, increasingly
dimly lit, steadily making her way to the rear corner of the huge
mansion. Deep in the private areas, distant from the reception
rooms and their noise, the back parlor gave onto the gardens at
the rear of the house; Honoria often sat there of an afternoon,
watching her children play on the lawn below the terrace.

Eliza finally reached the end of the last corridor. The
parlor door stood before her. She didn't hesitate; turning the
knob, she opened the door and walked in.

The lamps weren't lit, but moonlight poured through the
windows and glass doors that gave onto the terrace. Glancing around and seeing no one, she closed the door and
walked deeper into the room. Perhaps he was waiting in one
of the armchairs facing the windows.

Nearing the chairs, she saw they were empty. She halted. Frowned. Had he given up and left? "Hello?" She started to turn. "Is there anyone—"

A faint rush of sound came from behind her.

She whirled—too late.

A hard arm snaked about her waist and jerked her back against a solid male body.

She opened her mouth—

A huge palm swooped and slapped a white cloth over her mouth and nose. And held it there.

She struggled, breathed in—the smell was sickly sweet, cloying . . .

Her muscles went to water.

Even as she sagged, she fought to turn her head, but the heavy palm followed, keeping the horrid cloth over her mouth and nose . . .

Until reality slid away and darkness engulfed her.

Eliza swam back to consciousness on a sickening sway.

She was rocking, swinging; she couldn't seem to stop. Then her senses steadied and she recognized the rattle of coach wheels on cobbles.

A coach. She was in a coach, being taken . . .

My God—I've been kidnapped!

Shocked surprise, followed by pure panic, shot through her. And helped focus her wits. She hadn't yet tried opening her eyes; her lids felt weighted, as did her limbs. Even shifting a fingertip took effort. She didn't think her hands or feet were bound, but as she could barely summon enough strength to think, that was of little immediate relevance.

Besides, there was someone . . . no, two someones, in the coach with her.

Remaining as she had been when she'd awoken, slumped in a corner, her head hanging forward, she reached with her other senses. When that told her no more than that there was a person on the seat beside her, with another on the seat opposite, she let her head loll with the next big sway of the coach, then forced her lids up enough to look out from beneath her lashes.

A man sat opposite, a gentleman by his dress. The planes of his face were austere, rather long, his chin square. His hair was dark brown, wavy, well cut. He was tall, well built, lean rather than heavy. She suspected it was his body she'd been hauled back against in the back parlor. His large hand that had held that horrible-smelling cloth over her nose . . .

Her head throbbed; her stomach pitched at the memory of the vapor from that cloth. Breathing deeply through her nose, she pushed the remembered sensations aside and shifted her attention to the person alongside her.

A woman. Without turning her head, she couldn't see the woman's face, but the gown covering the woman's legs suggested she was a lady's maid. An upper-class lady's maid, a dresser, perhaps; the black fabric of the gown was of better quality than a mere housemaid would have.

Just as with Heather. Her sister had been provided with a lady's maid for her kidnapping as well. Their family had taken that as proof that it had been an aristocrat behind the kidnapping; who else would have thought of a maid? That seemed the case this time, too. Was the man sitting opposite her their aristocratic villain?

Studying him again, Eliza suspected not. Heather had been abducted by hirelings, and although—from what she could see compared with Heather's descriptions—this man, and the maid, too, looked to be a cut above those who'd kidnapped Heather, they nevertheless struck Eliza as people employed to do a job.

Her mind was clearing; it was becoming easier to think.

If this was a repeat of Heather's kidnapping, they would take Eliza north to Scotland. Shifting her gaze, she surveyed the street beyond the coach's window. Still feigning unconsciousness, she surreptitiously watched; it took some time, but finally she was certain the coach wasn't on the Great

North Road. It was following the road her family took when visiting Lady Jersey at Osterley Park.

They were taking her west. Or were they not taking her far from London at all?

If they didn't take her north, would her family know in which direction to search for her? They would assume she'd been taken north . . . when they eventually realized she'd been kidnapped at all.

Whoever these people were, they were bold and clever. Eliza's brothers and cousins had been watching her, of all the Cynster girls, most assiduously, but the one place in which they'd assumed she would be safe had been St. Ives House, and they'd relaxed their vigilance.

No one would have imagined that kidnappers would dare strike inside that house, of all houses, and especially not tonight. The mansion had been teeming with guests, with family, with the combined staff of various Cynster households, all of whom knew her.

Despite her earlier griping, she would have given a great deal to see Rupert or Alasdair, or even one of her arrogant cousins, come racing up on a horse.

After being such pests, where were her protectors now that she needed them?

She frowned.

"She's awake."

It was the man who'd spoken. Clinging to her pretence, Eliza let her features slowly ease, as if she'd frowned in her sleep. Letting her lids close fully, she made no other movement, gave no sign she'd heard.

The woman shifted nearer; Eliza sensed she was peering at her face.

"Are you sure?"

The woman was definitely a dresser; her diction was good, her tone that of an upper servant to an equal.

Which confirmed Eliza's suspicion that the man was a

hireling, too, not the mysterious laird they'd thought had been behind Heather's kidnapping.

After an instant, the man replied, "She's faking it. Use the laudanum."

Laudanum?

"You said he told you no drugs, no harm to her."

"He did, but we need to move fast and we need her asleep—and he'll never know."

He who?

"All right." The woman was rummaging in some bag. "You'll have to help me."

"No!" Eliza came to life, intending to convince them not to drug her again, but she'd overestimated her recovery. Her voice was a hoarse whisper. She tried to push away the woman, black-haired, dark-eyed, leaning toward her with a small medicine glass containing a pale liquid, but her arms had no strength.

Then the man was on her; manacling her wrists in one hand, with the other he caught her chin, tipped her face up.

"Now! Pour it down her throat."

Eliza fought to shut her mouth, but the man pressed his thumb to the corner of her jaw and the woman deftly tipped the dose between her lips.

Eliza tried not to swallow but the liquid trickled down . . .

The man held her until her muscles went lax and the laudanum dragged her down.

The next time Eliza managed to gather her wits enough to think, days had passed. How many, she had no real idea; they'd kept her drugged, propped in the corner of the coach, and had driven on, as far as she knew without any real halt.

Her whole body felt ridiculously weak. Keeping her eyes closed, she let her mind slowly sort through and align the jumbled snippets of information and sparse observations she'd managed to glean in the fleeting moments between the long stretches of drugged insensibility.

They'd taken her out of London on the westward road; she remembered that. Then . . . Oxford at daybreak; she'd caught a brief glimpse of the familiar spires against a lightening sky.

After that first dose of laudanum, they'd been judicious in its use, forcing her to down only enough to keep her woozy and sleepy, unable to do anything, much less escape. So she had faint memories of passing through other towns, of church spires and market squares, but the only place she recalled with any certainty was York. They'd passed close by the Minster . . . she thought it had been earlier that morning. The pealing bells had been so loud the sound had hauled her to wakefulness, but then the coach had turned and passed out of the town gate, and she'd slid back into slumber.

That had been the last time she'd woken. Now . . . letting her head loll, with her lids still too weighty to lift, she reached with her other senses.

And smelled the sea. The distinctive briny scent was strong, the breeze slipping past the edge of the carriage door sharp and fresh. She heard gulls, their raucous caw unmistakable. So . . . past York and out along the coast.

Where did that leave her?

So far from London, once off the Great North Road her knowledge of the region was spotty. But if they'd traveled to Oxford, then to York . . . it seemed likely her captors were indeed taking her into Scotland, but avoiding the Great North Road, no doubt because her family would search its length for her.

If her captors had avoided traveling along the major highway entirely, it was possible that no trace of her would be found, not along the highway itself. Which, she suspected, meant that there would be no one riding to her rescue . . . or at least that she couldn't count on her family arriving to save her.

She was going to have to save herself.

The thought shook her. Adventures weren't her forte. She left such things to Heather, and even more Angelica; she, in contrast, was the quiet sister. The middle sister. The one who played the pianoforte and harp like an angel, and actually loved to embroider.

But if she wanted to escape—and she was quite sure she did—she would have to act, by herself, for herself.

Drawing in a deeper breath, she forced her lids open and carefully looked at her companions.

It was the first time she'd had a chance to study them in daylight; they usually noticed she was awakening and quickly drugged her again. The female guard—the one she'd originally taken for a dresser—she now suspected was a nurse-companion, the sort wealthy ton families hired to look after ageing relatives. The woman was neat, efficient, well spoken, and in appearance well presented. Her bountiful dark hair was drawn back in a severe bun at her nape; her pale face and features suggested she was perhaps gentry-born but had fallen on hard times.

There was definitely a hardness in the lines of her face, and even more in her eyes.

The nurse was, Eliza judged, of similar height and build to herself on the tall side of average height, middling to slender build—and perhaps a few years older. However, being a nurse, the other woman was significantly stronger.

Eliza shifted her gaze to the man who throughout the journey had remained seated opposite her. She'd seen him at closer quarters several times, when he'd held her so the nurse could drug her. He wasn't the mysterious laird; she'd recalled the description Breckenridge had gathered of that elusive nobleman: *"a face like hewn granite and eyes like ice."*

While the man sitting opposite had clean-cut features, they weren't especially rugged or chiseled, and his eyes settled the matter; they were dark brown.

"She's awake again." It was the nurse who'd noticed.

The man had been looking out of the window. He swung his gaze to Eliza.

"Do you want to drug her again?" the nurse asked.

The man caught and held Eliza's gaze.

She looked back at him and said nothing.

The man tilted his head, considering. After a long moment, he replied, "No."

Eliza surreptitiously exhaled. She'd had more than enough of being drugged.

The man shifted, rearranging his limbs, then looked at the nurse. "We need her in her customary excellent health by the time we reach Edinburgh, so we'd better cease drugging her from now."

Edinburgh?

Lifting her head, straightening her slumped shoulders, then settling back against the coach's padded seat, Eliza openly and rather haughtily studied the man. "And you are?"

Her voice was hoarse, still weak.

The man met her gaze, then his lips quirked, and he inclined his head. "Scrope. Victor Scrope." His gaze shifted to the nurse. "And this is Genevieve." Looking back at Eliza, Scrope continued, "Genevieve and I, and our coachman-guard, have been sent by your guardian to fetch you back from wicked London, to which you had fled from his isolated estate."

Eliza listened as he outlined essentially the same tale Heather's kidnappers had used to ensure Heather's compliance.

"I've been told," Scrope continued, "that you are, as your sister was before you, intelligent enough to comprehend that, given our tale, any attempt to attract attention and plead your cause to anyone en route will only result in you irretrievably damaging your own reputation."

When he arched a brow at her and waited, Eliza curtly nodded. "Yes. I understand."

Her voice was still weak, soft, but its strength was returning.

"Excellent," Scrope said. "I should add that we will shortly be crossing into Scotland, where any attempt to gain help will be even more futile. And in case you were too incapacitated to notice, we've avoided traveling on the Great North Road. Even if your famous family search up and down its length, they'll find no trace of your passing." Scrope caught her gaze, held it. "So there's no likelihood of rescue from that quarter. The next few days will be much easier for us all if you accept that you are my captive and that I will not be releasing you until I give you into my employer's hands."

His calm, cold confidence brought to mind an iron cage.

Eliza nodded again, but her mind was, somewhat to her surprise, already reviewing, assessing, searching for some way out. Scrope's reference to Heather confirmed that his employer was indeed the same mysterious laird believed to be behind Heather's kidnapping, and Eliza was perfectly sure she didn't want to be handed over to him. Waiting to escape until after she was in the laird's hands might well be akin to waiting to drop from the frying pan into the fire before reacting to the heat. So . . . if she couldn't count on any help from her family, how was she to escape?

Turning her head, she looked out at the passing scenery, in the distance, beyond rocky cliffs, she could see the sea glimmering under the weak sun. If they'd passed through York this morning . . . she wasn't sure, but she suspected that whatever coach road they were on, they would have to pass through at least one major town before the border.

She didn't want to wait until after crossing the border to do whatever she was going to do; as Scrope had intimated, being in Scotland would only further reduce her prospects for rescue.

And it was rescue she needed. With her captors' tale at the ready, attempting to directly free herself would only lead to social disaster.

Like Heather, she needed her hero to appear and whisk her out of danger.

Heather had got Breckenridge. Who would come for her? No one, because no one had any idea where she was.

Breckenridge had seen Heather kidnapped; he'd followed her from the start. No one, Eliza felt certain, had any idea where she'd gone.

If she wanted someone to rescue her, she was going to have to do something to make that happen.

She wished she had Angelica with her; her younger sister would be bursting with ideas, jigging with enthusiasm to try them out. Eliza, in contrast, couldn't think of any clever plan beyond the obvious one of exploiting the single loophole in her captors' tale of fetching her for her guardian.

If she could attract the attention of someone who knew her, someone of the ton, then her captors' tale would never stand. And given her family's wealth and influence, there was every chance that the shocking fact of her being in her captors' hands for days and nights could subsequently be buried.

But any such rescue would have to occur this side of the border; once in Scotland, her chances of sighting anyone who knew her, and their ability to talk her out of her captors' custody, would be greatly reduced.

Shifting back into her corner of the coach, she trained her gaze forward, scanning the occasional vehicles traveling toward her. If she saw anyone likely . . .

In this far distant corner of England, she knew only two families well—the Variseys at Wolverstone, and the Percys at Alnwick. But if her captors continued to avoid the Great North Road, her chances of sighting any member of those households wouldn't be high.

Looking at Scrope, she asked, "How long before we cross the border?" She managed to make the question sound idle enough.

Scrope glanced outside, then pulled out a fob-watch and

consulted it. "It's just after midday, so we should be in Scotland by late afternoon." Tucking the watch back into his pocket, he glanced at Genevieve. "We'll halt at Jedburgh for the night, as planned, then go on to Edinburgh tomorrow morning."

Eliza looked outside again, staring out at the road. She'd been to Edinburgh twice. If they left Jedburgh in the morning, they'd be in the Scottish capital by midday, and from what Scrope had let fall, that was where they planned to hand her to the laird.

But if they weren't going to cross the border until late afternoon, and it was just after midday now, she was fairly certain that the coastal road they were on would take them through Newcastle-Upon-Tyne, the nearest major town to both Wolverstone and Alnwick, and, if she remembered correctly, the coach would have to traverse the entire breadth of the town to pick up the road to Jedburgh.

If it was market day, or even if it wasn't, rolling slowly through Newcastle-Upon-Tyne would be her best chance to attract the attention of someone she knew, in a town where that someone could readily command the support of the authorities.

Adventure might not be her forte, but she could do this. She could manage this.

Relaxing against the squabs, she gazed out at the road and waited for the roofs of Newcastle to appear.

The sun broke through the clouds and beamed down; the warmth made her sleepy, but she fought off the temptation. She wriggled, straightened, stretched, then settled back. The glare off the next section of road, wet after a passing spring shower, hurt her eyes.

She closed them, had to, just for a moment. Just until the stinging eased.

Eliza woke with a jolt. For a second she didn't remember . . . then she did. She recalled what she'd been waiting for, glanced at the window, and realized that more than an hour had to have passed.

They were crossing a reasonable-sized bridge; the different sound of the wheels on the wooden planks had woken her.

Heart pounding, she sat up and looked out to see houses lining the road. Relief poured through her. They must be heading into Newcastle-Upon-Tyne. She hadn't missed her moment.

Wriggling on the seat, she eased her shoulders and back, then, spine now straight, settled to once again stare out of the window.

Willing someone she knew to be there, walking the pavements of the town. Perhaps Minerva, Duchess of Wolverstone, might be there shopping.

Preferably with her husband.

Eliza couldn't think of anyone more able to effect her rescue than Royce, Duke of Wolverstone.

She felt Scrope's watchful gaze on her face but paid him no heed. She had to keep her eyes peeled. Once she saw someone, she would act, and it would be too late for Scrope to stop her.

Only . . . the further they went, the houses thinned, then finally ceased altogether.

She'd woken only as they'd left the town, not, as she'd thought, as they'd rolled into it.

She'd missed her chance.

Her best, and very likely last, chance to attract the attention of someone who knew her.

For the first time in her life, she actually felt her heart sink.

All the way to the pit of her stomach.

She swallowed; slowly, she eased back against the seat.

Her mind in turmoil, she didn't look at Scrope, but sensed when he looked away, when he relaxed his vigilance.

He knew there was little likelihood she could do anything to upset his plans now.

"That," Scrope said, ostensibly speaking to Genevieve, "was the last large town before the border. It's mostly open country between here and Jedburgh—Taylor should have us there well before dusk."

Genevieve made a humming sound in acknowledgment.

Eliza wondered if Scrope could read her mind. If his purpose was to deflate and deject her, he'd succeeded.

She continued looking out of the window, staring out even though she'd lost all hope. This was definitely not the Great North Road; she'd traveled the stretch from Newcastle to Alnwick several times. She'd never traveled this way before, but fields already bordered the ditches. What roofs she spied belonged to cottages and farmhouses.

The coach bowled steadily on, carrying her further north, its wheels rumbling in a constant, unrelenting rhythm. Now and again, another conveyance rolled by, mostly farm carts.

Gradually, the road narrowed. Every time the coach encountered another vehicle going the opposite way, both had to slow and ease past.

Eliza blinked. She didn't straighten, instead counseling herself to remain relaxed—dejected. To give no sign that might trigger Scrope's watchfulness.

If by any chance at all someone useful might happen along, in a carriage, gig, or cart driving south to Newcastle . . . she was sitting on the right side of the coach to attract that person's attention.

Her situation was desperate. Even if she saw a country squire—any gentry at all—she had to be prepared to seize the moment and scream for help. As matters stood, her family wouldn't know where she was being taken. Even if the person she alerted did nothing more than write to someone in London, that would be enough. Someone would tell her parents.

She had to believe that.

She had to alert someone, and this stretch before the border was her very last chance.

If an opportunity presented, any opportunity at all, she had to seize it.

Gaze fixed, apparently unseeing, on the road ahead, she vowed she would. She might not possess Heather's stubborn determination, she might not have Angelica's reckless lack of fear, but she'd be damned if she'd allow herself to be handed over to some Scottish laird without making even one bid for freedom.

She might be the quiet one; that didn't mean she was meek.

Jeremy Carling tooled his curricle around a sharp bend, then settled to a steady pace heading south on the first leg of his long journey back to London.

He'd left Wolverstone Castle at midday, but instead of heading east via Rothbury and Pauperhaugh to join the road to Morpeth and Newcastle-Upon-Tyne, the route he had, as usual, used to reach the castle, he'd elected to take the westerly route along the northern edges of the Harwood Forest, joining the lesser road to Newcastle just south of Otterburn.

He enjoyed seeing fresh fields, as it were, and although the less-traveled way over the hills had slowed him, the views had more than compensated.

With a better surfaced road beneath his curricle's wheels, he let his latest acquisition, a high-bred black he'd named Jasper, stretch his legs. About him the afternoon was waning, but he would still reach Newcastle and the inn he usually patronized well before dark. Freed from the need to think about anything practical, his mind drifted, as it usually did, to the contemplation of ancient hieroglyphics, the study of hieroglyphics being the cornerstone of his life.

He'd first become fascinated with the esoteric word-pictures when, on the death of their parents, he and his sister Leonora had gone to live with their widower uncle, Sir Humphrey Carling. Jeremy had been twelve at the time and insatiably curious, a trait that hadn't waned. Humphrey had, even then, been widely recognized as the foremost authority on ancient languages, especially Mesopotamian and Sumerian scripts; his house had been littered with scrolls and musty tomes, with papyrus bundles and inscribed cylinders.

Easing Jasper around a bend, Jeremy thought back to those long-ago days and smiled.

The ancient texts, the languages, the hieroglyphics, had captured him from the instant he'd first set eyes on them. Translating them, unlocking their secrets, had rapidly become a passion. While other gentlemen's sons went to Eton and Harrow, he, established from an early age as an able and impatient scholar, had had private tutors and Humphrey, a remarkable scholar himself, as his mentors. Where other gentlemen his age had old school friends, he had old colleagues.

And that life had suited him to the ground; he'd taken to it like the proverbial fish to water.

As both Humphrey and he were independently wealthy, in his case via a sizeable inheritance from his parents, he and his uncle had happily immersed themselves, elbow to elbow, in their ancient tomes, largely to the exclusion of polite society and, indeed, most company other than that of like-minded scholars.

Had matters allowed, they would probably have continued in comfortable seclusion for the rest of both their lives, but Jeremy's assumption several years ago of the mantle Humphrey had for decades carried had coincided with an explosion of public interest in all things ancient. That in turn had led to frequent requests for consultations from private institutions and wealthy families attempting to verify the authenticity and standing of tomes discovered in their collections. Although Humphrey still consulted occasionally, he'd grown frail with the years, so running the increasingly businesslike enterprise of consulting on matters ancient for society at large fell mostly on Jeremy's shoulders.

His reputation was now such that owners of ancient

manuscripts frequently offered outrageous sums to secure his opinion. In certain circles it had become all the rage to be able to state that one's ancient Mesopotamian scroll had been verified by none other than the highly respected Jeremy Carling.

Jeremy's lips twitched at the thought. And the one that followed; the wives of the men who sought his opinion were every bit as keen to have him visit, to be able to claim the cachet of having entertained the famous, yet so-reclusive, scholar.

In social terms, his eschewing of society had rebounded on him. Given he was well born, well connected, well respected, reassuringly wealthy, and tantalizingly elusive, to many hostesses his very reclusiveness made him a major prize; the machinations to which some had gone to attempt to socially ensnare him and keep him a permanent captive had amazed even him.

None had succeeded, and none would; he liked his quiet life.

Although consulting for wider society was lucrative and often satisfying, by choice he spent most of his time buried in his library translating, studying, and publishing on works that either found their way into his hands or were brought to him, as a renowned scholar and collector, by the various august public institutions presently engaged in the serious research of ancient civilizations.

Such academic studies and contributions would form the bulk, the meat, of his scholar's legacy; that sphere would always remain his principal interest.

In that, he and Humphrey were two peas in a pod, both perfectly content to sit in the massive twin libraries—one each—in the home they shared in Montrose Place in London and pore over one or another ancient tome. The only lure guaranteed to tease either of them out of their scholarly seclusion was the prospect of discovering some unknown treasure.

Scholars such as they lived for such moments. The thrill of identifying some ancient, long-lost text was a drug like no other, one to which they were, as a species, addicted beyond recall.

It was just such a lure that had drawn him all the way into the far reaches of Northumberland to Wolverstone Castle, the home of Royce Varisey, Duke of Wolverstone, and his duchess, Minerva. Royce and Minerva were close friends of Leonora and her husband, Tristan Wemyss, Viscount Trentham; over the years, Jeremy had come to know the ducal couple quite well. Consequently, when Royce had been cataloguing his late father's massive library and had discovered an ancient book of hieroglyphics, it had been to Jeremy he'd turned for an opinion.

Grinning to himself, Jeremy flicked the reins and sent Jasper the Black pacing on. His luck had been in; Royce's book had been a fantastic find, a long-thought-to-be-lost Sumerian text. Jeremy couldn't wait to tell Humphrey about it, and he was equally keen to get started on compiling a lecture for The Royal Society from the copious notes he'd made. His conclusions would cause quite a stir.

Expectant pleasure a warmth in his veins, his thoughts focused ahead, throwing up a mental picture of his library, of his home.

The peace of it, the comfort and quiet of it.

The emptiness.

Sobering, he was tempted to push the thought aside, to bury it as he usually did, but . . . he was in the middle of nowhere with nothing else vying for his mind. Perhaps it was time he dealt with the problem.

He wasn't sure when or why the restless undercurrent of dissatisfaction had started. It had nothing to do with his work—the outlook there was positively glowing. He still felt riveted by his chosen profession, still as absorbed as ever by his longtime interest, his chosen field.

The restlessness had nothing to do with hieroglyphics.

The unwanted uneasiness came from inside him, a burgeoning, welling, unsettling feeling that he'd missed something vital, that he'd somehow failed.

Not in work, but in life.

Over the two weeks he'd spent at Wolverstone, the feeling had only intensified; indeed, in one way, it had come to a head.

Unexpectedly, it had been Minerva, Wolverstone's evergracious wife, who had forced him to see the truth of it. Who, with her parting words, had forced him to face what he had, for quite some time, been avoiding focusing on.

Family. Children. His future.

While at Wolverstone, he'd seen and observed what could be along those lines, had been surrounded by the reality.

Growing up without his parents, with only Humphrey—already a reclusive widower—and Leonora around him through his formative years, he'd never been exposed to a large, boisterous brood, to the warmth, the charm, and that other level of comfort. To the fundamental difference that made a house a home.

The house he shared with Humphrey was just that, a house.

It lacked the essential elements to transform it into a home.

He hadn't thought it mattered, not to him or to Humphrey.

In that he'd been wrong, at least with respect to himself. That error, and his consequent lack and refusal to pay attention and do something about it, was what lay beneath his restlessness, what drove it and, increasingly, gave it teeth.

Minerva's parting words had been, "You're going to have to do something soon, dear Jeremy, or you'll wake up one morning a lonely old man."

Her eyes had been kindly and understanding.

Her words had chilled him to the bone.

She'd put her delicate finger on the crux of what, he now recognized, was his deepest fear.

Leonora had found Tristan, and Tristan had found her, and

they, like Royce and Minerva, had made their own family, their warm and boisterous brood.

He had his books, but as Minerva had intimated, they wouldn't keep him warm through the years ahead. Most especially through those years after Humphrey, already old and frail, passed on. Would he then regret that he hadn't bothered to make the time to find a lady of his own to share his life, to have children like his nephews and nieces? To do what was necessary to hear children's voices, their laughter, rolling down the corridors, to have children of his own to watch and see grow.

To have a son to whom he could pass on his own knowledge, his accumulated wisdom, as he'd seen Royce doing with his eldest boys. Perhaps to have a son, or even a daughter, with whom he could share the fascination of ancient writings, as Humphrey had with him.

He'd long ago assumed he'd never want such things, yet now . . .

He was already thirty-seven, a fact Minerva knew, no doubt prompting her remark, although with his lean frame, which had only truly filled out in his thirties, he was thought by most to be younger. Yet there was no denying the truth of her observation; if he wanted a family like hers and Royce's, like Leonora's and Tristan's, then he needed to do something about it.

Soon.

He'd whisked through the hamlet of Rayless; a sign proclaimed that Raechester lay ahead. He had an hour of driving before him with nothing to claim his attention; he might as well use the time.

And decide what he wanted.

That took two seconds—he wanted a family like his brother-in-law had. Like Royce had. The details were there, glowing in his mind.

Next: How to get it?

Obviously he needed a wife.

How to get her?

His mind, widely proclaimed to be brilliant and incisive, stalled at that point.

So he did what any academic would do and rephrased the question. What sort of wife did he want, did he need, in order to lead to his optimal outcome?

That was easier to define. The wife he wanted and needed would necessarily be quiet, reserved, if not precisely self-effacing then at least of the sort who wouldn't take umbrage when he spent days with his nose buried in some book. She would be content to manage his household and bear and care for any children they might be blessed with. He could imagine that she might be shy, relatively reticent—a meek, mild, accommodating lady who would not seek to interfere with his scholarly pursuits, let alone distract him from them.

Slowing to trot through the tiny village of Raechester, he grimaced. His previous encounters with the fairer sex had left him very aware that such a paragon wouldn't be easy to find. Ladies, certainly all those he'd ever dallied with, liked attention. That issue, of all others, was the one that invariably led to him and them parting company.

That said, he had nothing against women per se; some, like the Cynster twins, Amanda and Amelia, he found quite entertaining. In earlier years, he'd indulged in various encounters with certain bored matrons of the ton, followed by three longer affairs, but ultimately he'd found himself both bored and resentful of the increasing demands of the ladies involved, so he had, as gently as possible, ended the liaisons.

Over recent years, he'd clung to his recluse's shield and kept his distance from all females, deeming any further dalliance likely to be more trouble than it was worth. Leonora had prodded him, insisting that his past experiences simply meant that he hadn't yet met the lady who, to him, would be worth the trouble, would be worth putting himself out to engage with.

Logically he had to concede the point, but he continued to

have severe doubts that such a lady might exist, much less that she would cross his path.

Intellectually, he was both wary and distantly dismissive of ladies. Wary because he occasionally wondered if they, operating on some different plane of rationality, actually knew more than he, at least about social subjects. Distantly dismissive because, when it came to reason and logic, he'd never met any whose abilities commanded his respect.

Admittedly, only a small cohort of gentlemen made that grade either.

Nevertheless, now that he'd decided—had he? Yes, he rather thought he had—to find himself a wife, he was going to have to . . . how would Tristan and his Bastion Club colleagues phrase it? . . . devise a campaign to achieve his goal.

His goal being to find, woo, and secure the hand of a lady of impeccable character with all the characteristics he'd described.

It wouldn't hurt if she was passably pretty, and of similar social station, too; he would be no help if the poor woman needed guidance in such complicated matters as who had precedence entering a room.

So, campaign goal in place, how to move toward it? His first step had to be to locate a suitable candidate.

Leonora would help in a heartbeat if he asked her.

If he did . . . the old biddies, Tristan's pack of elderly female relatives, would instantly leap into the fray, too. Nothing he, Leonora, or Tristan might say or do would be able to avoid that—and the likely subsequent catastrophe; while infinitely well-meaning, the old ladies had very definite ideas and were as bossy as they came.

So . . . if he couldn't ask Leonora for help, then he couldn't ask any female for help. He knew that much. Which left him with the males—Tristan and his erstwhile colleagues, all now good friends, including Royce.

He tried to imagine any help they might give, but other than their giving him tactical advice—which he'd already had over the years from them—he couldn't see them helping him identify and meet his specific young lady; they were all married, and, as he did, avoided society as much as they could. So no help there.

Reaching deeper into his acquaintance, there were several unmarried gentlemen he knew through his connection with the Cynsters, yet from their occasional meetings he'd got the impression that they, too, kept society—at least those circles in which unmarried young ladies swarmed—at a distance.

Hmm. Considering the issue more broadly, it appeared that all the gentlemen he knew, or had any affinity with, avoided the wider company of young ladies . . . until they needed to find one to marry.

He frowned. Slowing Jasper, he trotted into Knowesgate; immediately they were past the small knot of cottages, he eased the reins and let Jasper run.

There had to be someone he could appeal to for assistance in locating his necessary wife. The idea of finding her on his own . . . he wouldn't know where to start.

The thought of Almack's was enough to put him off the project altogether . . . so there had to be some other way.

A mile further on, he still hadn't thought of any useful option. He passed the lane that led to the hamlet of Kirk-whelpington and rattled on around a long, wide curve, keeping Jasper to a spanking pace.

A coach, the first he'd sighted that day, appeared ahead, rumbling steadily toward him around the curve.

"Damn." The road wasn't a major highway, and that stretch was too narrow to permit two carriages to pass at a clip.

Reining Jasper in, he slowed the curricle until it was rolling slowly, the horse at a walk. The coach slowed, too. Carefully angling his curricle's off-side wheel onto the verge, Jeremy raised a hand in brief acknowledgment to the coachman as the man edged his team as far as he dared the other way.

Jeremy was concentrating, managing the reins and watching like a hawk to ensure the coach's wheels and his curricle's wheels slid past without touching, when a thump on the coach's window made him look up—

Into a pale face. A woman's face.

Distressed, her eyes wide, she'd struck the window with her open palms.

He saw her lips move—distantly heard her scream.

Male hands grabbed her shoulders and she was hauled abruptly back.

Then the coach was past, and the road ahead lay empty.

Jasper, wanting to run, tugged at the reins.

Still stunned, his mind replaying what he'd seen, Jeremy absentmindedly lowered his hands, letting the black start trotting.

Then he blinked, turned his head, and glanced back at the coach.

It was rolling at speed again, but not rushing or racing, just steadily rumbling along at the same pace as when he'd first seen it.

Half a minute later, the coach rounded the curve and passed out of sight.

Facing forward, Jeremy let Jasper continue trotting.

While his mind swiftly sorted and compared.

He was an expert in ancient hieroglyphics, with a steel trap of a memory for such things. Faces were very like hieroglyphics, and he knew he'd seen that face before.

But where? He didn't know anyone in the area, other than the household at Wolverstone . . .

London. In some ballroom. Several years ago.

The scene came back to him in a rush.

"Eliza Cynster."

Even as he said her name, another memory was pouring through him—of Royce reading a letter he'd received from Devil Cynster on the day Jeremy had arrived at Wolverstone, about the foiled kidnapping of Heather Cynster and the belief that her sisters were still under threat. . . .

"Hell!" Jeremy hauled on the reins, halting Jasper.

Shocked, he stared down the road.

Heather Cynster had been taken by her captors into Scotland. The coach behind him was heading for the Scottish border.

And he'd made out the single word Eliza had screamed.

Help!

She'd been kidnapped, too.

Eliza slumped back into the corner of the coach into which Scrope had flung her. He'd snarled at her but then had quickly regained his composure, his previous stoic and stony expression cloaking the turmoil she'd provoked.

Genevieve had hissed at her, too. Talonlike fingers locked about Eliza's wrist, the nurse held on to her as if she might bolt.

Small hope of that.

Standing over her, keeping his balance with one hand on the coach's ceiling, Scrope stared coldly down at her, then reached up, opened the hatch in the roof, and spoke upward. "That curricle that just passed us—did the driver stop?"

After a moment, the coachman replied, "No. Glanced back once, puzzledlike, but then went on. Why?"

Scrope glanced at Eliza. "Our precious baggage tried to attract his attention. You're sure he isn't following?"

A moment passed. "There's no one behind us."

"Good." Scrope closed the hatch. Weaving slightly with the coach's motion, he stared down at Eliza.

She stared back, surprised to discover she felt no real fear. She'd done what she'd had to—and no longer had sufficient strength to do very much at all, even to be properly afraid.

Eventually, Scrope shifted and sat again opposite her. "As you've just demonstrated, there's no point in trying to create a scene—nothing comes of it, even if you do. So." He eyed her coldly, measuringly. "Do we have to tie you up and tell our tale at our next stop, or will you behave?"

Recalling the tack Heather had taken with her captors, letting them believe she was helpless and unable to accomplish anything on her own, Eliza let her muscles slacken in not entirely assumed defeat. "Clearly there's no hope, so I may as well behave."

As long as it suited her.

She'd allowed the weakness stealing over her, through her, to color her voice. She wasn't surprised when Scrope, after considering her for a long moment, nodded. He looked at Genevieve. "Release her. But if she shows any further sign of making our life difficult, we'll bind and gag her."

With a black look for Eliza, Genevieve unlocked her hold on Eliza's wrist and, with a muted humph, settled back in her seat.

The three of them went back to what they'd been doing before the drama—before she'd seen Jeremy Carling driving past.

Eliza knew she should have felt wretchedly disappointed, but summoning the strength even for that was a struggle. She'd assumed her ability to think had meant the laudanum had worn off. She'd thought she'd marshaled her strength, that she'd recovered and gathered enough of that commodity to, when and if her moment came, make a determined show, enough to convince whoever went by to assist her.

Admittedly, she'd had little hope of seeing anyone who might help, but then, wonder of wonders, she'd seen a familiar face.

She hadn't stopped to consider further but had flung herself at the window. She'd bashed the glass and screamed for help . . .

The instant she'd moved, her head had spun. But, desperate, she'd poured every ounce of strength and determination into that moment, into doing all she possibly could.

Now she felt drained. Literally wrung out.

And, it seemed, it had all been for nought.

Jeremy Carling. Of all the gentlemen fate might have sent her way, why had it had to have been him?

He was a scholar, a dreamer, a certified genius, but stand-offish, with a marked disinterest in social life; he was so absentminded she seriously doubted he would remember her name.

He might not even have recognized her enough to register that he knew her.

That was a distinct possibility. Although she'd been introduced to him formally at a ball several years ago, and had seen him several times in family drawing rooms since, she'd barely exchanged two words with him—and those had been at that first meeting years ago, when he'd appeared to be so *elsewhere* she'd quickly found some polite reason to quit the group he'd been with.

Still, there was nothing else she could have done; for good or ill, she'd had to grasp the opportunity when it had offered.

She heaved a deep, despondent sigh, uncaring if the other two heard. It would only add to the image of a beaten, help-less female . . . she wasn't quite that, but at that moment she felt close to it.

Closing her eyes, she tried to relax, to marshal her strength and determination again.

In her mind, a faint hope flickered.

She had, after all, recognized Jeremy Carling, so he, in turn, might—just might—have recognized her.

It was a slim hope, but it was the only sliver of hope she had. In her present dejected and worn-out state, she had to cling to whatever she could.

If he had recognized her, what would he do? He was a scholar, no hero—not a knight or a warrior to come riding to her rescue himself. But he would be concerned, surely, and would either send word to her family, or visit them himself when he returned to town . . .

If he was returning to town. She had no idea why he'd been this far north. Perhaps he was visiting friends?

Folding her arms, she settled deeper into the corner. She couldn't predict what Jeremy might do, but he was an honorable man—he'd do *something* to help her.

It took a full minute for Jeremy to convince his brain that this was really happening, that he wasn't dreaming, that the situation was *real*.

Then he started thinking. Furiously.

Jasper, finding him uninterested in going on, dragged the reins until he could lower his head and crop the grass of the verge.

Jeremy sat in the stationary curricle, reins in his lax hands, and stared unseeing down the road.

Assessing the situation, and what needed to be done, what was possible, what his options were.

He needed to get word to the Cynsters, or if not that, to Wolverstone. The thought of notifying anyone else occurred, only to be dismissed. He might be a social hermit, but he knew well enough that in such circumstances preserving a lady's reputation was high on the list of "things that must be done at all costs."

But if he drove south to Newcastle, the nearest town from which he'd be able to send a fast courier-rider south, or alternatively turned back to Wolverstone and Royce, all he'd be able to tell anyone was that Eliza had been taken in a coach across the border.

While he was sure her parents would like to know even that much, he was equally sure they would prefer that he followed and tried to help their daughter escape.

If he tried to send a message south, he would lose track of her and lose any hope of helping her directly.

And clearly she needed help. She wouldn't have tried to attract attention in such a way if she hadn't been down to her last reserves.

Help was what she'd screamed for. It wasn't for him to question the call, but to respond appropriately.

Especially as he doubted she would have recognized him, which meant she'd been reduced to soliciting help from any gentleman who might have ridden past.

Such actions in a young lady of her ilk smacked of abject desperation.

He thought back to the details of the kidnap plot that Royce had read out. It was believed that some laird, most likely a highland nobleman, was, for reasons unknown, intent on kidnapping one of the Cynster girls. A novel, and to Jeremy reassuring, aspect was that the laird, whoever he was, had insisted that Heather, once kidnapped, was taken excellent care of, even to the extent of providing a maid during the long journey north.

Breckenridge—whom Jeremy knew slightly—had by chance seen Heather seized in a London street and had given chase, ultimately rescuing her and leaving the laird empty-handed.

Now, it seemed, the laird had managed to seize Eliza Cynster. The question of how was intriguing; knowing the Cynsters, the males of the family, Eliza's brothers and cousins, Jeremy couldn't imagine how they'd come to let down their guard . . . but he pushed the fascinating question aside and concentrated instead on the more pertinent question staring him in the face—namely, what he should do. Now. This minute or the next.

The facts were clear: Eliza Cynster had been kidnapped and was in a coach that would shortly carry her over the border. Once in Scotland, her trail would be hard to divine, especially if her captors took her into the wilderness of the highlands. Finding her then would be close to impossible.

If he let her be taken across the border and didn't follow, she might well be lost, or at least find herself at the mercy of the mysterious laird.

If he did follow . . . he would have to rescue her, or at least do his best to help her escape.

He wasn't any sort of hero, but he'd spent the last decade

in the company of such men, with Tristan and the other members of the Bastion Club. He'd been involved in a few of their civilian adventures and had seen how they thought, how they approached problems and dealt with the exigencies of such situations.

That experience couldn't compare with proper training, but in this case it would have to serve.

As far as he could see, he was Eliza's only hope.

He'd been looking forward to going home and settling into his comfortable chair before the fire in his library to bask in the glow of his discovery of Royce's manuscript, then later applying his mind to solving the problem of how to find his ideal wife, but clearly all that would have to be postponed. He knew where his duty lay, what honor demanded.

Lifting his reins, he clucked at Jasper. "Come on, old son. Back the way we've come."

Turning the curricle in the empty road, he set Jasper pacing, then urged him to lengthen his stride. "It's the border for us, then Scotland beyond."

Absentminded scholar though he was, he had a damsel in distress to save.

Chapter Two

Eliza determinedly paced the wooden floor of an upper-story room in the coaching inn at Jedburgh. The stout oak door was locked, sealing her in. Her captors had supplied her with a tray of food, then gone downstairs to enjoy their dinner in the more convivial atmosphere of the inn's dining room.

Reaching the wall, Eliza swung around, her gaze falling on the tray set on a table on the other side of the room. Even though she'd had no appetite, she'd forced herself to eat all of the broth, and as much of the game pie as she'd been able to swallow. If she was to escape her three jailers—Scrope, Genevieve, and Taylor, the burly coachman—she would need her strength. The possibility of escape, however remote, was the reason she was pacing, hoping the exercise would help burn off the lingering effects of the laudanum.

Stepping out again, down the long room, she had to work to hold her balance. The drug was still in her system, still sapping her strength, leaving her muscles weak and wobbly, and her relatively helpless. They'd kept her drugged for three days—this was, they'd said, the third night after Heather and Breckenridge's engagement ball—so she probably shouldn't be surprised or too concerned that it was taking some time for the potent sleeping draft to completely wear off.

Reaching the tray, she paused to lift a glass and swallow a mouthful of water; she was fairly certain drinking water would help, too.

She was trying, quite desperately, to keep her hopes up, but . . .

Given all she'd recalled about him, having to rely on Jeremy Carling was hardly reassuring.

He was widely acknowledged as having a brilliant mind, but as that mind preferred ancient times to the present, and usually appeared to be distracted, dwelling on civilizations long gone to dust rather than paying attention to what was happening under his nose . . .

Setting down the glass, she hauled in a huge breath, held it until her nerves settled again. There was no sense in working herself into a state. Jeremy would either do something to help, or he wouldn't.

There was nothing she could do to influence that.

Pacing again, she tried to ignore the insidious, carping whisper that slid from the deepest recesses of her mind. *Heather got Breckenridge, her hero, as her rescuer. Who did I get? Jeremy Carling. How utterly unfair!*

Brushing the irrational complaint aside—at the moment she'd be happy to be rescued by anyone, never mind her hero—she doggedly marched across the room.

Her mind returned to that moment in the coach when, fast approaching the very brink of despair, she'd seen Jeremy and her heart had leapt. She could see him quite clearly in her mind's eye—sitting upright, broad shoulders square, his greatcoat, open, draping from said shoulders, framing a chest that, compared to her previous memory of him, appeared to have improved in both width and strength, or at least the impression of it.

Frowning, she paced on, remembering, recalling. She had to admit there was nothing in his present appearance that disqualified him as a potential rescuer. Indeed, dispassionately considering the recent image burned into her brain, she concluded that even absentminded scholars could eventually grow into the sort of gentlemen ladies noticed.

Regardless, as that little voice of darkness within her was

quick to point out, what he looked like didn't matter. Just because Heather's rescuer had turned out to be her hero was no reason to suppose anything of the sort would happen to Eliza.

Besides, all she knew of Jeremy Carling suggested he was infinitely more interested in any musty, dusty, ancient tome than he was or ever would be in any woman.

Reaching the wall, she sighed, tipped up her head, and spoke to the ceiling, "Please let him have noticed me. *Please* let him have recognized me. *Please* let him have *done something* to send help my way."

That was another issue; in her experience, absentminded bookworms were the second least decisive people on earth, only fractionally better than timid little old ladies.

Lowering her chin, swinging around, she paced steadily back across the room. The muscles in her legs seemed less wobbly than when she'd first started pacing.

Head down, she tried to put herself in an absentminded scholar's shoes, tried to imagine what Jeremy might do. "If he sends word to London, how long before—"

Tap.

Halting, she stared at the curtained window. She'd thought the sound had come from there, but the room was two floors up; she'd already evaluated her prospects of escaping via that route and found them to be nil. Admittedly, Breckenridge had first contacted Heather through a second-floor inn window, but really, how likely was that to happen with her? It was doubtless just her mind playing tricks on her. Wishful think—

Tap.

She flew to the window, flung open the curtains, and looked through the glass.

Directly into Jeremy Carling's face.

She was so thrilled to see him that she just stood there and beamed. Drinking in the fact that he had very nice eyes; she couldn't make out their color in the moonlight, but they were large, well set, giving him a wonderfully direct and open gaze.

His features were regular, a touch patrician, his nose distinctly so, his forehead wide, his cheeks lean and long; his chin was decidedly squared, but his lips looked like they belonged to a man who laughed easily.

Her gaze skimmed quickly down and, yes, his shoulders really were much broader, his overall build much stronger than when she'd last seen him.

The moon was full, pouring silver light over him; sitting on the ridge of the roof just below her window, Jeremy felt ridiculously exposed. But his logical mind reminded him that normally people rarely looked up. He just hoped none of the patrons leaving the inn fell too far outside the norm.

As it was just as bright outside the room as in, he could see Eliza's face clearly. See her features well enough to register her surprise, pleased though it was.

He could hardly take umbrage; *he* was surprised to find himself perched on the roof outside her window.

As she seemed momentarily frozen, he seized the chance to confirm that the impression he'd assimilated wasn't wrong; she was . . . not prettier, but more striking than he'd recalled. Especially now she wasn't so distressed.

He felt oddly pleased about that.

Raising a hand from the roof's ridge, he pointed at the catch on the casement window, twirled his finger.

She looked, then quickly obliged.

As she eased the casement open, he leaned back to let the frame pass by him, then leaned in, closer, to whisper, "Are you alone?"

Gripping the windowsill, she leaned nearer still. "For the moment. They—there's three of them—are downstairs."

"Good." He beckoned. "Come on."

Her eyes flared, then she leaned over the sill and looked down.

He stared at the profusion of honey-gold locks glimmering in the moonlight just below his chin, then blinked, and continued, "It's not as steep as it looks. We can brace against the wall to the edge of this roof, then it's only a small drop to the next, and from there we can cross part of the kitchen roof—it's a bit of a scramble, but—"

"I can't." Drawing back, still gripping the sill, she raised her eyes to his. "Believe me, I'd like nothing more than to go with you, but I . . ." She reached out and grasped his forearm.

Looking at her hand, he saw it shake as she tightened her grip just a fraction, but no more.

She released him on a sigh. Met his gaze as he lifted his eyes questioningly to hers. "That's the best I can do—the hardest I can grip anything at the moment. They gave me laudanum for the past three days and it still hasn't worn off. My legs are still shaky, and I can't hold onto anything. If I slip . . ."

A chill coursed down his spine. If she slipped . . . he might not be able to catch and hold her, and stop her from pitching over the roof's edge. She was tallish, admittedly slender, yet there was enough of her to make him question whether he would be strong enough to hold and save her. He grimaced; the truth was he didn't know his own strength—he'd never had occasion to test it before. "All right." He nodded, keeping both gesture and tone calm and even. "It won't help our cause if either of us falls and breaks a limb, so we'll think of another way."

She blinked as if taken aback, but then nodded. "Yes. Good." She paused, then asked, "Do you have any suggestions?"

Relieved that she seemed to be in a more rational state than he'd expected, not panic-ridden and, heaven forfend, weepy, he turned his mind to considering their options.

There didn't seem to be many.

He frowned. "Freeing you tonight would probably be unwise, anyway. It's pitch black out on the road, and going back across the Cheviots, even in a carriage, in the dead of night, possibly fleeing pursuers who might or might not have weapons, could end very badly. Given we don't know this area . . ." He stopped and looked inquiringly at her, but she shook her head. He concluded, "It would be wisest not to attempt to flee at night."

"We might get lost. We might run off the road."

"Exactly." He thought further. "You said there are three of them?"

Leaning her elbows on the sill, Eliza nodded. "Scrope is the leader—I think he was the one who was waiting in the back parlor of St. Ives House." She met Jeremy's eyes. "The room was dark. I didn't see him, but he drugged me—with ether, I think. They must have taken me out through the window—it gives onto an alley."

He looked at her intently, patiently waiting for her to continue.

"There's a woman—I'm sure she must normally be a nurse-companion. She's somewhere in her early thirties, and stronger than she looks. And the coachman, Taylor, is also part of the scheme. He's burly and strong, too, rather rougher than Scrope, who looks and speaks like a gentleman."

His eyes still locked on her face, Jeremy said, "So there's three of them and only two of us, so even in daylight we can't try anything direct, not unless we can get rid of at least one of them, if not two."

Both paused to think. After a minute ticked past, she shook her head. "I can't think of any clever way of even *distracting* two of them—they're very definitely not stupid."

Jeremy nodded. "Where are they taking you?" His eyes again met hers. "Have they said?"

"Edinburgh." Her lips firmed. "They've kidnapped me for some highland laird and they're planning to hand me over to him there—they said the day after tomorrow." She held his gaze. "You see, there's this Scottish nobleman—"

"I know all about it—about Heather's kidnapping and

who your family thinks is behind it." When she looked her surprise, he went on, "I was at Wolverstone Castle, evaluating a manuscript for Royce, when he got a letter from Devil telling him about the incident with Heather, explaining what they thought, and asking his advice. Royce read it to Minerva and me. That's how I know."

"Good." She let her relief color her voice. "I wasn't looking forward to explaining it all—it sounds so far-fetched."

"There's nothing far-fetched about you being here, locked in an inn room in Jedburgh."

"True." She grimaced. "This laird is clearly no figment of anyone's imagination." Leaning more heavily on the sill, she said, "So if I can't escape tonight—"

"I'll have to arrange to get you out of their clutches tomorrow." He made the statement sound like a fact. "As it happens, getting you free is likely to be significantly easier in Edinburgh than here."

She frowned. "Because Jedburgh's such a small town?"

"Partly." He met her gaze. "In his letter Devil mentioned a tale the kidnappers had concocted to ensure Heather couldn't easily get help, even from the authorities . . ."

She was already nodding. "About them fetching me for my guardian? Yes, they've mentioned it. Threatened it, as it were."

"Well, that's the other reason trying to rescue you while we're in or near Jedburgh isn't a sound idea. All they'd need to do would be to alert the garrison, and they'd have quite a force to throw against us—and it's possible they could close the border before we reached it, too."

"Definitely not a good option."

He hesitated; from his expression—definitely intelligent—she suspected he was thinking, assessing. "On top of that," he eventually said, "Edinburgh has pertinent advantages. It's a large city, so hiding ourselves in it once we have you free of them won't be such a problem. And even more helpfully, I have friends, good friends, in Edinburgh itself." He caught her gaze. "I'm sure they'll help."

He paused, searching her eyes, her face—she wasn't sure what he was looking for, much less what he would see—then he somewhat diffidently said, "If they head on tomorrow morning, as I think we're safe in assuming they will, they'll reach Edinburgh about midday. You said they expect to hand you over to the laird on the day after that, so they'll have to hold you somewhere in or very close to the town. Do you think you can bear to go on with them, at least until they halt wherever they intend to spend tomorrow night?"

She considered, then said, "Well, yes, I can manage—I really don't see that we have much choice."

He grimaced. "No good or wise alternatives, anyway."

She nodded. "So I'll play along and let them take me to Edinburgh." She caught his gaze. "Then what?"

"I'll follow, note where they take you, then I'll come and rescue you tomorrow night." His gaze was direct, open, and reassuringly steady. "We're not going to let them hand you over to this blackguardly Scotsman, so tomorrow night I'll come for you."

She looked into his eyes, sensed the determination behind his steady gaze, and nodded. "All right. But it will definitely need to be tomorrow night—it won't be like it was with Heather, where they waited for days for the laird to arrive. I overheard Scrope tell Taylor that he'd sent a message north before they even left London. Scrope is keen to get me off his hands and into the laird's as soon as he can."

"Wise man. It's definitely safer for him that way—he doesn't risk losing you as the others lost Heather."

"Hmm. So, your friends . . . are you sure—" She broke off, glanced at the door and heard footsteps approaching. Eyes wide, she turned back to him.

"Yes, I'm sure," he whispered back, already pushing at the casement.

52   Stephanie Laurens

She didn't have time to reply. She grabbed the window, hauled it shut, snibbed the catch, yanked the curtains closed, then managed to start walking toward the bed before the key scraped in the lock.

The door opened, revealing Genevieve. The maid saw her, took in her slow gait, then turned to murmur a goodnight to Scrope, whom Eliza glimpsed in the shadows of the corridor. The stealthy scrape of a boot on slate tile reached her ears, masked by the dual male rumbles that came in reply to Genevieve's words; Taylor was in the corridor, too. Reaching one of the two narrow beds the room possessed, Eliza slowly let herself down; listening carefully, she confirmed that one of the men went into the room to her left, while the other took the room to her right.

Scrope was taking no chances.

After casting her a sharp glance, Genevieve tidied away the tray, setting it outside the door. Then she closed the door, locked it once more, and, slipping the key onto a chain she wore around her neck, turned to survey Eliza. "Time for bed—please remove your gown."

Eliza inwardly sighed and complied, undoing the tiny topaz buttons down the front of her silk ball gown, now horridly crushed. Twisting to undo the laces down the gown's side, she saw Genevieve gather her cloak, as well as the one they'd kept Eliza wrapped in, fold both garments, and lay them beneath the head of the mattress on the other bed.

Recalling Heather's story of how her "maid" had taken and slept on Heather's as well as her own outer clothing every night, making escape through the dark hours virtually impossible, Eliza wondered if there was an instruction book for kidnappers, detailing the most efficient ways to ensure their captives didn't cause them trouble.

As she'd expected, once she wriggled out of her gown, shook it out, and laid it on her bed, Genevieve reached out and claimed it. Without a word, the nurse laid the gown out on the webbing under her mattress, alongside her own black day gown and the two cloaks, then dropped the lumpy mattress down. Looking up, she met Eliza's eyes and smiled smugly. "Now we can all get a good night's rest."

Eliza didn't bother replying. Clad in her silk chemise, she quickly got into bed, stretched out, then sat up, pummeled the lumpy pillow, and lay down again.

She stared at the ceiling as Genevieve got into the neighboring bed, then blew out the candle. The other woman settled on her side. Soon her breathing deepened, steady and even, and Eliza knew she was asleep.

Much good did that do her; as Jeremy had said, trying to flee at night would be inviting disaster, even if she could manage to get out of the room without alerting any of her three captors, even if she could lay her hands on clothes enough to be decent.

Meek, mild, and helpless; that was how she should behave until Jeremy contrived to whisk her away. Behaving so would ensure her captors saw no reason to place more difficult-to-circumvent safeguards around her.

Meek, mild, and helpless. Eliza uttered a near-silent hollow laugh. She had no doubt she'd be thoroughly successful in projecting that image, because she *was* meek, mild, and helpless. Certainly a lot meeker, milder, and a great deal more helpless than either of her sisters, than, very likely, any other Cynster female ever born.

Heather was the eldest, confident, assertive, and utterly sure of her place in the world. Angelica, the spoiled baby, was fearless, reckless, bossy, and ineradicably convinced that come what may, everything would always turn out the best for her. And it invariably did.

She, Eliza, was the quiet one. She'd heard herself referred to as that often enough, but even more, she *thought* of herself as that. She was the pianist, the harpist, the needlewoman, not exactly a dreamer but closer to that than any other Cynster in recent memory. She didn't favor physical pursuits; such activities were all very well, but they simply weren't for her . . . and she'd never excelled at, in some cases had never even attained a decent competency in, such endeavors.

Her sisters were both confident, outdoorsy types, as assured in the countryside as they were in a ballroom. In the country, while Heather's and Angelica's version of a brisk stroll was an energetic hike over hill and dale, hers was a gentle amble around the terraces and the paved paths of the formal gardens.

All of which left her hugely relieved that her escape was to occur in Edinburgh, and not out here in the middle of the countryside—worse, the Scottish lowlands, a region of which she had no personal experience.

She stared upward at the moonlit ceiling and felt something inside—determination and something more—quietly but steadily well, rise, and coalesce.

Meek, mild, and helpless she might be, but she was still a Cynster. No matter what happened, with Jeremy's help, or even without it, she would escape. She would get free.

She wasn't about to be delivered like some package to some heathenish highland laird.

Drawing in a deep breath, she closed her eyes and, somewhat to her surprise, found sleep waiting.

Half an hour later, Jeremy returned to the room he'd hired in a small tavern a hundred yards further along the road from the coaching inn where Eliza's kidnappers had halted for the night.

By the time he'd dropped to the ground after carefully climbing down the inn's roof, he'd realized that, given he wouldn't simply be helping Eliza out of the room and driving her south immediately, as he'd first assumed, he would need a plan in order to effectively and safely rescue her. A detailed, well-crafted, well thought-out plan. He'd spent the next hour reconnoitering the town, making sure he had its layout, the salient features, properly set in his mind.

He might not have had much experience of such endeavors, but he'd rubbed shoulders with Trentham and the other members of the Bastion Club long enough to know the basics of how to go about formulating such a plan. Information gathering was always the first step.

Setting down the single candle the tavern keeper had handed him on the ancient tallboy, he closed the door, locked it, then, shrugging off his greatcoat, he set the garment on the straight-backed chair beside the narrow bed.

Sitting down on the bed, he tested the mattress, found it adequate, then swung around and lay down, setting his hands behind his head, stretching his legs straight so his boots dangled off the bed's end.

Staring unseeing up at the ceiling, he reviewed all he'd learned of the town. Everything—the proximity of the garrison in the castle, the relative lack of effective cover in a town that was little more than a single street—confirmed that having Eliza go on with her kidnappers to Edinburgh was their wisest choice.

The only possible alternative that he could see was if, tomorrow morning, her kidnappers, being so close to their goal, relaxed sufficiently to make some mistake that gave him an opening to step in and whisk Eliza out from under their noses in some way that would ensure her and him a reasonable head start in driving for the border.

From all she'd told him of her captors, from what could be inferred given they'd successfully snatched her from inside St. Ives House, that scenario was beyond unlikely.

Nevertheless, he could almost hear Trentham, and the others, too, lecturing him that one should always be prepared and watching, ready to step in and take advantage of just such "beyond unlikely" situations.

So he would be there in the morning, in the inn yard, waiting and watching, just to be sure. And Eliza would, no doubt, find it comforting to have at least visual confirmation that he was, and intended to remain, close.

He lay still for some considerable time, his gaze fixed unseeing on the ceiling while his well-trained, logical scholar's mind worked through all the aspects, the possibilities and probabilities of what would ensue once the coach carrying Eliza reached Edinburgh.

Thinking further, he methodically listed all the pertinent alternatives, as well as all his advantages, his potential sources of help, his abilities, his knowledge of the city.

He'd lived there for nearly five months eight years ago, when the university had consulted him over the translation of a dozen old scrolls. He'd made two close friends at that time and had visited every year since, usually when consulting work again called him to Edinburgh.

As he'd told Eliza, in Edinburgh he would have friends he could rely on.

Of course, both Cobden Harris and Hugo Weaver were scholars, too, but they were hale and energetic, a year or so younger than Jeremy, and weren't without resources. Both were also local and knew the town, every wynd and twisting close, every tavern, better than the backs of their hands.

Jeremy entertained not the slightest doubt that they, and Cobby's wife, Meggin, too, would help in any way they could.

But exactly how to effect Eliza's rescue . . .

He was juggling potential scenarios when the light playing across the ceiling started flickering. Glancing at the candle, he saw it was close to guttering. Rising, he divested himself of his clothes, realizing as he did that he couldn't risk being seen by Eliza's captors while he was hanging around the inn yard tomorrow morning.

Following that thought further, he considered what Tristan, in the same position, would do, and amended his plans accordingly.

Snuffing the candle, he climbed between the sheets and stretched out, once again staring upward. This was the first time in his thirty-seven years that he'd engaged in a real-life drama where *he* was the one who had to make the plans. Where the mission, as it were, was his to run.

He hadn't previously realized what a challenge it would be, let alone that he might enjoy such an undertaking, but the truth was his mind saw the enterprise as an activity rather like chess—real-life chess without a defined set of pieces, board, or rules.

He'd forgotten what it had felt like all those years ago when he'd been caught up in the strange events at Montrose Place—the thrill, the enthralling tension, of engaging with a villain, of trying to win, to triumph over an adversary.

To fight on the side of right.

Lips curving, he turned onto his side and closed his eyes.

And admitted to himself that he'd forgotten there were other entertaining challenges in life beyond the ones contained in millennia-old hieroglyphics.

Chapter Three

Eliza was shaken awake by Genevieve in the morning. When she blinked her eyes open, the nurse pointed to the washstand. "Best get yourself washed and dressed. Breakfast will be served soon, downstairs, and Scrope wants to get on to Edinburgh without delay."

Groggily, Eliza pushed back the covers and sat up. The morning air was chill. Tugging the coverlet off the bed, she wrapped it about her shoulders, then shuffled across to the washstand. She wasn't a morning person; that, too, was Heather or Angelica, not her.

The water in the pewter ewer was lukewarm. Tucking the coverlet under her arms, she used both hands to lift the ewer and pour . . . considered the ewer's weight and solidity as she did. What if she called Genevieve over, used the ewer to strike her unconscious, then got dressed and rushed out of the room . . . straight into Scrope's arms. He, or Taylor, would very likely be waiting for her and Genevieve to appear.

Setting down the ewer, Eliza splashed water on her face, blinking, gradually coming fully awake.

Attempting an escape now, on her own, was unlikely to succeed and would alert Scrope and his minions to her underlying, disguised determination. And no good would come of that.

She dried her face with the thin towel provided. Her previous night's conclusion reached with Jeremy still held sound. She would travel on to Edinburgh and place her faith in him.

In an absentminded scholar.

Returning to the bed, and her thoroughly crushed evening gown, she reminded herself that he had climbed the inn's roof, an action of which she wouldn't previously have thought him capable; clearly he had hidden depths.

She could only pray that those depths were deep enough to manage her rescue.

As soon as Eliza was ready, Genevieve made sure she was enveloped in her cloak, then ushered her out of the room. Taylor was indeed waiting in the corridor to escort both women down the stairs to a tiny private parlor. Breakfast was consumed in rushed silence, then Taylor left to bring the coach to the door.

Scrope watched from the window; when the coach was in position, he looked at Eliza. "You know the tale we'll tell if you make a scene. There's no reason to make this more difficult on yourself than it needs to be. Behave, and we can proceed civilly."

Eliza forced herself to incline her head. They could take it as acquiescence if they chose. This was the first time she'd had to truly make a decision to go along with their plans; until now she'd been drugged, or still too weak to resist.

On the way to the parlor, she'd tested her limbs; to her relief, she'd regained full control, her normal strength. If she wanted to resist, she could, but . . .

Scrope held the parlor door, and Eliza followed Genevieve through, very aware of Scrope following at her heels. Logically she knew she should do as she and Jeremy had arranged and go forward without protest, yet when she stepped out of the inn's door and saw the dark maw of the coach waiting, innate resistance reared.

She halted on the inn's porch, then a movement to her left caught her eye. Glancing past Genevieve, who was waiting to usher her—push her if necessary—into the coach, she glimpsed . . .

Jeremy, in a scruffy-looking jacket with a cloth cap pulled low over his dark hair, its bill shading his face.

He lowered his head in an infinitesimal nod.

He was there, watching over her. He would follow the coach to Edinburgh, as he'd said.

He would rescue her.

Dragging in a deep breath, she looked forward and walked to the coach. She climbed in, Genevieve followed; Scrope paused to speak to Taylor, then stepped up into the coach and closed the door.

The coach lurched, then rumbled out of the inn yard.

They were away.

On the road to Edinburgh.

As soon as the coach turned up the highway, Jeremy quit his position in the yard and strode quickly back to the tavern.

Swiftly changing into his identifiably gentlemanly coat, raking his fingers through his hair then shaking his head to resettle the thick locks, he packed his bags, paid his shot, and went out to where a helpful young ostler, currently in his shirtsleeves, was holding Jasper the Black, harnessed and prancing, ready to be off.

With a smile, a word of thanks, and a coin, Jeremy returned the coat and cap he'd borrowed from the ostler. A disguise would do him no good while he was driving his elegant curricle with Jasper between the shafts; someone might even think he'd stolen the carriage. And once he reached Edinburgh, he might well need to command the usual attention gentlemen of his class garnered; a disguise might be counterproductive.

All he had to do was ensure he didn't get close enough for the coachman—Taylor, Eliza had named the man—to get a sufficiently good look at him to recognize him as the gentleman Eliza had tried to enlist.

Whose help Eliza *had* enlisted.

Pleased enough with how matters had thus far unfolded, he

climbed into the curricle, lifted the reins, then with a flourish sent Jasper pacing smartly out of the tavern's small yard.

Once he and Jasper had agreed on a nice, steady pace, Jeremy kept his eyes glued to the road ahead, just in case the coach had for some unforeseen reason slowed.

The one task on his list that he'd as yet been unable to accomplish was to send word to Eliza's family. If they'd been on the Great North Road, he'd have been able to send a message by the night mail, but there was no Royal Mail service along this lesser road. Locating a trustworthy courier to employ had likewise proved futile; such messengers plied the main highways and the major towns they linked.

He'd considered approaching the commander of the garrison, but, as he understood such matters, it was imperative that Eliza's days-long sojourn with her kidnappers be kept a complete secret, one shared with as few people as possible, as had been managed with Heather's disappearance; he himself only knew of Heather's kidnapping because he fell within a trusted circle.

In rescuing Heather, in protecting her reputation, Breckenridge had been exceedingly wary over entrusting the truth to anyone. In a similar vein, Jeremy had no confidence that even handing a sealed missive addressed to the Cynsters into the garrison commander's hands would be in Eliza's best interests.

Once he reached Edinburgh, he'd send word south—perhaps via Royce—as soon as he knew where they intended to hold Eliza. Jeremy was confident the Cynsters would understand his tardiness in doing so; no matter how worry might be eating at them, they would expect him to put Eliza's safety first.

Holding Jasper to their steady pace, he bowled along in the coach's wake.

As she couldn't avoid keeping Scrope and Genevieve company in the coach, Eliza decided to make the minutes count.

She ransacked her memory for every last fact gleaned from Heather's kidnapping and rescue, and picked the one she hoped would have the best chance of unsettling Scrope. As usual, he was sitting opposite her—close enough to seize her. She fixed her gaze on his face, waited until he cast her a glance to ask, "Is the Scotsman who hired you still using the name McKinsey?"

Scrope blinked. His hesitation suggested her supposition was correct. Eventually, he replied, "Why do you ask?"

"I was just wondering what name I should use to address him."

Scrope's lips curved slightly and he relaxed against the seat.

Eliza arched her brows, faintly patronizing. "I do know that's not his real name." Satisfied by the frown that flitted over Scrope's face, she asked, "What did he tell you about me and my family?"

Scrope considered, then replied, "He didn't have to tell me much about your family. The Cynsters are rather well known. As to you . . ." He shrugged. "All he told me was that he wanted you seized and brought to him in Edinburgh, and that you'd be ripe for the picking at your sister's engagement ball."

Eliza suppressed a frown; she didn't want Scrope to know how important her next question was. She kept her tone airy, as if vaguely flattered. "He asked specifically for me?"

Scrope's dark gaze grew more intent. A moment passed before he nodded. "Yes—you. Why?"

She saw no reason not to reply. "When my sister, Heather, was seized, he'd asked for one of us—a 'Cynster sister'— which could have meant Heather, me, Angelica, Henrietta, or Mary. It was just luck that Heather was the one taken."

Scrope's brows rose; his gaze shifted, grew distant as he leaned back into the shadows of the opposite corner. Softly, he said, "Well, this time, he wanted you—just you." After a moment, his gaze flicked back to Eliza; she could read nothing in his eyes as he said, "He specifically stipulated you."

His tone did nothing for her peace of mind. She racked her brain for pertinent questions, but before she could even formulate the first, Scrope, his gaze on her face, spoke again.

"Don't bother. I run a far tighter ship than your elder sister's captors. If you want answers to your questions, you'll have to wait and address them to"—his lips curved, faintly malicious—"McKinsey."

She narrowed her eyes at him, then turned her gaze to the window and kept her lips shut.

While her mind turned over the one new, and frankly unexpected, fact she'd learned. This time, McKinsey had wanted only her.

Whatever his reasons, she doubted that boded well.

And with every mile, with every rattling turn of the coach's wheels, Edinburgh and McKinsey drew inexorably closer.

She definitely needed to be out of Scrope's hands before McKinsey came for her.

They approached Edinburgh in the late morning, with a blue-gray sky overhead and a brisk breeze blowing. Carefully tooling his curricle along, Jeremy was a hundred yards back down the highway when the kidnappers' coach slowed, then turned in under the arch of a large coaching inn close by where South Bridge Street started its ascent into Edinburgh Auld Town.

He'd stayed far enough back over the journey to ensure that Taylor, the coachman, was unlikely to spot him if he glanced back; he'd kept other vehicles between his curricle and the coach for as much of the journey as he could.

But . . . what now? What was Scrope's plan?

There were two carts and another carriage, all rolling slowly along, between his curricle and the entrance to the coaching inn's yard. Raising his head, Jeremy searched both sides of the road ahead; as he'd thought, while there were many inns along this stretch of road, there were no major inns beyond the one the kidnappers' coach had stopped at.

The observation answered his questions. Scrope had halted at the coaching inn closest to the town proper, either because he intended to put up at the inn, holding Eliza there until the laird came to fetch her, or, and more likely in Jeremy's estimation, Scrope intended to take Eliza into the town, to some house or lodging in the narrow, twisting cobbled closes where carriages didn't go.

If the latter was the case, he needed to act now. He couldn't afford to let them take Eliza into Auld Town without being close on their heels.

Casting around, he saw another, smaller inn a bare twenty yards from the larger house, and on the same side of the road. Praying Taylor or Scrope didn't think to come out of the coaching inn's yard to check for pursuing gentlemen, he drove up to the smaller inn and turned into its yard.

Five minutes later, he slouched against the iron railings of South Bridge, one among the horde of people who used the bridge to go into and out of the town, and surreptitiously watched the coaching inn. He'd only just settled into position when Scrope, Taylor, and the nurse, closely escorting a slighter figure enveloped in a drab cloak, emerged and headed his way. The nurse had her fingers locked around Eliza's elbow, and Scrope walked close by her side, a fraction ahead of her. Taylor brought up the rear, with a porter toiling in his wake, lugging three large traveling bags.

Jeremy did nothing to attract their attention, but none of the three kidnappers looked to right or left. They walked with purpose onto and up the bridge, wordlessly declaring that they knew where they were going and were intent on reaching their destination as soon as possible.

Eliza kept her head down; with the cloak's hood up, Jeremy couldn't so much as glimpse her face. After watching her from the corner of his eye for several moments, he realized she was having to watch her feet, holding the over-long skirts of the cloak so she wouldn't trip, and placing her ballroom-slipper-shod feet carefully on the worn paving.

She didn't see him as they passed.

Pushing away from the railings, giving every indication of idly strolling, he followed some twenty yards to their rear. Given his height, he had no difficulty allowing others to fill the gap between. Ambling along, he kept the group in sight as they steadily climbed toward the Royal Mile.

Eliza had visited Edinburgh twice before, on both occasions with her parents to attend ton events. As she'd never imagined she would ever need to know, she'd paid little attention to the layout of the streets. While she recognized the wide sweep of the elevated thoroughfare they'd trudged up and the big church at the corner where that street finally met level ground—she thought the intersecting street was the High Street but wasn't truly sure—she was lost from there on.

The bustle in the High Street, if it was that, was considerable. Caught up in the melee, by the time her captors turned her down a narrow, descending street she'd lost sight of the mouth of the elevated street—the one that led south and eventually back to the Great North Road and England.

Glancing back at the last moment, she caught a glimpse of the spire of the big church and calmed herself with the thought that she could use that as a landmark if she needed to find her way later; the elevated street, South Bridge she thought it was called, ran down one side of that church.

Facing forward, she discovered, to her surprise, that the cobbled street they were leading her down was lined with new houses. The stone facing was crisp, the window glass gleaming, the paintwork glossy. The entire right side of the street was occupied by a newly built terrace, rising three stories above the cobbles.

She was so surprised she forgot Scrope's injunction on

leaving the coach, forbidding her to speak. "I thought all of Edinburgh was ancient."

Scrope cast her a sharp glance. "Except for the parts that burned to the ground not so long ago."

"Ah. I remember now." The town had been devastated by a massive fire in . . . "Five years or so ago, wasn't it?"

Scrope, ever the conversationalist, nodded.

Two paces on, he halted before one of the new houses, before the steps leading up to its narrow porch and glossy green front door. Pulling a keychain from his coat pocket, he mounted the steps. An instant later, he had the door open. As he walked inside, Genevieve urged Eliza to follow.

Climbing to the porch, instinctive reluctance mounting, she swallowed. Lecturing herself that she had nothing to fear, that Jeremy would have followed, and that any of the rooms in such a new house that they might lock her in would surely have a window through which she could escape, she clung to her veneer of obedience and stepped over the threshold. Not that she had any real choice with Genevieve and Taylor at her back.

Scrope had halted in a small front hall, in the doorway of what Eliza guessed would be the drawing room. With a gesture, he waved Eliza and Genevieve to the left. Genevieve guided Eliza forward, past Scrope and down a short corridor. A glance back showed Taylor blocking the front doorway and her view of the street as he paid off the porter.

Genevieve steered her into the room at the end of the corridor; it proved to be the kitchen. But instead of halting before the table that filled the center of the room, the nurse, using her grip on Eliza's arm, turned Eliza to face a door in the wall.

Scrope had followed them; he reached past and opened the door, revealing a set of narrow wooden stairs leading down.

Lifting a lantern from a hook alongside the door, Scrope lit it, adjusted the flame, then went quickly down the steps. "Come along."

Eliza's feet turned to lead. If they put her in the basement—

"Get moving." Genevieve emphasized her order with a sharp jab to Eliza's back. "Console your pampered self with the reflection that it is a new basement, and our orders are to keep you in comfort, if not style."

Eliza heard Taylor's heavy tread as the coachman-cum-guard joined them. She had no choice but to do as they said.

Slowly, step by step, she descended, eventually stepping onto a solid stone floor. Scrope had halted a few yards away, the lantern held high enough to shed a wide circle of light.

That light illuminated a short corridor and another door. This door looked even thicker than the one through which they'd just passed, and possessed a heavy iron lock fitted with a massive key.

Turning the key, Scrope pulled the door open. He half bowed and waved her in. "Your quarters, Miss Cynster. Not what you're accustomed to, I fear, but at least you'll have to spend only one night in such spartan surrounds."

Scrope raised the lantern, letting the beam wash through the doorway into the small room beyond. Roughly thirty feet square, the sparsely furnished room contained a narrow bed and a rickety washstand, with a tiny mirror on the wall above. A threadbare runner ran beneath the bed and across the stone floor. In one corner, a small screen stood angled, presumably hiding a chamber pot.

The best that could be said of the room was that it was clean.

Forced to the threshold by Genevieve, Eliza glanced at Scrope. She refused to quiver or show her reaction; the truth was that reaction was more anger than fear. Catching his eye, she asked with quiet dignity, "May I at least have a candle?"

Scrope's dark eyes held hers for an instant—no doubt while he tried to imagine how a single candle might help her escape—then he looked toward the steps; Taylor had remained at their top, in the kitchen. "Light a candlestick and bring it down."

Turning back to her, Scrope nodded toward the room.

Inclining her head haughtily, she moved into the small space. Walking the few paces to the side of the bed, she unlaced the rough cloak they'd given her and swung it off her shoulders.

Taylor appeared in the doorway and offered a candlestick bearing a single lighted candle.

She took it. "Thank you."

As Taylor stepped back, she looked Scrope in the eye. "You may go."

Scrope's lips pinched; the thinly veiled insult had hit its mark.

He closed the door with a barely restrained thud.

The key grated loudly in the lock.

Eliza listened to the footsteps recede, then set the candlestick on a corner of the washstand, sat on the bed, clasped her hands in her lap, and stared at the door.

At the solid timber panel that stood between her and freedom. That was the only way out of her basement room, the modern dungeon they'd locked her in.

She couldn't think of any easy way for Jeremy to get her out of there, but he'd already surprised her with his ingenuity, his willingness to attempt things she hadn't thought it likely he would try; she wouldn't, she lectured herself, give up hope yet.

But she couldn't quash the sliver of doubt that whispered through her mind. Did he even know where she was?

She didn't know, she couldn't tell, and that was the worst of it. The situation required her to have blind faith, not something she would readily accord anyone.

The weight of the pendant between her breasts impinged on her awareness. She reached for it, clasped the crystal through the fine silk of her bodice, and tried to tell herself she wasn't totally alone.

Tried to believe it.

She was grateful for the illusory warmth of the steady candlelight.

Her fingers around the pendant, her gaze fixed on the door, she waited.

Jeremy leaned against the area railings of a house across Niddery Street and three doors down from the one Eliza and her captors had entered. He lounged as if waiting for a friend, and pondered the newness of the terrace opposite and what that almost certainly meant.

He'd heard about the great fire from Cobby and Hugo, and also much about the subsequent rebuilding. Matching that information with what he saw before him raised an intriguing prospect, one, he decided, he should definitely pursue.

Eliza and her three captors had entered the house more than twenty minutes ago. He was about to push away from the railings and head for Cobby's house when the door of the kidnappers' house opened.

The man in charge—Scrope, Eliza had named him—stepped out onto the porch, closed the door, then descended the steps and strode back toward High Street.

His gaze on the house, Jeremy hesitated, evaluating the risks . . . reluctantly concluded that the coachman guard and the nurse were still inside, one too many for him to have any reasonable chance of overcoming.

Should he follow Scrope?

He glanced after the man and discovered he'd already lost his chance there. Scrope had quickened his purposeful stride and had already merged with the thronging masses in the main thoroughfare. Although readily recognizable when on his own, there was nothing about Scrope that would make him stand out in a crowd.

Had Scrope gone to summon the laird? Eliza had said they planned to hand her over the next day—not today—so presumably Scrope had gone to send word that they had her there, in Edinburgh, in their keeping.

Eliza needed to be out of the house and away before to-morrow morning.

Looking back at the house, Jeremy raised his gaze and studied every window on the upper floors, but saw no face peering out. He wondered if Eliza had seen him, if she knew he was there and so would know help was coming.

He didn't like to think of her imagining she was alone.

Pushing away from the railings, he walked back up the street. He knew Eliza's location; it was time to start arranging her rescue.

Reaching High Street, he turned right along the Royal Mile, toward Cannongate and Cobby's house in Reids Close.

Chapter Four

several hours later, Jeremy—garbed in a dun surveyor's coat that reached to his knees, his dark brown hair parted in the center, brushed back and slicked down, a pair of spectacles and two pencils showing in the coat's top pocket—followed his friend Cobby down the steps of the house next door to the one Eliza was being held in.

It had taken more than three hours to get everything organized and underway. His first action had been to stop at a courier office and send a letter to Wolverstone posthaste. Not knowing Eliza's parents' direction, he'd left it to Royce and Minerva to spread the word, confident they would convey his information to Eliza's family with all speed.

They had to be desperate for news of her.

He'd written explaining how he'd stumbled upon her, related what he'd learned of the kidnappers, and concluded with an assurance that he was presently arranging her rescue without allowing her identity or her time spent with her captors to become public knowledge. He'd closed with the information that he and Eliza would seek refuge at Wolverstone Castle, that being the nearest place of assured safety, as soon as they possibly could.

With the missive dispatched, he'd gone on to Reids Close and had been lucky enough to find not just Cobden Harris—scholarly scion of the Harris clan, known to all as Cobby—with his feet up before his hearth but also the Honorable Hugo Weaver keeping him company. Jeremy, Cobby, and Hugo had become firm friends during the five months Jeremy had spent in Edinburgh working for the Scottish Assembly, cataloguing various old works in their collections, some of which had been acquired by Alexander I and not looked at since. While Cobby was a scholar of ancient Scottish writings, Hugo was a scholar of ancient legal works, of laws, parliaments, and governance. The Assembly had invited the three of them to form a team; the result had been an association that had overflowed from the professional to the personal, and continued long after Jeremy had returned to London.

Naturally, the instant he'd told them—Cobby, Hugo, and Cobby's wife, Margaret, more commonly known as Meggin—his news, they'd been eager to throw themselves into the project: "The Rescue," as Hugo had dramatically dubbed it.

"That should do it." Consulting the ledger he held in his hands, Cobby—a few inches shorter than Jeremy and slightly more rotund, and presently dressed similarly—paused on the pavement and made a show of comparing the ledger entries with the notes on the papers attached to the board Jeremy was carrying.

When Jeremy had described the house on Niddery Street, the three locals had immediately confirmed his suspicion. Which was why Jeremy and Cobby, disguised as council inspectors, were currently inspecting the houses along the street, their aim to determine exactly where in the house Eliza was being held, while Hugo, who had a long association with all things thespian in the city, after suitably dressing the pair of them for the outing, was out searching through the wardrobes of the various theaters and otherwise arranging for all else they would need to pull "The Rescue" off.

Leaning closer, Cobby more quietly asked, "Ready?"

By way of answer, Jeremy nodded to the door of the next house. His disguise was good enough; he doubted Taylor would recognize him.

Swinging around, Cobby marched up the steps, raised his fist, and beat a smart tattoo on the door.

A moment later, it opened, revealing Taylor. He glanced at Cobby, then at Jeremy, then looked back at Cobby. "Yes?"

"Good morning." Cobby was all breezy officialdom. "We're from the town council, here to make an inspection of the works."

Taylor frowned. "The works?"

"Why, yes." Cobby gestured broadly. "The building. As per the new regulations instituted in the wake of the fire, every new structure must be inspected to ensure that the works are in keeping with the new town ordinances."

Taylor's frown hadn't abated. "We're not the owners—we've just leased the house for a few weeks. We'll be leaving any day." He made to shut the door. "You can come back—"

"Oh, no, no, sir." Cobby halted him with a raised hand. "The inspections are mandatory and cannot be put off. The owner would have been notified by the town clerk. If the owner failed to inform you of the pending inspection, you must take that up with him, but you must not impede us, officers of the council, in any way. As I'm sure you understand, in the aftermath of the tragic fire, public anger against poor building standards reached fever pitch, and the council cannot be seen to be wavering in this regard." Cobby gestured back along the terrace. "We've already completed the survey for most of this section and must finish here today, so if you will allow us entry, we will endeavor to accomplish our task and be out of your way as soon as possible."

Still holding the door, Taylor hesitated; shifting his weight, he said, "My master's out, but should return shortly. If you could come back in an hour—"

"Sadly, no—we are on a tight schedule." Cobby briefly paused, then offered, "If it will help, the police station isn't far. We could command the presence of two constables to lend gravitas to our demand, if that would help your standing with your master?"

Looking down, Jeremy squelched the inclination to smile. He'd rehearsed Cobby in what to say; his friend was very good at making people think him the soul of reasonableness.

As he'd expected, the option of having constables in the house made Taylor's decision much easier. The man's face blanked, then he shrugged. "If you won't be long, I don't suppose it matters."

He opened the door, and Jeremy followed Cobby inside.

They started their "inspection" in the attics, consulting the various forms they'd concocted, making notes, and steadily working their way through the house, room by room, cupboard by cupboard. When they reached the ground floor without detecting the slightest sign of Eliza's presence, they insisted on checking under the stairs, then Cobby dallied at their foot, supposedly making more notes, in reality ensuring that no one smuggled anyone—Eliza for instance—back upstairs while Jeremy embarked on a determined progress through the various ground-floor reception rooms.

All to no avail.

But Eliza had to be in the house. Them moving her in the few hours he'd been away, yet remaining there themselves, didn't make sense.

He also knew there was more to the house than was apparent from outside.

Eventually collecting Cobby, they again made a show of comparing notes, then Cobby led the way down the short corridor to the kitchen.

The dark-haired woman Jeremy had seen with Eliza—Genevieve, the nurse—was sitting at the deal table sipping from a cup when they entered. She looked shocked, then shot a surprised and concerned look at Taylor.

Almost imperceptibly, the big man shook his head and reported what they'd told him of their business.

Given the woman's reaction, Jeremy felt certain that Eliza was there, most likely in the basement room. Their inspection of the house next door had confirmed that the houses in the terrace had such a room, and all of the houses appeared identical in construction.

Under Taylor's and the woman's guarded gazes, they dutifully inspected the kitchen, paying special note to the chimney flue, and the construction of the back door and its frame. Then, after they'd conferred in hushed tones, Cobby pointed to the door in the wall to the left of the door through which they'd entered. "Right then. Just the basement and we're done. If you would unlock the door?"

Jeremy mumbled to Cobby, drawing his attention away from the door to some point in Jeremy's notes, making their expectation that the basement door would be unlocked without fuss transparent.

Across the deal table, Taylor and Genevieve exchanged a long look.

Jeremy gave them a minute to think—took the same time to think through the possibilities of the next moments himself—then he stepped back, releasing Cobby, who turned to Taylor and the basement door.

Seeing that Taylor had made no move toward the door, Cobby raised his brows. "Is there a problem?"

"Ah . . ." Taylor, his eyes again meeting Genevieve's, raised a hand to lift a key from a hook on the wall. "You might think so. We can let you down into the basement, but the owner's left the basement room locked, and we don't have the key. We assume he's put all his valuables down there—it wouldn't look good if we tried to force the lock."

"Oh, well." Cobby glanced at Jeremy. "That is unfortunate . . ."

"Perhaps"—seeing the danger, Jeremy stepped in, imitating Meggin's lowland Scots accent—"as it's hardly your fault the owner has done as he has, we should examine what we can, and then make a note for the clerk to deal with it." He glanced at the clock on the kitchen wall, then, lowering his voice, leaned closer to Cobby and said, "If we don't get on, we're not going to be able to meet the others at the pub."

Cobby glanced past him at the clock, then nodded decisively. "Right." He turned back to Taylor. "Perhaps if we just look down the steps so we can show we've done what we could."

Moving slowly, Taylor fitted the key to the lock, turned it, then opened the door.

Thinking furiously about what might happen next, Jeremy realized that if Eliza sensed that someone other than her captors was near, she might cry out, trying to attract their attention . . . if she did, Taylor and Genevieve would do all they could to ensure he and Cobby didn't leave the house.

Taylor's smile was forced as he held the thick panel open. "You can't see much—just the steps and that bit of corridor."

Jeremy sensed the rising tension; the woman behind him had stiffened and shifted her weight, ready to spring up and help Taylor push both him and Cobby down the steps.

Cobby stepped to the threshold and peered down.

Keeping his voice low so that while Cobby and Taylor would hear him, Eliza, if she was behind the basement door, wouldn't, Jeremy quickly said, "We don't need to see more. Those steps look safe enough—same as in the other houses."

Picking up the urgency in his tone, Cobby glanced back at him, then looked again down the steps at the short corridor and the heavy door they could just make out in the gloom. "Yes, you're right." Taking his cue from Jeremy, he spoke softly. After an instant more of peering into the deep shadows, Cobby stepped back and waved Taylor to shut the door—which he did far more quickly than he'd opened it.

Moving to Jeremy's side to look down at his notes, Cobby read, then nodded. "That should be sufficient."

"Good." Setting the key back on its hook, Taylor turned to usher them out.

With a polite nod to the woman, they left.

A minute later, they were out on the pavement again.

"Next house," Jeremy said. "They're watching through the window."

"We need to check the basement, anyway." Cobby led the way on, marching up to the next house's door and knocking briskly.

The old woman who lived there argued querulously but eventually let them in. Their inspection of her house was more cursory, but they still went from attic to basement, just in case Taylor or Genevieve thought to ask the old biddy what they'd done.

They'd hoped to get a good look at the basement room, especially its floor, but when the old lady pulled open the door, disappointment awaited them. The old woman had clearly moved from a much larger house and had kept all her furniture. It was stacked, packed, into the basement room; barely five square inches of floor were visible.

"Ah—yes." Cobby stared at the hotchpotch, glanced briefly around at the walls, then nodded. "Right. That'll do."

He turned to thank the woman, pouring on the Scottish charm. They left her almost smiling.

The instant they were back on the pavement and the door had closed behind them, Jeremy stated, "We need to know if we're right about the basement."

Cobby waved him on. "Next house, then. This close to High Street, they'll all be the same."

The next door was opened by an elderly gentleman, a retired soldier. He was gruffly genial and, leaning on his cane, happily conducted them about his house, chatting about this or that the whole time.

They humored him and were amply rewarded when he showed them into his basement room. "Same as all the others, of course." Setting the door open, he waved them in. Cobby lifted the lantern he held, playing the light over several pieces of old furniture stacked in one corner. Otherwise, the room was empty, the floor bare.

Both Cobby's and Jeremy's gazes lowered, following the lantern's beam as Cobby visually searched the stone floor.

Beside them, the old soldier chuckled. "Aye—it's the same

as in all the other houses along this terrace. I wondered if you knew to check for it."

His gaze on the wooden trapdoor set into the floor, Jeremy nodded. "We've seen it in some, but in other places—for instance in the old lady's house next door—we've been unable to confirm it or examine it ourselves."

"Go ahead." The man nodded at the heavy bolt set into the trapdoor's surface. "Just pull that back and you can take a look."

Eager to do so, Jeremy pushed past Cobby, who shifted the lantern to focus on the trapdoor. Jeremy wriggled the bolt loose, pulled it back, then lifted the panel. While it was inches thick and heavy, it was nicely weighted on good hinges; it opened easily enough.

Cobby stepped closer and shone the lantern down the gaping hole. The edges of the trapdoor were solid and sound; a neat, newish wooden ladder led down to the floor of the corridorlike space beneath. "Yes," Cobby said, "this is just like the last house where we could check, a few doors up the terrace."

"Oh, aye." The old soldier nodded sagaciously. "This whole terrace was built by the same builder—all the houses are as close to identical as makes no odds. Clever fellow left every house with an escape route in case of another big fire. Wouldna have been so many people died if they hadn't blocked off the access to the old tunnels there. Easy enough to go down, along, and out."

Jeremy smiled and looked across the open trapdoor at Cobby. "What a wise and helpful builder, indeed."

Genevieve, with Taylor at her back, shook Eliza from a sound sleep.

Shielding her eyes from the glare of the lamp Taylor held, Eliza blinked awake. A glance at the cold puddle of wax, all that was left of the fresh candle they'd given her when they'd come to take her luncheon tray away, suggested she'd been asleep for some time.

She struggled onto her elbows, watching as Genevieve set a faintly steaming pitcher on the washstand. "What time is it?"

"Seven o'clock." Genevieve turned to her. "Scrope's decided you should join us for dinner. Easier than making up a separate tray."

Setting a lighted, two-armed candelabra on the washstand, Taylor snorted. "It's the last night we'll be babysitting you. More like Scrope wants to celebrate."

"Regardless"—Genevieve nudged Taylor back toward the door—"we'll leave you to wash and tidy yourself. We'll come back in fifteen minutes to take you upstairs."

They went out and shut the heavy door again. Pushing upright, Eliza swung her legs over the side of the bed, listened, and heard the key turn in the lock. Sitting on the bed's edge, she tried to imagine what ulterior motives might lie behind the unexpected dinner invitation, then decided that whatever they were, she didn't truly care. Getting out of the tiny basement room even for a few hours wasn't a boon she was in any mood to refuse.

After her days in the coach, she'd welcomed their brisk walk through the town, but being incarcerated again in such a small room had made her long for wide and open spaces. Which felt strange given she wasn't overly fond of such places.

Rising, she paused for an instant, confirmed, to her very real relief, that the last vestigial traces of the laudanum had worn off. Her mind was her own, and so was her body.

Going to the washstand, she lifted the pitcher and poured the warm water into the basin.

Stripping off her much-abused ball gown, pushing the rose quartz pendant around so it hung down her back, out of her way, she quickly washed.

Briskly shaking out the golden gown, she donned it again, then turned to the mirror to do what she could to tidy her hair. The elegant style of honey-gold curls artfully arranged to tumble from a knot on the top of her head to form a shining crown was now a disarranged disaster. Swiftly plucking pins, she released the long tresses, used her fingers to comb the mass out, then plaited it into two braids, finally winding both around her head to form a coronet, and anchoring the ends with the pins.

Finally, she pulled the pendant back to hang between her breasts; she debated about leaving it on show, but the rose quartz clashed with the gold of her gown. "Better not to flaunt it, anyway." She tucked the pendant beneath her bodice, straightened the necklace from which it hung, rearranged her fichu and collar as best she could, then dipped and weaved before the mirror, checking the result.

It was better than she'd hoped, which made her feel more confident. More like the Cynster female she was, less like a bedraggled kidnap victim.

She was, she realized, looking forward to the dinner, to seeing what more she might tease from Scrope and his minions. As long as she didn't dwell on the vexing questions of whether Jeremy knew where she was, and how he might rescue her, assuming that he did, she would manage.

Hearing footsteps beyond the door, she swung to face it. Taylor pulled the door wide; he grinned when he saw her. Standing in the corridor, Genevieve looked irritated. She beckoned. "Come on. Scrope's waiting."

They conducted her up the steps into the kitchen, then along the short corridor to the dining room.

A rectangular table had been set for four. Scrope was standing before a tantalus by the wall, a glass of red wine in his hand. He turned as she walked in. His gaze took in her appearance, then he half bowed, playing the gentleman. "Miss Cynster. May I offer you a glass of wine?"

Although his expression remained uninformative, Eliza

sensed he was in a distinctly good, if not mellow, mood. "No, thank you, but I would like some water."

"In that case." Scrope waved to the table and came forward. Setting down his glass beside the place at its head, he came around and held the chair to his right for her.

Playing along—she saw no reason not to—Eliza sat, graciously inclining her head in response to his gallantry.

Taylor, mimicking Scrope, held the chair opposite Eliza for Genevieve. With both ladies seated, the men took their seats, and the meal began.

There were no footmen to offer the dishes, but everything had already been set on the table, large enough to accommodate six. The first course was a pea and ham soup, rather heavy for a dinner, but Eliza was starving. She made short work of emptying her bowl.

A fish course followed, supplanted by guinea fowl and partridges accompanied by various side dishes, before the silver dome was lifted from a platter of roast venison. With her appetite more than appeased, she dabbed her lips with her napkin and set herself to learning what she could. "I can see that this is, indeed, a celebratory feast—and a last supper of sorts for me." Lifting her water glass, she met Scrope's dark gaze. "I take it that, as you foreshadowed, McKinsey will come for me tomorrow?"

Scrope and his minions had been distinctly closemouthed, but presumably anything they told her now would no longer matter.

His dark gaze steady, Scrope considered her.

She sipped and did nothing more than faintly arch her brows.

Eventually, he nodded. "Your supposition is correct. I sent word to McKinsey, or whoever he is, before midday. I don't know how long it'll take to reach him—the delivery is not, you'll understand, direct—but he led me to believe he would be in Edinburgh, waiting for you to arrive."

From the other end of the table, Taylor, busy with a large

helping of venison, flicked a glance at Scrope. "So we don't have to wait for him to ride down from Inverness?"

"Inverness?" Eliza looked back at Scrope.

Scrope's lips tightened, his dark eyes narrowing on the hapless Taylor.

Glancing back at the now wary coachman-cum-guard, Eliza airily said, "We already knew McKinsey is a highlander." She shrugged. "Knowing he comes from Inverness is nothing new."

Inverness was the southernmost large town in the highlands.

Scrope looked down at his plate and all but growled, "He doesn't come from Inverness." He flung another irate glance at Taylor. "Inverness is just the place through which the message I sent to him before was routed."

Eliza considered that reply, then ventured, "You followed a message sent to him?"

Scrope turned his narrow-eyed gaze on her. "I like to know who I'm dealing with."

She nodded. "Understandably. Did you learn anything more of his identity?"

"No." Scrope's frustration assured her that he spoke the truth. "The man's as slippery as any damned highland nobleman ever birthed. The message vanished from the office in Inverness, and no one seemed to have the faintest clue as to where it went."

"Hmm." Eliza found Scrope's tale revealing. She, Heather, and Angelica had discussed and speculated on the character and person of the mysterious laird for many hours. Given such telltale acts of power, the sort of power Cynsters intuitively recognized and understood, combined with the picture the various snippets of physical description had drawn of him, there was no denying that the figure the laird cut was one of considerable elemental and visceral attraction.

At least to Cynster females.

Nevertheless, despite her curiosity, Eliza had no wish to

meet the man, at least not on his terms. Being hauled into the wilds of the highlands did not feature on her list of desirable diversions.

As for what he intended for her, *that* she was determinedly refusing to dwell on; Jeremy would rescue her first, so there was no need to imagine herself into a panic.

Eventually, Genevieve rose and, assisted by Taylor, cleared the table.

Scrope, reverting to his role of considerate host, offered Eliza a small glass of orgeat, which, on consideration, she deigned to accept.

"Tell me," she said, seizing the moment when the other two were elsewhere, "why do you, who I assume was born a gentleman, take . . . jobs, for want of a better word, such as this." She met his dark eyes. "I'm curious as to what drives you."

Whoever had arranged the dinner menu had known the basics of gentle living; she was quite sure it wasn't Genevieve, a lowly companion-nurse, who had chosen the dishes and arranged for them to be delivered in their warming pans and chafing dishes, as she assumed they must have been.

Scrope, she deduced, harbored gentlemanly aspirations. In her experience, gentlemen, if approached correctly, always liked to talk about themselves.

Sipping from the wineglass he'd kept filled throughout the meal, Scrope considered her, then, after flicking a glance toward the corridor door, quietly said, "I might have been born and schooled as a gentleman, but by a twist of fate I was left with no way of supporting myself as such." He met her gaze. "Some men in that situation take to the tables, hoping to find their salvation in the cards. Me . . ." His lips lightly lifted. "Fate sent me an opportunity to perform a singular service for a distant acquaintance . . . and I discovered a profession at which I excelled."

"Profession?" She arched her brows, faintly supercilious.

"Yes, indeed." Scrope took another healthy swallow of the wine; she felt certain it was assisting with the sudden loosening of his tongue. "Would it surprise you to know that there's a well-established trade in the professional services I offer?" When she made no reply, Scrope actually smiled. "I assure you there is. And there's a ladder of achievement within that profession, too."

Taking another swill of his wine, he eyed her over the rim of his glass, then lowered it and said, "And you, Miss Eliza Cynster, will take me, Victor Scrope, to the very top of that ladder." With his glass, he saluted her. "Handing you to McKinsey will raise me to the dizzying pinnacle of my professional tree."

She said nothing; Scrope had clearly set aside his usual, impenetrable demeanor. As witnessed by this celebratory dinner, he was beyond confident of success—of succeeding in handing her over to McKinsey tomorrow morning.

In that instant, she was looking at the man behind the coolly professional, impassive mask.

Scrope leaned forward, dark eyes fixing intently on her face. "So you see, my dear, it's not solely the money that motivates me, although to give McKinsey credit, he has in no way skimped on my fee. Our highland laird placed a very high price on your head. But that's not the most valuable boon I'll secure when I hand you to him tomorrow. Put simply, Miss Cynster, you will be my salvation. You'll give me my future as I wish it to be. With McKinsey's money, and even more with the fame your successful kidnap will bring me, I'll be assured of a wealthy and comfortable gentlemanly life for the rest of my days."

Leaning back, a gloating, almost manic smile on his lips, Scrope raised his glass to her once again. "To you, Miss Cynster—and to what tomorrow will bring."

Scrope downed the wine in one gulp.

Eliza stared and fought to suppress a shiver.

A sound at the door had them both glancing that way.

"Trifle or apple pie." Genevieve carried two dishes to the table.

"And there's clotted cream, too," Taylor said, setting a smaller bowl down and retaking his seat.

"So." Silver serving spoon poised, Genevieve looked from Scrope to Eliza. "Which will you have?"

"Both," Eliza said. She needed to take her mind off what she'd glimpsed in Scrope's eyes, and dessert was the only distraction available; it would have to do.

All three of them escorted her back to her prison not long afterward. Scrope allowed her request for fresh candles; he glanced around the room as if assuring himself she had adequate comforts, then he waved Genevieve outside and closed the door.

The last sight Eliza had of her captors was Scrope's face, demonically lit by a candle from below, his dark eyes glinting, and fixed on her.

Once the door shut, she allowed herself the instinctive shiver she'd until then suppressed. Almost as if someone had walked over her grave.

Shaking the sensation and all thought of graves aside, she finally turned her mind to what might happen next.

She had no assurance that Jeremy even knew where she was. He might have lost the trail of the coach, or he might have missed their route through Edinburgh. She had to be realistic and at least *try* to think of some way to escape if he didn't rescue her that night.

After pondering the likely opportunities, she realized her first decision had to be whether to try to escape Scrope's clutches, or wait until she was handed over and then try to escape from the laird.

It wasn't, she reasoned, a question of which one would be easier to outwit, so much as which one was more likely to make a miscalculation and give her the opportunity to flee.

Scrope had yet to give her any opening at all. And no

matter how overconfident he was, how certain he would suc-cessfully hand her into the laird's keeping, no matter how overweening his gloating, she couldn't imagine him stum-bling at the last hurdle.

Conveying her into the laird's hands tomorrow would be a carefully orchestrated and tightly monitored event. Scrope would not make any mistake, not with so much money and pride riding on the outcome.

As for what she knew of the laird . . . it was possible that if he was a nobleman, as seemed increasingly likely, then he might well suffer from the same male assumptions, the same male blindness when it came to females as she was used to dealing with in her brothers and cousins.

That would give her a chance. A chance she might be able to convert into an opportunity to slip away.

Against that, however, was the strong likelihood that he would cart her off into the highlands, and that was one land-scape in which she would be totally and impossibly out of her depth.

In the English countryside, she would have managed somehow; she might not enjoy hiking over hill and dale, but she knew she could do it. Hiking through glens, around lochs, and over possibly snowcapped peaks was another matter altogether.

People got lost in the highlands and weren't found for years.

She sat on the bed and stared unseeing at the door, and thought and thought as the candlelight dimmed, then flick-ered. Before she lost the light, she used the cold water in the pitcher to splash her face. As the candles started to gutter, first one, then the other, she toed off her slippers and got into the bed.

Pulling the thin blanket over her shoulders, she curled on her side.

There was no way out. None at all. There was nothing whatever she could do.

Whichever way she looked at it, her future depended on a man.

Scrope. The laird. Or Jeremy Carling.

Her fingers locked about the rose quartz pendant her sister had passed to her with such hope and assurances of happiness to come, Eliza knew who she hoped fate would choose for her.

Even if he was an absentminded scholar, she would cope.

Jeremy, Cobby, Hugo, and Meggin sat gathered around the table in the dining room of Cobby and Meggin's town house in Reids Close. The scene, Jeremy thought, looked like an artist's impression of exactly what it was—a convivial dinner hosted by a young, well-to-do, and well-connected Scottish couple for two of the husband's bachelor friends. Illuminated by the comfortably cozy glow of the chandelier suspended above the mahogany table, the room was well appointed, with dark wood paneling on the walls, and richly hued paintings of misty landscapes above the heavy sideboards. Silver candelabra and a matching multitiered fruit dish added their gleam, while the stag's head mounted above the fireplace, flanked by two massive, mounted trout, screamed Scotland to anyone with eyes.

In the great carver at the head of the table, Cobby's eyes danced and his smile was wide as he spoke with Hugo, seated on his left. With hair a similar color to Jeremy's middling dark brown, with hazel eyes and regular features, and now garbed in his habitual townsman's clothes, Cobby looked every inch the scion of a venerable Scottish clan.

Seated in the smaller carver opposite her husband, with tumbling black curls, twinkling blue eyes, and a dark blue silk gown, the very epitome of a sophisticated young matron, Meggin watched her husband with open affection.

The covers had been drawn, the dishes cleared away. It was time to get down to business.

Jeremy tapped the table. When the other three cast questioning glances his way, he stated, "We need to go over our plan."

They'd assembled it in bits and pieces—one making a suggestion, another seeing how it could be altered to better fit—like a giant cerebral jigsaw, titled "The Rescue."

He was rather pleased with the outcome.

Hugo, a chameleon of sorts with his Byronicly handsome features and artistically ruffled dark hair, his slender bones and slighter build often rendering his movements gracefully effeminate, was a good friend to have at one's back; he was equally at home trading supercilious barbs in some lady's drawing room as trading punches in a barroom brawl. Leaning back in his chair, Hugo waved at the clothes and wig he'd left on a straight-backed chair by the wall. "Now we have the last of our disguises, by all means let's review our campaign."

That was exactly what it felt like: a military campaign. One with a clear goal to attain.

"Just out of interest," Cobby said, "where did you find those?" With his head he indicated the clothes on the chair.

"The little theaterette at the palace." Hugo winked. "Don't tell."

Hugo's family, root and all its various branches, were longtime legal counselors to the palace; Hugo therefore had the entree to areas few others did.

"Let's start at the beginning." Clasping her hands on the table, Meggin looked at Jeremy. "How do you plan to get Miss Cynster out of that basement?"

The practical one, Meggin forced them to go through their plan step by step, insisting they fill in the gaps, all the minor details that, in their scholarly fashion, they were apt to take for granted.

"Are you sure they won't have drugged her again?"

Jeremy hesitated, thought. Eventually, he said, "I don't think so. In both cases—Eliza's and her sister Heather's—

the kidnappers were under strict orders to keep their prizes in good health. I suspect Scrope wasn't supposed to keep Eliza drugged at all."

"So if they're to hand her over to the laird tomorrow, they won't have drugged her tonight, so she should be able to walk out on her own." Meggin nodded decisively. "All right. Go on."

They did, rehearsing in their minds each act of their grand plan. After releasing Eliza from the basement room, the next stage was to whisk her out of the city.

"We'll leave here just before first light," Jeremy said, "and go down and hire horses. There's no point trying to ride out before there's light enough to see." From Niddery Street, they planned to bring Eliza there, to Reids Close. "Once we're away, we should be able to reach Wolverstone in a day—well, at least by evening."

Meggin looked doubtful. "That's hard riding by anyone's standards."

Jeremy grimaced. "Perhaps, but as long as we're over the border before nightfall, I know the roads from there to the castle well enough to navigate in the dark."

Meggin hesitated, but then nodded and let the matter slide.

Jeremy appreciated her tact. He'd realized, as she had, that in order to preserve Eliza's reputation from the socially damning slur of spending a night entirely alone with a gentleman not related in any way, they would need to cover the distance from Edinburgh to Wolverstone Castle in a single, nonstop journey. Normally that would be easy enough, but in this instance they had to take a circling, roundabout route the better to avoid any effective pursuit.

Nevertheless, he thought through the various points again but still concluded, "There really isn't any other way to accomplish our aim."

With that stage settled, Cobby and Hugo took over the discussion, going over their subsequent roles in "The Rescue," namely as decoys designed to lead Scrope and his team, and the laird, too, if he became actively involved, in the opposite direction from Jeremy and Eliza's route.

Jeremy and Meggin shared a glance at the exuberance Cobby and Hugo seemed determined to invest in their roles.

"Just be careful," Meggin finally said. "There's no need to call attention to yourselves as yourselves—I would remind you that you're both respected members of Edinburgh society now, not high-spirited schoolboys."

Both Cobby and Hugo contrived to look abashed, but their eyes were twinkling.

Meggin eyed them, then softly snorted, cynically unimpressed; she turned once more to Jeremy. "This is all very well, but I do have reservations about Miss Cynster's journey south. I'd accompany you myself if I could, but with the bairns to watch over, I can't leave." She glanced down the table at her spouse. "Especially not if Cobby's gone, too." She looked back at Jeremy. "Are you sure you shouldn't take a maid, to lend Miss Cynster countenance, as they say?"

All three men frowned. All gave the suggestion due consideration.

All valued Meggin's insights; they knew they were, all three of them, wont to ignore aspects they deemed irrelevant, such as society's strictures.

Eventually Jeremy pulled a face. He looked at Cobby. "I still think taking a maid is too problematic. For a start, if they don't take your bait and instead mount a wider search for us around town, our having a maid will call attention to us, which is precisely what we're striving to avoid. Secondly, a maid will mean we'll have to drive, and quite aside from then having three people, one a maid, in a carriage—precisely the combination of bodies they'll most likely be searching for—we'll need something bigger than a curricle or phaeton to accommodate the maid, and that will slow us down." He looked back at Meggin. "We would definitely need more than a day to cover the distance, and that will give them more time to come at us."

Meggin scrunched up her nose.

Jeremy shook his head. "No—I think our plan as we have it is our best option."

Both Cobby and Hugo nodded agreement.

Meggin sighed. "Very well." She glanced at the clock on the wall.

The others all looked, too.

"It's getting late." Jeremy met Cobby's, then Hugo's, eyes. "We should go."

No one demurred.

They rose from the table; in the front hall, the three men shrugged into their greatcoats and collected lanterns.

Meggin stood ready to unbolt the front door.

Jeremy looked at Cobby, then Hugo, then nodded to Meggin to pull open the door. "Let's get moving—it's time to get 'The Rescue' underway."

Time to get Eliza Cynster out of her captors' hands.

Chapter Five

The night seemed interminable. Eliza didn't even try to sleep. Once the candles guttered, darkness so intense she couldn't see her hand before her face closed in.

It weighed on her like a suffocating blanket.

She wasn't normally afraid of the dark, but this dark had a menacing quality. Despite the covers, she found herself shivering; the basement was cool, but the chill gripping her owed little to the temperature.

Time quickly lost all meaning.

She tried to keep her mind from the question of what would happen if the laird came for her before Jeremy did. What should she do? What could—

Rat-tat.

She blinked, glanced toward the door, but there was no sign of it opening. Not that her captors were likely to knock.

Not that they were likely to come for her at this hour, whatever hour it was.

Rat-tat.

Slowly sitting up, she frowned. The darkness was disorienting, but she thought the tapping was coming from . . . under the bed.

Rat-tat.

The rhythm was regular, a man-made sound. Throwing off the blanket, she groped on the floor, found her slippers, and slid them on.

Rat-tat. Rat-tat.

"I'm coming," she whispered, although she couldn't imagine . . .

Crouching beside the bed—a typical iron-and-wire-framed bed, the base a foot and more off the ground—she peered underneath. It took her an instant to realize that the reason she could see anything at all was that faint light was glowing through the worn fabric of the runner.

Grabbing the rug, she pulled it back, just as another *rat-tat* sounded.

Thin slivers of light outlined the sides of a square set into the floor.

For an instant, she stared at what her stunned brain informed her was a wooden trapdoor, then, hauling in a quick breath, she reached out and rapped her knuckles on the panel: *rat-tat*.

For an instant, nothing happened, then the trapdoor jiggled and pushed up from underneath, but clearly it was fastened in some way.

Her heart leapt, but she reminded herself that she had no idea who was on the other side. They might be burglars. Leaning close, putting her face near the edge, as loudly as she dared she asked, "Who is it?"

A pause followed, then came, "Jeremy Carling. We've come to rescue you."

Sweeter words, she'd never heard. Relief, gratitude, and a curious, eager excitement surged through her. "Just a minute. I have to move the bed."

Scrambling to her feet, she pushed and lifted the end of the bed away from the wall until the space above the trapdoor was clear, then she fell on her knees and felt along the edge opposite where the panel appeared to be hinged.

Her fingers fumbled along what seemed to be a simple bolt. "I have it." Finding the bolt's knob, she lifted it from its anchoring slot and drew the bolt back.

"Thank God!" Relief surged anew as the bolt slid smoothly free.

Using the knob as a handle, she tried to lift the trapdoor. The instant she did, hands beneath pushed it up. Sinking back on her heels, she watched as arms followed, swinging the trapdoor back until it came to rest against the wall.

Lantern light welled out from the open space.

Still on her knees, she leaned forward and looked down.

Directly into Jeremy Carling's upturned face.

Beyond delighted to see him, she beamed.

He stared rather blankly up at her for a moment, then blinked, frowned slightly, and quietly asked, "Is there anyone near who might hear?"

"No." She thought back, then decisively said, "After dinner, they brought me down here, locked me in and went back upstairs, and none of them have come down since."

"Good." He looked at her face again, then moved his gaze to her shoulders, barely covered by her hideously crushed fichu. "Do you still have that cloak you had earlier? It's chilly down here."

"Yes." Reaching out, she dragged the cloak from the bed; she'd been using it as an extra blanket.

Jeremy spied the edge of a thin blanket dangling from the bed. "Bring the blanket, too—it won't hurt."

Having swung the cloak around her, she tied its ties at her throat, then reached for the blanket.

"Is there anything else you need to bring?"

Folding the blanket, she shook her head. "They didn't even give me a comb."

"All right. Hand me the blanket."

She passed it to him; he took it and handed it down to Cobby, waiting at the base of the ladder.

Looking up at Eliza, Jeremy made a circling gesture. "There's a ladder here, but you'll need to come down backward." He retreated a few steps. "Take it slowly. I'll catch you if you slip."

She moved quickly to do as he'd said, easing down through the trapdoor, carefully feeling with her feet for each rung.

He continued to retreat as she descended. Eventually he stepped onto the rough stone floor of the tunnel; displacing Cobby at the ladder's foot, he reached up to take Eliza's elbow and steady her. "Almost there."

She stepped down to the tunnel's floor, then turned to bestow another of her blindingly brilliant smiles on him; as before, when their eyes met, a wave of heat, both pleasurable and discomfiting at the same time, rolled through him.

Reminding himself where they were, he turned to Cobby, who was hovering at his elbow. "Allow me to present Cobden Harris."

"Cobby, Miss Cynster." Cobby reached out and shook Eliza's hand. "Everyone calls me Cobby."

"And this"—Jeremy gestured to her other side—"is Hugo Weaver."

Hugo juggled the bag of tools he'd carried into his other hand, then took Eliza's and bowed gallantly over it. "Enchanted, Miss Cynster."

Releasing her, Hugo looked at Jeremy. "I suggest we get going before the natives grow restless."

Cobby stepped back and waved Eliza forward.

"Wait." Jeremy glanced up at the open trapdoor, then he looked at Eliza. "Did you say the bed was over the trapdoor?"

She nodded. "There was a rug over it, and the bed stood over that. I had no idea the trapdoor was there—and clearly neither did Scrope or the other two. They'd never have left me there if they had."

Jeremy flicked a glance at Cobby, then Hugo, then turned back to the ladder. "It's worth spending a few extra minutes to confound any pursuit."

He climbed quickly up, stuck his head into the basement room, and looked around. "Cobby—I'll need some light." Climbing up into the room, Jeremy waited until Cobby appeared on the ladder, holding up one of the lanterns so Jeremy could see, then he got to work setting their stage.

Five minutes later, after fluffing up the pillows and stuffing them under the sheet, then positioning the rug back across the trapdoor so it would lie flat, hiding the panel again once it was fully lowered, then, standing on the ladder and reaching out around the edges of the partially lowered panel, tugging the bed back into place, he finally lowered the trapdoor fully, then retreated down into the tunnel.

Resettling his coat sleeves, he grinned at Cobby and Hugo. "That'll leave them wrestling with the classic riddle of how someone vanishes from a locked room."

Cobby chuckled. "I've always wanted to leave someone with that mystery to solve."

Hugo briefly smiled, then nodded along the tunnel. "We need to go."

They shuttered their lanterns so that the light shone in narrow beams ahead of them, enough to light their path but hopefully not enough to disturb any of the denizens through whose abodes, as it were, they would pass.

Jeremy signaled Eliza to put up the hood of her cloak. Even in its presently disarranged state, the honey-gold of her hair gleamed in the light; far safer to keep it, and any suggestion of her quality, concealed.

Through the cloak and the blanket she'd slung about her shoulders, he located her elbow, lightly grasped it. He nodded to Cobby and they started off; Jeremy walked by Eliza's side, fractionally behind her, ready to steady her over the rough ground, or to protect her.

Cobby walked ahead of them. Hugo strode just behind.

The scabbard of the short sword Jeremy had strapped under his coat tapped his thigh with every step. Cobby, too, had a similar weapon; as they walked, his hand hovered over its hilt.

Hugo, behind them, had a truncheon and a dirk.

They weren't looking for trouble, but none of them were foolish enough to come into this area without being prepared for it.

Eliza recognized their protectiveness, guessed its cause. Even though she couldn't see the danger, she could sense its nearness, the unseen, unvoiced menace. The damp chill of the sometimes narrow, sometimes cavernous, tunnels through which they passed was insidiously laced with the potential for violence.

Clutching the blanket closer, she edged nearer Jeremy. "What is this place?" Her voice was the merest whisper.

Ahead of their little group ranged three youths in rough clothing who'd been waiting a little way back along the tunnel from the ladder down which she'd come; the youths occasionally held up a hand to slow them down, as if checking the way ahead, then they would beckon and continue on.

Leaning close so his words wafted across her ear, Jeremy seized a moment when their guides had waved them to a halt to reply, "These are the vaults—the vaults between the bridges' supports. When the elevated bridges leading north and south from High Street were built, those who later built houses against the bridges incorporated the spaces between the supports as multiple below-ground levels in the houses— second, third, and so on basements, one below the other."

He fell silent as they moved forward again, swiftly and silently crossing a large, much wider area.

Eliza sensed movement in the impenetrable darkness of the unseen space. As their way once more narrowed, she whispered, "Why are there people hiding in the dark?"

"Not hiding. They live here—we're walking through their homes."

She couldn't imagine it. "Why are they here?"

"When the fire five years ago burned down the original houses, removing all the levels above ground, the builders who built on the foundations of the burned-out shells simply sealed off the lower levels. Those lower levels—these tunnels—became a warren for the homeless, the dispossessed, the poor of every kind. Some, like the canny builder who built the terrace of houses your captors chose, left exits in the house basements in case of another fire. Most locals know of the vaults."

"I think Scrope is English, and the nurse and the coachman definitely are."

"Just so. They either rented a house or commandeered a house whose owner is away."

They reached a set of crude steps cut into the stone. Cobby and Hugo hovered, alert and on guard, while Jeremy helped her down.

"It's not far now," he whispered as they started off again. "We're descending the slope under the bridge—we're not far from the end."

Recalling just how long the bridge they'd walked up from the coaching inn to the High Street had been, Eliza thought of how many rooms must be hidden away, tucked underneath. How many people, families, groups. "At least they're out of the weather."

Jeremy didn't reply. Ahead of them Cobby had come to a halt at a wide opening beyond which stars appeared like pinpricks in the black fabric of the sky.

Halting, Jeremy murmured to Eliza, "Go on with Hugo. I'll join you in a moment."

She hesitated, clearly reluctant, but then Hugo stepped forward and touched her arm, and she allowed him to steer her on through the opening and out into the relative safety of the night.

Cobby waited just beyond the exit, glancing back as Jeremy pulled a small purse from his pocket. The three youths who'd hovered in the darker shadows instantly drew nearer.

"Here." Upending the purse in his palm, Jeremy showed them the coins he'd promised in return for their help navigating the vaults safely. "Your due, plus a tip."

The oldest youth glanced at the other two, then looked back at Jeremy. "Can you divide it for us?"

Jeremy obliged.

More than happy, the youths took the coins, saluted, and melted away.

Jeremy joined Cobby; a few steps more brought them to where Hugo waited with Eliza in the shelter of a doorway.

As soon as Jeremy neared, she retrieved her hand from Hugo's sleeve and grasped Jeremy's arm. She looked at Cobby, Hugo, then up at Jeremy. "I can't thank you enough. Scrope said he expects the laird tomorrow morning. I wasn't looking forward to meeting him."

Hugo smiled and swept her a bow. "Delighted to be of service."

Cobby grinned. "Truth to tell, we haven't had an adventure for far too long—it's we who are in your debt. Now!" Face alight, he swung around. "Let's leave this place for fairer climes."

Once more, Cobby led the way, and Hugo brought up the rear.

"Where are we going?" Eliza asked.

Jeremy glanced down at her through the dense shadows; she felt more than saw his gaze as it moved briefly over her features. "To Cobby's town house. It's not far."

Cobby patently knew his way; he led them unerringly through passages and tiny courtyards, through narrow alleys, and across larger lanes. Eliza kept up as best she could, but in ballroom slippers she had to be careful where she placed her feet.

Jeremy was unwavering in his solicitousness, in being ready with a hand, or his arm, to steady her. She would normally have found such constant attention irritating, yet tonight she was nothing but grateful. And surprised.

Surprised by just how aware she was of the man by her side.

He might be a scholar, as absentminded as they came, but he was also very tall, and quite . . . *manly* was the word that sprang to mind.

He possessed a great deal more physical presence than

she'd recalled, an aura she found distracting. That made her senses skitter and her nerves tighten, that made her awareness focus on him, rather than on her surroundings.

Yet even distracted as she was, she didn't need to be told that they'd entered, and were pushing further into, the better part of Auld Town. The houses changed; many were older, predating the fire; ornamentation on their stonework became increasingly more visible as the moon rose.

It cast more than enough light for her to appreciate the solid gentility that permeated the houses in the street they eventually turned into. The city's bells chimed and clanged twice each as they strode up the slumbering street. Fishing in his pocket, Cobby halted before a three-story town house, then, latchkey in hand, he ascended the three steps, unlocked the door, set it wide, and with a smile to match, waved them in. "Welcome to my humble abode, Miss Cynster."

Guided by Jeremy up the steps, she passed Cobby to step over the threshold, and he added, "Although your stay will be short, Meggin and I hope it will be comfortable."

Crossing into the front hall, into welcoming warmth and soft candlelight, Eliza found a lady much her own age, with lustrous black curls and laughing blue eyes, waiting to greet her.

The lady smiled and offered her hands. "I'm Margaret— Meggin to all. Welcome to our home."

Eliza found herself smiling broadly back. She put her hands in Meggin's, without hesitation leaned close to touch cheeks, and for the first time in days, relaxed.

The door shut and bolted, they repaired to the drawing room where a tray with tea, small honey cakes, and a plate of more robust sandwiches was waiting. While Meggin and Eliza sipped tea from china cups and nibbled the delicious honey cakes, the men sipped from glasses of whisky and made short work of the sandwiches.

"It all went exactly as we'd planned." Cobby waved a sandwich as he brought Meggin up to date. "We went straight to the High Street end, then counted back to find the right basement."

"We were lucky that the same builder built that terrace all the way from the corner," Hugo said.

"And that you found those youths to act as guides." Jeremy set down his empty glass. "We could have found our way without them, but we'd have attracted far too much interest along the way. Having them with us allowed us to go in and come out without hindrance."

Comfortably seated on the damask-covered chaise alongside Meggin, in a room whose amenity made her feel at home, for the first time since she'd walked into the back parlor of St. Ives House, Eliza felt her sartorial shortcomings. And the need of a hot bath. She glanced at Meggin, smiled rather wanly. "I wonder if I might trouble you for a change of attire?" Meggin was nearly a head shorter than she. "Perhaps you have a maid more my size . . . ?"

Meggin laughed and patted her hand. "Actually, we're going to do rather better than that. Water's already being heated for a bath—we weren't sure exactly when you would reach here, or it would have been ready sooner. However"— she glanced at Jeremy—"I suspect that you'd better hear the rest of the plan these gentlemen have concocted before you indulge." Meggin briefly met Eliza's eyes. "It's they who have arranged your wardrobe for today."

Puzzled, Eliza looked at Jeremy.

He met her gaze. "We need to get you away from Edinburgh to some safe house as soon as possible, and unless you can tell us of a nearer place, Wolverstone Castle is the closest I know."

She blinked, thought. "I've visited Edinburgh twice before, but we have no family or close connections here." After another moment considering, she nodded. "Yes, it would be Wolverstone. There's the Vale, of course, Richard and Catriona's home where Heather and Breckenridge sought refuge, but it's all the way across the country, and some way south—not as close as the border south of here."

"And Wolverstone's not far beyond the border, so that's where we need to go. Royce and Minerva are in residence, an added bonus."

She nodded again. "So how are we going to get there?"

Jeremy glanced at Cobby. "Do you have that map?"

"Left it in the dining room—I'll fetch it."

While Cobby went to get the map, Jeremy went on, "Before I forget, I sent word to Royce by courier yesterday, telling him I'd found you and that we would make for Wolverstone with all speed, and asking him to send word to your parents. Of course, by the time they receive any missive, we should already be safe with Royce. However, in order to reach him, we have to take into account that it's highly likely that Scrope will give chase."

"Once he realizes I'm gone."

"Precisely. Unfortunately, it isn't sensible to leave before dawn, and he may realize you've gone shortly after, so we thought it best to have some strategy to slow him down." Jeremy paused as Cobby came back in, carrying a large map, already unfolded.

Cobby laid it on a small table, then pulled the table between the chaise and Jeremy's chair. Hugo pulled his chair closer. Cobby followed suit, saying, "It won't hurt to go over it one more time."

"Right." Jeremy glanced at Eliza. "The plan we've come up with has two arms. The actual escape—you and me racing back across the border to Wolverstone—and the decoy."

"That's me and Hugo," Cobby informed her.

"The four of us will leave here a little before dawn," Jeremy went on. "We'll split up immediately. Cobby and Hugo will go down to the smaller inn on South Bridge Street near the coaching inn where Scrope left the coach. My curricle and horse are at that smaller inn. Cobby and Hugo, pretending to be me and you, will take my bag, collect my horse and curricle, then drive out along the Great North Road, heading at speed for the border—exactly as anyone would expect us to."

Leaning over the map, Jeremy traced Cobby's and Hugo's prospective route. "They'll drive via Berwick all the way to Wolverstone, carrying word that you and I will be coming via a different, less obvious route." He glanced up and caught Eliza's eye. "Meanwhile, you and I will go down Cannongate and along High Street to the Grassmarket and the stables there, to the southwest of the town, then head out along this road"—he pointed—"heading southwest to Lanark via Carnwath. But at Carnwath, we'll turn east." He traced the road eastward. "Going via Castlecraig, Peebles, Innerleithen, Melrose, Galashiels, and St. Boswells through to Jedburgh and the border beyond."

"The same border crossing they used on the way here," Eliza said.

Jeremy nodded. "We're wagering they'll assume we'll take the faster road with more traffic for cover. From their point of view, there's no reason for us to use the Jedburgh, or more accurately, the Carter Bar crossing, because they can have no idea that we're making for Wolverstone, which is actually more readily reached from that direction." He looked at her. "If we leave at dawn, making all speed, with luck we should reach Wolverstone by tomorrow evening."

Eliza frowned. "What I don't understand is why they— Scrope and his people, possibly even the laird—would follow a curricle with Cobby and Hugo in it." She looked at Jeremy. "Quite obviously neither of them is me."

Jeremy grinned.

Cobby looked smug, and Hugo looked triumphant.

"What our magnificent trio have failed to mention," Meggin said, "is that Hugo is a thespian of long standing."

Hugo's grin widened. "I have a wig that will match your hair well enough, and a gold silk evening gown much like yours. Add a little padding, throw your cloak over all, and

I'll pass as you easily enough—I'm not that much taller or broader, and I can assure you I've plenty of experience walking, gesturing, and talking like a woman, enough to pull the wool over most casual observers' eyes."

"And we only need to fool casual observers," Cobby put in. "The ostlers at the smaller inn's stables, and anyone else who might see us en route, who might be asked to point out where we've gone. I can pass for Jer well enough." He glanced at Jeremy, grinned. "I have before."

"In addition to that," Jeremy said, his gaze refixing on Eliza, his expression growing serious and a touch uncertain, "we were hoping you would consent to donning male attire—breeches, boots, shirt, and coat." Faint color rose in his cheeks. "In the interests of confusing Scrope and his people."

Her gaze locked with his, Eliza's lips curved, then she grinned as widely as Cobby. "That sounds like an excellent idea."

Jeremy felt a surge of relief. "Good." He glanced at Cobby and Hugo, then concluded, "So that's our plan for confounding Scrope, his people, and even the laird, and getting you safely to Wolverstone."

Eliza spent a glorious half hour relaxing in a hip-bath filled with hot water in a cheery upstairs bedchamber. Feeling clean and much more like herself, she reluctantly climbed out and dried herself. In a fresh chemise Meggin had loaned her, wrapped in a warm robe, she was kneeling before the fire drying her hair and quietly marveling at the turn of events—most especially at her new insights into an absentminded scholar who, viewed through his friends' eyes, seemed far less distant and detached from wider life than she'd thought—when a tap on the door heralded her accommodating hostess.

Smiling as she shut the door behind her, Meggin held up the pile of clothes she carried. "These are Hugo's contributions to your disguise." Bustling over to the bed, she started laying them out. "I suspect the silk shirt and neckerchief are his, but the jacket, breeches, and boots most likely came from one of the theaters."

Rising, Eliza joined Meggin by the bed. "How useful to be able to raid their wardrobes."

"Especially as he was able to get alternatives—we can pick which best suits." Meggin held up a tweed jacket. She wrinkled her nose. "That's simply too countrified—it will make you stand out." She looked down at the offerings spread on the bed. "You need to look unremarkable in every way."

They picked through the clothes, holding each garment up, discarding some immediately, leaving others to be tried on.

"The three of them have put a lot of effort into this . . . this adventure, as Cobby called it." Eliza met Meggin's eyes. "I'm truly in their debt, and yours, too."

Meggin waved. "We were happy to help, and truth be told, I haven't seen the three of them so animated in months, if not years. All three normally lead very . . . well, *cloistered* lives, even Cobby. An event like this that gets them challenged, enthused, and out and about, dealing with the world even if only for a short time, is no bad thing."

Eliza gestured to the clothes. "They seem to have thought of everything."

"I'm sure they have." Meggin sighed. "But they do have a tendency to assume that everything will go exactly as they plan. For instance, you and Jeremy reaching Wolverstone in one day by such a roundabout route. I have reservations, and raised them, too. I agree it's possible, and with both Scrope and this laird potentially on your heels, there'll be no time to dally, but that timing allows for no hurdles along the way, and in my experience nothing runs that smoothly." Meggin caught Eliza's gaze. "I did suggest that you and Jeremy take a maid with you, just in case, but they vetoed that on several counts, and I have to admit their reasoning is sound."

Eliza tipped her head, considering. "Along the lines of, what would a gentleman and a youth need with a maid?"

Meggin nodded. "Among other things. Most telling was that you and he wouldn't be able to travel as quickly as required while dragging an extra body along. Taking a maid would more or less ensure you had to pass the night somewhere along the road, and Jeremy is set on not allowing Scrope, or this laird, even that much chance to come up with you."

Eliza grimaced. "That's not something I would argue with."

Eventually, she donned new silk drawers Meggin had bought for her, and between them they used a silk cravat to bind her breasts. Eliza kept her necklace on, tucking the rose quartz pendant safely out of sight between her squashed breasts; the fine chain with its amethyst beads was concealed well enough beneath Hugo's silk shirt. The shirt fitted well enough in the body, but the sleeves hung past her fingertips. Meggin had brought needles and thread. They each took one cuff and, with a few quick stitches, shortened the sleeves.

"There. Try that." Stepping back, hands on her hips, Meggin watched critically as Eliza redonned the shirt. Then Meggin nodded. "Good. That will pass. Now for the rest."

Twenty minutes later, with rags stuffed in the toes of the boots to make them fit, Eliza stood before the cheval glass, settled the soft-brimmed hat over her tightly pinned hair, and surveyed their handiwork. "I really do make a passable young man."

Beside her, also looking into the mirror, Meggin nodded. "A youth on the cusp of manhood. As long as you remember to stride and not glide, you'll do."

Eliza glanced down at her feet, then, grinning, caught Meggin's gaze. "The boots will help with that."

Meggin laughed. "True. So, are you ready?"

"Yes." Straightening to her full height, chin rising, Eliza

nodded as imperiously as her brother Gabriel might. With a graceful bow, she waved Meggin to the door. "Lead on, ma'am, and I'll follow."

Chuckling, Meggin complied.

But when they reached the head of the stairs, Meggin stepped back and waved her on. "Go down first—they're eagerly waiting to see the results of their endeavors."

Lips curving, Eliza started down the stairs. The front hall came into view as she descended. She saw a pair of boots, then, as the legs in the boots were revealed, realized they were Jeremy's. He was standing closest to the stairs.

Meggin's reservations about the men's planning abilities replayed in her mind. For her part, she'd been surprised, delightedly so, by their resourcefulness thus far, but as Meggin had warned, perhaps she shouldn't expect too much of them—they weren't magicians. They were scholars, and such beasts didn't change their spots purely through an exercise of enthusiasm.

With every step downward, she saw more of Jeremy. With every inch revealed, it was conclusively confirmed that her memory of him physically had been well and truly superseded. The present reality was significantly different, in ways that still made her heart beat faster, made her breathing quicken, and sent awareness prickling over her skin.

Ignoring the effect, head held at a lofty angle, she descended the last stairs; stepping onto the hall tiles, she coolly met the men's widening gazes, then slowly turned, careful not to pirouette like a girl but half swagger around like a male.

Jeremy couldn't take his eyes off her; they'd fixed on her long, shapely legs, displayed to advantage by the breeches and boots as she, with slow deliberation, had come down the stairs step by step, and now wouldn't shift. As she continued her turn, he had to force himself to blink, force himself to haul in a breath—and only then realized he'd stopped breathing.

Despite his intentions, his gaze flicked unerringly to the curves of her derriere, subtly outlined beneath the skirts of the jacket she'd chosen.

His mouth dried. Another wave of heat washed through him, as it had in the basement when she'd smiled so dazzlingly at him.

His conscious mind, his logical, rational scholar's mind, arrogantly dismissed the reaction—yes, it was lust, pure and simple, but that just meant he wasn't dead—but some other, less rational part of his psyche knew there was a great deal more to it than that.

And he'd just volunteered to escort her, an unmarried Cynster princess, in her male guise, the two of them alone, over all the miles to Wolverstone.

His new insight cast the journey in a completely different light, more an ordeal than an adventure.

At least it would only last for a day.

He forced himself to meet her gaze as, completing her turn, she raised her eyes to his face. "You look . . . very plausible."

Cobby cast him a sharp glance, then smiled at Eliza. "Convincing," he declared. "Totally convincing."

"You'll do very well," Hugo said. "Especially if you remember to move like that."

If she continued to move like that . . . raising a hand, Jeremy rubbed his left temple.

"Come along, all of you." Meggin had followed Eliza down the stairs. She shooed them into the dining room. "There's an early breakfast waiting. You need to eat so you'll be able to race off, to hare out of Edinburgh the instant the sun's up."

Ignoring the intrigued look Meggin cast him, Jeremy stood back and let the others go ahead. He seized a moment to steel himself before following them in.

Over a hearty breakfast of pancakes, griddle cakes, sausages, coddled eggs, bacon, ham, kippers, and kedgeree, they went over their designated routes one last time. Jeremy was pleased to note that Eliza didn't restrict herself to tea and toast, as so many fashionable ladies did. She ate enough to see her well into the day, much to his relief; while potentially fleeing Scrope and the laird, a fainting female was the last thing he would need.

"With any luck, Scrope and this laird will hie after us and leave you two to make your way to Wolverstone unmolested." Cobby pushed back from the table. "Really, the odds have to be very much on our side. There's no reason whatever for either Scrope or the laird to look west, let alone cast their net wide enough to include a man and a youth."

Hugo had eaten quickly, then excused himself to don the gold silk gown he'd borrowed and the cloak Eliza's captors had given her; he reappeared in time to hear Cobby's last remark. Hugo struck a ladylike pose in the doorway. "Certainly not when they have a lady and a gentleman of precisely the description they seek to follow instead."

The others all stared.

Jeremy recovered first. "The gown suits you. It brings out the hazel in your eyes."

Hugo batted his lashes. "Why, thank you, kind sir."

"'Pon my word, you make a very dashing young lady, Hugo, m'lad."

Hugo pointed at Cobby. "Just remember to drop the 'm'lad.' "

"Well," Meggin said, taking stock of them all. "You're all nearly ready, which is just as well." With her head she directed their attention to the uncurtained window. It faced east, and the faintest lightening of the sky was spreading upward and outward over the roofs. Meggin rose. "Just wait one more moment while I fetch my contribution."

The other four exchanged puzzled glances. They drained their cups, put down their napkins, and rose.

They were waiting in the front hall, Eliza swirling a man's cloak about her shoulders, when Meggin came out through the door from the kitchens carrying three packed saddlebags. "These are for you." She handed one to Cobby, and the other two to Jeremy. "Just in case."

Cobby and Jeremy peeked under the bags' flaps.

"Food," Meggin informed them. "And there's a small knife in the bottom of each bag."

Just in case. Eliza met Meggin's eyes. "Thank you," Eliza said, then glanced at the others. "For everything."

Cobby saluted her. "We'll see you at Wolverstone this evening."

"We'll beat you there." Hugo took her hand in a manly grasp and shook it. "We'll be waiting on the terrace with a glass of wine in hand to greet you."

Eliza shook Cobby's hand, too, then enveloped the smaller Meggin in a warm hug. They touched cheeks, squeezed fingers.

Releasing her and stepping back, Eliza waited while Jeremy bussed Meggin on the cheek. "I'll come and visit again soon," he said. "Without the excitement."

"You must." Meggin's gaze flicked to Eliza, including her. "You'll need to tell me how all this works out."

Amid a flurry of farewells, the front door was opened, and Eliza found herself standing beside Jeremy in the street.

"Good luck!" Meggin waved from the open doorway.

They all waved back, then Eliza and Jeremy looked at Cobby and Hugo. The three men saluted; Eliza quickly mimicked them.

"Until Wolverstone." Jeremy turned up the street, gesturing for Eliza to follow.

"To Wolverstone!" Cobby and Hugo echoed as they swung away and, with Cobby carrying Jeremy's bag, walked off in the opposite direction, down the sloping street.

Following Jeremy, Eliza quickly climbed to Cannongate. Turning left, side by side they strode east along the Royal Mile, into High Street and past the Tron Kirk—the church beside South Bridge that she'd remembered—and on past the Cathedral of St. Giles and the Parliament.

She used the moments of pacing along the largely deserted main street to practice her manly stride. At first she found keeping her hips relatively still difficult, but by the time they were nearing the western end of the main street, she'd mastered the art of taking longer strides and letting her arms swing in a more natural manner.

One saddlebag slung over his shoulder, the other over one arm, Jeremy paced alongside her, acutely aware of what she was doing, that every now and then her gaze would drop to his hips, his thighs, as she used his stride as a model for hers.

Ignoring the distraction as best he could, he kept his gaze trained on the street, scanning ahead, probing every alcove, dissecting every shadow. His instincts were awake and alert, his senses alive in a way he couldn't remember ever experiencing. He told himself it was because he was protecting her—and it was—but he'd never imagined the simple act of protecting a female would generate this level of excitement, let alone the blend of suppressed tension and readiness for action that was presently coursing through him.

It was exhilarating; he was starting to comprehend how men like his brother-in-law and the other members of the Bastion Club might have grown addicted to this medley of sensations. It was undeniably a challenge to be in charge, to make the plans, give the orders, and play the knight-protector, but he'd never expected the accompanying thrill that came with success, with achievement, much less that it would have much effect on him.

He was a scholar through and through; what did he know of or need with such warrior-protector reactions?

Clearly there was another side to him, a dormant side with which he hadn't previously engaged.

The castle loomed ahead. Bumping Eliza's arm—as he would have if she'd been male—he veered left, striding down the curve of Grassmarket to where a collection of stables served the traffic that came into the city from the southwest.

As they approached the stable he'd selected as the most suitable for their purpose, he murmured, "Remember—I'm your tutor, you're my charge. Look bored and disinterested in what's happening about you. Don't speak unless you have no other choice."

She nodded. "Give me one saddlebag."

Halting outside the stable, he handed her the bag he'd been carrying; the other still over his shoulder, he left her by the roadside without a backward glance and went into the stables, hailing the stable master and engaging in a swift exchange of pleasantries before getting down to the business of choosing suitable mounts for them both.

Instinct constantly prodded, then more insistently pricked, urging him to glance back at Eliza; he had to keep lecturing himself that if she'd been the lad she was supposed to be, he wouldn't think to watch over her, not unless some commotion arose.

Gritting his teeth, he concentrated on the matter at hand. They needed two swift steeds to carry them along the roads, even, if necessary, across the fields, but their best time would be made on the roads. That said, they also needed strength and stamina; while they could and would change horses at least once along the way, he wanted to get as far as possible, Carnwath at least, before having to stop at another hostelry.

The stableman was experienced and, when informed of their needs, turned out two likely chestnuts, one heavier, the other a touch younger and sleeker. Jeremy inspected them and approved. Selecting saddles and tack was quickly accomplished. After paying the man, Jeremy led the horses out into the narrow yard beside the road.

At the sound of hooves, Eliza turned.

Her eyes widened.

He frowned. A quick glance back showed that the stableman had retired deeper into his domain.

Slowing the horses, Jeremy used them as a screen as he halted in front of her. "What's wrong?"

Dragging her eyes from the restive, eager horses, Eliza focused on her principal rescuer's face. "I, ah . . ." With an effort she suppressed the urge to wring her hands. "Wouldn't it be faster to drive? In a curricle with a pair of fast horses, for instance?"

His frown grew a touch more etched. "Possibly—possibly not. But the deciding factor is that a carriage of any sort will restrict us to the roads—passable roads—while on horseback, if necessary we can go cross-country."

Her gaze flicked to the horses again.

She felt Jeremy's gaze search her face. After a moment, he added, voice low, "If Scrope or the laird manage to find our trail and chase us, we need to be flexible, mobile, able to tack and turn like foxes. We need to be able to run, so we need to be on horseback, not in a carriage."

She dragged in a breath, shifted her gaze to his face, and forced herself to nod. "Yes, of course."

He hesitated, then asked, "You can ride astride, can't you? I've always heard that riding sidesaddle is harder."

"I've heard the same." She clung to the commonly held belief. "I've just never ridden astride before." Locking her gaze on the smaller horse, she hauled in another huge breath, fought to quell her suddenly pitching stomach enough to lift her chin and declare, "I'm sure I'll manage."

She would have to. He and his friends had gone to so much trouble to help her, and riding was clearly required to make their rescue work.

"Good." He angled the smaller chestnut before her. "I'll hold him. Can you get up on your own?"

"I think so." She'd watched her brothers and cousins mount more times than she could count; grimly determined, she placed the padded toe of her boot in the stirrup, grabbed the pommel, and hoisted herself up.

And was pleasantly surprised by the unexpected freedom her breeches afforded her; swinging her leg over, with commendable grace she came down in the saddle and quickly picked up the reins.

She could definitely get used to wearing breeches.

Jeremy adjusted the stirrups for her. The sensation of sitting astride the horse's back felt odd, yet far more secure than her usual position in a sidesaddle.

I can do this. Surely riding astride in her new male persona she wouldn't have any problem. She just had to believe; horses sensed the mood of their riders—she knew that well enough.

Jeremy attached both saddlebags, one before her saddle, the other before his, then swung easily up to his mount's back. He settled, then picked up the reins and nodded briskly at her. "Right. Let's go."

He led the way out of the stable yard. Eliza's mount followed its companion more or less of its own accord.

That was all right. She could manage that.

The next ten minutes had her slowly relaxing. Both horses seemed to be reasonably well mannered. Although eager to run, neither possessed the mettlesome tempers she was accustomed to having to wrestle with in Cynster-bred mounts.

Her neat chestnut obeyed her hand on the reins well enough. Even more reassuring, although it was barely dawn, there was sufficient traffic on the road—other riders, a few carriages, and lots of carts—to ensure their best speed was, at most, a slow jog-trot.

It wasn't that different from riding in Hyde Park.

I can do this. The refrain repeated in her head as they left Edinburgh, perched high on its rock, behind them, and trotted southeast on the road to Carnwath.

Behind them the sun slowly rose in the sky, warming their backs, and throwing long shadows ahead of them, while turning the sky from gray to pink, to a pale wash of yellow, and finally to a soft summer blue.

Eliza rode steadily on.

Scrope, Genevieve, and Taylor seemed like distant memories; so much had happened since last she'd seen them.

Jeremy rode beside and half a length ahead of her, keeping to a steady pace. The road stretched out in front of them, with nary a hurdle in sight.

With birdsong swelling around them, with the clack of hooves, the rattle of wheels, and the occasional voices of passing drivers competing for her ears, with the fresh breeze blowing in their faces, even with the sure knowledge that a long and physically tiring day lay ahead, she found herself amazingly content.

Her heart felt light, buoyed, free.

Even though she was riding a horse.

I can do this.

Smiling, she rode alongside Jeremy, away from Edinburgh.

Chapter Six

I'm off to wait for McKinsey in the square." Scrope walked into the kitchen of the town house where Genevieve and Taylor had just sat down to their breakfasts. Genevieve gestured to the platters on the table. "You don't want any?"

"I ate earlier. I want to get Miss Cynster into McKinsey's hands as soon as I can—and get my hands on our bonus. He said he'd be waiting first thing—let's see how keen and eager he is." Scrope looked at their plates. "As soon as you've finished, take a tray down to Miss Cynster—just tea and toast will do. Get her up, washed, dressed, and fed, ready to hand over to McKinsey when I bring him here."

Genevieve nodded.

Scrope turned for the front door. "Be sure she's ready when I get back."

Genevieve pulled a face at his back, then applied herself to her meal.

Once the front door clicked shut behind Scrope, Taylor grumbled, but he, too, ate as quickly as he could. Both he and Genevieve had long ago learned that it was better to humor Scrope in all things; his jobs were invariably the simplest, the most straightforward, and the best paid.

Stuffing her last crust into her mouth, Genevieve rose and started assembling a tray. When the kettle boiled again, she filled the teapot, then tipped the rest of the steaming water into an ewer she'd half filled with cold water. "That should do her."

Setting the kettle back on the hob, she wiped her hands on her apron and glanced at Taylor. "You ready?"

Swallowing a last bite of sausage, Taylor nodded. Pushing his plate away, he rose.

While Genevieve hefted the tray, he took the keys from the hook, unlocked the door to the basement steps, and hauled it wide. Reaching for the lantern, he quickly kindled it, adjusted the wick, then led the way down.

Genevieve followed more slowly. Balancing the tray, she halted outside the basement room door and waited while Taylor, having set the lantern on the floor, inserted the large key, unlocked the heavy door, and pulled it open. The light from the lantern showed them the outline of their prisoner, still lying in the bed.

Walking forward with the tray, Genevieve looked back at Taylor and tipped her head toward the kitchen. "Fetch the ewer and basin, will you, while I get her highness up?"

Taylor grunted and went, leaving the lantern on the floor.

The beam of light wasn't strong. Genevieve set the tray down, glanced at the figure in the bed, then went back to fetch the lantern. "Rise and shine, Miss Cynster. The day of reckoning has come." Seeing Taylor slowly descending the steps with the basin and ewer, Genevieve lifted the lantern, strengthened the flame, then turned back into the room.

"Come along, now." She advanced on the bed, playing the light over it. "It won't do you any good—" She broke off on a gasp. A second later, she rushed the last feet to the bed. "No!"

Dragging back the sheet, exposing the two pillows bunched and stuffed beneath it—exposing the complete absence of the young woman who should have been there—Genevieve let out a shriek. "*No*! How could this be?"

There was a clatter and a clang on the floor outside, then Taylor came rushing in. "What? What is it?"

Having comprehensively scanned the room, Genevieve turned a white face to him. "She's *gone*."

"Don't be silly—she can't be." Taylor looked around, then bent down and peeked under the bed.

"She's gone," Genevieve repeated. When Taylor straightened and lumbered back to his feet, she was clutching her elbows. "Scrope will have our heads!"

"Don't see why—it's not us who lost her." Taylor turned in a stunned circle. "She's just not here. She's vanished. From a locked room."

"You try telling Scrope that. He's going to think we've done some deal with the chit—taken money from her family to let her go."

That was a real possibility. Taylor wasn't used to thinking fast—that's why he worked for others like Scrope—but he was thinking now. "She was here last night. Scrope was the last to leave—he was the one who closed the door and locked it. He was up and in the kitchen earlier than we were . . ." Taylor met Genevieve's gaze. "Could he have already handed her over to this laird—and now he's just left us?"

Genevieve gave the matter due thought but eventually shook her head. "That's not his way. He never works alone, so he needs to hire us, or those like us. It won't do him any good if word gets out that he's crossed us."

Taylor nodded. "Right—you're right."

Still clutching her arms, Genevieve turned slowly, examining every inch of the room. "How the devil did she get out—of here, of the basement, even of the house?"

"Doesn't matter." Taylor saw the light. "Howsoever she got out, she's gone, but if she was here late last night, as we know she was, then no matter *when* she left the house, chances are she wouldn't have been able to leave the city until early this morning, once the sun came up and the stables opened."

Taylor caught Genevieve's gaze. "We've a chance of catching her if I go now. Right away." He swung on his heel and hurried out of the room.

Genevieve came to life and raced after him. "How can you know which way she's gone? Where to look?"

"Simple." Taylor didn't look back as he climbed the steps. "She'll have gone home—where else would a young lady like her go?"

Reaching the kitchen, he grabbed his coat off a peg by the rear door. "Even if she's found some fellow to help her, she'll be heading down the Great North Road, fast as ever she can."

"To the border." Genevieve nodded.

"I'm off to check the stables and coaching inns at the bottom of South Bridge Street—that's where she'll have looked for a carriage or a mail coach." Taylor turned to the door. "You stay here and tell Scrope. I'll be back with his package—or send word if I have to follow her along a ways."

Genevieve pulled a face, but there was no help for it.

Without waiting for any response from her, Taylor strode to the front door and clattered out into the street.

Following as far as the door, Genevieve heard Taylor's footsteps running down the cobbles. Closing the door, she stood in the hall, still absorbing the shock. "But how the devil did she get out?"

"Oh, fair and joyous day!" Hugo leaned back against the curricle's seat, golden wig twirling on one finger as with a sweeping gesture he expansively declaimed, "The sun is shining, our enterprise is prospering. What more can we ask of life?"

The curricle's reins in his hands, Cobby shot him a grin. "I suspect we should hope that Jer and Eliza have managed as well as we have."

"Doubtless they have," Hugo replied. "Why wouldn't they? Our plan is excellent. What could go wrong?"

Cobby shrugged. "Have to say this horse is a goer. Nice action and plenty of power."

"Jer's always had an eye for such things." Hugo glimpsed a coach approaching and set the wig back on his head.

"If we keep up this pace, we'll be in Dalkeith shortly."

Hugo twisted around to look back at Edinburgh, high on its rock, fading into the haze rising from the firth beyond, shrinking and receding as they sped along.

Turning back, the rattle of the curricle's wheels now joined by the deeper rumble of the approaching coach, Hugo drew Eliza's cloak closer about the gold silk gown he wore, let his shoulders fall, flipped the cloak's hood up and turned his head away, transforming in a heartbeat to a shy lady as the coach drew near.

Then the coach was past, and Hugo turned back, met Cobby's eyes and grinned. He remained in his female persona until they'd gone another mile, then, with no other travelers about to see, he threw back the cloak. "Onward!" Dramatically, he pointed down the road. "To Dalkeith, then Berwick. And then on to Wolverstone!"

"To Wolverstone!" Cobby clicked the reins, and Jasper obligingly stepped out.

"I'm looking for a young lady—English, fair-haired, in a gold evening gown." Taylor halted before two ostlers in the yard of the small inn just past the larger inn at which his own party had left their coach.

He was still catching his breath, having run all the way down from the house, but eyeing the two faces before him, watching the lads exchange a glance, it was clear the exertion hadn't been wasted. Hope surged. "Obviously you've seen her. Which way did she go?"

The older of the two looked up at him. "What's in it fer us?"

Taylor cursed and hunted in his pockets. Finding a shilling, he held it out. "Don't push your luck. So where did she go?"

The ostler took the coin, inspected it, then slipped it into his pocket. "She came in with an English gen'leman. He'd stabled his curricle and black here—came in yesterday, late morning. They took the curricle and set off at first light."

"Which way did they go?"

The younger ostler shifted. "Heard the gen'leman mention the Great North Road. Dalkeith and on from there."

"Thank you." Thinking furiously, Taylor fished in his pocket and found a few more coins. Handing them over, he asked, "Do you have a fast horse I can hire? And someone to run a message into Auld Town, too?"

"At last!" Jeremy loosened his reins and glanced at Eliza. "I thought the traffic would never thin. I had no idea we'd strike so many carts. At least now we can start moving."

He tapped his heels to his mount's sides and the bigger chestnut surged.

Eliza forced herself to ease her reins enough to allow her horse to respond. As it lengthened its stride, she instinctively tightened her grip—clamped her thighs to the saddle skirts, felt her stomach clench—tightened everything.

Every muscle tensed, and tensed.

She tried to stave off the burgeoning panic. Tried to remind herself she was now a youth, not a female. Especially not a female who couldn't ride well. *I can do this.*

Ahead of them, the road was finally clear. The flat surface stretched as far as she could see, beckoning and tempting any decent rider.

"We'll need to go at a cracking pace if we're to reach Wolverstone by evening," Jeremy called.

Clinging to the saddle, to her seat, to her composure, she told herself it wouldn't matter if they were a few hours late.

I can do this. I can do this.

She repeated the mantra to the quickening rhythm of the horses' hooves as she rose and fell awkwardly with her horse's gait.

I can do this.

She was managing, just, but she was still in the saddle. There, see?

I can do this.

A minute later, Jeremy called to her, "We've over a hundred miles more to cover. We need to start making up time—let's go."

"N—" Her throat seized, along with everything else.

Jeremy's chestnut fluidly shifted into a gallop.

Her horse stretched out, following its companion.

She felt like a block of wood, stiff, frozen, unable to relax, to do what she knew she should.

Panic welled and swamped her.

Her lungs seized. She couldn't breathe.

I can't *do this!*

She started jouncing, as she'd known she would, her panicked attempts to match her horse's stride quickly getting out of rhythm until she was bouncing, until her horse's stride broke, fractured. It started pulling, then tossing its head, trying to pick up the gallop and join its stablemate.

Gasping, panic a full-blown monster in her chest, she fought the horse, yanked and tugged and hauled—the beast slowed, swerved onto the grassy verge, back arching as she wrestled with the reins.

The horse abruptly halted and she tipped, then, helplessly flailing, trying to regain her balance, she slowly slid ignominiously sideways, toppling over the horse's forequarter, to land, staggering, on the grass, the reins still in her locked fingers.

Her legs wouldn't hold her. She collapsed, chest heaving, to the ground.

The bands binding her breasts didn't help in the least. Feeling faint, she drew up her knees and hung her head between.

Suddenly Jeremy was there. He crouched beside her. She felt his hand briefly touch her back, then sensed him glancing around.

"There's no one around to see." Jeremy looked back at her, astonished by what had happened, equally surprised by his own, highly visceral reaction. "Why did you come off?"

He'd looked around only in time to see her serve to the

verge, then fall out of the saddle. Ducking his head, he tried to look into her face. "Are you hurt?"

"No." Her reply was muffled. She kept her head down.

He looked at the horse, running his eyes over its head and legs. He couldn't see anything amiss with either beast or saddle.

Then he heard her drag in a huge breath and heave it out in a long sigh.

"I'm sorry." She raised her head and met his eyes. "I should have told you—I'm not a very good rider."

He blinked. Before he could halt the words, he blurted out, "But you're a Cynster."

Her eyes narrowed. "Believe me, no one knows that better than I. Regardless, despite the rest of the family's obsession with the beasts, I'm not terribly fond of horses. I would never choose to ride—I never do in the country. Naturally, given my family, I can sit a horse and manage well enough to walk through streets and slowly canter in the park. But . . ." She gestured helplessly. "That's the limit of my equestrian abilities. I can't ride well enough to gallop."

Seeing their wonderful plan crumbling before him, Jeremy shifted and sat beside her on the grass. Arms resting on his knees, he stared across the road. "You should have told me."

"I tried—at the stables."

"I meant before, when we were discussing the plan at Cobby's."

"I thought we were going to drive—that you'd hire another curricle, not two horses. You never mentioned riding."

He thought back, grimaced. "Sorry—you're right. I didn't say. I just assumed . . ."

Eliza plucked at the grass between them. "No. It's my fault. I should have spoken up at the stables, but I thought being dressed as a youth and riding astride instead of side-saddle might do the trick. I thought perhaps I could manage, and I didn't want to ruin your plan . . ."

And she hadn't wanted him to know of what she saw as her weakness, a weakness she usually managed to hide or avoid altogether. She dragged in a tight breath and let it out with, "I didn't want you to know I'm such a weak and helpless female that I can't even manage a horse."

"There's lots of women—lots of men if it comes to that—who can't manage strong horses. It's just bad luck you were born into such a horse-mad family." His tone was even, that of a professor relating known facts. "Not being able to ride well is no real reflection on you, or on your no doubt extensive other abilities."

She shifted. "But my not being able to ride, at least not fast enough, has ruined your plan, hasn't it?"

"Not ruined—just forced an alteration."

The biggest of which, Jeremy realized, was that they couldn't possibly reach Wolverstone in one day, not even if they traveled through the night . . . not unless they found other fast transportation.

The emphasis being on fast.

"Come on." Rising, he reached down, grasped both her hands, and hauled her to her feet. He looked into her face for a moment, then smiled encouragingly. "All is not lost—far from it. We'll go on at a slow trot as before, then, when we get to the next town, we'll do as you suggested earlier and hire a curricle. It'll be a race like no other, but we should still be able to reach Wolverstone tonight."

She searched his eyes, studied his face, then tentatively smiled. "All right." As he released her hands and she drew them from his, she added, "And thank you."

He was puzzled. "What for?"

"For understanding."

He made no reply, simply held her horse until she was settled in the saddle, then mounted his and brought the bigger chestnut alongside her smaller mount. "Slateford is the next town along. It shouldn't take us too long to get there."

She nodded and they set off, slowly trotting along.

* * *

"Tra-lee, tra-la! We're in the wilds of Scotland!" Hugo finished the song with a wild flourish of his wig.

Grinning, Cobby nodded ahead to where roofs were visible between low hills. "That must be Dalkeith."

"It is, it is." Hugo pointed to a sign that flashed past. "One mile on, apparently."

"We're making excellent ti—oh!" Cobby fumbled the reins as Jasper the Black suddenly misstepped, then slowed, his gait awkward. "Damn!"

Both Cobby and Hugo peered around the sides of the horse.

"He must have picked up a stone in his off-side hoof," Hugo declared.

They drew horse and curricle to a halt, climbed down, and examined the hoof in question. There was indeed a stone; they winkled it out with a penknife, but it was instantly apparent that Jasper was favoring the hoof.

"Double damn!" Hugo said. "The hoof's tender."

Cobby swore, then patted Jasper. "This is Jer's favorite horse. He'll never forgive us if we let him come to harm."

Hugo sighed. Raising his head, he looked down the road toward the distant roofs. "So we'll have to walk. We can stable Jasper in Dalkeith and get another horse put to."

"One mile." Cobby shrugged. "It shouldn't take us long."

Hugo bowed before Jasper, waving him on. "Come along then, Jasper m'lad—let's amble on and get you comfortable, before we set off again."

The two men and the horse started walking, the empty, well-sprung curricle rolling easily in their wake.

After a moment, Cobby said, "We haven't even come five miles."

Hugo shrugged. "Doesn't really matter. It's still so early I can't imagine Scrope would have even discovered Eliza's disappearance, much less be hot on our trail. We'll be off again long before anyone comes pounding along."

* * *

"You encountered no difficulties?"

"None at all." Scrope led McKinsey down Niddery Street. "We didn't halt for longer than it took to change horses until we'd reached Jedburgh on the night before last. We brought her here yesterday."

"She's given you no trouble?"

"None. Once I warned her of the tale you'd told us to use, she accepted there was little she could do."

"And her health?"

"Once the drug wore off, she hasn't complained, nor appeared to be sickening in any way."

McKinsey shot a shrewd glance at Scrope's too-bland expression. He'd been in Grosvenor Square himself, watching from the shadows as Scrope, his coachman-cum-guard, and the nurse he'd hired had removed Eliza Cynster's limp form from the back parlor of the Cynster mansion.

He'd followed the coach out of London, seen it head up the Oxford Road, then, deeming the most dangerous part of the kidnapping successfully accomplished, and his order that Eliza Cynster was not to be harmed in any way sufficient to keep her safe, he'd ridden north by a different route. He'd been in York, sitting on the steps of the minster, when the coach had passed. He'd glimpsed Eliza Cynster inside; she'd seemed to be dozing.

The time at which the coach had passed by had told him that Scrope had adhered to his instructions not to halt but to continue steadily along the route they'd agreed on. Accepting that Scrope had done exactly as requested, McKinsey had mounted his horse, Hercules, followed the coach long enough to ensure it was taking the road to Middlesbrough, then ridden cross-country, eventually traveling via the Great North Road to Edinburgh and his house near the palace.

He knew Edinburgh well; he had eyes and ears in many places. He'd been informed within ten minutes of Scrope and his party arriving.

He could have come for the girl yesterday, but he hadn't wanted Scrope to guess how carefully he'd watched him; he'd seen enough of the man to sense he'd be touchy about not being trusted to do his job. He wanted no argument with Scrope at this juncture, so, deeming twelve or so hours neither here nor there, he'd waited for Scrope's summons.

Once it had arrived, however, he'd seen no reason for further delay; he'd met Scrope just as Auld Town had been waking to the new day.

He would take Eliza back to his house, then take her north; all lay in readiness for the trip. Soon she would be in his hands, and through her, the goblet he had to regain would be within his grasp once more.

"This is it." Scrope halted outside a neatly painted front door. The entire terrace was new, replacing houses burned in the fire five years before.

Unlocking the door, Scrope pushed it wide. He stepped back as if to wave McKinsey in, then abruptly halted.

Looking past Scrope, McKinsey saw a woman dressed in black, the nurse, standing in the shadows of the hall and all but wringing her hands.

"What is it?" Scrope demanded.

The nurse's gaze had gone past him to McKinsey. She moistened her lips, then looked at Scrope. "She's gone. Disappeared. She wasn't in the basement when we opened the door."

Scrope rocked back on his heels. His face was expressionless. "But . . . the basement door was locked when I came down this morning."

"Inside." His own face showing nothing of his erupting fury, McKinsey all but pushed Scrope ahead of him. Stepping into the hall, he shifted to keep both Scrope and the woman in his sights.

The woman shut the door, then whirled to face Scrope. "*Both* basement doors were locked, as they should have been. You were the one to lock them last night, and you were the first one down this morning. Taylor and I came down at the same time, and both doors were locked then. Besides, there's no sense either of us taking the girl." She glanced briefly at McKinsey, waved at him as she looked back at Scrope. "We clearly haven't handed her over."

"She must be there!" Scrope said. "She must be hiding— you've missed her."

"Go and look!" The woman waved down the corridor. "When we couldn't find her we locked both doors again. The keys are on the table."

Scrope strode down the corridor. The woman turned and followed.

McKinsey walked slowly in their wake. He already had a very good idea of how Eliza Cynster had got out of the basement.

What he didn't yet know was where she'd gone, or who, if anyone, had helped her get free.

Entering the kitchen at the end of the corridor, he saw Scrope swipe up two heavy keys.

"Where's Taylor?" Scrope demanded.

The nurse was standing back, holding her elbows, her expression angry and defensive. "As soon as we found her gone, he raced off to check the stables and coaching inns that service the Great North Road. He thought that regardless of how she got out of here, that's where she would go, trying to flee back to London."

Scrope snorted and turned to fit the key to the basement door.

McKinsey caught the nurse's eye. "A sensible move on Taylor's part."

The woman thawed a fraction. McKinsey knew better than to terrify people from whom he might later need information.

Scrope hauled the door open, grabbed the lantern, and went quickly down the steps. McKinsey followed more slowly, ducking to pass through the doorway. In the short corridor below, he found Scrope, the lighted lantern at his feet, unlocking the second, even thicker, door.

"It's impossible!" Scrope muttered. "She couldn't have got through two locked doors."

"She didn't."

"What?" Scrope glanced at him.

"Never mind." McKinsey waved at the basement room door. "Open up and let's see."

Hauling in a breath, Scrope pulled open the door. Stooping, he picked up the lantern; holding it high, he stepped across the threshold, playing the light around the room.

It was instantly apparent that there was nowhere any young woman could be hiding. The room was spartan, but, McKinsey reflected, halting just inside, sufficiently comfortable for one night.

"I can't believe . . ." Utterly bewildered, Scrope swung the lantern around, desperately peering in every corner.

McKinsey looked down at the floor. After a moment, he stepped forward, crouched, caught the thin rug and drew it aside, exposing the stone flags. Then he glanced under the bed. "Ah."

Rising, he walked to the bed, lifted the end, and dragged it away, half across the room.

Both Scrope and the nurse watched, baffled.

McKinsey walked to stand looking down at the patch of floor that had been hidden by the bed. He pointed. "That's how she got out."

Scrope and the nurse moved to peer over the bed.

"A trapdoor?" Scrope's tone said he couldn't believe his eyes.

"All the houses in this terrace—and in other similar terraces built after the great fire—have them." McKinsey crouched and grasped the bolt. He lifted the panel, revealing a stout, permanent wooden ladder leading down to a dusty floor. "Note that this was unlocked." Lowering the panel, he shot the bolt home, then smoothly rose.

"Where does it lead?" The nurse looked up at him.

"Into the vaults—the spaces between the bridge supports and the tunnels that link them."

"But . . ." Scrope looked at McKinsey. "How could she have known?"

"I doubt that she did. Which means she must have had help." In the lantern light, he caught Scrope's gaze. "Did she have any chance to contact anyone?"

Scrope shook his head. "I can't see how." He looked at the nurse.

She, too, shook her head. "She hasn't spoken to anyone. No one at all. Only the three of us."

McKinsey stood for a long moment, letting nothing of his thoughts, much less his emotions, show. "Your coachman—Taylor—may yet gain some word of her. Until then—" He broke off, head rising; a distant tapping was followed by a bell jangling in the kitchen.

"That might be Taylor now." Scrope looked at the nurse. "Go and see."

The woman hurried from the room. Her shoes pattered up the steps.

Scrope shifted, then cleared his throat. "Sir—my lord—I know—"

"No, Scrope. Not yet." McKinsey made the statement absolute. "Let's see what we can learn, how far we can trace Miss Cynster, before I make any decision."

The last words carried enough power to silence Scrope.

A moment later, the nurse was back. "That was a messenger from an inn near the one where we left our coach. Taylor says our package left there with an English gentleman, who drove away in a curricle down the Great North Road at first light. Taylor's hired a fast horse and is giving chase."

McKinsey nodded. He glanced around, then walked to the door. "I take it that Taylor's armed but knows I wish no violence of any kind to be visited on anyone in relation to this business?"

"Yes, my lord." Scrope followed him out of the door.

The maid had already retreated up the steps. McKinsey followed, wondering how much trust he could place in Scrope's last answer. He also had no idea how strong Scrope's control over Taylor was.

Regardless . . .

On reaching the kitchen, he paused, his fingers lightly drumming the kitchen table. "Clearly we'll need to wait to hear what Taylor discovers, to learn whether he returns with Miss Cynster or not. Meanwhile, however, there are other inquiries I can make which will perhaps help determine who this unexpected Englishman is, and whether it was he who helped her escape."

He looked at Scrope, then the maid. "You two wait here. I'll be back within the hour."

The nurse nodded in ready acquiescence. Scrope, however, still looked stunned.

It had been, Jeremy now realized, a serious flaw in his planning. He hadn't thought of, let alone assessed, her abilities, nor what his plan as originally formulated would require of her. He hadn't really thought of her at all, not as an active participant.

He'd thought of her more as a manuscript to be fetched.

Seated beside him in the back of a dray, a pile of cabbages separating them from the farmer perched on the front axle guiding his horse, Eliza sighed softly. "I'm sorry. I know you expected to go much faster than this."

His gaze on the road reeling out behind them, he shook his head. "No—don't apologize. If you do, I'll have to apologize back." He shot her a smile he hoped was encouraging. "I should have explained our plan better and asked for your opinion. If I had, we could have hired a curricle and pair instead of the horses, and all would have been well."

They'd left the horses at Slateford. Even at a slow trot,

Eliza had been growing more and more tense and, he suspected, more fearful she would again lose control and be
thrown—which would have most likely ensured that she
would have been.

By the time they'd reached the village, that fear had in-
fected him, too. Broken bones or worse wouldn't aid their
flight. But the tiny tavern had had no carriages for hire, not
even a gig, but the farmer had been about to set out and had
offered to take them on to the next town. The farmer was
going as far as Kingsknowe and felt sure they'd be able to
get a gig there.

At least the farmer had already delivered most of his cabbages and his horse was strong; they were rolling along at a
steady clip, a touch faster than a slow trot.

So they'd improved their circumstances—the speed at
which they were traveling—but not by much. Against that,
however, Eliza was no longer in danger of taking a spill, and
both of them were a lot less tense.

At least on that account.

He was still finding it difficult to ignore her—or rather the
effect she had on him—in her new incarnation, still having
to force himself not to ogle her long, breeches-clad legs.

The tension that caused . . .

Dragging his mind from that distraction, he refocused on
the immediate problem. The morning was full about them;
it was pleasant enough rolling along in the cart, especially
with Eliza beside him, but going at such a slow pace, exposed and unable to take evasive action, if pursuit came
charging toward them, they would be the equivalent of sitting ducks. Pulling out his fob-watch, he glanced at the face.

Eliza leaned closer to look, too.

The fresh scent of her hair—rose and lavender—wreathed
through his senses; the suddenly closer, distinctly feminine
warmth, grabbed his awareness and wouldn't let go.

"Nine o'clock, near enough." She straightened, shifting
away.

. He wanted her back, close. Squelched the thought. "Yes." The word was weak. He cleared his throat. Looked down at the watch in his hand . . .

What had he been thinking?

He frowned, tucked the watch back into his pocket. "It's taken us three hours to get . . . not very far. We'll need to find a gig and drive like the devil. We'll probably need to readjust our plan, too, but we can't make any decisions until we know what our options are."

He felt her gaze on his face and turned to meet it.

Eliza smiled. "You're being very understanding. I appreciate it." He hadn't railed or ranted; he hadn't made her feel responsible, or made her feel even worse than she already did, about disrupting his plans.

He hadn't even made her feel stupid—more stupid—about not being able to ride well. He'd accepted both her and her shortcomings, and was reworking his plan without even a hint of contempt or sarcasm.

"Whatever we do, I'll do the very best I can not to slow us down."

He inclined his head, then looked back along the road. "I just hope our decoy is faring better than us and has drawn all pursuit far away."

After trading inventive expletives for the first ten minutes of their enforced trek, Cobby and Hugo were trudging along in silence, one on either side of poor Jasper, when the thunder of approaching hooves had them halting and looking back along the highway.

Several carriages and the early mail had lumbered past them, but this was the first rider to come their way.

They glimpsed the rider, coming on fast on a largish horse, before a dip in the road hid him from view.

Cobby viewed Hugo critically. "Your wig's askew."

On the verge-side of their equipage, Hugo righted the wig, then flipped up the cloak's hood and stepped closer to Jasper, so that the horse largely hid him from anyone on the road.

The horseman crested a rise a little way back.

Studying the rider, Cobby stiffened. "He's got a pistol."

"In a holster or out?" Hugo kept his head down.

"In his hand."

The horseman came down on them in a flurry of heavy hooves. Hauling back on his reins, he waved the pistol at them both. "Hold hard! Don't move!"

Cobby spread his arms, palms empty. "We've already stopped. Who the devil are you?" He did his best imitation of Jeremy's voice.

The horseman frowned. Pistol still in his hand, but not pointed anywhere in particular, he quieted his prancing horse, then looked searchingly at Cobby, then at Hugo, then raked the curricle with a knowing eye.

Frown deepening, he fixed his gaze on Cobby. "You take this curricle from the Rising Sun Inn on South Bridge Street?"

"Yes." Cobby nodded pugnaciously. "What of it? It's mine."

The horseman eyed him for a moment, then looked hard at Hugo. Lastly, he looked at Jasper, then shook his head. "Never mind. Thought you were someone else."

"Indeed?" Cobby set his hands on his hips. "Is that any reason to come bailing us up waving a pistol? As you can see, our horse has gone lame—"

The rider swore, kicked his horse around, and took off back toward Edinburgh.

Cobby stood in the road and watched him go.

Once the rider disappeared back over the crest, Hugo came around Jasper and joined Cobby.

The rider reappeared further along the road, riding hell-for-leather back to Edinburgh.

Cobby grimaced and reverted to his own voice to say, "Well, that didn't take long."

Putting back his hood, Hugo removed the golden wig and scratched his head. "I really thought our decoy mission would last longer—distract them longer—than just a few hours. I assume that was Taylor, the coachman-cum-guard."

"Do you think he recognized Jer's curricle?" Cobby turned to pat Jasper's long neck. "Or Jasper here?"

"He might have, but as they don't know who Jer is, they can't make anything of that." Hugo considered. "Most likely they'll just discard us as an unconnected coincidence—nothing to do with Eliza."

"When Taylor gets back with the news, they'll search again to see if they can pick up Jer's trail."

"No," Hugo said. "They don't know Jer exists. Or if they do, they think he's you. But they'll quarter the town for Eliza, or any sight of her, which, with luck, won't get them far."

Cobby shifted. "So what now for us?" He glanced across at Hugo. "What should we do?"

Both cogitated, then Hugo said, "I'd feel much more comfortable if I knew Jer and Eliza had got well away. Perhaps"—he swung around and looked down the road toward Dalkeith—"we should go on and get a fresh horse as planned, then drive back to Edinburgh and check with Meggin, and, if she's heard nothing to the contrary, check with the Grassmarket stables, too. If all seems to have fallen out as per Jer's plan, then we can drive out again along the Great North Road and still be at Wolverstone before him."

Brows raised, Hugo turned back to Cobby.

Meeting his gaze, Cobby nodded. "Good thinking. That's what we'll do."

It took McKinsey some time to locate the particular urchin he wanted, then another half hour for the urchin to seek and report back.

"Three flash gents h'escorted a lady through the tunnels last night. Well, h'early this morning, to be h'exact." Rabbit, so called because of his ears and his ability to scamper quickly through the vaults, added, "Three of the Dougan lads acted as guides-like. Said one of the gents paid them well."

Perched on the remnants of an old stone wall not far from the mouth of the South Bridge vaults—the tunnels weren't built for men of his size—McKinsey received the news with outward patience. "Did the Dougan lads say anything about the three men? Or the lady herself?"

"Just that the lady had bright gold hair. She had a cloak on, and put up the hood, but they saw her hair afore she did."

"And the men?"

"Seems they were well spoken, sort of quiet-like—not the usual roisterers come looking for a lark. Serious men. From how they spoke, two were from here—h'Edinburgh—but the other, the man who paid, he was h'English. Fer certain."

"Did anyone see where they went after they came out?"

"Nah." Rabbit nodded toward the town. "Just went out into the night, they did."

"In which direction? Palace or Castle?"

"Palace. Confidentlike—they seemed to know where they was going."

"Excellent." McKinsey reached into his pocket, sorted coins in his palm. "You've done well."

Rabbit—who knew exactly who McKinsey really was—straightened to attention and tugged his lank forelock. "Thank you, m'lord."

McKinsey held out several coins.

Rabbit received the small hoard in his dirty palms. "Always a pleasure doin' business with you, m'lord."

McKinsey laughed. He smiled at Rabbit, then rose to his feet. "Good-bye, Rabbit." He resisted the urge to ruffle the boy's dark hair. "Take care of yourself and your mother."

"I will, m'lord." Slipping the money into the inside pocket of his ragged jerkin, Rabbit snapped off a jaunty salute. "Until next time, m'lord."

McKinsey watched Rabbit scamper back into his burrow, then turned and climbed a short slope and stepped back into the world of the city's streets. He headed for Niddery Street.

It was now midmorning and while, courtesy of Rabbit,

he'd confirmed how his package had escaped the house, when, and with what escort, he still didn't know where she'd gone subsequently, or who, exactly, had come to her aid.

Given the social imperatives, however, he wasn't the least surprised that she'd set off back to England as quickly as she'd been able. Assuming, of course, that she was the lady who had left in some Englishman's curricle at first light. He wondered whether that Englishman was the same man who'd escorted her through the vaults in the wee hours.

What continued to puzzle him was how anyone had known where she was. Was it significant that one of the rescuers was English, and that she might well have fled south with him? The answer to that had to lie with Scrope and his people, even if they didn't realize it.

He refocused on what waited for him in the house in Niddery Street.

Since he'd left an hour ago, instinct had been nagging; finally considering why . . . it was Scrope's stunned bewilderment that had surprised him. The woman, the nurse, her reactions he'd understood, but Scrope's . . . the man was supposed to be a consummate professional, yet he'd been knocked totally off-balance and had shown no signs of quickly righting himself.

McKinsey had expected Scrope to be quick to reengage, to reassess and rejig his plans. To accept what had gone wrong and swiftly revise, replan, and be ready to move forward in whatever new direction was required to reach their ultimate goal.

Instead, Scrope had given an excellent imitation of a stunned mullet.

Comparing Scrope's behavior at the house with his reputation . . . according to the latter, Scrope had never failed in any of his questionable endeavors. Perhaps it was simply the looming reality of his first-ever failure that had so rocked the man?

McKinsey snorted. Coping with plans gone awry was

something he was becoming, as far as he was concerned, too expert at. He could certainly give Scrope lessons in the futility of raging against fate. One simply had to take the cuffs she handed out and roll with them. Then get back up, reassess, and come at the desired goal from some other direction.

The truth was, stubbornness combined with doggedness rarely failed. Not in the end.

So he had found.

Which brought him to where he was now, the situation he currently faced.

All things considered, all possibilities weighed, he had a lurking suspicion fate, that fickle female, was once again playing games with him. That she was, in a roundabout way, setting him up to fail again.

Unfortunately, he couldn't yet tell which outcome awaited him at the end of this act—triumph or defeat. Until he learned who had spirited Eliza Cynster away, until he knew what her view of her rescuer was—whether, as with her elder sister, Heather, there was, or would soon be, more between damsel and rescuer than mere mutual regard—he wouldn't know what his role in fate's current production would be.

He'd set the stage, then opened the curtain, but fate had taken over and was now running the show.

Reaching High Street, he strode along.

One way or another, Eliza Cynster had to come out of this with a husband; the social imperatives he'd brought into play would permit no other outcome. The only question he had on that point was whether said husband would be him—allowing him to go forward with his plan to reclaim the vital goblet from his mother—or the Englishman.

If the Englishman—until he learned otherwise, McKinsey would assume it was he who had rescued Eliza—proved to be a man of worth, one whom she wanted as her husband, and who wanted her, then honor, that quality McKinsey was determined to cling to no matter his mother's demands, would force him to draw back and let the pair escape.

Back over the border, and presumably to their wedding.

Where that would leave him, he didn't want to think. Literally did not wish to consider, not until he was forced to.

"Sufficient unto the day . . ." Jaw clenching, he turned down Niddery Street and strode for the house.

He needed to learn just how the Englishman had been drawn into this. And after that, he needed to locate Eliza and her rescuer, and determine whether the silly chit needed him to step in and save her from said rescuer, or instead, whether the Englishman was Eliza Cynster's ordained fate.

"I want to know how some Englishman learned you had Eliza Cynster in your keeping." McKinsey sat in an armchair in the drawing room of the terrace house, his gaze resting with cool, insistent, implacable command on Scrope, who sat on a straight-backed chair facing him.

The nurse sat on a chair alongside Scrope, her back straight, her fingers nervously twining.

Since McKinsey had left the house, Scrope had gone from bafflement to belligerence. He stared back at McKinsey. "I haven't the slightest idea. We didn't advertise her presence."

"Nevertheless, an Englishman assisted her escape from this house, and as we've heard from Taylor, an Englishman drove away from Edinburgh this morning with a lady of her description sitting beside him."

Scrope hesitated, then said, "There's no reason to believe that the man who took her out via those blasted tunnels is the same man who's driving her south. She might simply have talked some likely traveler into taking her. She has no money on her, but her name would mean something to another Englishman, enough to ensure he would help her."

McKinsey inclined his head. "All of that might be true, yet someone found out she was here and showed her how to escape. At some point someone saw her and, as you haven't taken her outside since you brought her here, they must have followed you here yesterday."

Scrope frowned, and McKinsey knew he hadn't been on guard against being followed when they'd walked Eliza Cynster to the house.

McKinsey fixed his gaze on Scrope's face. "Tell me all— every last detail—of your journey from Grosvenor Square to Edinburgh."

"I told you." Scrope gestured impatiently. "There's nothing to tell."

"Bear with me." McKinsey's response was no request. "You drugged Miss Cynster, carried her out of her cousin's house, bundled her into a coach, and drove out of Grosvenor Square. Start from there—what happened next?"

Scrope scowled but grudgingly obliged. "We drove out along the Oxford Road, through Oxford—"

"Had Miss Cynster revived by then?"

Scrope hesitated, then replied, "Yes and no—she was still groggy. She slept much of the way."

Scrope pretended not to notice the sidelong glance the nurse sent him.

McKinsey saw and suspected Eliza's grogginess had been arranged. Why else hire a nurse-companion to do a maid's job? Scrope had disobeyed his explicit orders in that, but that was now water under the bridge. "Very well—I take it Miss Cynster was too 'groggy' to have attracted anyone's attention while you drove through Oxford. At what point did she become more . . . shall we say, compos mentis?"

Scrope ignored the implication. "She started to stir as we left York, but then she slept again."

McKinsey had seen her dozing in York. "Very well— concentrate on the journey between Oxford and York. Go over each stage, each village and town you passed through. Was there any instance of any gentleman taking any interest at all in the coach and its occupants?"

At last Scrope stopped and thought.

The nurse thought, too.

Eventually, however, both shook their heads.

"No," Scrope declared. "There was *nothing*—nothing for us to report. No incident of any kind."

"No one who chatted to Taylor?" McKinsey asked. "Who lounged about and started up a conversation at any of your halts?"

"No." The nurse spoke up. "When he's making quick changes, Taylor rarely leaves the box."

"And he drove straight through?"

The nurse shrugged. "It's his job."

Scrope shifted. "I spelled him through a few of the lonelier stretches so he could catch a few hours sleep, but we didn't halt for any reason other than changing horses."

That married with McKinsey's estimation based on the time they'd passed through York. He kept his gaze steady, locked on the pair before him. "All right. So you passed through York without incident. What about the stretch from York to Middlesbrough?"

Again, both Scrope and the nurse considered; again, they shook their heads.

"You mentioned Miss Cynster stirring at York. When did she properly wake up?"

The nurse answered. "North of Middlesbrough. We spoke with her, then she dozed off again. She woke when we crossed the bridge leaving Newcastle."

"On either occasion, either on the road north of Middlesbrough, or as you left Newcastle, did she get close to the window, or make any attempt to attract someone's attention?"

"Not there," Scrope replied.

McKinsey fixed his gaze on Scrope's face. His tone was deceptively mild when he asked, "Are you telling me she did make a bid to attract someone's attention at some point?"

Scrope's scowl intensified. "Yes." He waved dismissively. "But nothing came of it."

McKinsey had grown very still. "Yet she's escaped."

"It had nothing to do with that. We were well out of Newcastle, only thirty miles from the border, and in wide-open countryside."

"On the road to Jedburgh?"

Scrope nodded. "Precisely. Forests and moors, and not much else. She appeared to be dozing again, slumped in the corner, then we slowed to let a curricle past, and she suddenly sprang to life."

"What happened?" McKinsey rapped out.

"She flung herself at the window, battered on it, screamed for help."

"And?" McKinsey couldn't believe he'd had to drag it out of them.

"Nothing came of it!" Scrope all but glared back. "We hauled her back from the window. The curricle was already past. I had Taylor keep an eye on it, but all that happened was that the driver turned around and looked back at the coach, then shrugged and simply drove on. Taylor kept watch for a while, but the curricle didn't turn and follow."

McKinsey pictured the scene in his mind. "Did either of you get a look at the curricle's driver?"

Both Scrope and the nurse shook their heads.

"Both carriages were moving," the nurse explained. "They'd slowed, but the driver still whisked past the window very quickly. Miss Cynster's effort lasted no more than a moment—an instant—before we pulled her back, but even then the curricle was long past."

"But she . . ." McKinsey considered the picture in his mind. "She was sitting in the corner, deep in the corner, so she would have seen the curricle driver as he approached, going the other way. She had time to see him, recognize him, and act."

Scrope snorted. "More like that was the only curricle, or even carriage or cart that we passed. She saw the curricle and grasped what she saw as her last chance—that was all there was to it. No reason to imagine she knew the driver."

Yet she's gone. McKinsey eyed Scrope but didn't bother to

point out the obvious. What Scrope thought no longer mattered.

Still, it paid to be thorough. "Other than that incident, was there any point at all where Miss Cynster could have come to the attention of a gentleman, English or Scottish or of any other stripe. Whether you saw it happen, or don't think it did—*think*. Could she have been recognized at any point after the incident with the curricle? While walking up South Bridge, for instance?"

Scrope replied coldly, defensively, "No. There was no other incident of any possible relevance, and when we walked her here, we kept her hemmed between us with her hood over her head and pulled low. It was crowded. No one took the slightest notice."

McKinsey stared levelly at Scrope. Had it been the curricle driver or some chance sighting in Edinburgh that had led to Eliza's escape?

Before he could decide if there was any sense in further interrogating the increasingly hostile Scrope, a heavy knock landed on the front door.

"Taylor." The nurse rose and hurried out into the hall.

A second later, McKinsey heard his alias being whispered as Taylor was warned that he was there. A silent moment passed, then a large man in coachman's garb filled the doorway, his hat in his hands. Seeing McKinsey, he bobbed, then glanced at Scrope.

Scrope waved him in and somewhat peevishly demanded, "Well? Did you find her?"

Taylor halted, squared his shoulders. "I found the gentleman in the curricle that passed us yesterday, down the other side of the Cheviots."

Scrope came to his feet, his face paling. "He was here?"

"Apparently. After I left here, I checked down South Bridge Street—didn't have to go further than the smaller inn just down from the coaching inn we used. The ostlers said the gentleman had come in yesterday late morning, and he left at first light, along with an English lady with fair hair and a gold gown. Sounded like our package, so I sent that message back to you and gave chase."

"And?" Scrope demanded.

"I ran them to earth this side of Dalkeith—that nice-looking black had gone lame and the pair of them were walking him on."

"Never mind the damned horse!" Scrope yelled. "What about the woman—and the man, this Englishman?"

Taylor studied Scrope, then went on, "Looked like the same fellow we passed yesterday, far as I could make out—but I recognized that horse and the curricle right enough, so it had to be him." Taylor transferred his gaze to McKinsey. "But the lady definitely wasn't Miss Cynster. Soon as I saw her—the lady with the Englishman—I came racing back. I checked up and down the coaching inns along South Bridge Street—all those that service the Great North Road. No one's seen any other fair-haired English lady. She definitely didn't go out in any of the public coaches, nor yet the private ones that set out this morning." He paused, then ventured, "She might still be in Edinburgh."

McKinsey didn't reply. Although he was tempted to ask why anyone would go to the trouble of arranging a demonstrably excellent decoy if not to deflect attention from a flight in a different direction, he had better things to do. That the English gentleman and the lady in the gold gown that Taylor had run down constituted a decoy was beyond question; how many fair-haired ladies in gold gowns were likely to leave Edinburgh on the Great North Road in an Englishman's curricle on one morning?

The Englishman Eliza Cynster had recognized driving his curricle down the Jedburgh Road had rescued her. McKinsey didn't know how he'd accomplished the whole, only that he had. And it was therefore now McKinsey's role to hunt the pair down.

His present position was very much an unwelcome case of

déjà vu. Just as had happened with Heather Cynster, he now found himself in the ridiculous position of being cast as a Cynster chit's protector. He would have to find her, determine whether she was in danger or not, whether he needed to step in and rescue her or not, or whether he could with honor intact withdraw and turn his mind to what next he would have to do.

Scrope and his two assistants had been watching him, waiting for his verdict, to see what orders he would give.

He focused on Scrope. "A word."

With a jerk of his head, Scrope sent the other two out of the room. Both bobbed courtesies to McKinsey before obeying; Taylor shut the door behind them.

"She has to still be here." Scrope wheeled and started pacing. "We'll scour the city—"

"She's already left."

Halting, Scrope stared at him. "You can't know that."

McKinsey looked up at him. "Ah, but I do." Reaching into his coat, he drew out a purse and tossed it at Scrope.

Scrope caught it, knew from the weight that it wasn't the reward he'd hoped for. "What's this? My work for you isn't finished."

"Sadly, it is. I'm paying you off and dismissing you. You no longer have any role to play in this game."

Scrope's dark eyes flared. "No!" He stepped closer, standing over McKinsey. "I won't—"

McKinsey rose, fluidly, gracefully. Fully upright, he looked down at Scrope. Asked, quite quietly, "What was that?"

Scrope was tall, but McKinsey towered over him. Where Scrope was well built, McKinsey was huge, all heavy bone and solid muscle.

Scrope didn't swallow and back away, as most men would have; he was, apparently, made of sterner stuff. He did, however, moderate his tone. "This was *my* assignment, my undertaking. Until it's finished, until I deliver Miss Cynster into your hands, it's still mine to carry out."

"So you believe, but I say otherwise, and, you might recall, I'm your client in this."

Scrope nearly ground his teeth. "You don't understand— this is my work, my profession. *I don't fail.*"

"You have this time, but rest assured I'm unlikely to spread the word."

"That's not the point!" Scrope's hands fisted, as if physically holding back his welling rage. He was all but erupting; when next he spoke, the words came through clenched teeth. "I will not be bested by a silly chit, even with some gentleman to help her. If I walk away from this, my reputation will be shredded. I will not let it—let her—go."

McKinsey didn't bat an eyelash. He studied Scrope's eyes, his face; he could understand professional pride, but there was more than that at work here. "This is not about you, Scrope. It never was. Let me make myself clear. Obey me in this, and no one will ever hear of your failure. Pursue Miss Cynster further, and I'll ensure you will never work in this town, or any other, for the rest of your days."

He couldn't tell from Scrope's eyes, now so dark they seemed to burn blackly, whether the man was even taking his words in. "Do you understand?"

The answer took a moment to come. "Perfectly."

"Excellent." McKinsey held Scrope's gaze for a moment more, then stepped around him and walked to the door.

Scrope's gaze burnt a hole between McKinsey's shoulder blades. Reaching the door, and foreseeing an eventuality he hadn't yet countered, McKinsey grasped the knob, then glanced back and met Scrope's gaze. "I'd wager Miss Cynster is long gone from Edinburgh, but if fate proves me wrong and you should find her in the town, I would counsel you to remember that my injunction against any harm befalling her still applies. One scratch, one bruise, and I will come for you, and I will not be merciful. If she falls into your hands, treat her like porcelain, and send word to me in the usual fashion. If you succeed in that, I'll double the reward we previously agreed on."

McKinsey considered Scrope for a long moment more, then evenly said, "You believe Miss Cynster is still within the town. I believe otherwise, so let's put it to the test. You look for her here, I'll look elsewhere. If you prove correct, as I said, I'll double the reward."

Lips pinched, his gaze burning darkly, Scrope offered nothing in reply.

McKinsey opened the door, stepped into the hall, and shut the parlor door softly behind him.

Seconds later, he was striding up Niddery Street.

Crossing High Street, he plunged into the warren of closes and wynds, ducked through passages and alleys so narrow he had to turn sideways to pass through. The erratic path ensured that no one—Scrope, for instance—followed him.

Once he was striding along more genteel streets, his mind meandered back to Scrope. Could he trust the man to desist in his pursuit of Eliza Cynster?

While he was reasonably certain Scrope had circumvented his instructions regarding Eliza's treatment on the long journey north, by and large the man had stuck to the letter of the orders he'd been given.

Now McKinsey had not just challenged him but he'd also made it very much worth his while to remain in Edinburgh and search for Eliza Cynster there.

While McKinsey was sure she'd already quit the town—there was no point in sending out a decoy if one wasn't going to act at the same time—the chance that she hadn't, Scrope's own conviction that she hadn't, plus the sizeable potential reward should serve to keep the man safely tethered.

McKinsey had to admit he hadn't liked the odd, almost fanatical look in Scrope's eyes, but on balance, he felt that Scrope now had sufficient incentive to remain in

Edinburgh—not least the prospect of proving him, Mc-Kinsey, wrong.

McKinsey turned up the street in which his own house stood.

He'd done enough, dangled bait enough, to ensure that Scrope toed his line.

Chapter Seven

Jeremy's respect for his brother-in-law and his Bastion Club colleagues was increasing by the minute. How did one remain outwardly calm when disaster was looming nearer and nearer?

It was nearly noon and they'd only just reached Kingsknowe.

A wheel on the cart they'd been riding in had split, tipping the cart sideways, almost into the ditch. Quite aside from disentangling themselves and recovering from the shock—and, on his part, subduing the unruly impulses evoked by being tossed on top of Eliza—they'd felt obliged to dally to help the poor farmer get the cart horizontal again. Then the farmer had taken his horse and ridden off to find a blacksmith, leaving the pair of them to walk on.

Worse, on reaching Kingsknowe they'd inquired at both the small town's inns, only to discover that while each had had a gig for hire, both conveyances had already been in use. Neither inn had had any other suitable equipage available. Nothing that would have traveled faster than an unladen farm cart.

That, once again, had been their only option. That, or hiring horses again, but one look at Eliza's apprehensive expression had put paid to that idea.

They'd been directed by the stableman at the second inn to a farmer who would soon be traveling on. The farmer had just ordered an early lunch in the inn's tap; he was going as far as Currie and had readily agreed to let them ride in the back of his dray.

Although they'd had food in their saddlebags, Jeremy, starting to think ahead, had suggested that, as they had to wait for the farmer to finish his meal, they might as well let the inn feed them, too.

Which was how they came to be sitting at a corner table in the small tap, plates bearing the remains of a decent game pie pushed to one side, with the map Cobby had given them spread out between them . . . and carefully not talking about the single issue that unquestionably loomed largest in both their minds.

Tracing their path thus far—more than five hours gone and so few miles covered—Jeremy tried to find the right words to address the near certainty that, given their slow progress, they would be forced to spend at least one night on the road, together, alone . . . but his mind simply balked.

After trying for several minutes and advancing not at all, he abandoned that subject and concentrated instead on getting on. "We'll have to replan—that's all there is to it."

Eliza grasped the straw of distraction. "This was the way we were going to go, wasn't it?" She traced the route to Carnwath, then east across to Melrose and Jedburgh before turning south across the Cheviots. "Perhaps we can shorten the journey by heading east earlier? Perhaps taking this road here."

Jeremy followed the tip of her finger, grimaced when it reached the Great North Road. "No—we can't do that. All that will accomplish is to take us in a wide sweep around Edinburgh and put us on the Great North Road only a few miles out of the town—more or less in exactly the spot where Scrope and company will search."

Eliza wrinkled her nose. She peered more closely at the map. "There are so few other roads east."

"It's the Pentland Hills. Once they rise on the left of the

road, which follows the western flank of the hills, there's no road that crosses them, not until we reach Carnwath."

"So we have to stay on this road until then."

"Unfortunately, yes." Another aspect of their original plan that, in hindsight, could have been improved. Given the possibility of pursuit, it would have been helpful to have had useful alternative routes sooner, closer to Edinburgh, than later. As it was, the first viable alternative way forward didn't eventuate until Carnwath. Jeremy tried to sound positive. "So Carnwath it is. We'll just have to be especially careful until then, but on the bright side, we'll definitely be able to hire a carriage there. We can check in the villages we pass on the way, too."

Eliza looked into his brown eyes, plain brown but warm, a color she associated with rich caramel, or perhaps expensive, well-aged brandy. At the pace they were going, even if they managed to find a faster cart, they still had no hope of reaching even Carnwath that night. Which meant they would have to find shelter, and that might prove problematical in more ways than one.

Another apology hovered on her tongue, but rather than utter the useless words she resolved instead not to make his life harder. They didn't need to discuss how they would spend the night until they knew what their choices might be. Sufficient unto the hour the problems—and they had problems enough to deal with as it was.

Noticing the farmer rising from his table and looking their way, she raised her hand in a manly salute and reached for the map to fold it away. "Also on the bright side," she said, determined to do her part to keep their mutual spirits up, "we haven't yet had Scrope on our heels."

"Or the mysterious laird." Having seen her salute and repacked his saddlebag, Jeremy stood.

She rose, too. He started to extend a hand to help her, then remembered and let his arm fall.

Catching his eye, she smiled.

His lips curved lightly in response, then he tipped his head toward the door. "Our carriage awaits."

She led the way and he followed. Minutes later, they were seated side by side in the back of the dray, boots swinging over the rear edge, the road unraveling like a ribbon beneath their feet as the farmer's cart rumbled along, down the road to Carnwath.

The city's bells had just rung the noontime peal when the laird presently calling himself McKinsey walked into the third of the string of stables located below the Grassmarket.

The decoy Taylor had discovered along the Great North Road strongly suggested that Eliza Cynster and her gentleman-rescuer had left town by another route that morning. Given that their ultimate destination was unlikely to lie deeper in Scotland, the laird had dismissed the roads to the north or northwest. Likewise, he felt certain they wouldn't have headed east or southeast; those roads lay too close to the Great North Road; indeed, some even branched off it.

That left the road directly south, or those to the southwest. From either initial direction, the fleeing pair could circle around and pick up the Jedburgh Road. If it had been him, he would have tried for that border crossing; given they'd elected to avoid the Great North Road and its crossing north of Berwick, the Carter Bar crossing south of Jedburgh offered the nearest, most open, and uncrowded route into England.

The prospect of remaining unobserved by hordes of other travelers would, he imagined, appeal to his fugitives.

He'd toyed with the idea of trusting to his instincts, riding south to Jedburgh, waiting there for his quarry to come past, then falling in on their heels. However, there was an outside chance the pair had decided to make for the Vale of Casphairn, to the far southwest in Galloway, to—as Heather Cynster and her rescuer, Breckenridge, had done—seek refuge with Richard Cynster and his wife there.

Given he needed to observe Eliza Cynster and her rescuer, to determine what manner of man said rescuer was and what the relationship between the pair might be in order to decide his own next move, he couldn't afford to risk losing them. Hence, he had to follow them, whichever way they'd gone.

The stableman saw him darkening his doorway and came forward. "Good day, my lord. Can I help you with a horse?"

The laird smiled. "No, not a horse. Two travelers. I'm looking for an English gentleman and a young lady, also English. They left town this morning, most likely early. They were going to hire transport—a fast carriage or horses—but I'm not sure which road they intended to take. Did you see them, or better yet hire to them?"

Wiping his hands on a rag, the stableman shook his head. "No lady and gentleman, not English, least ways. Two of my regular couples came in midmorning, locals wanting gigs for the day, but no other ladies."

The laird inclined his head. "Thank you. I'll continue searching."

He was turning away when the stableman said, "Funny, though—I did have two English here at the crack o'dawn, but it wasn't any young lady."

"Oh?" The laird turned back, one black brow rising.

"A young gentleman and his tutor. They hired two fast horses and headed for Carnwath."

"Did you speak to the younger man?"

The stableman shook his head. "Didn't even get a good sighting of him, now I think of it. It was the tutor came in and selected the mounts and tack, and saddled up both horses. The younger one hung about out there"—with his chin, the stableman indicated the narrow yard at the front of the stables—"holding one of the saddlebags, until the tutor took the mounts out to him, then they mounted up and trotted off down the road. Mind you, I don't know how fast they'll go—the young one was that stiff in the saddle. No horseman, that one. I remember thinking that perhaps that was the reason the tutor had them up so early—just to reach Carnwath will likely take them the whole day."

Head rising, the laird stared unseeing across the stable for a moment, then refocused on the stableman and smiled. "Thank you." Fishing a coin out of his waistcoat pocket, he flipped it to the man, who eagerly snatched it out of the air.

"Thank you, m'lord." The stableman saluted. "Sure you don't want that horse?"

The laird laughed. "I thank you, but no. My own mount would be jealous." So saying, he strode out of the stables and up to the Grassmarket.

Climbing swiftly back to High Street, he strode for his home, his stables, and Hercules. His quarry might have nearly six hours' head start, but he had no doubt that, mounted on Hercules, he would easily run the pair down.

"There." Scrope dropped two pouches on the kitchen table. "We're square."

Seated at the table, Genevieve and Taylor took one pouch each. Scrope waited while both opened the pouches, upended them, and counted the coins. "Your full payment as agreed."

About them, the terrace house was silent and still, the curtains drawn, all trace of their recent sojourn removed. All three had packed; each had their traveling bag on the floor beside them. This would be their last meeting before they went their separate ways. Although Scrope had worked with the other two as a team before, they were individual practitioners, hiring out their services job by job.

He waited impatiently, eager to leave.

Sliding the coins back into his pouch, Taylor looked up. "But we lost the girl."

Scrope forced himself to shrug. "McKinsey terminated our services. He made it very clear he didn't want us to pursue the matter—or the young lady—further."

Taylor looked his surprise. "He paid the full reward?"

Scrope expended considerable effort not to grind his teeth. "No. He didn't. But he paid us enough for our services to this point. We can't complain."

Taylor's expression had shifted from surprise to incredulity. "So you're just letting her—and the money—go?"

Not a chance.

Scrope drew a steadying breath. "As McKinsey pointed out, he was our client, and providing services to our client is the nature of our business. Doing everything the client wants is the overriding standard we have to meet, and, in case it escaped your notice, McKinsey, or whoever he is, is not the sort of gentleman any sane man would cross. Not this side of the border, anyway."

"Nor even on the other side." Genevieve tugged the strings of her pouch tight. "You're right. McKinsey's in charge. If he says leave her, we leave her." With a shrug, Genevieve stood. "I'm off." She looked at Taylor. "You coming?"

After staring at Scrope for an instant more, Taylor nodded and lumbered to his feet. "May as well."

Scrope inwardly railed at the note of derision he detected in Taylor's tone. His reputation was already being questioned, and not just by Taylor. Genevieve's agreement had come far too quickly, too pat. Both would wonder; eventually, both would talk. Word would get out—

But he would put a stop to that.

Bags in hand, the three of them left the house. Scrope locked the door, turned to the others. "I'll take the key back to the agent."

Genevieve nodded. "Until next time." She turned away and started down the street.

Taylor saluted Scrope, then followed her.

Scrope turned and climbed up the street, turned right onto High Street, then lengthened his stride.

The agent's office was along his way; leaving the key there took less than a minute.

Five minutes later, he was sitting in a small coffeehouse

staring out of its dingy window at one of the major stables on the north side of Auld Town.

He'd never managed to follow McKinsey back to his house, but by sheer luck, he had, a week ago, discovered where the man stabled his horse.

McKinsey would hunt for the girl; of that Scrope entertained not the slightest doubt, and, realistically, such a man had advantages over a nonnative like Scrope when it came to extracting information from the townsfolk of Edinburgh.

McKinsey would turn every stone to find the Cynster chit's trail. Why bother searching himself when McKinsey insisted on doing the legwork for him?

When McKinsey discovered the girl's direction, he would return to the stables across the road for his horse.

And when he rode away, Scrope would follow.

And then, when the time was right, Scrope would step in, do what he did best, and reclaim the troublesome chit from the hands of her rescuer.

He could all but taste the triumph he would feel when he presented the woman to McKinsey and claimed his reward, and, in so doing, reaffirmed and underscored his reputation.

His reputation was all—it was who he was.

Without it, he'd be nothing. A no one.

McKinsey hadn't understood that; he hadn't appreciated the fact that Scrope, having been hired to capture Eliza Cynster, had the right to accomplish the deed and, in quiet triumph, hand her over to his client.

That was simply the way the world, Scrope's world, operated.

Those fleeting moments of ultimate triumph were the moments in life he most savored. In those moments, he was king.

In the end, McKinsey wouldn't care; to him, all that mattered was getting his hands on the girl.

Scrope would make sure he did, and that it was Scrope who presented her to him.

* * *

It was midafternoon when the laird, mounted on his massive chestnut, Hercules, rode into the yard of the second of the two inns in Kingsknowe.

A young ostler came running, eyes widening as the boy took in Hercules's might.

About to dismount, the laird paused, then leaned forward, stroking Hercules's neck as the big chestnut allowed the boy to hold his bridle.

When the lad managed to drag his gaze from Hercules to his rider, the laird smiled.

The young ostler smiled back. "Yes, m'lord?"

"I'm looking for an Englishman and his charge, a younger man. They're traveling down from Edinburgh to Carnwath and beyond. They've been looking for a gig to drive on in—I wondered if they'd stopped to ask here."

He'd tracked his quarry to Slateford but had been met with puzzling news there. For some reason, the pair had left the horses they'd hired for return to the Grassmarket stables and, after finding no carriage available for hire, had gone on in a farm cart.

The young ostler's face lit. "Aye, m'lord. They were here. Came in just afore lunchtime wanting to hire a gig, but ours was already out."

"Where did they go?"

"They stopped for a bite in the tap, then went on with old farmer Mitchell. Last I saw they were sitting in the back of his dray rolling off down the road." The boy tipped his head toward Carnwath.

Straightening in his saddle, the laird fished for a coin in his waistcoat pocket, then tossed it to the lad.

Releasing Hercules's bridle to snatch the silver shilling from the air, the boy saluted. "Thank you, m'lord."

About to wheel Hercules, the laird paused. "How long ago did they leave?"

"An hour, maybe two."

With a nod, the laird swung Hercules around, trotted out of the inn yard, then set out down the road.

On the heels of his quarry, who, for some incomprehensible reason, weren't riding.

They were fleeing; on horseback would have been the obvious best choice. Even a carriage would be a poor second best, restricted to the roads and easier to trace. But a farm cart? Whoever heard of a pair fleeing by farm cart?

"The young one was that stiff in the saddle. No horseman, that one." The words of the stableman from the Grassmarket. The laird wondered if therein lay the truth.

He'd assumed Eliza Cynster—a Cynster born and bred—would be able to ride and ride well.

If she couldn't . . . catching up with them would be so much the easier, but it was another consideration that flooded his mind. If she hadn't been rescued, and instead his plan had come to fruition, he would have ended up with a wife who couldn't ride.

The thought . . . was enough to make him shudder.

Perhaps fate hadn't, as he'd thought, been playing games with him so much as giving him a solid nudge to get him off a path that would have led to disaster.

Despite his focus on catching up with the fleeing pair and, beyond that, regaining the goblet he needed to save his estate and his people, beneath his preoccupation with those tasks, the deep-seated fatalism he'd inherited from his highland ancestors was solidly at work.

It hadn't escaped him that, once again, he'd been forced to assume the mantle of protector to a Cynster girl. As had happened with Heather, he now felt honor bound to ensure that whatever arose out of his kidnapping of her, Eliza suffered no true harm. That she came out of the experience hale, whole, and respectably married, if not to him as per his original plan, then to her rescuer. The choice was hers, and he was willing to abide by her decision.

If, as he now suspected, she couldn't ride, he would be

perfectly happy to let her go, even in the face of what that meant.

The more he dwelled on all that had, once again, gone awry, the more certain he was that fate was telling him, very clearly, that Eliza Cynster wasn't for him, and he wasn't for her.

Beyond that, however, fate's clear message seemed to be that he wouldn't be allowed to reclaim the goblet without sacrificing the one thing he'd tried so hard to cling to, to avoid having to lay on the altar in meeting his mother's demands. His honor was an intrinsic part of him. Directly kidnapping a Cynster chit himself was the one line he'd drawn and had tried to hold to.

Fate, apparently, wasn't prepared to let him get away with that, with standing aloof, above the dirty work. He was going to have to do the deed himself, accept the ignominy, the stain on his soul, instead of stepping in at the last, almost as a rescuer.

The role of rescuer came easily to him—he'd been playing it for most of his life; in hindsight, he should have realized fate would never let him off so easily, merely doing what came naturally.

No. If he wanted the goblet back, he was going to have to balance the scales by doing something he didn't want to do, by sacrificing something that was precious to him.

Which meant . . .

He shifted in the saddle and thrust the consequent thoughts away. Later. He didn't need to deal with the "what next's" now.

Refocusing on the road ahead, he wondered where his quarry would next halt to inquire after a gig, and whether they would find one. Even if they did, with Hercules beneath him, he'd come up with them before nightfall.

And then he would see.

He would observe the pair and decide if Eliza's rescuer was a worthy protector, and, if they had a deeper understanding, whether their feet were already treading the path to the altar, or shortly would be. If that was so, he would step back and let them go, perhaps watch over them from a distance long enough to see them to some safe place.

Once he caught up with them, he'd soon know how matters stood.

And what fate, fickle fate, intended for him.

Jeremy and Eliza farewelled the farmer and his dray in the tiny village of Currie. Eliza kept her head down and mumbled her few words as deeply as she could; the farmer patently suspected nothing, tipping his hat and addressing her as "young sir."

"Come on." As the farmer rumbled off down a smaller lane, Jeremy nodded at the single tiny inn the village boasted. "I don't hold much hope, but we can at least ask if they have a gig for hire."

They crossed the road, the main highway to Carnwath, Lanark, Cumnock, and Ayr beyond, and entered the inn yard.

Eliza hovered in Jeremy's shadow, literally and metaphorically, while he spoke with the stableman. As they'd feared, there was no conveyance of any kind to be had.

"We've horses aplenty," the stableman said.

Jeremy glanced at her, but he seemed to sense the trepidation that surged through her. Turning back to the stableman, Jeremy shook his head. "We'll have to rethink our plans."

Nudging Eliza with his shoulder, he started them back to the road.

Eliza glanced up at him, took in the firm set of his lips, his chin. "What now?"

He glanced at her, considered her for a moment. "We need to stop and think." He looked around. "Let's find somewhere out of the way, off the road."

She swung slowly around, looking, too, then halted, her back to the road. "How about that church?"

Jeremy followed her gaze and saw the square tower rising behind the houses bordering the road. "Perfect."

About to take her elbow, he stopped just in time, lowered his arm. "Let's go."

Each carrying a saddlebag over one shoulder, they walked back along the road, then down a narrow lane. The church stood surrounded by its graveyard, a wide swath of green dotted with monuments and stone-clad graves, many a testament to the congregation's age. A solid stone edifice with a heavy oak door, the church appeared quietly prosperous and well tended.

Reaching the arched doorway, he grasped the latch, grateful when it lifted freely. Pushing open the door, he led the way inside.

At that time of day there was no one about, but when Eliza moved to pass him and go into the nave, he touched her arm. "One moment."

She obligingly halted, watching as he crossed to the base of the tower, to a small door set into the wall.

It, too, was unlocked; opening it, he found, as he'd hoped, stairs leading upward. Looking back at Eliza, he tipped his head. "Let's take a look at our surroundings first, before we try to come up with a new plan."

Head rising, she strode across quite eagerly. A shaft of sunshine beamed down through a clerestory window, turning the hair that showed beneath her hat to a rich, bright, beaten gold. He could only give thanks that she'd kept to the shadows and kept her head down when they'd been near others. No man getting a clear view of her face would ever imagine her a male.

Instinct gripped; he stepped back and let her go before him.

Climbing the narrow spiral stair in her wake, he lectured himself over the telltale error. If she'd been the male she was supposed to be, he would have led the way.

If he had, he wouldn't have been tortured by the sight

of her hips swaying before his eyes in a distinctly unmale way with every steep stone step. Even though her figure was screened by Hugo's cloak, he still knew what he was seeing.

But as they stepped out onto the tower's roof, instinct of a different sort surged to the fore, swamping all inclination to lascivious thought. He hadn't truly appreciated that he had such instincts, such warrior impulses, before this adventure; he was still learning how to deal with them, with how to define whether to yield to their prompting or suppress them.

With each successive setback that morning, his newfound instincts had risen and grown. Now, with him and Eliza at midafternoon no further than Currie, those new instincts were screaming.

The sensation wasn't simply a ruffling of the hairs at his nape but an actual prickling, as if someone or something was literally behind him, sword drawn, about to strike.

He had to, simply had to, look behind him.

And the tower roof was perfect for that need. Walking to the chest-high battlemented wall, he looked out over the countryside, spread model-like below them, saw the road leading back to Edinburgh laid like a ribbon across the fields. The nearer stretches were in clear view; from their vantage point, coaches, carts, and horsemen looked like children's toys.

Eliza raised a hand to her eyes and looked south and west, toward Carnwath.

Pulling the saddlebag from his shoulder, Jeremy hunted through it, eventually locating the spyglass Cobby had lent him. Drawing it out and setting the saddlebag at his feet, Jeremy opened the glass to its full extent, put it to his eye, and focused on the road they'd recently rattled along.

The spyglass was an old one, not especially good, yet . . .

Jeremy looked, looked again, then bit his tongue to hold back a curse. Spyglass still trained, he asked, "That mysterious laird of yours—did Heather or Breckenridge say what he looked like?"

To his relief, his tone made the question sound like a scholarly query; none of his welling agitation showed.

"Tall, large . . . very large. Black hair—real black, not dark brown. Pale eyes. 'Face like hewn granite and eyes like ice'—that was the description from one of the men who'd spoken with him." Eliza glanced at him. "Why?"

Adjusting the spyglass, he ignored the question, asked instead, "His horse—I vaguely recall some mention about a horse."

Eliza drew nearer. "A huge chestnut. Massive chest." An instant passed, then she asked, "Is he near?"

Not, he noted, is he following us?; she'd already realized that. "A man fitting his description, on a horse of the right type, is riding this way at a good clip. He's less than a mile away."

"If he stops in the village and asks, he'll realize we're close. He'll search."

"Did the stableman notice which way we went? I didn't see."

She paused. "I don't think so. But he might have."

"We need to get out of here."

"We can't go back to the road—he'll see us."

Lowering the spyglass, Jeremy swung around, then strode to the opposite side of the tower. Looking out at the countryside in that direction, a significantly different landscape, he grimaced. Shutting the spyglass, he stuffed it back in his saddlebag; pulling out the map, he unfolded it.

Beside him, Eliza grabbed one edge and helped hold the map open. One glance at her face told him that she was frightened, fearful, but still thinking, still rational, not panicking.

Which was a relief. Inside he was panicking enough for them both.

Next time he felt that prickling sensation on the back of his neck, he would react a lot sooner.

He jabbed at the map. "Those"—lifting the same finger,

he pointed to the purplish hills that rose, a backdrop to the fields directly behind the village—"must be the Pentland Hills. If we continue along the lane we took to the church, we'll head toward them, but according to the map the lane will end soon, and after that, there's nothing but hills, not until we cross them."

Eliza was following, searching the map for what lay further on. "But once we cross the hills, there's a highway—no, *two* highways on the other side." After a moment of looking further afield, she said, "Penicuik is a fairly large town on a highway. Surely we'll be able to get a gig there, and then we can drive to Peebles, and we'll be back on the route we originally planned to take to Wolverstone."

But they would be a day late. This, however, was not the time to discuss that, not with the laird all but breathing down their necks.

"Right." Jeremy caught her eyes. "Are you game to try walking across the Pentland Hills?"

Her chin firmed. The look on her face reminded him that she was a Cynster through and through. "I am not going to wait here until the laird catches up with us." Eyes sparking, she raised her head and swung toward the stairwell. "Let's go."

Hurriedly stuffing the map back into his saddlebag, he swung the bag up to his shoulder as he stalked, grim-faced, after her; catching her up before the open door, he grasped her arm, drew her back, and went down the stairs ahead of her.

There was no danger lying in wait in the church foyer.

"He'll be nearing the first cottages." Hauling open the church door, he looked back toward the highway, saw with relief that bushes along the edge of the graveyard screened them from view.

Stepping out onto the path, he waved Eliza ahead of him. After one glance toward the highway, she strode, all but ran, down the path, around the back of the church, down to a side gate, then stepped through into the lane once more.

He joined her. After one last glance back toward the highway, they walked quickly, side by side, away from civilization toward the looming Pentland Hills.

A little way along the lane curved, hiding them completely from anyone on the highway. They exchanged a glance, then lengthened their strides.

It wasn't easy going.

The lane had petered out not all that far from the church. They'd pushed through a low hedge and into the field beyond and continued on, pausing every now and then to mark the higher line of the hill and look back at the church tower, the landmarks they were using to keep their course.

Eliza gave fervent thanks she was wearing breeches and boots; had she been in a gown, she would have been staggering. The freedom of male attire had a great deal to recommend it; each stride in her boots would have taken two or even three had she been restricted by skirts.

As the ground rose, they encountered banks of heather. Although not yet in bloom, the bushes were abundant and plentiful. Sheep tracks wended through the thick masses, but her and Jeremy's direction did not always match those of the sheep.

Halfway up the first ridge, they came to a stream. At Jeremy's suggestion, they walked along the bank a little way and found a place where rocks set in the bed allowed them both to cross easily enough.

Without wasting breath on words, she slogged on. Jeremy kept pace alongside, occasionally pausing to glance back and check their direction.

The way grew steeper. Harder. Determined not to whine or give any hint of censure, she set her jaw and walked on, ignoring the unaccustomed heat, the burning sensation in her thighs, her calves.

She was completely as one with Jeremy on the need to flee the laird, and as, thanks to her, they had no other option but to do so on foot, she was not going to let a single word of complaint pass her lips.

Reaching the top of the ridge, she bent from the waist, braced her hands on her thighs, hung her head, and tried to catch her breath.

After a moment of unladylike wheezing, she felt the weight of the saddlebag, still over her shoulder, ease.

"Let me take that."

Feeling her legs wobble, she staggered to a flat rock and collapsed upon it.

Jeremy stood just below the ridge, far enough below so he wouldn't be outlined against the sky should anyone think to look. He set the saddlebags by his feet, then drew out their map again.

After a moment of consulting it, he glanced at Eliza and saw her staring onward, across the shallow valley before them.

The look on her face was horrified. "Good God—that was only the *first* ridge." Turning to him, she demanded, "How many are there?"

"Only one other." He nodded at the ridge before them. "That one. Once we're over that, it's all downhill."

"Thank God for small mercies."

Hiding a wry smile at her faint voice, he looked again at the map. "We're heading in the right direction." Glancing across the shallow valley, he gauged the distance, then looked over his shoulder at the western sky. "The light's already fading, and as we go further into the valley, we'll be descending into shadow."

"Can we get over the next ridge before nightfall?"

"I don't think so, and this isn't the sort of country to go walking through at night." He scanned their surroundings. "We need to start looking for shelter."

The one aspect of their flight they still hadn't discussed.

Yet instead of embarking on recriminations, something Jeremy had steeled himself to hear, Eliza sighed and pushed up from her rock. "Let's start walking and look about us while we do. I can't see any roof at present, but there must be huts, or cottages, or something around here."

He had a suspicion "something" would be the best they would find, but as she'd already started off, he hefted the saddlebags, settled one on each shoulder, and followed her down the slope.

When the laird reached the village of Ainville without sighting his quarry, he drew rein on a curse.

"Damn. I've lost them."

Hercules paid no heed.

Sitting the horse in the gathering gloom, the laird mentally reviewed the miles between Ainville and the last news he'd had of the pair. The stableman at Currie hadn't seen which way they'd gone, but given they'd been heading south, the laird had continued in that direction, but had learned of no other sightings along the road.

He'd stopped and asked at every inn, but no one had had any tidings of any kind.

It was possible some coach had halted and they'd persuaded the occupants to take them up.

But he'd ridden steadily, especially over the last long, straight, very empty stretch of road. A coach would have to have been rattling along for him not to have caught even a glimpse of it ahead of him.

Unless the coach had turned off the main road, but intersecting lanes were few and far between along this particular road.

An inn lay just ahead. Deciding that night was too close upon him to continue further pursuit that day, he nudged Hercules into a walk and headed for the stable yard.

Tomorrow, he'd have to backtrack and inquire about coaches and carriages that might have taken the pair up.

The inn proved to be surprisingly comfortable. Leaving his bag by the stairs, he walked into the tiny tap and had the barkeep pull him an ale.

Leaning on the counter, he glanced idly around and saw an old man, wrapped in knitted shawls and with a plaid cap covering his bald head, tucked in a corner of the bay window, looking out at the road.

The old man's head was bobbing, but his eyes were open, his gaze, when it flicked briefly the laird's way, alert.

Picking up the mug of ale the barkeep placed by his elbow, the laird nodded at the old man. "What's his drink?"

"Porter."

"Give me a mug for him."

The barkeep grinned and complied.

Carrying the mug of porter as well as the mug of ale, the laird walked to the table before the window.

The old man looked up, dark eyes bright in a wrinkled face.

"For you." The laird set down the porter.

The old man considered him for a moment, then reached for the mug and nodded to the bench on the other side of the table. "Thank you, m'lord."

The laird sat, stretched out his long legs, then took another draft of the ale.

After taking two sips of porter, all the while regarding the laird over the rim of the mug, the old man chuckled. "So, what can I do for you?"

The laird smiled. "You can tell me what you saw this afternoon. I'm trying to catch up with two acquaintances who were supposed to have traveled down this way today, but I fear I've missed them. Then again, they might have hailed some carriage and been taken up, and so still be ahead of me."

The old man nodded his understanding, sipped again. "Well, you must have missed them along the way, because since noontime, no one—on horse or in any sort of carriage, not even on foot—has passed this window."

"Thank you." The laird inclined his head. He stayed chatting to the man, exchanging the usual countryman's news, until he'd drained his mug, then, with a polite nod, he rose and headed for his room.

A good dinner, a decent night's sleep, then tomorrow he'd backtrack and find his quarry's trail.

Tracking was an accomplishment at which he excelled, and unless he missed his guess, his fleeing pair had resorted to shank's pony. On foot, they'd be easy enough to track, easy enough to come up with.

And then he would observe, and see what he could see.

Chapter Eight

The light was failing, and Eliza was starting to believe they would be sleeping on the open ground when Jeremy, walking half a pace ahead of her, halted and put out a hand to stop her.

Glancing up through the dimness, she saw he was peering toward a stand of trees ahead of and to the right of their path.

"Is that a roof?"

She peered, too. After a moment, she made out a patch of what might have been gray tiles, a shadow of a different quality in the gloom beneath the trees. "I . . . think it is."

Jeremy surveyed the shallow valley into which they were descending. "I can't see any other habitation of any kind. This whole valley looks deserted."

Eliza nodded toward the copse. "Except for that roof and whatever's beneath it."

He looked again at the trees. "It might be a woodcutter's cottage. Those trees look like they're managed for firewood. Let's take a closer look." He stepped off the path and headed for the trees.

She followed. "What if the woodcutter's there?"

"We'll ask if we can share his cottage. But"—he peered between the boles—"I can't see any sign of life. No light, and it's dark enough anyone inside would have lighted a candle by now."

They picked their way through the thick blanket of leaves, twigs, and branches littering the ground beneath the trees. Signs of recent logging could be seen here and there, but the closer they got to the cottage the more certain he was that it lay empty. "Most likely the woodcutters only stay here while they're harvesting the logs. This land and the copse probably belong to some nearby estate."

Eliza didn't reply but stayed close behind him, her hand occasionally brushing the back of his coat.

He was acutely aware of her nearness, and of them being together, alone in the wilds with no chaperon of any description in sight, but in that moment his newfound protective instincts were simply reassured knowing that she was near.

They had to circle to descend into the dip in which the cottage stood. A small, doubtless single-roomed abode fashioned of rough stone and split logs, it nestled against the rising hillside behind it, protected by both the hill and the thick trees all around.

At the edge of the small clearing before the cottage, he paused and scanned the shuttered windows again. Detecting no sign of life, he cautiously crossed to the door.

He knocked once, then again.

No answer came.

Exchanging a glance with Eliza, he shrugged, grasped the latch, lifted it, and opened the door. Pushing it wide, in what little light remained to penetrate the dimness, he took stock.

Eliza peered past him, then stepped across the threshold and walked into the tiny cottage. "It looks neat and quite clean."

"Almost certainly an estate cottage." Spying a candle in a simple holder on a shelf by the door, he lifted it down, then, seeing no tinderbox, hunted in his pockets for his own.

Outside, the last of the daylight died, and night fell like a blanket around the cottage.

The candle flickered, then flared to full life; once the flame settled, he raised the candlestick and took inventory of their surroundings.

A roughly made dresser stood against the wall opposite the door. Two wooden crates of logs and kindling sat on either side of the narrow hearth. A small square table took up the middle of the floor, with three simple wooden chairs set about it. On the far side of the cottage, filling the quadrant furthest from the door, lay a straw-filled pallet covered by coarse blankets.

Eliza had halted looking down at the pallet; taking off her hat, she turned and sat, sinking down. She leaned down and sniffed. "The straw smells fresh."

He managed to keep his voice even, his tone bland. "The woodcutters probably come up here once a month or so, at least during the summer. We must have just missed them."

Her brows arched fleetingly. "That's just as well."

Walking forward, he set the candlestick on the table, then shrugged off the saddlebags and set them over the backs of the chairs. His gaze fell on a metal pitcher sitting on the dresser. "I saw a well outside." Picking up the pitcher, he walked back out.

Eliza followed him to the door. She watched as he crossed to the tiny stone-sided well, then went to join him. "I'll hold the pitcher. You haul the bucket."

"All right."

She took the pitcher from him, waiting while he let the bucket down on its rope and more slowly hauled it back up, then she held the pitcher for him to fill.

Leaving him to empty and reset the bucket, she carried the pitcher back to the cottage, found metal mugs, and filled one for each of them.

Jeremy reentered the cottage to see Eliza seated at the table, sipping cold water, eyes closed, and a blissful expression on her face.

Hearing him, she opened her eyes and smiled. "This might as well be the finest wine."

His mouth dry, he managed a grin, then turned to shut the door. Seeing an iron bolt set above the latch, he slid it home with some relief. At least no one could sneak up on them during the night.

"Thank goodness Meggin insisted on packing some food." Setting down her mug, Eliza opened one saddlebag and rummaged inside.

"What have we got?" Jeremy opened the other bag.

Between them, they unearthed a passable repast of rolls, cold chicken, cheese, and figs. There was also an apple each, but they decided to save those for the morning.

With the candle between them, they sat on the chairs and ate, listening to the light wind playing through the branches outside. An owl hooted.

The food gone, still they sat, sipping the last of their water.

Peace, an aura of stillness and quiet, of comfort and safety, enveloped them; Eliza sensed it, felt it, knew she wouldn't have if he hadn't been sitting opposite her.

She glanced at him, and their gazes met.

Held.

All too aware of the subject she—and presumably he, too—was avoiding, she cut her gaze to the empty fireplace. "Should we light a fire, do you think?"

Her body was exhausted, her mind in no fit state to discuss the social ramifications of them spending the night alone.

After a fractional hesitation, he replied, "We could, but if the land is anywhere near, the smoke might lead him this way."

"True, and it's not really cold."

"It would be best not to."

That settled, she sighed wearily and rose, feeling twinges in her thighs and calves. "If I don't lie down soon, I'll fall asleep where I stand." She turned to the straw pallet, their makeshift bed.

He rose, too. "You take the bed. I'll—"

"Don't be nonsensical." Swinging to face him, she heard the sharp edge to her words but made no attempt to soften it. "I hate it when people insist on being unnecessarily self-sacrificing, especially on my behalf." Dropping onto the bed, she fixed him with a challenging look and waved at the pallet. "This could sleep three with space to spare, and we're both fully clothed. And cloaked, too. There's more than enough space for us both to lie down, and there's nowhere else you can sleep. We'll have to walk again tomorrow, and there's no telling what we might need to do, so you'll need to be at your best, which means you'll need your sleep." She held his steady gaze uncompromisingly, fractionally tilted her chin. "I rest my case."

His lips, until then set in a noncommittal line, kicked up at the ends before he straightened them. Still standing by the table, he hesitated, frowningly considering her, then lightly grimaced. "All right." Picking up the candlestick, he came around the table. Waved at her. "You take the side closer to the wall."

Further from the door in case anything comes through it.

Jeremy kept the words to himself, grateful when, without further argument—indeed, probably because she considered she'd won that round—she shifted across, then stretched out full length on the far side of the bed.

Setting the candle a safe distance from the bed, he sat, went to pull off his boots, then decided against it. If he was called on to defend them, he would need to be ready instantly. Without glancing at her, he murmured, "Good night," and blew out the candle.

"Good night." Her voice came through the ensuing darkness. She already sounded sleepy.

He shifted, then stretched out full length on his back.

She wriggled, then he sensed her turn onto her side, facing the wall. She twitched the folds of her cloak closer, then, on a soft sigh, relaxed.

He couldn't imagine getting much sleep with her within arm's reach, but that hadn't been an issue he'd wanted to discuss, especially not with her. Falling in with her wishes had seemed the easiest way; as she'd pointed out, the bed was wide enough. Nothing inappropriate was likely to occur.

Not, of course, that it needed to; them being alone, together, in such isolation, was inappropriate enough.

Arms at his sides, he dragged in a deep breath, closed his eyes as he exhaled. Cast about in his mind but couldn't summon reason enough, let alone will enough, to pursue the question of where, given this night, they now stood vis-à-vis each other.

She was worn out; so was he. He could hear her breathing, already even and slow. She was already asleep . . . and so was he, so close to the edge that just the thought was enough to send him tumbling over, into oblivion.

Scrope waited until it was nearly midnight and the landlord of the inn at Ainville had started his rounds, checking the windows before he locked up for the night. Only then did Scrope emerge from the darkness of the copse twenty yards up the road and walk his horse to the inn's tiny yard.

The innkeeper was ready enough to hire him a room and send a sleepy boy out to see to his horse.

Scrope kept his voice low; all the other guests, including McKinsey, had retired more than an hour before, but there was no sense taking chances. "If at all possible, I'd like a room at the front of the inn." From where, in the morning, he could watch McKinsey leave.

The innkeeper grunted. "One left, as it happens." Turning, he lifted a heavy key from a board, then handed it to Scrope. "Room on the left at the top of the stairs."

Scrope accepted the key. "Seeing I'm so late getting in, I won't be leaving early. I'll come down for breakfast eventually."

"As you wish, sir. We can do breakfast for you anytime."

Scrope took the candle the man offered and started up the stairs, growing increasingly cautious as he ascended. He'd wager McKinsey was in the inn's best room, most likely another room overlooking the inn's forecourt. Very possibly the room next to his.

He'd followed his erstwhile employer from Edinburgh, hanging back as far as he'd dared. He wasn't about to underestimate McKinsey, but by the same token, just by being the sort of man he was, the laird himself had weaknesses. Scrope was counting on McKinsey being so accustomed to giving orders and having them obeyed without question that it wouldn't occur to him that Scrope might ignore his order to let the girl be.

Reaching his door, Scrope inserted the key and, as quietly as he could, unlocked the door, opened it, went inside, then, setting down his saddlebag, locked the door again.

He crept about the room, then undressed and got into the bed.

For a moment he lay on his back staring upward, reviewing his actions of the day, and planning, as well as he could, those of the next.

To his mind there was no question about his right to follow and capture Eliza Cynster. He was Victor Scrope; once put on the scent of a particular prey, he never failed. McKinsey had hired him precisely because of that reputation, so now McKinsey would simply have to bear with the natural outcome.

Closing his eyes, Scrope grimly smiled. He would succeed in this, as he always had before; that was written in his cards. This was merely a new challenge—a novel and unexpected hurdle—and in ultimately triumphing in spite of it, he would raise his professional standing to new heights.

He would seize Eliza Cynster, then hand her over as agreed to McKinsey.

In doing so he would claim his bonus and salvage his pride, but most importantly he would shore up, and possibly even increase, the professional standing of Victor Scrope, a standing this episode had threatened to undermine.

Of all the issues involved, that was the most important.

His reputation was all. It was him. It defined him.

Without it, he was nothing.

Without it, he'd be lost.

No one had any right to attack or damage it. And no one would.

At the end of this tale, the name of Victor Scrope would shine among those in his singular profession. No other would have overcome such hurdles; no other would be seen as so powerful. As so omnipotent in his field.

As sleep drifted nearer, Scrope's grim determination solidified.

He would do whatever was necessary to protect his reputation; that was his inalienable right—one he would exercise without compunction.

Jeremy came gradually, slowly, awake, lured to awareness by the sensation of his nose being lightly tickled.

As the fogs of sleep lifted, his senses reported the warm weight of a woman in his arms. Soft, alluring curves fitted snugly against his side, cradled his hip, caressed his thigh.

Which was beyond pleasant, but how could that be? He never fell asleep in any woman's bed, and he couldn't recall inviting any woman into his . . .

He came fully awake with a start. Eyes flying open, without moving his head or any other limb, he looked down.

Felt triumphant, if utterly misplaced, satisfaction course through him at the sight of Eliza snuggled comfortably in his arms.

Even as, delightedly stunned, he gazed wonderingly at her, she stirred.

Before he could decide whether to release her with all speed, plead his innocence and apologize profusely, or adopt a man-of-the-world sophistication, she froze, then on a small gasp pulled back and away.

Wide hazel eyes found his. For a split second she stared, then gushed, "I'm so sorry!"

Pushing up to sit in the shifting straw, Eliza glanced at the bed behind her, confirming that she was the one at fault.

"I . . . ah . . ." Horrified, but not at all in the way she'd expected, she felt color mount in her cheeks. Looking back at Jeremy, she found his rich caramel eyes reassuringly warm and not at all shocked or embarrassed.

His lips curved, again reassuringly, not as if he was laughing at her, and he raised his shoulders in a light shrug. "It's all right. We probably both slept better being closer, sharing our body heat. It was probably that that lured you nearer in your sleep."

She wasn't at all sure that was true, but he was gallantly giving her an easy way out of the embarrassing situation, and she wasn't too proud to take it. "Yes, well." Sitting fully upright, she pushed back her hair, which had slipped loose from her pins and was now tumbling everywhere. "I didn't think of that. But then I don't normally sleep with anyone else in my bed."

He pressed his lips tight and nodded. "Naturally not."

She narrowed her eyes on his dancing ones, but she, too, was fighting a grin. After an instant of staring into those lovely brown eyes, she said, "I can't believe I said that. Stated such an inanely obvious thing."

He grinned. "Don't take it back on my account."

She simply looked at him, amazed and fascinated—by him, and herself, by his reaction to her, and hers to him.

Another second passed, then he glanced toward the front of the cottage. "Looks like we might have overslept. It's full daylight outside."

Swinging his long legs from the bed—and leaving her legs feeling suddenly abandoned and the strange, oddly intimate moment broken—he sat up and ran his hands through his hair.

She fisted her hands against the urge to reach out and ruffle the thick locks herself, then comb them down.

He, of course, left his hair sticking up in every direction. Rising, he headed for the door. "Let me check outside first. Don't come out until I get back."

Now he sounded like a lot of the males she knew.

Unbolting the door, he lifted the latch, opened the door halfway and checked, then pulled it wide and walked out.

By expending considerable willpower, Jeremy cleared his mind of the distraction of all that had just happened. He stood just outside the door and searched the surrounds, both with his eyes and his senses.

Tristan and Charles St. Austell had taught him how to be silent and just listen, to every rustle, every twig, every chirp.

A minute passed, and he heard not a single note out of place. Reasonably confident there was no one nearby, he nevertheless circled the cottage, climbing up through the trees to pass over the bank behind it, then down across the path they'd walked the previous evening.

He returned to the cottage to find Eliza in the doorway; she'd pinned up her hair again and had crammed her hat over the golden locks. "I didn't see anyone. We appear to be safe."

She nodded. "I've made the bed and tidied, and repacked the saddlebags. I left out the two apples for our breakfast, and we still had water in the pitcher, so I've poured two mugs." She peered into the trees. "And now I'm going out."

He pointed to the side. "There's reasonable cover around that way."

"Thank you." She strode out and headed around the cottage.

Shaking his head, he went inside. She continued to puzzle him. What he'd gathered of her before, what he knew of her reputation, had suggested a pampered princess, if anything one more delicate than her sisters.

Her lack of equestrian ability had seemed to confirm that, yet beyond that she'd given him no cause to think her weak, wilting, or in any way unable. As in any way less than his sister, Leonora, who had been and continued to be a strong female force in his life.

He knew a lot of strong, willful, independent ladies; he

hadn't expected Eliza Cynster to figure among that choir, yet he was starting to suspect she did. She'd already adjusted to a situation that would have reduced the average ton miss to tears and unreasoning fright, which would have made his task as her rescuer that much harder.

Other than riding—and even there she'd tried—she'd risen to every challenge that being kidnapped had flung her way.

As for that morning . . .

He heard her footsteps briskly returning, realized he'd been standing by the table staring at the newly made bed for uncounted minutes.

Rapidly thrusting his thoughts aside before he blushed and gave himself away, he seized one apple and took a sizeable bite, then dragged the map to him and spread it open.

When she stepped through the doorway, he was frowning down at the map, finally doing what he'd meant to, considering their onward route.

"I can't see any way around it—we'll need to cross two streams at least before we start to climb the next ridge. The larger stream connects two small lakes—lochs, I suppose I should say. We could go all the way around the northern loch, but quite aside from taking us too far out of our way, there's an old hill fort near the northern tip, and just at the moment I'd prefer to avoid being seen by anyone in authority—meaning anyone who might have the authority to hold us."

She'd drawn near, bringing a light scent he now recognized as her. She pored over the map, then nodded. "I agree. The streams it needs to be."

He waited until she straightened, then met her gaze. "I don't want to lose you if you stumble. Can you swim?"

She smiled intently. "Yes, I can. Quite well, as it happens. It's only horses I'm hopeless with."

He inclined his head and refolded the map. "Right, then." Slipping the map into one saddlebag, he reached for the other, but she was before him.

"No—let me carry this one, at least to begin with. Now we've eaten the food, it's much lighter."

He caught the look she sent him, as if expecting him to fuss over her being a female and too weak to carry the bag. Instead, he nodded and said, "Give it to me if it gets too heavy."

She beamed at him. Swinging the saddlebag to her shoulder, she swiped up her apple and turned to the door. "Right. Let's get going."

Shaking his head to dispel the paralyzing effect of that brilliant smile, he followed her out into the weak sunshine.

They continued descending through the trees, keeping to the cover as long as they could, but eventually they had to walk out into more open, rock-strewn country. He glanced around frequently but saw no one, most especially no one following them.

The first stream was a minor one; they found a shallower part and splashed their way across.

The second stream would have caused them serious trouble, but some kind souls had swung a long log across from bank to bank. He went first. He nearly landed in the swiftly moving water; with wild flailings and much cursing, he managed to keep his footing long enough to leap for the bank, where he landed in a sprawl.

To the sound of tinkling, chimelike laughter.

He'd never heard her laugh before, not like that, unrestrained and uninhibited. Turning over, he was about to send her a mock scowl. Instead, he lay on his back and watched in abject appreciation as, balancing the saddlebag so one pocket hung over each shoulder, she all but danced across the log, landing lightly on her feet beside him.

She looked down at him in princessly triumph, then grinned and tipped her head toward the ridge. "Come on, lazy bones—we've another ridge to climb."

He groaned and got to his feet.

She laughed again, as he'd hoped she would, then she set

off, striding along in her man's boots, and he fell in alongside.

They went up the second ridge with confidence and speed.

Once over the crest, they halted to pull out the map, match the markings with what they could see, and confirm their route.

A middling-sized road ran along the bottom of the valley below them. He pointed to a cluster of roofs a little way along. "That will be Silverburn." He consulted the map. "According to this, it's about two miles on." He looked up and pointed directly east. "And that's Penicuik, about five miles away." He glanced at her. "We can make straight for Penicuik, or go to Silverburn first. Via Silverburn will be a little bit longer, but we could most likely get a bite to eat in the village."

Eliza considered, not just for herself but for him as well. Despite her earlier view of him, he wasn't a small man, being neither skinny nor short. She was fairly certain she could march to Penicuik without further sustenance, but she had two large brothers and knew how they ate.

And she was under no illusions about who would need to save them if danger threatened. She might help, but she would be following his lead.

"Silverburn," she declared. "We need food, and we have no idea what the rest of the day will bring. This might be our best chance to eat all day."

"True." Slipping the map away, he tipped his head down the slope toward the village. "Let's go."

Less than an hour later, they were seated in a rear corner of the Merry Widow's taproom, addressing plates of ham, eggs, kedgeree, and sausages. Eliza did her best, then, when the barman was looking the other way, swapped Jeremy's empty plate for hers.

When he looked his question, she murmured, "No youth would leave a breakfast half eaten."

His lips twitched, then he applied himself to cleaning her plate, too.

They were on their way shortly after. While in the inn, Eliza had had to remind herself that she was supposedly male; she'd remained largely mute, responding with grunts or snorts whenever she'd been forced to give some response. Once they were out of sight of the village and striding through open country again, she felt as if a weight slid from her shoulders and she could be herself again.

A hill rose ahead of them, some way off.

Jeremy pointed. "Penicuik's on the other side, but approaching from this direction, we can go around the southern tip of the hill."

"Good." She glanced up and met his eyes. "I don't mind walking, but avoiding hills is appreciated."

He grinned and looked forward. "Not just by you."

They came to another stream. Not that wide or deep, but too wide to leap and too deep to splash through. They followed the bank along and finally found a set of stones that would serve their purpose, but when Jeremy tried them, some wobbled, and others were slippery with slime.

He started to slip and launched himself across, landing safely on the opposite bank. Turning to her, he beckoned. "Come halfway, then take my hand."

She readily complied, clutching his offered fingers before stepping onto the difficult rocks. Like him, she started to slip from the slimy one, but with a yank, he pulled her on, up, and to him; she swallowed a very unmalelike yelp.

Her senses flared in anticipation, but just before she slammed into his chest, he caught her about her waist and halted her.

To her surprise, her unruly senses gnashed their teeth. She blinked.

"There." With a satisfied smile, he released her, clearly oblivious to the distinctly risqué impulses surging through her. "Come on."

He turned and led the way up the bank.

But he didn't let go of her hand.

She told herself that he was only keeping hold of her fingers so he could help her up the slippery bank.

But once they were back on level ground, he set off over the field, her fingers still firmly clasped in his.

Striding beside him, enjoying the freedom of breeches and boots that allowed her to do so, she wondered if he'd forgotten that he held her hand, but she decided he wasn't nearly as absentminded as she'd earlier—long ago—assumed.

Which meant he was holding her hand on purpose. Because he wanted to.

She thought about that and decided she wasn't going to mention the liberty. Much less protest. She liked feeling his strong, hard fingers clasped about hers. The distinctly male touch conveyed a sense of reassurance, of comfort and protection.

A sense of being together in this, in their dangerous flight from dangerous men.

Feeling her lips spontaneously curving, she tipped her face up to the weak sun and reminded herself to make sure he let her go before they came within sight of the road, or any habitation, or anyone who might wonder why a gentleman was holding the hand of a youth.

The laird reached the woodcutter's cottage in midmorning.

He'd left Ainville just after dawn and had enjoyed himself galloping back up the road to where he'd had his last reported sighting of his fleeing pair in Currie. He'd stood on the road before the small inn at which they'd stopped, and, putting himself in his quarry's boots, had looked around.

The church tower had caught his eye.

In the lane before the lych-gate he'd found boot prints, one pair large, one much smaller, both heading into the churchyard.

The paved paths and stone flags of the church wouldn't have held any telltale clues, so he'd walked the perimeter of the churchyard and had found more boot prints from the same two pairs of boots laying a distinctive but hurried trail eastward along the lane.

Away from the highway, toward the Pentland Hills.

Remounting Hercules, he'd glanced back at the church tower. He had a strong suspicion the pair had seen him—and had known enough to recognize him as the man behind the kidnappings. He should, he supposed, have taken greater care to remain hidden while following Heather Cynster and Breckenridge weeks before, but that was water under the bridge. The relevant point was that Eliza and her gentleman would run if they saw him; if he wished to locate and then observe them, he would need to stay concealed.

From the churchyard on, he hadn't lost their trail, not even through the banks of heather. Rocky ground was little impediment to him; out in the wilds of Scotland, any wilds of Scotland, he was in his element.

He drew rein just outside the copse.

The rude cottage sat nestled among the trees. All was silent, quiet; no smoke curled from the squat chimney. Dismounting, he tethered Hercules to a low-hanging branch, then, making no effort at stealth, walked beneath the trees and into the clearing. He knocked at the door. When no answer came, he opened it and went in.

It took him mere minutes to read the signs and extract all he could from them. Someone, certainly, had spent the night at the cottage—two someones, to be precise. The pitcher still had water in it, and two glasses were free of all dust. The surface of the wooden table had also had things placed on it, spread upon it, disturbing the fine layer of dust that had previously covered it.

He eyed the neatly made pallet, then crossed to it and drew back the coarse blankets. Some attempt had been made to even the straw, but it was still possible to see that the man—the heavier, larger body—had lain on the side closer to the door, and the slighter figure had for the most part lain curled by his side.

The laird frowned. The evidence could be interpreted as suggesting some degree of intimacy, but on the other hand, the relationship between the pair could just as easily have been that of close friends. Compatriots forced by circumstance to share a bed and warmth.

He couldn't—shouldn't—make too much of it.

Replacing the blankets, he cast one last comprehensive glance around the sparsely furnished abode, then walked back out into the weak sunshine. Closing the door, he noted the route by which the pair had left the clearing, then returned to Hercules, mounted, and circled the copse to pick up their trail.

He followed it down to a stream.

As he sent Hercules splashing across, he wrestled with the question that had plagued him since the day before. Why were they traveling by such slow means? Could Eliza Cynster truly not ride?

With every passing hour they were in greater danger of being caught; for all they knew, Scrope was hot on their heels. Yet he'd gained sufficient respect for whoever had rescued Eliza Cynster from her basement cell and whisked her out of Edinburgh, confounding the expert and until-then-unchallenged Scrope, to accept that this cross-country trek might well be the best they could do.

Although the lowlands was not his territory, he knew the area well enough not to need a map to guess where his quarry was heading.

He leaned forward to pat Hercules's sleek neck as the big chestnut picked his way down to the valley floor and the larger stream that bisected it. "Penicuik—that's where they'll make for." He narrowed his eyes. "They should be able to hire a gig there, and then drive for Peebles, then across . . . yes." He smiled, and with his heels nudged Hercules to a faster pace. "That's what they'll do, and that's where we'll find them. Come on, my lad—let's hie ourselves to Penicuik."

* * *

Hidden among the trees, Scrope sat his horse and watched McKinsey ride up the next ridge.

He stayed where he was, biding his time. There was no cover to be had once he left the trees, and the last thing he wished was for McKinsey to see him.

Admittedly, the man had thus far lived up to Scrope's expectations. It hadn't occurred to the laird that Scrope might disobey his orders and follow; not once had he glanced back. Yet Scrope wasn't prepared to take the risk that this time, on reaching the top of the next ridge, McKinsey might rein in for a moment, idly glance back, and spot him; he would wait until his erstwhile employer disappeared over the ridge before venturing forth and following.

Scrope was keen to let McKinsey continue in ignorance of his pursuit. The present arrangement, albeit unwitting on McKinsey's part, was simply too good to risk losing. As matters stood, McKinsey was performing as an expert tracker for Scrope. The ease with which McKinsey had found the pair's trail, then followed it so unerringly, spoke volumes as to the man's skill. Scrope was professional enough to accord such talents due respect.

"A damned shame he's not someone I can hire."

Scrope glanced behind him, through the trees to the woodcutter's cottage. He debated using the enforced sojourn to search it, but McKinsey would have taken note of any useful signs.

Facing forward again, he saw that McKinsey had surged up the ridge and was disappearing over it.

Scrope lifted his reins, waited until McKinsey's dark head finally dropped out of sight altogether, then spurred his horse out of the trees and on.

He needed to cross the valley and reach the top of the ridge while McKinsey was still in clear sight.

He wanted Eliza Cynster, and McKinsey was his sure and certain route to locating her.

Chapter Nine

Later that morning, once more firmly in their assumed roles of tutor and charge, Jeremy and Eliza walked into Penicuik and discovered it was market day.

There was no market square as such, but the road they'd followed into the small town widened considerably, allowing horses, carriages, and carts to pass in two opposing streams to the right, while a hotchpotch of market stalls filled the extra space to the left.

Pausing alongside Jeremy, Eliza surveyed the colorful, bustling, pleasantly noisy sight.

"There's an inn further on." Jeremy nodded to a swinging sign hanging from a gable beyond the stalls. "Let's see if they have a gig and horse for hire."

Eliza nodded and fell in by his side. The easiest way to preserve her disguise was to speak as little as possible. Dropping her voice to a deep enough, gruff enough register was a last resort; she'd discovered it took constant effort to keep such an assumed tone even and believable.

Reaching the inn, The Royal, situated on a curve in the road, they continued on around the building's side in search of the stable yard and found even more market stalls sprawled beside the road on that side of the inn.

A second, large posting inn lay beyond the stalls, further up the gently rising road.

Jeremy tipped his head toward the other inn. "If they can't help us here, we'll try there."

But when appealed to, The Royal's stableman said the words they'd hoped to hear. "Aye—I've got a nice gig should suit you."

Eliza met Jeremy's eyes, then turned to idly view the market stalls, cloaking her relief behind a show of adolescent male disinterest, leaving Jeremy to negotiate over gig and horse.

Many of the stalls before her sold fresh fruit. Some sold pastries and pies, while others sold nuts, or cheeses and hams. One stall sold freshly baked bread rolls.

Her mouth was watering just from looking.

The sight of a public water pump reminded her that the pottery water bottles in their saddlebags were almost empty again. Of course, they would be leaving in the gig, and presumably would reach Wolverstone tonight, yet . . .

Jeremy joined her, a satisfied look on his face.

She waved at the stalls. "Perhaps we should replenish our saddlebags, just in case."

He nodded. "It'll take the ostlers fifteen minutes or so to have the gig ready. I said we'd wander around the stalls and come back." Drawing out his fob-watch, he consulted it, then said, "It's early yet. If we bought some supplies, we could get underway, then stop for lunch along the road."

"An excellent idea." Eliza felt his fingers brush her elbow, but then he remembered and his hand fell away.

He gestured at the stalls. "Lead the way." Dipping his head, he spoke more softly, "You'll have to direct me in what to buy."

She nodded and proceeded to pause before various stalls, artfully making the sort of suggestions a hungry youth might.

For his part, Jeremy played the resigned tutor, and with just the right show of reluctance, bought all she wished for.

There was so much to choose from that inevitably they bought more than they would need, but, Jeremy decided, it was better they have too much than too little, and as they now had a gig, they wouldn't be lugging the increasingly bulky saddlebags themselves.

The thought sent his mind ranging ahead, to the road they would follow, to how long it might take to reach the border. To the possibility that they might have to spend another night together, alone.

Not that spending a second night together, alone, would materially alter their situation, a situation that, he assumed, had already been decided by their first night together, alone. In the ton's eyes, one night was enough; subsequent nights were neither here nor there.

The tangle of social expectations was something over which he always felt at a loss; he knew the strictures existed, and that some were absolute, absolute enough to bind both him and Eliza irrevocably, but there were always exceptions, and he had no firm idea just how their circumstances translated . . . pushing such useless meanderings from his mind, he concentrated instead on what his brother-in-law and Tristan's ex-brothers-in-arms would counsel him to do.

Weapons. If they ran into the opposition, a weapon or two wouldn't hurt. He was an excellent shot, but he seriously doubted the small town boasted even a general gunsmith, let alone a pistolmaker; there were certainly no guns of any sort on the stalls.

There was, however, a gypsy stall selling some nicely balanced knives. The small knives Meggin had put in the saddlebags would do to attack fruit, and possibly cheese, but not much else.

He paused before the stall, reaching out to tug Eliza's sleeve as she ambled on, oblivious.

She turned, saw what he was looking at, then reluctantly returned to stand alongside him.

One glance at her face showed she was frowning in a disapproving way. Surreptitiously, he tapped her boot with his and held up a knife. "Nice knives."

From the corner of his eye, he saw her blink, then she realized and made a show of youthful male interest, picking up various knives and weighing them in her small hands.

Jeremy quickly engaged the stallholder, praying the man wouldn't notice those too-delicate hands.

The gypsy was more interested in driving a hard bargain.

They'd reached agreement when Eliza cleared her throat and rather gruffly said, "I wouldn't mind this one."

Jeremy looked at the knife she held—one with a short, tapered blade, one she could carry reasonably safely in the small leather sheath that came with it. Briefly meeting her eyes, he took the knife from her and set it alongside the two he'd chosen. "Very well." He captured the stallholder's gaze. "Throw that in as well."

They haggled again, then, price decided, Jeremy paid, handed Eliza her knife in its sheath, and tucked his two into his belt.

Moving away from the stall, back into the thickening stream of pedestrians passing between the stalls, he ducked his head and murmured, "Keep the knife hidden. You never want to advertise that you have a weapon on you—it's best kept as a surprise."

She shot him a grin, nodded.

He didn't know where, exactly, she'd put the knife; it had disappeared somewhere beneath the cloak she wore over her male attire.

"Water." She pointed to the pump, and they took their turn filling their water bottles. They paused in the shadows by a wall while he stowed the bottles back in the saddlebags and settled their other purchases.

She glanced around. "I think that's all we need."

Straightening, he swung the heavier saddlebag across his shoulder. "We've been longer than I'd expected—they should have our gig ready and waiting."

His gaze rose to her face—he froze. "What is it?"

Her gaze was locked over his left shoulder; she was staring up the street, toward the other inn.

She looked like she'd seen a ghost. Eyes wide, she whispered, "Don't move—don't turn around. It's the laird. He's just ridden in and halted, and now he's sitting his huge horse and looking over the stalls."

"Can he see us clearly?"

"Not clearly. There's half the market between us—he's at the other end."

Resisting the urgent compulsion to glance over his shoulder, he grasped her arm, intending to turn her and walk evenly back to the inn's stable.

"Wait." She resisted his tug. A second later, relief flooded her. "He's turning away." She glanced at Jeremy's face, then, easing her arm from his hold, she turned toward the stable, quietly adding as she walked by his side, "He was just looking generally over the place—he didn't tense but just turned and walked his horse into the other inn's stable yard."

Jeremy lengthened his stride. "We need to get our gig and get out of here now."

They reached the inn's stable yard. It was difficult to banish the grimness from his expression, to keep his face set in easygoing lines, and not race to sling their saddlebags into the gig, clamber up to the box, and snatch the reins.

Once the reins were in his hands and Eliza was settled beside him, he guided the bay gelding he'd chosen out of the stable yard and into the street as fast as he dared.

Given the traffic, that wasn't all that fast. As they finally rounded the curve in the road, he glanced back up the street—

And saw the laird, large as life, standing, hands on lean hips, staring down the road at them.

"Damn!" He urged the horse on as fast as he dared.

"What?" Eliza shot him a scared look. "Did he see?"

Jeremy hesitated, but then nodded. "Just our luck the traffic thinned along the road behind us just at that moment."

Eliza made a snorty, disapproving sound—then the sound all but strangled in her throat.

She gripped his arm, started to point and stopped herself, but her gaze was fixed ahead. "Scrope. He's riding behind that coach-and-four coming toward us."

They were heading back out along the road they'd come in on, but the road they needed to take them south, away from the town, lay just ahead. Jeremy weaved, ducked, peered, and glimpsed the legs of a horse following close behind the heavy carriage lumbering slowly toward them. He glanced ahead, measuring distances, estimating angles. "Pray," he advised. "If we time this just right . . ."

He adjusted the gelding's stride, held the horse back while the carriage drew nearer, then turned sharp left into the road south, using the carriage as cover so Scrope wouldn't see them until he was looking directly at their backs. "For God's sake, don't look back."

"I won't." Beside him, Eliza sat bolt upright, trying to appear taller than she was. Her heart was thudding high in her throat. "The laird and Scrope both—they must be searching together."

She glanced at Jeremy; his expression was set and unrelievedly grim. With a flick of the whip, he sent the horse trotting on, increasingly swiftly.

A stone bridge spanned the river south of the town. They clattered over it. The way south opened before them.

There'd been no shouts, no sound of thundering hooves behind them.

"Scrope didn't see us, did he?" she asked.

"He might have, but I don't think he realized it was us."

Before she could even start to relax, Jeremy abruptly swung the horse left, down a narrower road leading away from the main road. She gasped as they plunged down a short dip; the low-lying road wended this way and that between stands of birch. Jeremy whipped up the horse and they rocketed along. The gig rocked; the wheels rattled, flicking loose stones in their wake.

"I thought we were going south to Peebles." Clutching the gig's side, she flung him a glance.

"We were." His face and tone remained beyond grim. "But now he's seen us, that's exactly where the laird will assume we're going. And assuming Scrope saw us—two people in a gig—driving out of town, Scrope will confirm our route. They'll be after us as soon as the laird mounts up."

"Ah." Maintaining her white-knuckled grip on the gig's side, she looked ahead. "So we'll leave them to ride to Peebles and search for us there." After a moment, she drew breath, asked, "So, where are we going?"

"This road straightens out soon and runs more or less east." Jeremy paused, then added, "If we keep going east, we'll eventually hit the road we want, the one through Jedburgh."

He hadn't studied the map far enough ahead, hadn't explored the alternative routes in this direction. Another lesson learned the hard way. "We'll stop further along and work out the best way to go, but first . . ."

The road they were following had risen again. Cresting a rise, he drew on the reins, slowed the horse to a trot, then halted it alongside a high stile. Applying the brake, he tied off the reins, then reached to their feet and pulled up the saddlebags, letting her take one. "The spyglass."

She searched as quickly as he; it was she who pulled the cylinder out and handed it to him.

He stepped out of the gig, leapt up the stile. Balancing on the top board, he focused the glass.

The vantage point was better than he'd hoped. He could see the road leading south from a point above the bridge, across the bridge, and a good way past the spot where they'd turned off it. He could see all but a short stretch of the road they'd come racing down instead.

He sensed Eliza draw near, a feminine warmth that reached for him and claimed his senses, realized she'd climbed the lower rungs of the stile. He could feel her gaze on his face.

"Well?" A species of imperious concern filled the word. "Can you see them?"

He refocused his attention, searched for a moment more, until he was sure no rider was racing along the short stretch he couldn't see, then he lowered the glass and grinned at her. "No. I can't see anyone at all."

She blinked up at him, then reached for the glass. "Let me see."

He let her take the glass, stepped down two rungs on the other side of the stile.

She climbed up, balancing precariously.

Throwing caution to the winds, he grasped her breeches-clad hips and steadied her.

"Thank you." The words were a trifle breathless. She didn't look down but instead kept the spyglass to her eye.

After several moments, she murmured, "I can't see either of them. Not on this road, or the other. Have we lost them, or did they not realize it was us?"

Jeremy thought, then admitted, "The laird . . . I don't know how he knows us, but I'm sure he recognized us in the town."

"If they followed us as quickly as they could, they would have passed further down the road to Peebles before we stopped."

"Either way—if they're still in the town, or have already passed further south—they've missed us."

She lowered the glass, faced him, and beamed. "We've lost them!"

He fell into her smile, into the warmth of her eyes.

She laughed, did a happy little jig, then flung her arms about his neck and kissed him.

Pressed her lips to his in sheer, overflowing, exuberant relief—then froze.

For a heartbeat.

So did he, too shocked, too lost, to do anything else.

Her lips firmed; slowly, deliberately, they firmed against his as she kissed him.

Intentionally.

He kissed her back.

Time stopped. Simply halted.

He couldn't hear; he couldn't think.

His entire awareness was trapped in the simple communion of her lips moving on his, on the intense thrill when he returned the pleasure and she accepted the caress, then returned it again.

She leaned closer, but wobbled and pulled back.

He let her, steadied her; knew his own reluctance, but sensed hers, too.

For a second, they looked into each other's eyes. With her on the top step and him two lower, their faces were near level, their eyes inches apart.

He waited for the fluster, for the garbled apologies; once she started, he'd have to reciprocate, and it would all degenerate into awkwardness . . .

But she said nothing at all, only gave a quick, small, intensely feminine smile, then drew out of his hold and backed down the stile.

Surreptitiously, he blew out the breath he'd been holding. *Well, then . . .*

She turned for the gig. He quickly climbed over the stile and followed.

She threw him a glance as she climbed up to the seat. "Shall we drive on, then find somewhere to stop and eat, and look at the map?"

Stepping up and sitting beside her, he briefly met her gaze, then nodded. "That sounds like a workable plan."

A pleased little smile curled her lips. Facing forward, she waved. "Onward, then. But you might want to spare the horse."

He grinned. Still faintly giddy from the lingering effects of an entirely unexpected pleasure and wondering if this was what a conqueror felt like, he flicked the reins and sent the gelding pacing on.

* * *

Nearly an hour after sighting his quarry driving out of the marketplace, the laird rode out of Penicuik, satisfied enough with his morning's endeavors.

Given his intention was to observe rather than capture, he hadn't raced to catch the fleeing pair. Instead, he'd left Hercules enjoying the amenities of The Crown's stable and had walked down to have a word with the stableman at The Royal.

Deployment of a little easygoing charm had yielded similar information to what he'd gained at the Grassmarket stables. The man with the youthful charge was definitely English, definitely a gentleman, and by all accounts was a straightforward, polite, personable sort. The impression the laird received was that of a quiet, intelligent man, possessed of a degree of inner strength, of understated reserves.

After that, he'd wandered through the market, chatting with the stallholders, using his brogue and the tale of two English friends who might have passed through a short time before to good effect. He'd discovered that they'd bought victuals, and, interestingly, three knives—two for the man, and a smaller one for the lad.

While he took due note of that, he was more interested in what he'd gleaned of the pair's characters.

Briskly trotting over the bridge south of the town, on reaching the open highway beyond, he let Hercules stretch into an easy, loping canter. Once the big gelding settled into his stride, the laird allowed his thoughts to return to the mental pictures he was assembling of the pair fleeing for the border ahead of him.

The descriptions he'd gained, and even more the asides, the unsolicited comments people offered of the pair, left him increasingly convinced that, should he find himself confronting Eliza Cynster and her gentleman-rescuer, his most appropriate response would be to shake the gentleman's hand and wish him well.

The man had, after all, stepped in and taken the lady off his hands. She was no longer his responsibility but that of the as-yet-unidentified brave gentleman.

As for Miss Cynster herself, she sounded a handful, although in a different way from her older sister. Eliza appeared to be the sort of female he mentally dubbed "soft and spoiled," perhaps not brattishly so, more in the nature of tonnish young ladies born of wealthy, aristocratic, Sassenach families, and she seemed a tad delicate to boot, neither of which would have suited him.

A lady who was gentle as well as gently bred, accustomed to every luxury and lacking in fortitude, would make a disastrous wife for him.

Which left him in two minds about the failure of this latest kidnapping attempt. On the one hand, his inability to take Eliza Cynster north and parade her before his mother as "ruined" meant he'd yet to satisfy his mother's requirements to secure the goblet he needed to save his estate and his people. And on that score, time was running short.

Against that, however, he'd avoided having to marry a lady who wouldn't have liked him, and who would have had a dismal time as his wife. A lifetime of misery for himself was a price he'd accepted he might well have to pay, but having to stand by and all but force a lifetime of misery on some innocent lady . . . that would have sat very ill with him and deepened his own misery to a truly dreadful degree.

So him not having to marry Eliza Cynster was a matter for celebration, on both his and the lady's parts.

Indeed, the only reason he was still following the pair was to, if possible, obtain a better look at the two of them together, the better to convince himself beyond all reasonable doubt that her gentleman-rescuer was a suitable consort, and that he was treating and would always treat her well.

He'd done the same with Heather Cynster and her gentleman-rescuer, and his eyes hadn't deceived him there. She and Breckenridge had announced their engagement shortly after their trek through Scotland, and all he'd since gleaned from his contacts in London had assured him the affianced couple were truly happy, somewhat to many observers' surprise. By and large, the ton hadn't seen that match coming.

As he rode on through the late morning, the faint wind of his passing ruffling his hair, he grinned at the thought that if Eliza Cynster, too—at the beginning of this adventure twenty-four and still unwed—had through his kidnapping found her fated husband-to-be, then instead of "ruining" the two Cynster sisters he'd been forced by his mother's scheme to kidnap, he'd instead played cupid for them in a convolutedly bizarre way.

That was an irony that truly was sweet.

He savored it for a full minute, before reality intruded and reminded him of what, given the failure of this second kidnapping, now lay before him.

In his philosophy of life he'd always accepted that fate existed as a true, formative force. If he'd ever needed evidence that fate was female, he had it now; only a woman would put a man through this.

He was brooding over what his immediate future would be once he saw Eliza and her gentleman-rescuer safely over the border when Hercules's long strides took them over a damp patch where a burn had flooded across the road.

Four strides on, he registered what he'd seen—or rather what he hadn't. "Damn!"

Slowing Hercules, then wheeling him, he rode back to the damp patch. Leaning from the saddle, he examined the imprints left in the dirt that had spilled across the road. Finally sitting up, he cast his mind back to that moment in Penicuik when he'd seen the pair driving away, focused his memory on the gig's wheels . . . the usual style of wooden wheel with a beaten metal rim.

He glanced down at the tracks in the road. "Not again. They didn't come this way."

With a sigh, he shook Hercules's reins. "Come on, old son.

Back we go. At least we didn't ride halfway to the border before realizing they'd slipped sideways."

He let Hercules enjoy a good gallop. It wasn't that long before the roofs of Penicuik appeared ahead of them, perched on the higher, north bank of the North Esk.

Slowing Hercules as they approached the bridge over the river, the laird was consulting his memories of the roads in the area when a fleeting movement—a quick, startled, furtive movement on the other side of the bridge—caught his eye.

Scrope.

His erstwhile employee had seen him coming and had dived for cover.

"As well he might." Inwardly grim—he did not appreciate having direct orders flagrantly flouted, yet he wasn't totally surprised—the laird drew rein on the south side of the bridge. Leaning on his saddle bow, he sat as if pondering, apparently studying the roofs of the town. From the corner of his eye, he could see the thick bushes where Scrope, mounted on a decent gray nag, was concealed.

He'd already noticed the wheel tracks he'd been searching for turning down the road to his right. That road led southeast. He could imagine that, knowing he was on their trail—and for all he knew the fleeing pair might have known Scrope was chasing them, too—and pressed for alternatives, the pair had taken the southeast road. It seemed to head in the direction they needed. Unfortunately, if they continued following it, they would find themselves running out of road once they reached the shallow foothills along the western flank of the Moorfoot Hills. And there were no roads through the Moorfoots. They would have to turn either north or south; either route would take them out of their way, but on the other hand, taking the southeast road had succeeded in keeping them clear of both him and Scrope, and ultimately they would be able to find their way around to the road he was increasingly sure they were making for, the road through Jedburgh.

If anything, he should be pleased; there was now no chance the pair could reach the border that day. They would have to spend another night, and at least another day, making their way south; he would have all the time he needed to observe and satisfy his picky sense of honor that Eliza Cynster's gentleman-rescuer was an appropriate protector for a Cynster miss. A satisfactory husband-to-be in lieu of him.

That was now his only concern—getting absolute confirmation of the gentleman's caliber and the couple's potential relationship—but what was he to do about Scrope?

He couldn't sit there all day staring into space. How had Scrope found the pair, in Penicuik of all places?

The irritating thought that Scrope might well have been following him firmed to a certainty the more he dwelled on it, compounding the man's sins.

But he really didn't care all that much about Scrope.

Unfortunately, however, he was a complication.

"Blast the man."

If he led Scrope astray at this point, he'd almost certainly lose his fleeing pair. Once they found themselves having to turn north or south, he might not be able to track them easily, depending on where exactly on the road they realized they had to turn. And they could go either way.

Time was steadily slipping past. He had to decide.

Straightening in his saddle, he nudged Hercules into motion and turned the big gelding down the dip into the southeast road.

He could deliberate while he rode.

At present, he was between Scrope and their quarry; as long as Scrope remained at his back, Eliza and her gentleman weren't in any danger.

Nudging Hercules into a canter, mind ranging ahead, he thought, and planned.

Ideally, he decided, he would find the pair, hang back long enough to see all he wished, then he would let the pair go on while he turned back and captured Scrope, and, in his quietest, coldest, most intimidating voice, inquired what the devil the man thought he was about.

Lips curving in anticipation of that last, the laird rode steadily on.

Keen to get as far as they could from the laird and Scrope before they stopped to eat and consult the map, Jeremy had driven for nearly an hour, following the road, little more than a lane but decently surfaced, that had been leading so helpfully southeast.

They'd crossed over two other, somewhat larger, roads, but both had been signposted as leading directly back to the southerly road to Peebles. With no wish to run into the laird and Scrope, they'd happily continued southeast.

The kiss they'd shared played over and again in Jeremy's mind. He told himself not to make too much of it; it had just been one of those moments that had simply happened. They'd both been swept up by triumph over losing the laird and Scrope . . . well, she had, at least. He . . . .

Determinedly hauling his mind from its obsession, he focused his attention on the lane ahead and saw that a little way on, it turned sharply northeast.

He slowed the horse, then angled it onto the grassy verge. "We might as well stop here." He glanced back. "We've neither seen nor heard any sign of pursuit. I think we're safe for the moment."

"Good." Eliza pulled the saddlebags up onto her lap. "I'm famished, and you must be, too."

Truth to tell, it wasn't food he was all that hungry for . . . *Stop it!* Stepping down from the gig, he held out his hands for the bags, took them both, and walked a little way from the already cropping horse.

A nearby bush afforded them a modicum of shade. He set the saddlebags down, then, when Eliza came up and dropped to her knees on the other side of the bags, immediately falling on them and rummaging inside, he sank down to the grass, stretching his legs out before him.

They ate, drank, then, munching on an apple, he pulled out the map. Flipping it open, he drew his legs up; sitting cross-legged, he spread the map on the ground before him.

Eliza moved the saddlebags aside, shuffled up, and sat beside him. "Where are we?"

Fighting the compulsive awareness of her, so close beside him, he stared at the map, then, reluctantly resigned, placed his finger on the pertinent spot. "We're here."

She leaned closer to look; from beneath her hat, the fragrance of her honey-gold hair rose and wreathed his senses.

"This road . . ." Her voice held the same disappointment he felt. Glancing up, she met his eyes. "It doesn't go southeast."

He grimaced. "No. For some incomprehensible reason, it turns and heads back toward Edinburgh." She drew back as he pointed. "Well, near enough. It meets the Edinburgh-Carlisle road near Gorebridge."

Eliza wrinkled her nose. "Carlisle's no use to us."

"No. Aside from being on the wrong side of the country, with the border much further away, there's no one there with whom we can beg shelter. No safe place we can go, and neither the laird nor Scrope will halt at the border—they'll follow us on."

She nodded. "Wolverstone is still the safest place to make for—the closest safe place." Peering again at the map, she glanced over her shoulder to where, twenty yards on, the road made its northeast turn. "It looks like there might be a minor road going the other way." Without looking back at the map, she vaguely pointed. "See?"

Jeremy looked, then pushed to his feet. "It's marked as a track, but let's look."

Leaving the horse where he was, they walked the few yards down the road to the opening of what proved to be little more than a sheep track.

Her shoulders slumped. "We can't drive on that."

"No." Jeremy turned and looked along the continuation of their road, a well-surfaced stretch leading, unhelpfully, in the wrong direction. "Where's a good Roman road when you need one?"

She smiled faintly, but any humor quickly faded. "So." She drew in a breath. "What now?"

He studied a farmhouse to the left of the road a little way past the bend, glanced at the hills to their right—the hills that, if they wanted to reach the Jedburgh Road, they had to either drive around or walk through—then waved back to where they'd left the map. "Let's see what options we have."

Back near the gig, they sat side by side in the long grass and pored over the map.

After a moment, Jeremy glanced up at the sky. "It's only early afternoon." He looked at her. "We have to assume that the laird and Scrope eventually pick up our trail and follow us here." He glanced around. "They'll see we stopped here and sat on the grass, and, assuming we drive on, they'll come on fast. But they're on horseback, and we're in a gig—they'll be able to travel faster for longer, and take shortcuts we can't."

Looking at the map, he traced a route. "If we drive on along this road, we'll get to Gorebridge, then we'll need to turn south and drive like mad through Stow to Galashiels, then across via Melrose to St. Boswells on the Jedburgh Road. From there, it's not far to the border."

Gaze on the map, she stated the obvious. "They'll come up with us long before Jedburgh."

Lips setting grimly, he nodded. "I agree."

She could see only one alternative and knew why he wasn't suggesting it; he was leaving the decision to her. So be it. Jaw firming, she looked up and met his eyes. "Can we make them think we've driven on, even if we don't?"

His quick grin of approbation felt like sunshine beaming through clouds.

He tipped his head toward the farmhouse around the bend. "We'll drive on, but only as far as that farm. We can leave the gig there, and I'll pay them to keep it out of sight and return it to Penicuik tomorrow. If we make sure there's no tracks leading into the farm yard, there's every possibility our pursuers won't know they've lost us until Gorebridge or even later, and once they do realize, there won't be anything to tell them which way we've gone. For all they know, we might have decided to circle back to Edinburgh."

She nodded. "Good. So with them confounded and out of the way, we walk on." She traced a route on the map, then raised her arm and pointed east. "Over the damn hills and all the way to Stow."

Their gazes met, locked, held. After a moment of searching her eyes, her face, he asked, "Are you sure?"

She knew precisely what he was asking. He was alluding to the subject that hung over their heads like Damocles' sword; patently he saw it as clearly as she. They'd already spent one night together alone; perhaps that might have been accounted for somehow, but by accepting the certainty of another night spent in some woodcutter's cottage or the like, alone with him, rather than fleeing in a curricle down country roads at night . . . perversely society might accept the latter idiocy, while condemning them for taking the former, infinitely safer option. With a little nod, she pushed to her feet. "I'm sure."

Dusting down her breeches, she found a smile. "I'm getting quite fond of these." She held out a booted foot. "And my boots. They're so much less restricting than skirts."

Jeremy was folding the map preparatory to stowing it in one of the saddlebags. Picking up the other, she headed for the gig. "I'm sure we'll be able to find some cottage or the like. Somewhere sufficient to sleep for the night."

A frisson of expectation ran through her at the thought. She hadn't allowed herself to dwell on that kiss. That eye-opening, fascinating, absorbing kiss. If she did, she'd start to think of other things, subsequent things, and then she'd blush . . .

Setting her saddlebag in the gig, she went to the horse's head. *Keep your mind on the matter at hand.* "Perhaps we should walk him around to the farm yard—without our weight in the gig, the tracks will be even less."

Jeremy set his saddlebag in the gig alongside hers. "We want to leave tracks here, to show we left. Get in and we'll drive around the bend to the farm gate, then we'll get out and I'll lead him in. You can check and obliterate any tracks."

Fifteen minutes later, with the horse and gig safely hidden away in the barn and the helpful farmer sufficiently satisfied with the largesse Jeremy had offered to assure anyone who inquired that he'd seen them drive on, they left the farm gate and crossed the road, careful to leave no telltale boot prints.

"The laird had to have tracked us from Currie." Shouldering one saddlebag, Jeremy followed Eliza as she struck out across a field to the rise of the first hill. "There's no other likely explanation for him finding us. If he's a highlander, as your family think he is, then most likely he hunts game, and so might be especially experienced at tracking."

She humphed. "I defy him to find any tracks back there. I made sure the ground inside and outside the farm gate was pristine."

He tapped her shoulder, then pointed to a sheep track that led more directly up and over the first hill. "Let's get over the first rise as fast as we can. I'll check from the crest to see if there's any sign of our pursuers, then we can forge on with greater confidence. Once we're over the first hill, we'll be largely out of sight."

They did precisely that. From the first crest Jeremy scanned the road but could find no trace of pursuit. Lowering the spyglass, he shut it. "Nothing yet."

Neither of them doubted the laird at least would come. But dipping down into, then crossing, the next shallow valley, they strode steadily on, secure and largely relaxed, knowing no one could spot them from the road.

They exercised greater caution slogging up the next hill, but on looking back they discovered the first hill blocked their view of the road; they couldn't see the farm where they'd left the gig. Which meant no one along that part of the road could see them.

With increasing confidence, they pushed on, tramping along sheep paths between banks of heather, splashing across a stream. The afternoon remained fine, the air fresh and clear as they climbed.

Landmarks were scarce. Jeremy kept them on a southeasterly course using the arc transcribed by the sun, and the position of far distant peaks.

They found their way over a larger stream and headed on, keeping the glinting waters of a big lake to their right. The line of the Moorfoot Hills themselves still lay ahead of them; they were presently traversing the slowly rising land, the foothills of the hills, as it were.

Eliza strode along, feeling intensely, and utterly unexpectedly, light of heart. That was the only way she could describe the inner sense of buoyancy, the near effervescence that showed in the brisk spring in her step. She looked about as she walked, drinking in the wide vistas that every now and again opened up between the enclosing low hills. Even the air seemed to taste fresher and better up there.

She never would have imagined she would enjoy striding about the heather. Let alone with a villain like Scrope in pursuit, much less the even more frightening unknown of the laird. Yet she was confident they'd lost their pursuers, at least as far as today was concerned, so she felt entitled to enjoy the moment; the wonder of it was that she could.

Walking had never been high on her list of exciting things to do, but striding along freely in breeches and boots, with the world wide about her and Jeremy Carling pacing alongside seemed somehow, in that moment, a tiny slice of heaven.

She would enjoy it while she could.

The thought brought to mind something else she'd enjoyed. That kiss. She couldn't stop thinking about it, which fact alone set it apart from any other kiss she'd ever experienced. Of course, it was true that they were both, in a fashion, out of their accustomed world, set adrift for the moment in a world of high adventure, and kisses—kisses that ordinarily could never have been—could be, could happen, could exist in this temporary world they were striding through.

But she wanted more. She knew she did; she was already thinking of how to bring a repeat engagement about. How else could she learn what it was that was so different, what it was in his kiss—Jeremy Carling the bookworm's kiss—that had so easily captured and fixed her senses?

If she was truthful, it was more than her curiosity that had sparked. But whoever would have thought a bookworm could kiss like that? Beguiling and tempting—tempting in a way she suspected she might find very difficult to resist.

Resist enough to turn her back and walk away.

Which was why she'd decided there was no point whatever worrying about what would happen when they reached civilization, and tonnish society, again. Yes, there might well be pressure brought to bear, in various guises and forms, for them to marry—but what if she and he actually wanted to of their own accord?

Such a felicitous outcome was possible. Heather and Breckenridge had found their way to the altar, and no matter the circumstances, there had been no coercion involved.

She glanced sidelong at Jeremy, pacing beside her. Every now and then, he would glance back and around, keeping watch. It was comforting to know he was so alert while she enjoyed the view.

And that view . . . she let her gaze briefly fall, skimming over his long frame, then determinedly looked ahead. The scholarly bookworm image had faded, replaced with a reality that was significantly more potent. Distinctly more alluring.

Even more intriguing was the man behind the mask. There was so much about him, so many quirks of character and nuance that she'd never imagined might be there.

His protectiveness, for one; she'd recognized it instantly—with brothers and cousins like hers, she was an expert on that trait. Yet his protectiveness was . . . softened wasn't really the word for it—informed might be nearer the mark—by an unexpected understanding and acceptance that she was an adult, too, that she had a mind of her own and might have views of her own regarding what she, and they, should do.

He'd consulted her rather than simply decreed; that was what was different.

His protectiveness she could accommodate, unlike that of her brothers and cousins.

There was also a certain hint of chivalry, old-fashioned perhaps, but attractive nonetheless.

And, of course, there was his exceedingly sharp mind, something she hadn't before considered a requirement in a man, but there was definitely something to be said for not having to explain her own thinking—and for his converse assumption that she could think her way through things, too.

She glanced his way again, then looked ahead, smiling softly to herself. She wasn't all that bothered over spending another night alone with him, because she'd set her mind on learning more about him, and indulging in at least one more kiss.

Another twenty yards brought them to the base of the main line of hills. They scouted around and found a rocky path leading up and over the summit. Without a word, Eliza started up it.

Jeremy glanced back and around one last time, then followed in her wake.

The going was considerably harder, the slope much greater than the ground they'd already traversed. The westering sun warmed their backs as they climbed; in places the rocks were more like huge steps, slowing them considerably.

He kept expecting Eliza to complain, but instead she toiled steadily upward. He was, heaven knew, no expert on the subject of tonnish ladies. He might have had several mistresses in years past, but for the current crop of younger ladies he had no real guidelines for behavior, at least not under stress.

The next time he could, he glanced at her face. Despite the effort of the climb, her lips were lightly curved, her features relaxed. She didn't seem to be worrying . . . about anything.

Not about them—him and her—spending yet another night alone. Not about that kiss.

A kiss that had left him . . . not wary so much as uncertain.

He was a scientist of sorts; he didn't like uncertainty.

But when it came to that kiss, he simply did not know what to make of it. As he'd read it, she'd initially kissed him unintentionally, driven by an excess of exuberance, but then she'd realized . . . and instead of pulling away, she'd kissed him again.

How was he supposed to interpret that?

Would she like it, allow it, if he kissed her? Again. She'd seemed to approve when he'd returned her kiss, but was that the same?

He was going to give himself a headache if he kept thinking about it.

Lips thinning, climbing doggedly in her wake, equally doggedly keeping his gaze from the enticing view just ahead and slightly above him, he told himself he should simply admit—to himself—that he was confused but interested, and that that interest, the fact he felt it so strongly, was a puzzlement all its own.

The last lady he would ever have imagined capturing his interest to this degree would have been Eliza Cynster. From the one occasion on which they'd met, he'd come away believing she hadn't liked, or perhaps hadn't approved of, him. What it was about him she'd taken against he'd had no idea, but that had been his clear impression.

Of course, he had come to her rescue, so she was honor-bound, so to speak, to smile at him now. But he honestly didn't think lukewarm gratitude would be enough to make her kiss him.

Perhaps she just hadn't known him well enough, and courtesy of their adventure, that lack was being rectified?

The crest loomed ahead. He banished all thoughts of her and him, and followed her onto a small plateau at the top of the gently rounded peak.

Halting, then sinking onto a rock, she swung her saddlebag to the ground and pulled out her water bottle.

Still standing, he pulled his own bottle out, took a long gulp, then, stowing the bottle, drew out the spyglass.

He searched and finally found the farm at which they'd left the gig. From this elevation, they could see most of the ground they'd covered since leaving the road.

"Anything?"

He shook his head. "I can see as far back as the stretch of road just before the bend, and I can't see any sign of them."

"So they've either gone past and continued northeast on the road, or not yet reached the bend. Either way, we're well away from them."

Lowering the spyglass, he looked west. The sun was hidden behind clouds, but it was already sliding beneath the horizon. "The light will be gone soon. We should get on."

He turned as she rose, lifting her saddlebag from the ground. He held out a hand. "Here—let me take that." Before she could argue, he added, "It's downhill from here."

She inclined her head in thanks and handed the bag over. "Once the light goes, they won't be able to track us."

"No, they won't." Greatly daring, Jeremy reached out and took her hand. Without meeting her eyes, he walked to the eastern edge of the small plateau. He looked down, into the deepening shadows that now cloaked the east-facing flank of the hill. "For tonight, we're safe, but"—glancing at her, he finally met her eyes—"we need to find shelter before night falls."

She nodded and waved him on. He led the way down, holding her hand to steady her over the steeper sections, walking by her side when the going was easier.

They descended into a high, shallow valley.

"The Scottish hills seem to be very deserted," she said. "All I can see is heather, rocks, and sheep."

He nodded. "There's a road of sorts down there, in the bottom of the valley, but I can't see any settlements along it."

They continued walking for some time, then Eliza shivered.

A compulsion gripped him, an urge unlike any he'd felt before, as if it was imperative he find shelter for her . . . he gave up trying to understand it, or fight it. Glancing around, he saw a rocky outcrop hugging the side of the hill twenty yards away. Releasing her hand, he shrugged off the saddle-bags and hunted in them for the spyglass. "Wait here." With his head he indicated the pile of rock. "I'm going to climb up there and see what I can find."

She nodded. Pulling her cloak closer, she waited, watched.

It took him a few minutes to scramble up to the top of the conglomerate of rock. Reaching the pinnacle, he balanced atop it and put the spyglass to his eye. The light was fading increasingly rapidly; urgency gripped him as he scanned . . . there!

Lowering the spyglass, he looked, squinted, then checked through the spyglass again, looked again.

The tiny hut was barely visible in the gloom, but it was there.

He scrambled down.

Eliza was waiting with the saddlebags at the outcrop's base when he dropped to the ground. "Something?"

"A hut—probably a shepherd's hut." He lifted the bags and slung them over his shoulder. "I saw no smoke from the chimney, and God knows what state it's in, but at least we'll have a roof over our heads."

She smiled and reached for his hand. "In our present straits, that sounds perfect."

Returning her smile, he closed his fingers around hers. "It's over there." He pointed as they started off. "Just around past those trees."

Daylight was waning when the laird reached the spot just before the sharp bend in the lane where the fleeing pair had clearly sat for sometime; the grass was flattened, and boot prints abounded in the soft dirt bordering the verge.

He'd been forced to waste time checking both north and south along two crossroads, just to make sure he didn't miss the clever pair again. The last days had been fine and the road itself was mostly dry, so finding tracks along it wasn't a simple matter.

In both instances, Scrope had hung well back, watching from cover, then had followed him on when, satisfied he was on the right track, he'd urged Hercules on along the southeast lane.

"So, they reached here." He glanced around. "It's possible they didn't realize their predicament until they got here. Once they did, what did they do?"

Hercules bobbed his head, as if indicating the hills to the east.

"Yes," the laird murmured, "I think so, too. But where's the gig?" He eyed the nearby farmhouse. "Very likely there, but before we investigate and confirm, what am I going to do about Scrope?"

While he'd been riding he'd had time to consider the pertinent facts. That Scrope was following in his wake and making no attempt to get in front of him, closer to their mutual quarry, combined with Scrope's giving every indication of being city-bred, suggested that Scrope had no real ability to track and needed him to point the way.

Taught to track game of various sorts from the time he could walk, McKinsey rarely failed to find a trail through any country. If Eliza Cynster and her gentleman-rescuer had headed into the Moorfoot Hills, he would find them easily, but if he did, Scrope would follow, and the hills were distressingly isolated, largely devoid of habitation or humans. Leading Scrope to the pair in such a landscape didn't seem at all wise.

He trusted Scrope rather less far than he could throw him.

And he didn't, in fact, need to follow the pair's trail directly. If they had quit the road and gone into the hills, he was willing to wager as to where they would come out. Such a direction would confirm his increasingly strong conviction that they were making for the Jedburgh Road, and the border crossing at Carter Bar. From their perspective, there were several advantages in using that crossing, and he'd wager there were others he didn't know.

Given he was convinced they were heading that way, there was no need for him to climb over the hills in their wake. He could, instead, follow the road northeast to Gorebridge, and use the time to lose Scrope there. There was no need whatever for Scrope to come up with the pair; if, as he suspected, they'd bravely marched into the wilds of the Moorfoots, he would seize the opportunity to rid them all of Scrope.

That accomplished, he would ride south to St. Boswells. A few miles north of Jedburgh on the main Jedburgh road, the town was well known to him and would suit his purposes very well. He would simply wait there until the pair came down the road, then fall in on their heels, close enough to observe and satisfy himself that despite his failure, Eliza Cynster's future was assured. Simultaneously, he could act as an extra guard for the pair, just in case Scrope continued to follow.

It didn't take long to make up his mind.

Shaking his reins, he nudged Hercules into a slow walk. He made a show of checking the verges as they rounded the bend. Frowning increasingly blackly, he eventually drew rein level with the farm gate and stared up the road toward Gorebridge. "Surely they didn't drive on?"

He'd come to see the pair as intelligent; he'd expected

them to be courageous enough to leave the gig there and take the physically more demanding route through the hills, understanding that if they drove on, he at least—and Scrope if they knew about him—would catch them up all too soon.

But there were no tracks. None. No boot prints heading toward the hills, no wheel tracks turning in at the farm gate . . .

He stared at the ground leading to and past the farm gate. It was unmarred by tracks of any sort. Which was simply ridiculous. Indeed, when he peered more closely, the surface looked as if someone had used a pine branch to sweep it even.

He was willing to wager someone had.

"Very clever. In this case, just a tad too clever for your own good, but it'll serve." Edging Hercules on once more, he scanned the verge on the opposite side of the road— and found very faint signs of the grass being crushed, just enough to allow for two pairs of boots to have carefully passed that way.

"Excellent." Straightening, he lifted his reins and sent Hercules into a trot, then a canter.

The pair had gone into the hills, but there was no chance that Scrope would see, let alone correctly interpret, such carefully concealed signs.

Scrope would follow him to Gorebridge and, with any luck, that was the last the three of them—him, Eliza Cynster, and her gentleman—would see of the iniquitous Scrope.

Chapter Ten

The cottage proved to be a shepherd's hut, presently untenanted, but whoever normally lived there hadn't been gone long and, quite possibly, given the pots of herbs growing on the windowsill, expected to be back soon.

Eliza followed Jeremy through the wooden door and into the single room. Built of split logs and stone, with a sound thatched roof, the cottage was larger than it had at first appeared; as well as a deal table and chairs, kitchen benches and a tin sink arranged around the single window, and the stone hearth, there were two pallets on rough-hewn wooden frames, one large, one smaller, and three narrow cupboards of different sizes set against two walls. There was even a washstand with a chipped pottery basin and ewer. Glancing around, she noted a general neatness and cleanliness. "Perhaps they've gone down to the nearest town for supplies."

Setting the saddlebags on the table, Jeremy nodded. "Very likely. I wonder if there's anything we might use for dinner—we can leave payment for anything we take."

Eliza caught his eye. After a moment, she asked, "Can you cook?"

He blinked slowly, started to shake his head, then stopped. "I've never tried, but how hard can it be?"

Coming to the table, she opened the bags and pulled out everything edible they still carried, laying each item on the table. "We've bread, fruit, not much cheese. A handful of nuts." She looked up to see Jeremy poking in the shadows behind the still open door. "What is it?"

Still rummaging, he replied, "I'm not woodsman enough to rig a snare for a rabbit, and I don't think trying to butcher a sheep or a lamb would be wise—assuming we could even catch one. However"—he emerged, brandishing a long pole wound about with thin twine—"I might just be able to catch us a trout or two." Meeting her eyes, he grinned. "I heard a stream nearby—I'm going to see what I can manage before the light goes altogether."

Almost as eager as he, she followed him out of the cottage. He strode across the small clearing before the door, then paused and, with his head, indicated a ring of stones in the center of the space. "Why don't you see if you can get a fire going—it'll be easier to cook any fish I might catch out here, rather than on the hearth."

She nodded. "All right."

"Tinder's in the other bag." He went off through the trees.

She followed as far as the edge of the clearing and saw the stream leaping down the hillside, gushing and splashing over several large rocks before spreading in a wide pool below. The pool was no more than twenty yards from the cottage. "Presumably that's why the cottage is just here."

Seeing Jeremy pause by the edge of the pool and fiddle with the end of the twine, presumably attaching a hook, she left him to it—she knew nothing about fishing—and scouted under the nearby trees for firewood.

It was only just May and they were high in the hills; although the evening air was decidedly chilly, it remained dry, and the long twilight was an added bonus. She'd never lit a fire outside by herself, but she finally succeeded in starting a small blaze. By diligently feeding it, she created a passable campfire, then scurried about gathering a pile of branches to keep it going.

Jeremy had still not returned; when she peeked down at the pool, she saw him standing by its edge, silent and still, the pole between his hands gently swaying. There was still light enough to see, and the moon was sailing free in the black sky, etching a silvery edge on every line.

Returning to the fire, she considered the next step. How, exactly, were they to cook a fish? Going into the cottage, she found a candlestick, went back to the fire to light it, then searched through the various cooking implements arranged around the hearth.

She'd just set up the iron spit she'd found—it had taken her a good few minutes to work out which bits went where— when Jeremy appeared, pole in one hand and two nice-sized trout dangling from the other.

Grinning, he paused by the fire, holding up his catch for her to admire.

She dutifully did. "Perfect!" She looked up at him. "What now?"

Setting down his rod, he laid the fish down on the thick grass. "I gutted them down by the stream, so all we need do . . ." Picking up the long spit, he demonstrated, sliding the thin bar through one fish's open mouth, then pushing it through and out near the tail. "We'd best do them one at a time."

Reaching out, he set the rod in the apex of the two tripods she'd set up, one on either side of the fire pit. "There." Drawing back, he settled on the grass beside her.

Shoulder to shoulder, they watched the fish heat, steam, then start to cook.

Picking up a stick from her pile, Jeremy used it to spread the burning branches more evenly in the pit. "The trick is," he murmured, "not to try to cook it too fast. We don't want it charred."

She nodded. He glanced at her face, saw the smile curving her lips, and felt remarkably content.

After a moment, she stirred and got to her feet. "I'll get some plates and the bread."

He stayed where he was, his arms loosely draped over his

raised knees, his hands lightly clasped, and watched the heat from the flames slowly sizzle the fish's skin.

When she returned with two tin plates, two plain forks, two tin mugs of water, and her knife, he helped her set their al fresco table and couldn't remember ever feeling so simply happy, so pleasantly content, in all his life.

Oddly for him, some primitive impulse insisted he didn't analyze or question; as a scholar he tended to do both instinctively, without fail. But for some reason the man within this time felt no hesitation in yielding to the moment, and simply being.

Simply wallowing.

Some wiser, more fundamental part of him knew that such moments in life were too rare to waste with worrying and poking; they were to be embraced and enjoyed without hesitation, equivocation, or care.

They timed it perfectly, slipping the tin plates under the fish just at the moment it parted from the bone. With soft laughter and cheers at their victory, they paused to set the second fish to cook, then fell on their plates with gusto, with appetites given an edge by the moment, by their surroundings, by their day.

When she licked her fingertips, then, eyes closed as she savored, murmured, "I've never tasted fish as wonderful as this," all he could do was agree.

The fresh spring water tasted as fine as the most coveted wine.

The second fish went the way of the first. Finally replete, they left their plates on the grass and simply sat, shoulder to shoulder, side by side, and stared into the rosy flames.

Eventually, Eliza glanced at Jeremy. "Tell me about your family." *Tell me about you.*

He glanced along his shoulder, met her eyes. "You've met Leonora."

She nodded. "But if I recall aright, you live with your uncle, don't you?"

"Humphrey." Facing the flames, he went on, "We—Leonora and I—went to live with him when our parents died. I was twelve. Humphrey lived in Kent then, but within a few years, he moved the whole household to London, the better to pursue his research."

"What does he study?"

"Ancient manuscripts, like me."

Distracted by the play of the firelight over the austere planes of his face, she searched for her next question. "Do you, and he, specialize in some particular form?"

"Not so much form as language. It used to be Sumerian, and I suppose that's still our favorite, but we're both comfortable consulting on any of the hieroglyphic-based scripts."

"Is there much call for that?"

And so it went on. She gradually built up a picture of what his life was like, how he spent his days; the information that he usually spent a few months every year traveling at the invitation of Europe's great institutions left her envious.

"It was Prague last year. And there's talk of a request coming through from Vienna—we'll see."

She sighed and asked how he liked the traveling. Bit by bit, question by question, she learned more of a lifestyle significantly different from any she'd known, yet at the same time overlapping her familiar world.

Thinking of that overlap, she fixed him with a direct look. "I can't recall meeting you at any ball except for that once, long ago. Lady Bethlehem's, I think it was."

He pulled a face. "I don't remember where it was. In those days Leonora insisted on dragging me out, introducing me around. I let her for a year or so, but balls aren't really my forte."

She arched a brow. "Not even if the venues have excellent libraries?"

He chuckled, nodded. "I tried that for a while, but Leonora, and others, too, quickly realized where to find me, and so the libraries—and therefore the balls—lost their allure, so to speak."

She grinned. His revelations had distracted her nicely from the increasing closeness—an intimacy not physical—that the firelight and the darkness and his nearness had engendered. She was congratulating herself on having gained a surprisingly detailed account of his life with very little effort when she caught him looking at her, a far too knowing look in his eyes.

"Your turn," he said. "I know about your family in general terms, but how do you see them?"

Wrapping her arms about her calves, she laid her chin on her knees and fixed her gaze on the flames. "You know the family well enough to have a sense of our characters, at least in general. My sisters . . . they're more . . . I suppose the word is *active,* than I am. I'm the quiet one. As you know, I don't like riding—until today, I didn't even know I liked walking. I don't, usually, but I think it might be the weight of the skirts. I'll have to experiment when I get home—to the Quantocks and Casleigh, I mean. Heather often walks there, and Angelica rides a lot, even more than Heather."

He tipped his head so he could watch her face. "So what do you do during a country sojourn there?"

She smiled faintly. "I embroider—I actually enjoy it. Aunt Helena is a wonderful needlewoman, and she taught me. I also practice a lot—the harp, mostly. The pianoforte is easy, relatively speaking." She slanted him a glance, met his eyes. "I'm the one always asked to sing first at *those* sort of family gatherings."

He smiled back. "There has to be someone to take on the role."

She looked back at the flames. "Yes, well—that's me."

"But you spend most of your year in London, don't you?"

When she nodded, he continued, "What's an average day there like—what do you do?"

She hesitated for an instant, but the warmth of the fire, the ease of his company, the simplicity of the moment, swept aside her reservations. Settling more comfortably, she gave herself up to answering his questions—responding to his interrogation—with the same candor he'd offered her.

It was a strangely heady experience; she—and she suspected he, even more—wouldn't normally have answered such questions. Normally she wouldn't have been asked such questions, let alone felt free to reply with so little reserve.

It was the circumstance, the situation, the isolation softened by the glow of the fire. She told herself that, and in part it was true, but had he been anyone else, anyone who had been less honest with her . . . she couldn't imagine revealing such things, and feeling so at ease as she did.

Gradually the night beyond the fire deepened. His questions ceased, and they simply sat, ineffably at ease with each other.

Nothing needed to be said; she felt no compulsion to make conversation, and he seemed as relaxed as she.

A silent communion enfolded them, imparting comfort and reassurance. Calm, peace, serenity; all were there in the darkness of the night, in the flames slowly dying to glowing embers.

Jeremy wasn't sure if that soothing blanket was real or imaginary, but he was content to accept it and continue to sit in the quiet with her. Enjoying the night with her.

The silence, the wild emptiness, and by contrast the togetherness.

He appreciated silence—on some level his soul drank it in—but he'd never met a woman, let alone a lady, who was as comfortable with silence as he.

Then again, he'd never had cause to be as close to a lady outside of the customary haunts of society.

He didn't want to break the stillness, the peace, yet . . .

they would soon need to go inside, and there was one thing he wished to say.

Lifting a stick from the pile, he slowly spread the coals. "Often, in situations such as ours, people—people like us—think too hard." He glanced briefly her way, saw he had her attention. Transferred his gaze back to the embers. "We invest the moment with meanings it may not necessarily have. We constrain and limit the potential outcomes by imposing external expectations, by imagining and anticipating how others will see things, what they might say . . . when in reality none of that might matter."

They were sitting close, her shoulder touching his. Turning his head, he met her gaze.

Her hazel eyes, only inches away, were serious, her gaze direct. "What happens, happens?"

"What might happen should be allowed to happen." He hesitated, then went on, "The wisest people are those who don't prejudge, who don't assume they know how matters will play out, especially when there's more than just themselves involved. The wise let situations play out without wasting energy organizing to battle outcomes that may never eventuate. They let the dice roll, and let them settle before deciding how they should cope with the result."

For a long moment, she held his gaze, then her lips very faintly curved. "I take it you'd prefer to be wise?"

He nodded. "Perhaps it's simply the scholar in me, but I can't see any point in going the other way. The usual way."

She held his gaze; a long moment ticked by.

He forced himself to remain as he was, his arms, like hers, loosely clasped about his knees. The fading warmth given off by the dying embers seemed to his wayward senses to be replaced, superseded, by the warmth of her, by the alluring temptation of her nearness.

Then she inclined her head. "I agree." Her eyes remained on his as she freed one hand, raised it. "So let's roll the dice, and see what comes."

Her hand touched his cheek, framed, caressed, then, lids lowering, she leaned closer, nearer, and her lips met his.

And she kissed him again, openly, directly, with no possibility of doubt as to her intent.

Lids falling, he savored the contact, so amazingly sweet. He'd kissed women enough over the years, but never had a simple kiss been this addictive. Shackling the fingers of one hand about his other wrist, forcing himself to remain as he was, he kissed her back, then tempted her further.

And she came.

Swiveling up to her knees, Eliza deepened the kiss, instinctively surrendering her mouth, luring him to take. She pressed nearer, her breasts firm against his upper arm, the hard edges of the rose quartz pendant still safely tucked between her breasts impinging on her senses.

Urging her on. She leaned in, with her lips pressing for more . . . then he moved.

Shifting, he broke the kiss and drew her into his embrace, swinging her down across his hard thighs, his lips following hers to engage again.

To capture, sup, and savor again.

Drawing her back, drawing her on, into the steadily deepening caress.

The moments spun out in giddy delight, in gentle if illicit pleasure. They traded caresses, the reins shifting between them so that first one commanded, demanded, made their wishes clear, leaving the other to respond before stating their own agenda.

The firmness of his lips, the heated stroking of his tongue, the roughness of his stubble against her palm, the silk of his hair as her fingers explored, wreathed through her senses and filled her mind.

She kissed him back, increasingly boldly, increasingly confident that, as he'd stated, they should simply flow with this tide—

Whoot. Too-whoot.

They broke from the kiss, both looked about, then their senses caught up.

"Owl." Jeremy looked back at her, at rosy red lips, at hazel eyes in which pleasure was alive . . . the thought of what should come next welled and filled his mind. But . . . it was too dangerous out here, in the middle of nowhere.

Before them, the fire had all but died.

She blinked. He saw no regret in her eyes, not even any awkwardness, yet . . .

He steeled himself. "We should go inside. We've a long way to walk tomorrow."

She looked at him, then nodded. "Yes, you're right." Her voice was husky and low.

She moved to rise. He helped her to her feet, then got to his.

He glanced at the spit, still hot, at their plates set to one side. "We can clear this up in the morning, when we can see well enough not to fall in the stream."

She laughed softly and turned to the cottage door. "A pertinent consideration."

Returning with the candlestick, she let him take it and kindle the wick on the last of the embers. He handed the candlestick back to her. While she slipped into the bushes, he considered one of Charles St. Austell's stories about upending the night in some isolated spot in enemy territory.

Last night, despite the bolted door, they'd been vulnerable while they'd slept.

When Eliza returned, he waved her inside, waited until she lighted a second candle, then took the first and circled the cottage several yards out, laying dry brittle sticks in any spot where a man could tread.

Finally satisfied that he'd done all he could to ensure her safety, he entered the cottage and bolted the door.

Two minutes later, with him stretched out on the larger bed and her on the smaller, within arm's reach, he blew out his candle, closed his eyes, and lectured his unruly body not to get ahead of him.

There was no need to overwhelm themselves all at once.
He needed not to think but to assimilate. To absorb.
Before they moved on.
Following the dice she had, with full intent, started rolling.
One step at a time.

The next morning they started out bright and early to walk through and out of the hills. According to the map, they had most of the Moorfoots still to conquer, at the very least a good morning's walk before they reached Stow.

Although the sun shone, the air was bracing. The lighter saddlebag over her shoulder, Eliza tramped in Jeremy's wake. The Moorfoots seemed to be a series of knobbly folds; they climbed up and down constantly, tacking first to follow the flank of one largely barren, moorlike hill, before turning to skirt the next.

The walking wasn't so much hard as demanding. They had to negotiate fern fields and leap countless little burns. They passed a small shooting lodge tucked into a narrow valley between two hills; at one point they walked through a stretch of forest where the shadows were so dense she shivered.

There was more than enough to see and do, to keep her mind occupied simply with getting on, to avoid thinking about the events of the evening, yet time and again her mind slid away to do just that. To consider, circle, poke, and prod at whatever this was that was happening between them.

This—being with a gentleman like this, entirely cut off from their normal world, only to discover a connection neither she nor he had thought likely—was beyond any situation she'd expected, anticipated, or even dreamed of.

In this, she had very little in the way of experience, her own or any of her mentors', to guide her.

Eyes on the ground, she followed in Jeremy's tracks. That morning, when they'd woken, availed themselves of the nearby stream to wash, then, working side by side, had quickly cleaned, straightened, and neatened the cottage, she'd kept expecting some moment of awkwardness, some sudden attack of self-consciousness on her or his part.

It hadn't happened. Instead, she'd been aware that he'd been watching her with the same expectation. Again and again their eyes had met, and they'd waited . . . the entire morning had passed off without one hint of real awkwardness between them.

Before they'd left, Jeremy had laid a gold sovereign on the deal table. He'd looked at her in query. She'd nodded her approbation, then had led him from the cottage and they'd set off.

She couldn't quite understand why, with him, she could behave as she was, and he could behave as he was, and somehow it seemed right. They were working together in a manner she would never have imagined might be between a tonnish gentleman—and no matter his scholarly reticence, Jeremy Carling was definitely that—and a distinctly tonnish lady.

They'd reached a difficult-to-negotiate rocky rise. She grimaced. Without any discussion, she halted, waited while Jeremy scrambled up, then held up her hands. He grasped them and pulled her up.

In perfect harmony without needing any words, they fell back into line and continued on.

She was starting to think that she and her family ought to thank the mysterious laird. If he hadn't sent Scrope to seize her and whisk her all the way into Scotland, she wouldn't now be walking the Moorfoot Hills alone with Jeremy Carling, enjoying herself hugely and learning far more about herself and him than she'd had any idea existed to be learned.

Their exchange before the fire pit had been enough to confirm that, amazing though it seemed, he and she were thinking along similar lines. That neither was yet sure what the outcome of their deliberations would be, what the destination of the road they were currently metaphorically walking down, together, hand in hand, would be.

To her mind, that slow, deliberate progress was perfectly acceptable; she wasn't the brave, adventurous sort like her sisters—she needed to feel her way through things.

To discover that he felt the same, that he saw such an understated, undramatic, stage-by-stage assessment as their most sensible way forward, was not just a relief—it was a revelation.

Her gaze rested on the windblown locks of his dark hair, then skated over the breadth of his shoulders. She wasn't the least bit bothered that, given their present trek through the morning, it was highly unlikely they would reach the border that evening, and would therefore have to spend another night, together alone, somewhere along the way.

Walking steadily on, she turned her mind to what the evening, and the night, might hold.

They emerged from a cleft between two hills and halted.

They were still high on the flank of the range, but the ground before them fell gently away across a wide valley, silver burns wending their way around progressively lower gentle hills to join the thickly treed line of a river. The river lay on the other side of the valley floor, closer to the rise of the next range of hills.

Having unfolded and consulted the map, Jeremy squinted across the valley. "The river's the Gala Water, and that"—he pointed—"is our destination. Stow." He refolded the map. "We should be able to hire another gig there and head south at a better pace."

At various high points along their route, he'd paused and looked back, scanning the hills behind them for any sign of pursuit.

Eliza glanced at him. "The laird isn't following us anymore, is he?"

He met her eyes. "Difficult to be sure—we can't look back far in this terrain. But if he was still on our trail, I would have expected him to catch up with us before now."

Resettling her saddlebag, she looked down across the

valley. "Let's assume we've lost both him and Scrope." She glanced at him. "Which way now?"

He nodded to a shimmer of silver not far ahead. "The easiest route will be alongside the burns. Every little streamlet will join a bigger one, and eventually they all run into the Gala Water. According to the map, the largest tributary, the one this little stream will eventually join, flows into the main river near the bridge we want—the one near Stow."

"Right, then." Stepping out, she headed for the stream. "Let's get to it."

Hiding a grin, he followed. He'd only known her like this, out of society, for a handful of days, yet in that time she'd transformed, changed . . . or, as he was more inclined to believe, the demands of her escape and their flight had drawn another side of her, a different set of skills, a deeper, more innate strength, to the fore.

From what she'd let fall the previous evening, he gathered she viewed herself as somehow less than her sisters. Less an outgoing, willful, impatient, and unwilling-to-be-denied sort of young lady. In society's and even in her family's terms, that might be true, but there was a great deal more to her than that, she had a great deal more to offer than that, and, to his mind, what she lacked was more a blessing than a curse.

They halted near the stream and finished off the nuts, then continued walking while munching their last two apples. The sun beamed down as they crossed the valley, following one stream to the next, steadily descending toward their goal.

The way was easier than their morning's hike. Jeremy remained behind Eliza, following her through the increasingly lush, if narrow, water-meadows bordering the river's tributaries.

He drew level when they finally stepped onto the lane leading to the bridge over the river. He had to quell the impulse to take her hand. Instead, side by side, they strode across the bridge.

He tipped his head toward the buildings gathered about a church tower a little way to their right on the opposite shore. "That's Stow."

She nodded.

He'd noticed she limited speaking whenever possible while they were in public—while she was masquerading as a youth. Which was unquestionably wise. Her normal voice was light, musical, enchantingly feminine, and didn't readily convert to anything male. She covered by speaking gruffly, generally incomprehensibly.

Stow held no unpleasant surprises. The tidy little town boasted several inns. Jeremy and Eliza chose one, arranged for a gig and horse, then went inside.

The taproom was reasonably crowded. Jogging Eliza's elbow, Jeremy pointed to a table by the wall near one window. She nodded and led the way to it. Sliding the saddlebags from their shoulders, they sat.

A buxom serving girl materialized all but immediately. "Right then, sirs—what'll you have? There's a good mutton pie, or if you've a mind to it, there's game pie, too."

"Game pie," Eliza mumbled, head down.

Fighting a grin, Jeremy nodded. "The same. And an ale for me." He glanced at Eliza.

"Water," she grumbled.

"Watered ale for the young sir, is it?" The serving girl made a note on her slate.

Jeremy arched a brow at Eliza.

Her eyes had widened, but after a fractional hesitation, she nodded.

He looked up at the serving girl. "That will do nicely."

The girl beamed. "I'll be no more'n a few minutes, sirs. Make yerselves comfy." She bustled off.

Jeremy grinned at Eliza. "Watered ale?"

She shrugged and kept her voice gruffly low. "Why not? I've never had watered ale before—Heather said she had some when she was off with Breckenridge. I suspect I should try it."

The serving girl returned as quickly as she'd said, sliding plates of pie and gravy before them. Jeremy asked for the reckoning and paid.

"Just in case we need to make a rapid exit," he murmured in reply to Eliza's questioning look.

The pie proved to be excellent, and the ale refreshing, if a trifle bitter.

Their exertions of the morning had sharpened Eliza's appetite. Somewhat to her surprise, she cleaned her plate and drained her mug.

Jeremy had already finished eating and had pulled out their map. He'd been frowning down at it in a considering way. When she pushed her plate aside, he glanced at her, then shifted the map so they could both study it.

"Here's Stow." He pointed. "There's Jedburgh, and the border beyond. Wolverstone's here—we can reach it by these lanes. That's the way I left."

She nodded. "The way that put you on the Jedburgh Road when the carriage came past with me."

"Yes—so that's our route to safety. It's already afternoon, so we can't expect to reach even Jedburgh by tonight, and if it's all the same to you I'd rather not hit the Jedburgh Road itself until we're ready to race straight over the border."

"In case Scrope or the laird, having lost our trail, decide to wait along the road to see if we go past?"

"Exactly." Starting at Stow, he traced the road on, then tapped the map. "We can get a good way on today—past Galashiels and through to Melrose. But I think we should stop there, or somewhere near there, while we're still off the Jedburgh Road, but close to it, with nothing but good, well-surfaced road between us and the border."

She nodded again. "So we find ourselves somewhere to stay near Melrose, then tomorrow morning we make our run for the border."

Across the map, he met her eyes. "You're agreeable to that?"

He was asking whether she was happy about spending another night on the road—together alone. She smiled. "Yes. Perfectly content." And she was.

Tonight . . . she was increasingly certain it would behoove her to push for rather more exploration. Especially if it was to be their last night, together alone, before they returned to society's arms.

Envisaging the evening, she frowned. He was refolding and stowing the map. She glanced to either side, confirming that no one was near enough to hear, then leaned forward and caught his eye as he looked up. "How are we managing for funds?"

She hadn't given the matter the slightest thought, but she should have. They'd already hired horses, two gigs, and had paid for meals at various places.

His lips kicked up. "Remember I told you I worked for a while in Edinburgh?"

She nodded. "That's how you came to know Cobby and Hugo."

"Yes, well." He swung his saddlebag over his shoulder. "Consequently the bank in Edinburgh knows me quite well. I called there before we rescued you. As I didn't know what might happen, what charges we might have to meet, I drew out a sizeable amount." He grinned as he eased his chair back. "I tend to overestimate in practical matters. We've more than enough coin to get us to London in a private chaise if need be."

She relaxed. "Good." Ducking her head, her saddlebag in hand, she slipped out from behind the table and followed him as he headed for the door. As they crossed the inn's front hall, she murmured, "I had a sudden vision of having to mop floors and wash dishes to pay for our next stay."

He chuckled as he opened the door and stepped out. When she joined him on the pavement, he glanced down at her. "It won't come to that, but even if it did, we'd manage, you and I."

She looked into his eyes, saw the easy acceptance and the warmth therein, and returned his smile in full measure. Then, nose rising, she stepped down from the stoop and led the way into the inn yard. "Onward once again. Let's see how far we can get today, and where we can find to spend our last night."

The horse harnessed to the gig was a raw chestnut, dancing on his feet and ready to run. After stowing the bags, Jeremy joined Eliza on the seat, took up the reins, and tooled the beast out onto the main road.

As they rattled out of the town, he flicked the reins and coaxed the young horse into a ground-eating trot. They whisked along, Eliza holding onto her hat and swaying with every turn, her shoulder brushing Jeremy's.

The well-surfaced road twisted and turned, following the curves of the river, still the Gala Water, as it wended its way south. They were rarely out of sight of the well-treed banks, and the birds that swooped and dipped above the rippling waters and flitted about the surrounding meadows.

The drive was ridiculously pleasant. It was easy to forget that they were fleeing pursuit by a villainous kidnapper and a powerful laird whose motives remained a mystery. With the sun beaming down and the breeze whipping past, with the scents and sounds of the countryside filling their senses, they grinned with delight and rolled smoothly along.

As they swept past the turnoff to Buckholm, Eliza started singing.

A few verses on, Jeremy joined in. While her voice was a light soprano, his proved to be a baritone; their voices blended and harmonized as they sang their way through several country songs.

Both river and road swung east and they followed, bowling into the larger town of Galashiels. They slowed as they entered the center of the town. "Keep a sharp lookout," Jeremy warned, "just in case."

But there was no danger lurking. They rattled on through

the town without incident, following signposts that directed them straight on toward Melrose. The Melrose road ran directly east; it initially followed the course of the Gala Water, but the distance between road and river gradually widened. Eventually, they lost sight of the river altogether.

Eliza sat back, then blinked and peered ahead. She pointed. "That's not the same river, is it? That's much larger."

Jeremy looked. "That's the Tweed. We'll cross it a little way along."

Soon, the Tweed curved up to run alongside the road.

"We go through a wood." Jeremy nodded at the thick stands of trees flanking the road ahead. "That looks like it. Just past that the road should curve south, and there's supposed to be a bridge."

There was, quite a picturesque one built of rosy bricks and gray stone, with twin arches spanning the wide river. They rattled across, then turned right along the southern bank. At an intersection a little way along, a signpost directed them straight on to Melrose.

The sun was sliding down the sky behind them, throwing their shadows ahead of the gig.

"Melrose should be no more than a mile further on." Jeremy glanced at Eliza. "Do you have any suggestions for what we should do—where we should seek accommodation?"

She thought, then said, "It's unlikely that the laird or Scrope will be waiting for us in the town, is it?"

"I wouldn't expect them to have come this way. They're either waiting for us further on or have lost our trail entirely, given up, and gone home."

"I hope it's the latter," she returned with feeling. "However, as they won't be in Melrose, there's nothing to stop us driving around the town. Once we see what's available, we can make our choice."

Jeremy nodded. "Sound thinking." After a moment, he added, "I've heard that the ruins attract quite a lot of interest. There might be smaller places we can stay—lodgings rather than putting up at an inn. If Scrope or the laird do happen this way, they're less likely to look for us in such places."

"Ruins?" Eliza looked at him. "What ruins?"

In the end, nothing would do but for them to put up at a small lodging house directly opposite the ruins of the old abbey. After the landlady had shown them to their room and departed, Eliza stood at the window and stared out. "Those are quite the most romantic ruins I've ever seen."

"Scotland has quite a few romantic ruins."

She whirled to face him, her eyes alight. "Can we go and explore? We can, can't we? It's not nearly dark yet, and Mrs. Quiggs said dinner would be another hour and more."

There was no hope for him, he decided, looking into her animated face. "All right." He waved her to the door, then fell in on her heels.

They spent more than an hour clambering about the ruins. He knew more than enough of monastic life to satisfy her curiosity over this and that, over what the monks had used each area for, enough to explain the details of the architectural embellishments over which she oohed and aahed.

He followed her as she wandered about, drank in her often rapturous expression, and was sincerely grateful there were no other visitors about to see and wonder at a youth who behaved so oddly.

When at the last, with the light fading and the smells wafting from the kitchen of the lodging house luring them back, they crossed the lane from the abbey's ancient graveyard, he caught Eliza's eye.

She arched her brows in innocent query.

"Don't forget—you're a youth, not a romantically inclined damsel."

She smiled another of her beaming smiles, then composed her features into a suitably bored mien. Facing forward, she slowed her steps, losing the exuberant bounce in her stride. Nearing Mrs. Quiggs's door, she sighed, patted away a bogus yawn, then gruffly opined, "Well, that was unutterably boring. I hope the dinner's better."

Suppressing an appreciative grin, he followed her into the house.

At much the same hour, in a comfortable inn in St. Boswells at which he was well known, the laird sat down to a succulent dinner of fresh salmon, venison, partridge, baked ham, and leeks. There was an excellent burgundy to complement the food.

All in all, he had nothing to complain about. Once he'd reached Gorebridge, losing Scrope hadn't been hard. The man had very little sense of direction; McKinsey had led him straight through Gorebridge and continued eastward, along a lane that, if Scrope continued following it, would eventually see him back on the Great North Road. With any luck, Scrope would imagine McKinsey was still ahead of him and continue on that tack, believing their mutual quarry had cut across to take the usually preferred route to London.

Well and good. Now all he had to do was keep watch tomorrow to see the fleeing pair come driving past, then fall in behind them and observe.

In truth, given Eliza's gentleman-rescuer's behavior to date, he harbored little doubt of the caliber of the man. He'd acted decisively, intelligently, honorably, and effectively. From his single sighting of the fellow, he'd appeared well set up, handsome enough, and protective.

He'd acted protectively, too. Just that one look across the cobbles of Penicuik's high street had been enough to communicate the man's view of Eliza. As far as her gentleman-rescuer was concerned, she was his.

Which was something of a relief. As the outcome of the botched attempt to kidnap Heather Cynster had proved, the only effective means of shielding a kidnapped Cynster chit's reputation was through marriage. In Eliza's case, as it had been with Heather, the choice was between marriage to her rescuer, or marriage to him.

While courtesy of that brief moment in Penicuik he had a fairly clear notion of where Eliza's rescuer stood on that question, honor demanded he confirm Eliza's view. Was she as happy with the prospect of marrying her rescuer as her rescuer was with the prospect of marrying her?

With luck, his observations on the morrow would answer that question in the affirmative. Then . . . while he could pull back and head home to the highlands, honor appeased, he rather thought he'd see them safely over the border first.

Assuming they'd be driving, once they were past him, the border wasn't that far on. If everything fell out as he hoped, he'd be on his way north tomorrow afternoon.

The meal concluded, the laird called for a whisky. When it came, he sat back, raised the glass in a silent toast to Eliza and her gentleman, wherever they were, then sipped and slowly savored, content for the night.

Chapter Eleven

I t's so *wonderfully* atmospheric."

Jeremy shut the door and turned to look at Eliza. She was standing by the window, its curtains parted, looking out—presumably at the abbey ruins. She'd set aside her coat and let down her hair; the honey-gold tresses swirled about her shoulders, clinging to the ivory silk of her shirtsleeves.

On quitting their landlady's dinner table, he'd elected to stretch his legs in a short stroll down the street, giving Eliza the privacy to wash and refresh herself in their room.

"The moonlight gives it such a mysteriously melancholy air. I wonder if there are ghosts." She glanced at him. "Perhaps the wind will moan through the ruined cloisters in the night."

"Don't start hares—you'll give yourself nightmares."

She grinned. After one last look at the view, she drew the curtains shut.

He glanced at the bed, then looked away. It was a decent-sized bed with a thick mattress, wide enough to be deemed adequate to sleep both a tutor and his charge. Of course, given his and her disparate weights, he was very sure that if they stretched out on the mattress, she would end in his arms.

Walking to the chest of drawers on which he'd left the saddlebags, he accepted his lack of resistance to the notion. He'd intended leaving the knives he'd carried since Penicuik with the bags, but he thought better of it and instead set both on the small table by the bed.

Eliza had left two candles burning, one on each bedside table.

He glanced across as, with a sigh, she sat on the mattress, her back to him, and leaned down to ease off her boots.

His eyes on the fall of her hair, gleaming a deeper gold in the candlelight, he hesitated, then diffidently said, "If you'd rather, I can sleep on the floor."

She swung around so abruptly that her hair fanned out around her. She narrowed her eyes on his face. "I thought we'd settled such nonsense at the woodcutter's hut."

He read her certainty in her face, in the belligerence in her gaze, lightly shrugged. "I just thought I should offer."

Lips firming, she nodded. "Duly noted, and thank you, but no." Turning away, she added, "I'd rather you slept in the bed. With me."

He studied the back of her bent head for a moment, then shook his and turned away. Shrugging out of his greatcoat, he set it over a nearby chair, eased out of his coat and waist-coat and set them aside, too, then unwound his cravat. He sat on the bed to pull off his boots, just as her second boot hit the floor.

She blew out her candle, then rolled onto her back and stretched out full length behind him. He heard and felt her rustle about; setting one of his boots down, he glanced briefly over his shoulder. She'd settled on top of the quilt, her hands folded over her waist, her head sunk in the soft pillow, her eyes fixed on the ceiling.

She looked like she was thinking . . . perhaps planning.

Bending to pull off his other boot, he tried to predict what.

What she was thinking, what she was planning.

What might come next.

He was all but certain as to their eventual destination—the altar seemed difficult to avoid. What he wasn't so certain of was the route by which they'd get there. They seemed to have embarked on an adventure running parallel to the physical one, that went with it hand in hand. An adventure into the unknown, for him even more, he suspected, than her.

Lust was something he'd felt before, but it had previously been a minor distraction, sometimes inconvenient, sometimes less so, yet always an itch he'd been able to ignore if he wished. But the desire he felt for her, and the way it was escalating, hour by hour, incident by incident—that was something new.

Something compulsive, a near-obsession that had a disturbing power to fix his mind on her. On having her.

And while that left him uncomfortable, in more ways than one, it also sparked his curiosity.

Curiosity killed the cat.

Perhaps, but a scholar without that basic trait wouldn't get far.

Of course, there was very little about his present curiosity that could be labeled academic.

His second boot removed, seeing no viable alternative he blew out the second candle, swung around and lay down, his head on the second pillow, his legs stretched out alongside hers but with a foot of clear space between. Then he let his body relax.

As much as he was able, which wasn't all that much.

The bed dipped, as he'd predicted, but she'd been prepared and didn't immediately roll into him.

With both candles snuffed, the room was dim but not dark. Two small square windows set high in the wall above the bed let moonlight seep in, bathing the room in a faint but strengthening silver-pearl wash.

"How far is it to Wolverstone?"

He replied in the same matter-of-fact tone she'd employed. "Somewhere between fifty and sixty miles. If we leave first thing in the morning, we should reach there in the early afternoon."

"Hmm. So by tomorrow evening, we'll be back in the bosom of society, so to speak." One hand clamped to the

edge of the bed to stop herself sliding into him, Eliza raised
one leg, studied the length of her breeches-and-stocking-
clad limb. "I'll be back in skirts and petticoats, and playing
the lady again." Lowering her leg, she glanced sidelong at
Jeremy. "And you'll be the gentleman-scholar again."

He hesitated, then raised his arms and locked his hands
behind his head. "Perhaps, but I rather think I won't be quite
the same gentleman-scholar I was when I left Wolverstone. I
can barely believe that was only four days ago."

"Rather a lot has happened in those days." Her gaze once
more on the ceiling, she added, "I know I'm not the same
young lady who attended Heather and Breckenridge's engagement ball."

She felt his gaze touch her face and linger.

"How have you changed?" He'd lowered his voice; the
question sounded almost intimate.

She turned her head and briefly met his eyes, lightly
smiled. "For a start, I know I can walk up hill and down dale
for hours upon hours—I honestly wouldn't have imagined I
could. And, despite not having any staff supplying my meals
and meeting all my needs, I've still managed well enough."

His brows rose. "I never imagined you wouldn't."

"Didn't you?" She thought for a moment, then said,
"Whether it was simply a matter of *assuming* I couldn't, and
never having put it to the test, it was still a . . . pleasant surprise to discover I wasn't as helpless as I'd thought."

He snorted and looked at the ceiling. "You're no more
helpless than your sisters—you just have different areas of
interest. A bit like me and Leonora. We both have an eye for
detail, for organization, and a great deal of stubbornness and
determination, but we apply those talents in different arenas,
namely those in which our interests are strongest—mine in
books and manuscripts, hers in family." Glancing at her, he
waited until she looked his way to add, "You have more in
common with your sisters than you think."

She stared into his caramel eyes, searched, saw, and

weighed his conviction. Murmured, "You may be right." She was certainly thinking along very Heather- or Angelica-like lines. Very much bolder lines than she'd imagined herself ever considering. She wasn't, after all, the venturesome sort. Yet . . .

Looking upward once more, she wondered . . . then, taking his assessment to heart, she cleared her throat and dived in. "I've been thinking . . ."

Having begun, she didn't know how to go on.

"So have I." A quiet but steady admission.

She grasped the opening. "About what?" Glancing at him, she met his gaze.

His lips firmed a touch. "Ladies first."

She couldn't look away. For an instant, she hovered, teetered, vacillated, then she girded her loins and took a bold step forward. "I've been thinking . . . about what we talked about last night. The point you raised about people like us, in situations like this, limiting themselves by assuming they know what will come to be . . . and therefore, perhaps, ignoring what is, or what else could be." She paused for a second, but his gaze didn't waver. "It occurred to me that if tonight is the last night we'll be spending alone, then"—if she'd been standing, the movement she made would have tipped up her chin—"this will most likely be the last chance we'll have for examining, exploring if you will, what that 'else' might be. Tomorrow, once we're back in society, back to being the people others expect us to be, we'll no longer be free—we won't have the opportunity. We'll be caught up in"—she gestured—"the expected outcome."

He waited, but when she held his gaze and didn't go on, he tipped his head in acquiescence. "I wouldn't argue with that assessment."

So tell me what our next step should be. When he said nothing more but again seemed to be waiting—her turn again, she supposed—she drew breath and, deciding she might as well be hung for a sheep as a lamb, suggested,

"Perhaps, in the interests of not making the mistake inherent in thinking too much and in the wrong way about our situation—indeed, in our own best interests, if your theory is sound—we should make some attempt to assess that 'else' . . . the alternative outcome, as it were."

His eyes locked with hers, Jeremy kept his fingers clenched tight behind his head to keep himself from reacting, from acting without some clearly stated invitation. He thought he understood her; thought they were thinking along the same lines, but she was a female, and he'd long ago learned caution in dealing with the species. When she again fell silent, and waited, he bludgeoned his brain, sadly distracted and overwhelmed with thinking of what he hoped would be. Slavering over the prospect. "That—" He broke off to clear his throat; his voice had grown gravelly. "That would probably be wise."

She studied him for an instant, then frowned and spoke a great deal more crisply. "Actually, I think exploration is mandatory. It certainly is from my perspective." She pushed up on one elbow, her frown still in place. "So I was thinking we should try this again."

She leaned over and kissed him.

At last! The barely civilized warrior inside him cheered, then broke ranks.

Drawing his hands free, with one he cupped the back of her head, with the other pushed aside the fall of her hair to frame her jaw. And hold her steady.

To kiss her back.

Lips to lips. A second later, she parted hers and it was mouth to mouth, tongue to tongue, and glory beckoned.

For a brief moment they clashed, dueled, an elemental battle of wills and wants—his and hers, whose to take precedence—but in the next heartbeat they found their rhythm, an accommodation, a dance of sorts where she took a step, then ceded the lead to him.

Back and forth, him, then her again, they whirled into the ever-deepening kiss, step by tiny step, caress by caress.

The result was an absorbing, intriguing descent into passion.

He couldn't recall that kissing any other woman had ever been like this. The usual underlying tension was there, subtly escalating with each kiss, each increasingly heated breath. Yet there was no unseemly haste but instead a devotion to each moment, to exploring, as she'd said, paying each progressive exchange its due attention.

Every exchange, every shifting pressure of their lips, every slow, heated caress of their tongues was beyond sweet; heady, intoxicating, riveting—the engagement snared his senses as nothing ever had, not even the rarest of Sumerian scrolls, not even a long-lost Mesopotamian tablet.

She pressed closer; he let her lean more completely over him, his inner self greedy for the feel of her soft flesh and firm, feminine curves impressing themselves on his harder muscled body.

Delight. This, he decided, was true delight. Why he'd never felt it with any other woman he had no idea, but in gratitude he willingly lay beneath her and allowed her to explore as she wished.

She was leaning on his chest; her small hands had risen to cup his face. Now her fingers trailed over his cheeks, along his jaw, tracing, learning, even as her mouth supped from his, as her lips, already plump and swollen, teased and tempted.

While she explored, his hands drifted from her head, to her shoulders, then he sent them skating lightly over the long planes of her back. He had to shackle a sharp urge to grip her hips and lift her fully atop him. Through the warm haze of burgeoning pleasure deliciously clouding his mind, he reminded himself that while this was familiar territory for him, it was her first excursion into this domain; for her, it was all new. All fascinating.

That was the import of the small, eager, but contented sound she made as she broke from the kiss and drew back—just an inch.

Just enough to open her eyes, all slumberous and heated, and look down into his.

She stared into his eyes as if she could see to his soul, then the tip of her tongue moistened her lips and she murmured, "More." She studied his face for a moment, then went on, "I was thinking . . ."

When she didn't continue, he managed to find his voice. "Yes?"

She nibbled at her lower lip. "That this time we shouldn't stop."

He'd refocused on her lip, on the urge to offer to nibble it for her; it took a moment to register what she'd said. When he did, his immediate response was *hallelujah,* but then he saw the conflict in her eyes—need and desire clashing with uncertainty. "We'll go as far as you wish. We'll stop whenever you want, whenever you say."

The words fell from his lips without conscious thought. Even as he said them, he wondered what had possessed him to promise a restraint, a control, he wasn't sure he could wield. He'd never had to before. His past lovers had been, if anything, even more eager than he; he had no experience gentling virgins through their first time, had no notion if he could simply stop whenever she shied. Given the strength of the desire already pounding, steady and sure, through his veins, he had to wonder if he could . . . yet even as the thought formed, as he gazed into her hazel eyes now sparking with reassured anticipation, he knew that for her, he would.

For her, he would move mountains.

His gaze fell to her lips; as they lowered to his, he clasped the back of her head in one palm and brought her the last inch to him.

Took the lead and kissed her. Freed by her words, by her clear wish to go further, he sent his other hand exploring, tracing first, then fondling, increasingly explicitly.

Eliza urged him on, with her lips, with soft murmurs.

A rising beat in her blood drove her on; recognizing it as desire, plain, simple, yet powerful, she gloried and let it sweep her on.

The silk of her shirt and the silk cravat binding her breasts muted his touch. Worse, her breasts were tight and aching beneath the restricting band. Between them, they dealt with the buttons down the front of the shirt, then, intrigued by what she could see in his eyes, by the blatant heat in his gaze, she let him peel the garment from her, inch by inch revealing her pale skin.

He frowned when he saw the binding, not just concealing but squashing her breasts nearly flat. He made an inarticulate sound of disapproval, a low growl of disapprobation, even as his hands quested, caressing her through the tight silk.

Catching her breath on a gasp elicited by the sensations his large hands sent searing through her, she raised one arm, exposing the knot securing the band.

He fell on it, swiftly unpicking the knot. Between them they unraveled the band, unwinding it, round and round, until it fell from her. Slid from her curves. Hands propped on his shoulders, she closed her eyes as she drew in a deep breath; relief coursed through her as he drew the material away. Slowly. And tossed the silk band over the side of the bed.

Slowly.

He seemed to have stilled.

Opening her eyes, she looked down at his face.

At his gaze fixed on her breasts.

At the flames smoldering in the burnt-honey brown. She felt the flames' heat as his eyes caressed her, as definite as his hands had earlier been. Her nipples ruched tight; her skin felt hotter, much tighter, too.

His features were set, austere, classically chiseled. As if feeling her stare, he murmured, "I feel like I'm unwrapping a treasure. A very precious treasure."

Without shifting his gaze, he raised one hand, set his palm to her breast.

She shuddered at the touch. Closed her eyes again.

His other hand gripped her nape, and he drew her down, back into his distracting, enticing, alluring kiss. To his lips that promised pleasure, scintillating delight, and delectable elucidation of the mysteries she'd never known.

She gave herself up to him, to his kiss, let herself sink back into it. As his lips claimed hers, as his tongue once again swept confidently in and claimed her mouth, his large, warm hand closed and claimed her breast.

Even then, he didn't rush her, didn't race ahead and leave her floundering, overwhelmed by passion and sensation. Instead, time and again, he drew back from the kiss. Enough for her to savor the delight of his touch fully, to murmur her responses when, his voice a gravel growl, he asked if she liked this caress, or that, if his gentle rolling of her nipples met with her approval, if she liked the sharp sensation that lanced through her when he tweaked.

Deeper and deeper, they sank together into the tantalizing intimacy.

Closer and closer they drew, until their breaths mingled as he explored, and she savored.

He gave her time enough to raise her lids and see, to watch as his hands shaped her flesh, as he stroked, caressed, and learned. To watch herself as she offered herself up to the moment, to the delight of the subtle and the passion of the direct.

To the heat and the hunger.

She could sense it in him, a nearly vibrating tension. Could feel it in herself, an appetite she'd never before entertained, never before experienced, let alone appeased.

Tonight . . .

She forced her lids, weighted by welling desire, up, and looked down at him.

At the increasingly clear stamp of passion on his features.

His hands swept down, over the planes of her now exposed back, before swooping up and forward to capture her breasts once more.

His hands closed, and she started to shut her eyes in anticipation of another wave of pleasured delight, but then she noticed his shirt. She was naked to the waist, but his shirt still lay between his skin and hers, to her mind an unacceptable barrier.

Summoning her will, focusing it, she put her fingers to the buttons and set about removing the offending garment. His hands slid to her waist, and he lay back and let her.

Encouraged, increasingly bold, she worked down the placket, tugging the shirt free of his waistband to get at the last button. The instant it slid undone, she grasped the shirt and spread the sides wide . . . exposing an expanse of muscled chest that looked like the product of her dreams. There was patently more to scholarly gentlemen than she'd thought.

The errant notion made her lips curve, but she couldn't drag her eyes from their visual feast. From surveying the bounty she'd uncovered. A line of crinkly dark hair trailed across the width, screening the flat discs of his nipples; another line arrowed down the middle of his chest to disappear beneath his breeches.

Of their own volition, her hands followed the track her eyes had blazed, touching lightly at first, then, when he twitched and his skin flickered, more firmly stroking, testing the resilience of steely muscle beneath the taut skin, then she gave into temptation and boldly possessed.

Jeremy watched her; his features were too tight, desire too rampant for him to manage a smile, yet the sight of her eagerness, of the innocent passion lighting her face as she looked and touched and learned him, much as he had her, held him in effortless thrall.

He allowed her as long as he could, but the insistent beat in his blood was rising, rising. He'd never been so aware of it as he was tonight with her. Never before had he been so sensitive to, so subject to, its compulsion.

When he saw the notion of sending her lips to cruise the path her hands had taken bloom in her eyes—they were so wonderfully open, a mirror to her thoughts, to her moods—he reached up, caught her nape, and drew her down for a kiss; drew her to him, drew her into the kiss, then tipped her, turned her, rolled her onto her side beside him.

Eased her onto her back as he rose to hang over her as she'd previously leaned over him.

Holding her to the kiss, he let the hand at her nape ease, then slide, fingers trailing down the long line of her throat, over the thudding pulse at its base, down over the upper swell of her breast, then he cupped the firm mound and claimed it again.

Distracted her with his touch, then drew his lips from hers and sent them skating down the path his fingers had traced.

Bending his head, he laved the pulse point at the base of her throat, heard her gasp. Felt her fingers tangle in his hair as he quested lower. And lower. Until, shaping her breast with his hand, he set his lips to the peak, touched, caressed, then laved. Then suckled.

Lightly at first, then more strongly.

Eliza gasped, managed to strangle the scream of pleasure that rose up her throat. Vaguely thought that he should have warned her as her body bowed and streams of white-hot sensation lanced through her, deep into her, coursing down to tighten something low in her body, to pool and spread there.

His ministrations went on; he continued to feast, leaving her struggling to draw breath, let alone think beyond a dazed, *Oh, yes!* Her scholar had studied in this arena, too.

She had wondered . . . but as his lips continued to cruise her swollen breasts, applying just the right amount of suction to her acutely sensitive nipples, any thought that he wasn't experienced in this sphere evaporated.

Then he paused. He drew back from her breasts, blew

gently on one tightly furled nipple, then glanced at her. In the moonlight streaming through the windows above the bed head, stronger now as the moon had fully risen, she saw him clearly. Saw the broad shoulders, leanly sculpted in muscle, the delectable width of his chest, the square jaw, and the tawny brown eyes that seemed to see her—the real her that even she hadn't known was there.

He looked down, laid one large hand, splayed, over her bare midriff, then looked up and caught her gaze. "Further?"

She blinked, took in the question. "Yes." The word was on her lips before she'd thought. Then she did; she consulted the pulsing, yearning heat washing through her, the promise of deeper fulfillment that had taken root somewhere in her pleasure-soaked mind, and couldn't see any reason to amend her reply.

His lips twisted in a grimace that was not quite one of pain. "Are you sure?"

That grimace that wasn't a grimace told her all; he didn't want to call a halt any more than she did, but he felt he had to make the offer—honorable scholar that he was. Because if they continued, there would be no going back, at least not without a great deal of angst . . . but most likely there would be no going back, no way out, anyway.

"Yes." This time the word rang with her certainty. "I need to learn more—I need to learn all. We both need to know—it'll help, later, if we know whether we suit in this sphere." Eyes locked with his, she tipped her head slightly. "Won't it?"

Jeremy couldn't argue. But . . . "If you'd rather wait until later . . ."

To his abject relief, she shook her head, her lips coming as close to a mulish cast as barely suppressed passion would allow. "Later—when we're back with our families, back living in our respective homes? No." Desire still had her firmly in its grip; her voice was thin, yet she managed to instill it with determination. "I need to know, you need to know, and this is our last chance to find out before we go back to being our usual selves. This is a moment I don't wish to squander—and neither do you."

Without warning, she cupped his nape with one hand, lifted her head and pressed her lips to his—not gently, not temptingly, but with blazing passion.

A passion that until then he hadn't known she had within her.

A passion that was all fire and feminine heat.

A passion that literally curled his toes with wanting—then her other hand found his erection through his breeches, lightly shaped, then boldly stroked . . .

He broke from the kiss, caught her hand, chest heaving as he struggled to catch his breath and shore up his suddenly tenuous control.

From a distance of mere inches, he met her gaze.

Her eyes burned belligerently. "More. Now."

He would have laughed if he could have. "All right." The words were pure gravel, ground out and tense. "But"—he held her gaze, let his fingers stroke the wrist he'd captured—"from this point on, I hold the reins. I drive . . . and you just lie back and go along for the ride. Agreed?"

Her eyes narrowed, but the passion between them had barely cooled from before, and her bold caress had shot heat through them both and set the flames raging once more; the last thing either of them wanted at this point was an argument. "Agreed."

She tried to tug him down, but he resisted. Slowly, he pressed her wrist down to the pillow beside her head, then smoothly shifted, lifting over her, then, slowly, his eyes locked with hers, he lowered his body to hers.

He watched her eyes flare, watched them widen and darken. Saw passion swirl in their depths and rise higher.

Fully upon her, his hips trapping hers, his shoulders and arms caging her, propped on his elbows he bent his head and captured her lips.

And waltzed them back into the fire.

Eliza couldn't catch her breath, couldn't still her whirling head. Her wits spun away; her senses, suborned, danced to his tune, to the rapidly escalating call of desire. To the symphony of passion unleashed.

That was what it felt like, an orchestrated medley of sensation and delight.

Of their own volition, her hands responded, spearing into his hair to hold him to their increasingly ravenous kiss, then sliding away to greedily spread and splay and pay homage to the broad muscles of his shoulders, to grip and seize his upper arms when his own hands drifted and razed her senses.

Her breasts were hot, sensitized to his touch, swollen and aching and needy. The crisp hair on his chest rasped her nipples and she gasped, her body arching evocatively, provocatively, under his.

Then one of his hands slid down, over her midriff. His fingers found the buttons at her waist, both those of her breeches, then those of the silk drawers she wore beneath; she felt the tug and release as he undid them.

His fingers quested, pushing under the garments, sliding lower, over her taut belly, quivering with a desire she could barely contain, to touch the curls at the apex of her thighs.

To brush, stroke, then slide past. His fingers pressed further, until they were stroking the soft flesh hidden behind the tight curls.

Like a dam breaking, the heat that had pooled, molten and liquid, deep in her belly, welled and swelled; it rose through her, engulfing and filling, until all she knew was the compulsive beat that rode its currents.

Passion, desire, need, and want—all came together in that swirling sea of pleasure.

A sea he drew forth, called forth, and immersed her in. Held her in.

He lifted slightly from her, settling on one hip beside her, one long thigh pressed alongside hers. His other knee slid between hers, parting her thighs.

Giving his fingers better access, access he immediately took advantage of to touch her where she was slick and hot and wanting.

He held her to their kiss, held her in that sea of unrelenting pleasure, and stroked, caressed, possessed. He traced the soft, swollen folds, and she learned his touch, learned his patience, too, as he drove her wild with anticipation, for exactly what she wasn't sure but she knew he knew.

With desperation closing in on her, with fire surging in her veins, she caught the side of his lip and lightly nipped. He responded with heat; angling his head, reclaiming her lips, he changed the tenor of the kiss to one of outright possession as his hand shifted and he cupped her fully.

Then one long finger slid deep into her sheath.

She stilled, caught in a vice of indescribable pleasure. Of shockingly novel sensation.

He pressed deeper, slowly stroked.

Stroked again, and something within her tightened.

Tightened, coiling, inexorably coalescing with every heavy penetration, every successive caressing stroke, until flushed and heated, yearning and desperate, she stood teetering on some invisible precipice, waiting.

Waiting . . .

His hand subtly shifted, then he stroked again—and she fractured. Simply came apart, her senses shattering beneath the force of sheer, undiluted pleasure.

She cried out, but the sound was trapped between their lips; he supped, and drank it down.

The pleasure spun out, flushing through her, down every nerve, every vein, spreading, golden, bright, and scintillating, as it sank into her flesh, as it comforted but, to her surprise, didn't appease. Didn't slake the growling hunger within.

If anything, that empty, heated hollow had deepened, expanded. Grown.

Jeremy wrestled with her breeches and drawers; he'd never made love to a woman in trousers, and breeches were even more difficult to strip away.

Still trapped in the kiss, her hands lacking their previous urgency yet still intent, she reached down and helped him; he felt absurdly grateful as he finally drew the garments away and sent them flying over the edge of the bed.

Breaking from the kiss, he stripped off her stockings, then left her for an instant, swiftly dispensed with his own breeches and hose, and returned.

To her.

To the molten gold and emerald of her hazel eyes. From beneath heavy lids, she'd watched him, waiting, ready, all but thrumming with passion.

To her arms. She held them gracefully wide in welcome, wrapped them about his shoulders as he joined her.

To the wonder of her body, all moon-kissed curves and shadowed hollows. Awed, he let himself worshipfully down upon it, pushing her thighs wide and making a space for himself where he needed to be. Bending his head, he found her lips, took them and her mouth in a long, slow, achingly desperate kiss. Felt the scalding wetness of her entrance bathe the distended head of his erection.

Unable to hold back an instant longer, he flexed his spine and sank slowly, so slowly, into her.

She caught her breath, stilled beneath him; he paused, waited, but sensed no resistance, no panic, from her. Only expectation. Anticipation.

The same feelings rode him with sharpened spurs.

He pushed on and came to the expected barrier, paused for a bare second, then thrust swiftly, cleanly, through. He sensed rather than heard the small yelp she uttered; trapped between their lips, it didn't escape.

Riding the powerful thrust to its natural end, he sheathed himself fully in her bounty.

She clamped around him, and he nearly died.

Breaking from the kiss, he bowed his head; his hand, sunk in the pillow beside her head, fisted as he fought for some semblance of control. Eyes closed, he dragged in a slow, tight breath, then eased back, pried himself from the wondrous clasp of her body, then slowly, *slowly,* returned.

If he kept the pace slow, perhaps he would manage. Manage not to lose himself totally in her.

In the glorious body that, after the slightest of pauses, rose beneath him, joined with him and answered desire's call.

He withdrew and thrust in more forcefully. Reassured by her urgent and immediate response, he set a steady pace of thrust and retreat, of blatant but reined possession.

She clung to him and plainly gloried. Eager and wanton, abandoned to the moment, she held nothing back, but went with him, rode with him, into the fire, through the flames, into the heat and the glory.

Her hair a writhing mass of gold spread about her head, her lips, swollen and rosy, parted as she panted, as the force of his thrusts rocked her and she whispered delirious nothings, all flagrantly encouraging, and her eyes, green fire set in gold, captured him, held him, enslaved him.

Drove him on through the landscape of their escalating need, her nails sinking into his upper arms as desire and passion melded and tightened, coalesced and strengthened. Until the combination whipped them on and ever on, to the pinnacle of physical desire.

And further yet, racing, hearts pounding. Reaching, wanting.

Until they burst through the conflagration to that heart-stopping moment of soaring . . .

To the ultimate culmination.

He reclaimed her lips just in time.

She shattered beneath him with a soft, keening scream, clinging, then gasping, her lips and mouth surrendered, her body all his.

He held back as long as he could, for as many seconds as

the powerful contractions of her slick sheath allowed him, marveling at the openness, the unadulterated, unshielded honesty of her passion.

In the instant when the insatiable pull became irresistible and she drew him over the edge, he felt something inside him give, like the link on a chain snapping open, sliding free.

Then he was flying, too, with her, within her, into the exquisite oblivion that waited in her arms. They closed around him as he broke, as he shuddered and his body emptied into hers.

He hadn't intended that, had intended to withdraw and at least spare them that final link in the binding chain, but . . . some part of him knew, simply knew, that there was no reason anymore. No reason to even imagine that he would—could—ever let her go.

The small part of his rational mind that still functioned couldn't follow the logic in that, but the rest of him didn't care.

As of tonight, their die was cast, irrevocably and forever.

They slumped together. He hung over her, his weight on his elbows, his forearms caging her head and shoulders; her arms were wrapped around him as far as they could reach, small hands spread on his back, holding him.

Their breaths sawed; their lungs labored. For his part, his senses still spun. Finally managing to raise his lids, he looked down into her face.

And saw glory dawning.

Her eyes were closed, but as he watched, her lips slowly curved upward in the smile of a well-pleasured madonna.

That smile was a benediction that touched his soul.

He drank it in, wallowed in it, enshrined it in his mind.

Eventually, she sighed, an exhalation of inexpressible contentment, and eased beneath him.

Holding back his own, too-revealing groan, he gently disengaged, tugged the disarranged covers from beneath them, wrestled the sheets over them, then slumped in the bed alongside her.

She turned to him, reached for him, trustingly snuggling.

Settling on his back, he eased one arm around her, watched as she laid her head on his chest, in the hollow below his shoulder. Almost immediately felt the tension in her muscles fall away.

Letting his head slump back on the pillow, he closed his eyes, intending to think, to consider what had happened, all that had been so unexpectedly different, to analyze and weigh; instead, he found sleep waiting, bliss-filled and deep. It ambushed him and dragged him under, and he went.

Eliza woke to darkness in the deepest hours of the night. The moon had long gone, yet not even a lark stirred beyond the window.

For uncounted moments, she simply lay there, wrapped in the warmth of a naked male—her naked male—and marveled. Who would have thought, indeed!

His lean but steely strength had been a welcome confirmation, the desire that had shone so clearly in his eyes reassuring, confidence building, and the care he'd taken to ensure her pleasure had set the seal on her approval of him.

As for the unimaginably erotic feeling of him deep inside her, moving so surely, filling her so deeply, that had been utterly astounding.

Just the memory sent a ripple of awareness coursing through her.

The event had been more, much more, than she'd expected. More earthy, more physical, more intimate.

More absorbing. More fascinating, more exciting, more enthralling, and definitely more tempting—the sort of experience that, once experienced, made one want to do it again.

Which left her wondering . . .

Taking stock, she tensed this muscle, then that, and discovered that other than a twinge or two, she'd weathered her deflowering in excellent shape. Better than excellent if one counted the pleasant, oddly glowing feeling that still lingered in every muscle. Satiation, she supposed.

She could certainly get used to the sensation.

Which sent her mind shifting to the cause of said sensation. He was lying on his back; she'd burrowed against him, pillowing her head on the wide muscle of his chest. One of his arms lay about her shoulders, holding her in place. The fingers of his other hand rested lightly on her arm . . .

Those fingers shifted, then she felt a tug on the chain around her neck.

"What's this?"

She couldn't see—it was all but pitch dark—but could tell he was turning the rose quartz pendant between his fingers.

He'd seen it when he'd unwrapped her breasts, but had, gratifyingly, seemed much more taken with her than the pendant.

Shifting her head, she looked toward where she knew his face to be. "How did you know I was awake?"

He didn't immediately answer, then she felt him lightly shrug. "I was already awake. I just knew."

Jeremy wiggled the hexagonal pendant. When he'd woken it had been lying on his chest, over his heart. The stone had felt oddly warm.

"That"—she raised a hand and followed the chain to the pendant and his fingers—"was passed on to me by Heather. She had it through her . . . ordeal. I suppose you might say it's a talisman of sorts."

He released it. "When I saw it earlier, it looked quite old." He'd barely glanced at it, absorbed with other things, but he had registered that much. That he hadn't been diverted by something old said quite a lot.

"It is." She shifted and slid the pendant down between her breasts.

He'd been awake for some time; his eyes were as adjusted to the dark as they were going to get, but he still couldn't see her as much more than a paler shape amid the shadows. He knew when she settled her elbows on his chest and turned her face to his again more by touch and movement than by sight.

"I was wondering . . ."

So was he. He'd been lying in the dark for the last however many minutes wondering whether he'd made a serious miscalculation over exactly what the nature of the relationship between him and her was going to be.

He'd sensed the potential from the instant he'd set eyes on her—or more accurately met her eyes—in Jedburgh. He'd subsequently assumed, given the circumstances of her kidnapping and rescue, given they'd been forced to spend first one, and now three, nights together alone, that marriage was the all but certain outcome. An outcome that would see her as his wife, that, at least in his mind, would subsequently result in children, and them creating a family.

That outcome, those results, had been entirely to his liking. He'd liked her, and the past days during which he'd watched her cope with the exigencies of their flight had only deepened his regard. His initial view, formed that night in Jedburgh—that even without any social imperative forcing them to the altar, a marriage between him and her would work—had been correct.

From their admittedly unspecific discussion of the matter, she'd seen the situation in much the same light.

So what had happened last night? Several hours ago, when they'd taken a step that, in the greater scheme of their already predetermined future, shouldn't have meant all that much?

Them being intimate shouldn't have changed anything.

Yet it had.

He now felt like he was standing on the brink—no, had already stepped over some unforeseen brink into . . . a situation he didn't understand. Didn't fully comprehend.

He didn't feel entirely himself anymore . . . or rather,

he felt like himself but with something added, or perhaps enhanced. As if the otherwise straightforward act of intimacy with her had brought some heretofore unknown and unsuspected part of him to the fore. And entrenched it in his psyche.

No previous intimacy had had that effect.

She tipped her head—he saw the paleness of her face move—and he realized she'd been waiting for a response. He replayed her last words. "About what?"

"About whether, now we've . . . indulged once, given that later today we'll be at Wolverstone and then doubtless on our way down to London, all in situations where further indulgence might be problematical, whether, given we are both wide awake, we shouldn't seize the opportunity to indulge again."

He couldn't see her expression, not even a hint, which meant she couldn't see his. Just as well. God only knew what might be showing in his face.

Lacing her fingers, she leaned her chin upon them, staring through the darkness. "What do you think?"

That he might as well be hung for a wolf as a sheep.

When he didn't immediately answer, she eased back a fraction. "Don't you want to?"

"Yes." The word came out in a rush, as if something within him was scrambling to reassure her, horrified by the notion that she might get the wrong idea. Regardless, there was no point lying on that score. All she'd have to do was shift her sleek, silken thigh a few more inches over his and she'd discover he was more than ready for another round.

He'd been half aroused before she'd woken, and hard as a post since she'd first spoken. His body, at least, knew precisely what it wanted.

Perhaps he should take his own advice and stop thinking so much.

"Are you sure you're not too sore?"

"I'm not." Eliza was grateful for the darkness; it hid her

blush. "And I really would rather know`. . ." Reaching out with one hand, she found his jaw, let her fingers slide further, into his hair, gripped lightly and, using that to guide her, eased up, leaned closer, and touched, brushed, her lips to his. Drew back just enough to breathe across them, "I'd really like to know if the second time will be as good as the first."

"It won't be." He surged up, flipped her to her back, and came down on top of her, pinning her beneath him. He looked down into her face; she couldn't be sure, but she thought his lips curved in a distinctly male smile. "The second time—" He bent his head and brushed her lips, a return of the tantalizing caress she'd given him. But then he hovered with no more than a breath separating their lips to state, "Will be even better."

He closed the gap and kissed her. Kissed her until her head was reeling, until her wits were waltzing and her senses singing.

And proceeded to demonstrate that he knew what he was talking about.

Chapter Twelve

They set out immediately after an early breakfast. Eliza sat on the seat of the gig and tried to keep her smile within bounds. She was grateful she didn't have to sit a horse, but other than a small degree of chafing in a very sensitive spot, she was feeling on top of the world.

On top of her world, at any rate.

Jeremy had been rather quiet, as if he had a lot on his mind, but she assumed he was absorbed with thinking through the details of their route to Jedburgh and Wolverstone beyond, and she forbore from teasing him.

The chestnut between the shafts seemed to have come to some accommodation with Jeremy; the horse paced steadily on, carrying them swiftly down a minor lane that curved southeast to the small town of Newtown St. Boswells.

"Not exactly a new town at all," Eliza remarked as the gig traveled briskly down the main street. "Some of these buildings have to date from centuries ago, at least."

Jeremy glanced briefly at the buildings, some clearly ancient. "At least."

They were soon through the town and rolling along the last section of the country lane he'd chosen, the better to keep them off the main roads where danger might still lurk, when Eliza closed her hand on his arm. "Stop, please." She pointed ahead to the right of the lane. "Just across from those bushes."

He grunted and obliged, without asking why.

She threw him a grateful smile. As soon as the gig rocked

to a halt, she slipped down to the road. With an "I won't be long," she rounded the gig, crossed the lane, and pushed through the bushes; the clump was high and thick enough to hide her from anyone on the road.

The reins in his hands, Jeremy looked forward, to the junction with the main Jedburgh road just ahead. Fifty yards, and then they'd have to dash. He intended to drive as fast as he could south, all the way to the border. Once over it, the turnoff to Wolverstone wasn't all that far.

He tried to keep his mind on the journey, but within seconds his obsession with what was developing between him and Eliza had reared its head and snared his thoughts. Somehow, some element he hadn't foreseen had slipped into the mix, and now he didn't know what sort of cake they were baking. Certainly not the marriage of calm reason based on mutual affection that he'd thought had been in his cards.

His recipe had mutated.

Somehow.

Last night.

Yet this morning, when they'd woken late and rushed to get downstairs in time for the breakfast Mrs. Quiggs had promised them . . . everything had seemed so normal. So stable and settled. Eliza had been so happy and content that he'd found it easy to go along, to follow and smile . . . as if nothing had been awry at all.

Perhaps nothing was.

Confusion wasn't normally his middle name.

On the other side of the bushes, Eliza rose, much relieved, and wrestled her breeches back up her thighs. This was the one activity that was distinctly more difficult in breeches than in skirts. Still . . .

Her thoughts halted as she stared down at her boots. At the sliver of light that was playing over them.

She looked up, aghast. Searched in the direction from which the beam had come. And saw, not far ahead, not far away at all, a man sitting a black horse.

"*Scrope*." The word came out in a hoarse whisper. She stared for a second more, then turned. "Oh, God!"

She fought her way back through the bushes to the lane. Wrestling with the buttons at her waistband, she pelted across it. Raising one hand, she pointed. "Scrope! He's waiting just ahead—along the main road on the right."

Jeremy lifted the reins as she scrambled up beside him. "Did he see you?"

"Yes! The damned man had a spyglass. That's why I noticed him—I saw the reflection."

Contrary to her expectations, Jeremy made no move to turn the gig. "Will he know it's you? You're still in disguise."

She blinked, then met his gaze. "I think it's safe to say he'll have realized I'm not a youth by now. He wasn't that far away."

"Ah." Despite his stoicism, Jeremy's mind was racing. It took no more than a few seconds for him to see and weigh all their options.

And decide that none were good.

"Scrope will have seen you racing back—he'll already be on his way." He caught Eliza's gaze. "Can he come directly across country to where we are now?"

She thought, then shook her head. "No. I don't think so. Not unless he can jump a very high hedge. He was on a small hill beyond it."

Jeremy faced forward. "So he'll come for us via the road—for him, that's more sensible anyway. He'll be at that junction and coming for us at any minute." He shoved her with his elbow. "Out! Get the bags. Quick!"

The instant she lifted the bags from the boot, he turned the horse and gig, looped the reins, leaving enough play for the chestnut to run with, then jumped out of the gig, slapped the horse's rump, and raced to Eliza. The horse and gig went rattling back along the lane, going faster as the horse realized and relished the lack of weight.

Jeremy took the saddlebag Eliza held out to him, swung

it over his shoulder, and grabbed her hand. "Come on!" He leapt across the narrow ditch, waited until she joined him, then pushed into the line of trees bordering the lane.

The bushes beneath the trees were thick enough to hide in if they crouched. Half bent, they raced across the narrow strip of land to the edge of the main road. Jeremy halted in the cover of the bushes. "Wait," he murmured. Releasing Eliza, he edged forward, looking down the main road, the highway to Jedburgh.

There was a curve just beyond, hiding the entrance to the lane they'd been driving down. He didn't see Scrope come thundering up and veer into the lane, but he heard him.

Had to assume it was indeed Scrope.

Jeremy beckoned urgently to Eliza. She joined him without a word, offering her hand. He grasped it. Tipped his head forward. Hand in hand, they sprinted across the highway.

They raced into the trees on the other side of the road. Jeremy paused briefly to take stock, then urged Eliza on, away from the road. "We can't afford the time to check the map, but I think these woods stretch all the way to the river. Once we reach it, we can follow it south to St. Boswells."

She strode quickly on, deeper into the trees. "Scrope will catch up with the gig, won't he?"

"All too soon. Then he'll be hot on our trail."

She didn't ask anything more, but when they reached older woodland and the trees grew larger, the trunks more widespread, she glanced at him, then started to jog.

He kept pace with her, glancing back every now and then, occasionally correcting their path so that they continued more or less perpendicular to the road, putting as much distance as they could between them and Scrope.

The trees did, indeed, run all the way to the riverbank; they halted beneath a large branch, looking down a sharply undercut bank to the swiftly rushing water.

"Which river is this?" Eliza asked.

"The Tweed." Jeremy eyed the distance to the opposite bank. "I hadn't realized it would be so wide."

A sharp but distant *crack!* came from behind them. They glanced back, but the trees and a dip in the land concealed their pursuer.

Jeremy tweaked her sleeve, whispered, "Come on."

Together they set off at a run, following the river south.

Twenty yards on, the trees to their right thinned, leaving only a meager line along the riverbank to screen them.

Jeremy paused under some low-hanging branches and peered back, across the open expanse of some farmer's paddock.

"There!" Beside him, Eliza pointed back along the edge of the field.

Jeremy looked and saw Scrope running down the line of the trees, pistol in hand, ducking and checking under the branches as he came.

Pistol?

Jeremy grabbed Eliza's hand and tugged her on.

She'd seen the pistol, too. They both ran as fast as they could. With only open pasture to their right and a narrow line of trees to hide them, they followed the river south.

Then the trees ahead thinned even more. And beyond, between Jeremy and Eliza and the roofs of what had to be St. Boswells, lay a large field, recently plowed.

Wide-open terrain, with not even a bush to conceal them.

Jeremy halted. He felt fairly certain Scrope wouldn't be carrying a pistol just for show. If they ran on . . . they'd never reach the town before Scrope caught them.

Jeremy turned to the river. "There has to be some way . . ."

Standing on the lip of the bank, sharply carved by winter flood waters leaving a drop of ten feet to the present summer water level, he looked south. The river looped in a large curve just ahead, swinging away to the east and passing out of sight. The bulk of St. Boswells lay along the opposite bank, along the east-flowing section.

"If we had any sort of craft, we could get out of sight that way." Eliza grimaced. "Please don't say we have to swim."

He turned and looked north. And grasped her hand. "We won't." He kept his voice at a bare whisper. "We're going to cross"—with his chin he directed her gaze back up the river—"there."

Thirty yards back along the river, a collection of four silt islands—the larger two, in the river's center, thickly covered with scrubby bushes—offered the equivalent of stepping stones.

Scrope was near enough for them to hear him thrashing branches.

"He'll be here soon," Eliza mouthed. She pointed. "How do we get down?"

Jeremy crouched, then jumped down to the lower bank, a yard or more of rocks and sand edging the riverbed. He landed easily and immediately stretched up, waving Eliza to him.

She sat on the edge of the upper bank, then, lips pressed tight, wriggled forward and let herself fall . . .

Jeremy caught her, steadied her on her feet, then took her hand and hurried her on ahead of him, back along the river. The rock-strewn sand was sufficiently compacted; they made little noise and the burbling river masked what sound they did make. They could hear Scrope clearly as he continued searching along the upper bank. Luckily, even if Jeremy stood upright the upper bank was high enough—or the level of the riverbed was low enough—to keep them hidden.

Once he was sure Scrope had passed their position and was continuing to search southward, increasing the distance between him and them as they hurried north along the river's edge, Jeremy risked murmuring, "He won't think of us crossing the river, not until he realizes we're not ahead of him, which he will as soon as he reaches the plowed field. Then he'll backtrack, but luckily it hasn't rained recently— we shouldn't have left any evidence that we got down to the riverbed, and the ground here is so rocky we're not leaving any obvious tracks."

He glanced back, then urged her on even faster. "But when he does realize and comes looking, we need to be concealed on one of those larger islands, out of his sight."

The distance they had to traverse might have been only thirty yards, but it was pitted with rocks; they had to step carefully or risk turning an ankle, or worse. They went on in a mad, panicked, but silent scramble, steadying each other as best they could.

Finally they drew level with the first of the silt islands.

Jeremy held Eliza back, stepped out into the open, and searched back along the raised bank as far as he could see. Without looking at her, he waved her on. "Go."

He sensed her leap over the narrow strip of water onto the first island. Seeing no hint Scrope had yet started to search down at river level, he quickly turned and followed.

They made it onto the second island, one of the two thick with bushes, easily enough. Jeremy silently directed Eliza around the north edge of the island, keeping them screened from Scrope as best he could.

The central channel between the two larger islands was wider than the channels closer to shore, and the water was running swiftly.

"Careful." He steadied Eliza on the crumbly, rock-and-sand edge of the island, gauging the danger. He had cause to thank Hugo for her breeches; in skirts, she'd never have been able to manage the leap. Glancing up and back at the higher bank further downriver, and seeing it still empty, devoid of Scrope, he drew her to the midpoint of the island's shore, then lifted the saddlebag from her shoulder. "Pull back a little, then when I say, run and leap." He pointed to a bush on the island opposite. "Grab that branch if you need to steady yourself, then get through the bushes as fast as you can and crouch down on the other side."

She met his gaze and nodded.

Dragging a breath deep into her lungs, past the constriction fear had placed around them, Eliza focused on her target bush on the other side of the rushing water.

Sensed Jeremy peering down along the riverbank. Waited . . .

"Now!"

She took three running steps and launched herself across the rushing river. In midflight she had a fleeting moment of wondering what the hell she was doing—she wasn't the venturesome sort, remember? Then she landed, boots firm on the gravelly soil. She swayed, grabbed the branch as instructed, righted herself, and burrowed straight on through the bushes, her attention already split between what lay ahead—hopefully nothing and what lay behind her.

Reaching the other side of the bushes, she crouched in their lee, and, heart thudding, waited. The moments stretched to a minute. She couldn't see Jeremy from where she was, but that also meant Scrope couldn't see her.

She shifted, anxiety rising. She told herself Jeremy was too clever to get caught.

Restless, straining her ears, she waited . . .

She heard a soft thud. A second later, Jeremy pushed through the bushes and crouched beside her.

"Did Scrope see you?" She mouthed the words rather than said them.

He made a show of listening, but no yells or shouts, and thankfully no shots, reached them. He leaned close, whispered in her ear, "He's there, not far back along the bank, but I don't think he saw me." After a moment, he added, "We'll have to stay here until we're sure he's gone." He tipped his head backward, at the rising bank beyond them. "There's no way we can get up that without him seeing us."

She swung her back to the bushes, slid down until she sat, and studied the bank in question. It was less steeply cut than the one they'd jumped down. Beyond the next silt island, a smaller, narrower one covered in coarse grasses and otherwise bare, the bank rose in a series of narrow terraces; climbing it would be easy enough, but while doing so they would be totally exposed. "Do you know what's up there, on this side of the river?"

He shook his head. After a moment, he grimaced. "I checked the connecting roads, and the surroundings of all the roads we were going to take. I didn't check the land over there. We'll have to go up, then find someplace to stop and look at our map. Too noisy, too risky, to try it down here."

She glanced back toward the bank down which they'd come but could see nothing lower than the trees' canopies; the bushes hid them well. Leaning close, she whispered, "Once he's gone, we could find a way back up that side and continue into St. Boswells."

Again he shook his head; this time his expression was grim. "Scrope will have left his horse somewhere near. Once he leaves the river, he'll fetch it—and then he could come upon us fast, on horseback, while we're on foot. We're lucky we've been able to avoid him this time. We don't want to meet him again."

The sight of the pistol in Scrope's hand had changed Jeremy's view of her erstwhile kidnapper from dangerous to insanely dangerous. What manner of man came waving a pistol as he chased an unarmed lady and an almost certainly unarmed gentleman?

More to the point, what did Scrope envision doing with said pistol?

They'd been speaking in tones low enough to be inaudible over the *whoosh* of the river. Two seconds later, Jeremy heard the heavy tramp of boots on the upper bank across from them.

He glanced at Eliza, met her wide eyes. They remained utterly still, protected from Scrope's sight by the thick bushes behind which they crouched.

A minute passed, then Scrope moved on, moved away. The sound of his heavy footsteps faded.

They both let out the breaths they'd been holding.

Another minute passed in silence, then Eliza tensed to rise.

Jeremy clamped a hand on her arm and shook his head at her. Leaning closer, he whispered, "If I were him, I'd draw back and watch, and wait to see if we emerge from hiding. We need to wait for a while before we can risk climbing up and going on."

Eliza searched his eyes, then nodded.

Side by side, they settled on the rocky, sandy ground, to wait out Scrope.

In an ornamental folly perched high above the southern bank of the Tweed just at the point where the river cut a wide loop and headed east, the laird stood, a spyglass to his eye, and roundly cursed Scrope.

"What the damned hell does he think he's doing? Especially with that pistol?"

After a moment, the laird muttered, distinctly savagely, "Why couldn't he have taken the hint when I lost him at Gorebridge?"

He'd been in position since nine o'clock that morning; he was a natural-born hunter—he could always summon patience enough when tracking game. From the vantage point of the folly, located in the gardens of a manor house owned by a family he knew to be in Edinburgh for the Season, he'd been waiting for his fleeing pair to come driving past. Instead, he'd witnessed the entire Scrope-provoked performance.

Initially, he hadn't been able to see Scrope, waiting in hiding on the other side of thick trees on the opposite side of the highway from the folly; if he had, he would have been tempted to do something about the man—removing him to the nearest magistrate's cell, for instance.

Instead, waiting in the perfect position to watch the pair come driving past, so he could then fall in behind them, he'd had to stand and watch Scrope force them off their course.

Again.

"Scrope has become exceedingly tedious." The clipped words did little to alleviate his temper.

He'd had the pair in sight from the moment they'd rushed, on foot, across the highway and dived into the cover of the trees. Thereafter, he'd tracked their progress more through Scrope's blundering down the tree line than by any direct sighting.

But then the fleeing pair had walked out of the trees to the very edge of the bank, separated only by the length of a plowed field from his own position. A sudden fear had gripped him, that, after all his machinations, he might be forced to watch, helpless, as Scrope shot Eliza's gentleman and reclaimed her.

Instead, to his very real relief, the gentleman in question had taken excellent evasive action, jumping down to the riverbed and inducing Eliza to jump down into his arms . . . that she had so readily spoke well for the trust she placed in him.

Which trust appeared to be well-founded. Under the gentleman's guidance, the pair had successfully evaded Scrope.

The laird watched as, having lingered in the area, parading back and forth along the tree line as if expecting his quarry to fall from the branches into his hands, Scrope finally gave up; head hanging, he started trudging back to where he'd left his horse, near where the pair had crossed the highway and rushed into the trees.

Swinging the spyglass back to Eliza and her gentleman, patiently and very wisely remaining concealed on the island, the laird waited . . . another ten minutes passed before, finally, they slowly rose. Carefully, clearly wary, they left their hiding place, leapt across to the next island, then climbed the more graduated eastern bank.

They didn't linger but went quickly on, into the grounds of Dryburgh Abbey. From his vantage point, he watched as they slid like shadows from one tree to the next, eventually reaching the ruined remnants of the old abbey. After a moment of watchful study, they slipped behind a ruined wall and went to ground.

Lowering the glass, the laird considered all he'd seen. Scrope might be a blessed nuisance, but through his interference he'd engineered precisely the sort of situation the laird had been waiting to observe. He'd been able to watch Eliza and her gentleman—watch how they reacted under the threat of real danger, always a revealing situation. And what he'd seen . . .

It was the little things that told the story. Like the way Eliza's gentleman constantly watched over her, seeing to her safety before his own. The way his hand hovered at her back, if he wasn't holding her hand instead, the way he constantly scanned their surroundings for danger. And Eliza trusted him, implicitly and without reserve; she didn't question, didn't argue. She did make suggestions.

The pair interacted with each other in ways the laird recognized; he'd seen exactly the same manner of physical and verbal communications, of togetherness and shared purpose, between his late cousin Mitchell and his wife. Theirs had been a match made in heaven; the laird saw nothing in the way Eliza and her gentleman behaved toward each other to suggest their relationship was any different.

On that score, he could rest easy.

The only complication that remained was Scrope.

The laird looked again in the direction in which Scrope had gone. Having unleashed the man on Eliza, McKinsey couldn't very well turn his back and walk away, much as he might wish to. They might manage to escape Scrope on their own; thus far, the Englishman, whoever he was, had shown an aptitude for thinking on his feet and acting effectively. But if they didn't escape . . .

If Scrope reclaimed Eliza, he'd presumably drag her to Edinburgh and offer her up to him, McKinsey, but at what cost? If Scrope harmed the Englishman, possibly even killed him . . . "What a damned melodramatic tragedy that would be."

The very last thing he wanted was a bride who hated him—who had loved another and lost that other because of a scheme he'd set in motion.

Quite aside from honor, on its own a sharp enough goad, that prospect convinced him he could not yet leave the pair to their own devices, not until he was sure they'd escaped Scrope's desperate and patently determined attacks.

If Scrope hadn't flagrantly disregarded his orders, he'd have been able to head home to the highlands at this point, to start planning his abduction of the Cynster sister that allowing Eliza to escape with her gentleman rendered absolutely necessary. Lips tightening in frustration, the laird raised the spyglass to his eye once more.

The pair hadn't emerged from the abbey ruins. Considering what, if he'd been in their shoes, he would do, he looked further east, searching for a place where they might be able to cross the river.

"Dryburgh Abbey." Jeremy pointed to the spot on the map. "The ruins thereof. That's where we are."

Sitting beside him on the ground in the lee of one of the few sections of walls still standing, Eliza studied the map he'd spread across his knees. "So where should we go from here?" She waved toward the river, now lying to their south. "St. Boswells is just there, on the other side of the river, but how do we cross over?"

"That's a pertinent question." Jeremy leaned over the map. "Another is whether we change our route and instead of going through St. Boswells and then south via Jedburgh, we head east from here, through Kelso to Coldstream, and cross the border there."

She considered the route he traced. "That's much further, and by that route, once we get over the border, we'd have even further to go to reach Wolverstone."

Jeremy humphed. He took another gulp from his water bottle, then stoppered it and stowed it back in the saddle-bag. They'd already demolished the cheese and bread Mrs. Quiggs had kindly pressed on them, saying she knew how young men needed to eat. Had she but known it, young ladies, too; at least Eliza's appetite hadn't dwindled with fear.

Resting his back and shoulders against the cool stone, he glanced at her. She'd seen the pistol Scrope had been waving, had recognized the danger, but other than a heightened tension visible in the way she every now and then checked their surroundings, she hadn't panicked. For which he was truly grateful.

Pulling out his fob-watch, he consulted it. "Nearly one o'clock." He tucked the watch away. Leaning his head back against the wall, he murmured, "It's peaceful here."

She glanced at him, then looked around, surveying the expanse of grass dotted with fallen stones and columns, the trees, many large, that shaded the ruins. "It's hard to appreciate the tranquility while knowing Scrope is somewhere near."

"Hmm." He risked closing his eyes for a moment, eliminating the distraction of the sight of her in an effort to think more clearly. "I wish we knew how Scrope found us. Did the laird send him this way after catching sight of us in Penicuik, knowing that other than the Great North Road, this was the way we'd most likely come? And if Scrope is here, where is the laird? Did we lose him at Penicuik, as we'd thought? Even if we did, has he come to this area, too, to join Scrope? While avoiding Scrope, do we have to keep an eye out to ensure that we avoid the laird, too?"

When she didn't reply, he opened his eyes and found her regarding him.

"That's a lot of questions to which we don't know the answers." She tilted her head. "The only reasonable way forward is to decide on the best route, then forge ahead—and deal with whoever, if, and wherever they rise up in our path."

Lips curving, he inclined his head. "Well put." Lifting the map again, he studied it. "We can't go back and find the gig. I suspect the horse would have stopped before he reached Newtown St. Boswells, but Scrope is almost certainly in that area. We can't risk tangling with him again."

"No. I could happily live my life without setting eyes on him again."

"Amen. So for my money our best route is still via the crossing at Carter Bar. If we can get ahead of both Scrope and the laird, we can barrel along to Wolverstone, and there'll be little chance of them catching us up—the road is more or less straight, and even after we turn for Wolverstone, relatively direct, with no real chance of them taking another route and coming at us from the side. However, the trick will be getting clear of Scrope, and the laird if he's lurking nearby."

"Right, then." She rose, dusting down her breeches, then reached for the other saddlebag. "Let's go into St. Boswells, hire another gig, and get on the road before Scrope, or the laird if he's near, sees us."

Nodding, he folded the map, then got to his feet. While he stowed the map back in his bag, she looked around.

"So, how do we get to St. Boswells?"

Reaching out, he took her hand, then remembered that she was still masquerading as a youth and that someone might see. Squeezing her fingers, he turned her south, toward the river, then released her. "The abbey grounds are contained within the loop of the river, and the town's directly on the other side of the lower, southern, end of the loop. There doesn't seem to have ever been a bridge, but there must have been a crossing of some sort, even if only a ford, to connect the monastic and secular communities. We know it wasn't on the western arm of the loop—the stretch we crossed in fleeing Scrope. So the crossing must be to our south or east. With luck, Scrope assumed we didn't cross the river and is now off searching the fields and roads to the west. There are no roads along this section of the river on either side, so we should be safe skirting the bank and searching for a way across."

Side by side they walked through the abbey church, pausing without a word to take in the single soaring arch rising high behind where the altar would have been, then they continued on, through a gap in the side wall and down a long, slight slope. The going was easy. The sun shone fitfully, warm when it struck through the branches of the huge, old trees. Eventually they reached a line of denser trees and bushes beyond which the river flowed swiftly on.

Thick shrubs edged the top of the bank, giving them excellent cover as they tramped along above the southern section of the river's loop, traveling west to east. All along that stretch, the banks were high and steep, almost vertical, and from what they could see, the river ran deep.

There was nowhere to cross along that stretch.

Pulling back, they angled through increasingly dense woodland, striking out for the eastern arm of the loop. Even before they came within sight of the bank, the ground started to slope downward and the vegetation thinned. "This should be it." Jeremy lengthened his stride. "Our crossing."

Sure enough, when they reached the river, they found a shallow ford. Designed for carts or horses, the surface lay beneath six inches of swiftly running water, but a line of flat-topped stones—looking suspiciously like stones from the abbey ruins—had been laid in the riverbed along one edge of the ford. They were some distance apart, but large enough for Eliza to jump from one to the next.

They both reached the other side without getting their feet wet, and shared a grin.

Resettling the saddlebag over his shoulder, Jeremy looked up, around, then nudged Eliza's arm. "That way."

There were a few farmhouses dotting the fields before them, but the roofs of St. Boswells now lay some way to their right.

As they walked along the country lane, more a cart track than a road, he said, "Scrope will be concentrating on the highway end of town—the highway sweeps past on the western side. We're walking in from the opposite direction, so all of St. Boswells lies between us and the highway and, we hope, Scrope. With any luck, we'll be able to find an inn and hire a gig, then slip out and start our race south before he has any idea we're near."

"Hmm." Eliza walked on, constantly scanning the way ahead. She was more concerned with avoiding Scrope than she was with reaching Wolverstone. Her priorities had changed the instant she'd seen the pistol Scrope had been waving. While she would be happy to reach safety tonight, it was more important that she and Jeremy reached safety together. She had no fear that Scrope would shoot her. It was Jeremy, her rescuer, Scrope would have in his sights.

The realization had shaken her more than she'd expected, but, as Jeremy was—quite clearly, to her mind—her intended hero, then she supposed she'd have to get used to being subject to such fearful concerns regarding him.

She certainly wasn't about to let Scrope harm him, take him from her, or to in any way interfere with their future.

A species of belligerent determination had her firmly in its grip as they reached a larger road and turned toward the town.

They trudged on through the early afternoon. Cottages became more frequent, increasingly bordering the road, but the town wasn't large. Reaching a wide curve and starting around it, they saw the usual shops and businesses of a small country town lining the road ahead.

They slowed, both increasingly cautious. Increasingly wary.

Ten paces ahead of them, a shop door opened. The tinkle of its bell halted them in their tracks.

A man stepped out, his back to them as he pulled the shop door closed behind him.

Giving them an excellent view of him from the rear.

Black-haired. Tall. Very tall. Massive shoulders. Long, strong legs.

A topcoat that, in reserved tones, declared its owner's station in life was teamed with buckskin breeches and well-made riding boots.

Without glancing their way, the laird walked, with an easy, long-legged stride that screamed of unassailable confidence, further on, angling across the road.

Not daring to so much as breathe, Eliza dragged her panicked gaze from him and realized she and Jeremy stood beside a narrow alley running between two shops. Sinking her fingers into Jeremy's sleeve, she gripped, tugged, and stepped carefully sideways into the alley.

After a fractional hesitation, Jeremy slid silently into the alley alongside her. Once safely concealed, he peered out.

Eliza leaned back against the alley wall and silently gave thanks. If they'd been half a minute faster, the laird would have stepped out of the shop on top of them.

Jeremy drew back again. Like her, he slumped against the wall. "He's gone into the hotel just along the street."

She swallowed. "Well, we can't go that way, then—on down the street."

"No." Reaching into the saddlebag, Jeremy drew out the map. "Not only that"—he could hear the grimness infusing his voice—"we won't be able to hire a gig here, either. If he's been doing the rounds of the hotels and inns . . ." Glancing up, he met Eliza's eyes. "He saw us in Penicuik. If he's given people a good enough description of us, then as soon as we walk in and ask for a gig, they'll keep us there and send someone to fetch him."

She sighed. "I was going to suggest we might see if we could get a better look at him, but it's too dangerous, isn't it?"

"Much." He unfolded the map. "Aside from him being half my weight again, if all the signs read true and he is a damned Scottish nobleman, then falling into his hands would be the worst thing we could do."

"He might claim I was his runaway ward and cart me off to his highland castle while leaving you in some magistrate's cell?"

"And that's the best outcome we could hope for." Jeremy held the map so she could see it. "Here's where we are." He pointed to the spot. "Here's where we want to go." He pointed to the road south of the border, just beyond Carter Bar. "The highway runs directly from here to there, but with both the laird and Scrope patrolling it, I can't see how we can risk staying on it. If the laird is here, keeping watch, chances are Scrope has already gone south."

Eliza grasped the map, brought it closer so she could make out the finer lines, the lanes and tracks. "We know there's no sense going east—by that route Wolverstone's simply too far. But . . ." Angling her head, she traced a route with her eyes. "Could we, do you think, head west? Down this lane"—she pointed—"to Selkirk, and then hire another gig there." She glanced up and met Jeremy's eyes. "Neither Scrope nor the laird will expect us to go that way."

Jeremy frowned. "But—" He broke off and bent closer, studying the map more acutely. "Ah—I see."

"Precisely." Eliza felt faintly triumphant. "From Selkirk, we can drive to Hawick—if they do happen to pick up our trail and think we're making for Carlisle so much the better. But at Hawick we can turn off the main road, and take the lane to Bonchester Bridge, and on."

"All the way to Carter Bar." Jeremy raised the map, angling it to the light that shafted into the alley. After a moment, he nodded. "You're right. That, indeed, is the only reasonable way forward. I hadn't even noticed that tiny lane, but it'll keep us off the Jedburgh Road until a bare few yards of the border." He met Eliza's eyes. "I can't imagine either the laird or Scrope will be hanging about the border itself. They'll want to stop us ahead of it, out of sight of any soldiers who might be quartered there. That close to the border, even if we haven't actually crossed into England, we could still summon Wolverstone. His name carries weight enough for us to be safe."

She smiled. "Excellent. So"—she tipped her head down the alley, away from the main street they'd walked in along—"let's work our way around to the lane to Selkirk."

It took them another hour of being extremely careful, of hiding behind hedges, searching all around before they crossed any roads, exercising extreme caution when they finally raced—thick bushes to thick bushes—across the highway itself, but their luck held. Neither the laird nor Scrope spotted them; no one came thundering after them.

The sun hung in the sky before them when, having finally gained the lane to Selkirk, they set out at a brisk pace. They soon found their way lined with hawthorn hedges; dense and in full leaf, with the lane gently wending this way, then that, the hedges quickly hid them from anyone following.

Half a mile or more on, Jeremy halted. "The hedges hide us, but they also keep us from spotting anyone following us." He nodded to a small grassy knoll crowned with less dense scrub. "I'd rather play safe. Let's take a short break and watch the road."

They did. They watched for half an hour, but no horseman or carriage came by.

"We're safe." Eliza stood and dusted off her breeches. She looked down at Jeremy and smiled. "Come on—it's Selkirk for us." He rose with an answering grin. As together they strode down the knoll, back toward the road, she added, a smile flirting about her lips, "And once there, who knows what we'll find?"

In midafternoon, the laird left the hotel at which he'd stayed in St. Boswells. Mounted on Hercules, he rode east, out along the country road, then turned left into the lane the helpful barman who'd recently come on duty had described.

The lane led directly north, ending within sight of the Tweed's banks. Dismounting and leading Hercules forward and to the left, the laird discovered the old ford easily enough—along with the tracks of two people, one boot large and heavier, the other much smaller and lighter, heading toward the town.

The river water had long since dried out of the boot prints.

"They've been quick enough." He'd made an educated guess that despite Scrope's actions, the pair would attempt to get back on the highway to Jedburgh. They weren't that far from the border, and the alternative route via Kelso and Coldstream was significantly out of what seemed to be their chosen way.

While he was pleased to have his reasoning borne out, he was less happy that he was, it seemed, already hours behind them.

Remounting Hercules, he followed the tracks back toward the town. Increasingly slowly; with the ground hardening and the verges thick, the closer he got to the town, the harder it was to be sure the tracks he was following were the ones he wanted.

He thought he'd lost them in the main street, but by sheer luck he glanced down a narrow ginnel and saw clear evidence, imprinted in the softer, damper earth, that his fugitive pair had stood there for some time.

The proximity of the ginnel to the coffeehouse where he'd first inquired as to a possible river crossing, and had subsequently been directed to the hotel across the street, told its own tale.

"Damn!" Stalking back to Hercules, he swung up to the gelding's back. They'd seen him. And, of course, not knowing that all he now wished was to see them safe back over the border and free from Scrope's pursuit, they'd fled in the opposite direction.

They'd walked away from the main street, down the ginnel and out the other side, but Hercules was too wide of girth to take the same path. Swallowing his curses, he turned the big gelding and rode back out along the road, to circle the block and pick up the errant pair's trail.

An hour and a half later, utterly disgusted by the latest turn of events, the laird sat atop Hercules at the junction of the highway with the main road through St. Boswells and debated his next move.

He had no idea where his fleeing pair had gone.

He might be an expert tracker, but he still needed some tracks—some hints at least—to follow, but the roads and lanes in this district had hardened with the sun and no longer held impressions sufficiently well for him to distinguish his quarry's boot prints from the imprints left by the many other boot-wearers in and around the country town.

The pair had left the ginnel and headed around, through the minor lanes running off and parallel to the main road in the general direction of the highway, but beyond that, he knew no more. He'd checked the obvious places, casting a wide net over and around the various possible minor routes they might have taken toward Jedburgh, even riding east as far as Maxton and the lane leading across Ancrum Moor, but he'd found nothing.

On the off-chance they'd gone back for whatever transport they'd used to reach the highway earlier, he'd ridden north, back along the highway, to the lane from Newtown St. Boswells. Just inside the lane, he'd found evidence, not of the vanished pair but of a horse following close behind a gig.

Scrope, he surmised, had gone back and found a gig—presumably the one Eliza and her gentleman had used to get that far and had abandoned on spotting Scrope ahead of them. Searching further, he'd found sufficient signs to verify his reading of what had occurred to send the pair rushing through the trees toward the river. On finding the gig, Scrope had tied his horse to its back and driven south.

McKinsey had followed the gig and the telltale closely following hoofprints back to the junction at which he presently sat. Scrope's trail led on. Scrope had removed the pair's ability to travel south at speed, at least until they could find another gig, and had gone on to wait for them at Jedburgh.

Nudging Hercules forward, the laird cantered a hundred yards south. Reining Hercules to a halt again, he looked west down the lane to Selkirk.

If he'd been Eliza and her gentleman, he would have gone that way.

Alternatively, they might have circled back into St. Boswells and sought shelter for the night with some cottager there; if so, short of knocking on every door and asking, locating them would be difficult.

He could head out along the lane to the west, and possibly somewhere along it he might find their tracks, and be able to follow them on.

Possibly. Against that, he had Scrope's tracks clearly before him.

His purpose—the only purpose keeping him in the lowlands—was to appease the demands of his honor and his conscience by preserving Eliza and her gentleman from Scrope's misguided, and potentially malicious, attentions. He could do that just as easily, possibly more so, by following Scrope and ensuring his erstwhile henchman did the pair no harm.

Much simpler.

Courtesy of Scrope's actions that day, he'd already reached the point of feeling confident in otherwise leaving Eliza's safety and care to her gentleman-protector—another Englishman, no less.

Shaking his head at the irony in that, with a flick of the reins the laird sent Hercules cantering on, leaving St. Boswells and the lane to Selkirk behind. He knew of a nice, comfortable inn in Jedburgh; with any luck, Scrope would stop in Jedburgh for the night.

Chapter Thirteen

I t was late afternoon when Jeremy and Eliza walked over a rise and saw the roofs of Selkirk before them. The ribbon of a major road snaked out of the town, then ran along the nearer edge of the settlement, right to left, leading south to Hawick.

Halting, Jeremy drew out the map and studied it. "Hawick's more than twelve miles from Selkirk." He grimaced. "It's a bit late, but we have two options. We could walk into Selkirk, hire a gig, drive to Hawick, then find some place there to spend the night, or"—raising his head, he looked toward Selkirk—"we could stay somewhere in Selkirk, then set off tomorrow."

Eliza didn't need to ponder her choice; what with fleeing Scrope, avoiding the laird, and the last few hours' brisk walking, she was starting to flag. "Selkirk and tomorrow have my vote."

Jeremy nodded. "Mine, too." Refolding the map, he tucked it away. "We seem to have successfully lost our pursuers, and whether tomorrow we start our run for the border from Selkirk or Hawick will make no real difference—we'll still reach the border by tomorrow afternoon. There's no real advantage in pushing on today." He met Eliza's eyes, smiled and waved her on. "Selkirk, it is."

They strode down the last stretch of the lane, debated, then crossed the main road and continued down a lane that promised to lead more directly into Selkirk proper.

Their judgment proved sound; the lane led them to the

high street, which in turn opened into the marketplace. Once again they'd entered a town on market day; there were dozens of small stalls and booths clogging the irregularly shaped space at the center of the town. The crowds still thronging the area allowed them to stand back and take stock of the two inns at either end of the marketplace, and the tavern along one side, without attracting undue attention.

"I don't think the tavern qualifies for our list of possible places to find a room, but"—Jeremy grimaced—"with all the people in town for the market, the inns might well be full."

"Hmm." The sight of a stall selling clothes had brought a thought that had been lurking in the back of Eliza's mind to the fore. "I wonder . . ." Catching Jeremy's eyes, she directed his gaze to the clothing stall. When he looked, then glanced back at her, she arched her brows. "Perhaps we should buy a nice plain gown for my twin sister? As a present. Then we might walk back to the church just back there, which is sure to be deserted at this hour, and then . . . well, if Scrope or the laird come searching this way, they're going to ask about a gentleman and a youth, aren't they?"

Jeremy's slow smile warmed her. "That's a brilliant idea."

"Well, then." Smiling herself, she started across the cobbles toward the clothing stall. "Let's see what we can find that might fit my sister."

They bought a simple petticoat and a plain cambric gown in a shade of brown that would, Eliza informed Jeremy as they walked back to the church, make her blend into any crowd. Personally, he doubted it; without the hat she'd been wearing as part of her disguise, her gleaming hair would catch anyone's eye, as would her fine features, features that would make it difficult for her to pass as anything other than the well-bred young lady she was.

Keeping watch in the nave while she changed in the vestry, he considered that point. When she finally emerged, retransformed into a woman, he pushed away from the wall against which he'd been leaning—and stared.

The gown fitted her well, its simplicity only emphasizing her height, her sleek curves, the regalness of her posture. Rather than dim the brightness of her hair, the plain brown of the gown made the heavy waves appear a richer, deeper shade of honey-gold, made her hazel eyes appear more vivid.

It wasn't that he'd forgotten what she looked like in skirts so much as he'd forgotten what the impact she had on him in that guise felt like.

Like he'd been clouted over the head.

He shook his brains back into place as she came toward him, still, he noticed, striding quite freely.

She saw his gaze slide down to her feet and grinned. "I know I've still got my boots on, of course, but I'm going to have to remind myself to glide like a lady and not swagger like a youth anymore."

He merely nodded and reached for the saddlebag she'd taken into the vestry with her. It now bulged with the clothes and hat she'd stuffed into it. "I'd better take that."

She handed the bag over, then, with a happy little sigh, swung the cloak she'd carried over one arm about her shoulders. "I feel so much . . . well, lighter, now I can breathe freely again."

He remembered the silk band she'd had him help her retie about her breasts that morning, thought of her unraveling it, recalled what she looked like without it . . .

Hauling breath into lungs distinctly constricted even without any binding, he dragged his gaze upward from the relevant part of her anatomy and fixed it on her face. "Now you're a lady again, when we get a room—"

"We'll need to pretend to be man and wife." She nodded and reached for his arm. "But that should only make our new guise even less conspicuous, don't you think?"

"Yes, I do." He walked with her to the head of the aisle but halted there. "Which is why I think you should wear this." He held out his hand, the signet ring he normally wore on his little finger resting on his palm. "It'll make matters easier and bolster our disguise."

Without the slightest hesitation, she picked up the ring. She slid it onto the appropriate finger, held it up, then showed him. "It fits."

He glanced at the ring—one that had belonged to his late father, which he thought of as very much his own—now circling her finger, then looked at her. Met her gaze.

Her lips curved, just a little, as if she knew what he was thinking. "Thank you."

He hesitated, words crowding his mind, but now was not the time. He tipped his head toward the town. "We'd better get on and find somewhere to stay."

Smiling more definitely, she slid her arm into his and waited until he settled the saddlebags on his other shoulder, then they walked out of the church and back along the high street.

They stopped at the first inn. Jeremy arranged for a gig to be waiting for them the next morning, but when he glanced into the inn itself, he drew back. "Too many people." *Too many rough-looking men.* He steered Eliza back into the inn yard.

His gaze fell on one of the ostlers, a middle-aged man, waiting by the entrance to the stable. "Hmm." He guided Eliza toward the man; she'd put up her hood, hiding her hair. "Try to look timid and shy."

She duly dipped her head and hung back a trifle, as if slipping into his shadow.

Drawing nearer the ostler, he nodded to the man. "Can you recommend anywhere, other than the inns and tavern, where my wife and I might find a quiet bed for the night?"

The ostler returned his nod politely and directed them to a lodging house across the marketplace. "Mrs. Wallace is a widder—keeps her rooms neat and clean, and she'll do you a good dinner, too. Good cook, she is, and a nice woman, too.

You'll find her sign up on the corner of yon lane there—she's three doors down on the right."

"Thank you." Jeremy tossed the man a coin, then turned and escorted Eliza across the cobbles and into the lane.

Mrs. Wallace and her lodging house proved to be as excellent as advertised. The room the widow showed them to was small, but airy and cheerful, with chintz curtains at the window and a matching counterpane on the brass-framed bed. After supplying them with towels and an ewer of warm water, Mrs. Wallace left them to make themselves comfortable. "Dinner will be less than half an hour, my dears," she warned as she turned back to the stairs. "I ring a bell so all my lodgers know."

"We'll come down as soon as we hear it." With a grateful smile, Eliza shut the door, then turned to survey the room. Jeremy carried the heavy ewer to the dressing table; he'd earlier slung their bags on the end of the bed.

Crossing to the bed, she set the towels down beside the bags, then sat and bounced lightly. The mattress was thick, the quilt beneath the counterpane stuffed full of feathers. Her gaze fell on her left hand. She stared for a moment, then raised her hand and studied the ring on her finger.

"It worked," Jeremy said.

She looked across to see him turn from placing the ewer in its matching basin.

He met her eyes. "Mrs. Wallace looked for the ring. Once she saw it, she was happy."

Eliza nodded. "She believes we're a married couple—she didn't question that at all." Returning her gaze to the ring, she murmured, "It's almost like we're . . . practicing."

Sliding his hands into his pockets, Jeremy halted at the end of the bed. He studied her for a moment, then said, "We're not going to think too much, remember?"

She looked up, met his gaze. "Yes, I know." She paused, then went on, "And I think you're right—we need to . . . just be. Just let ourselves be as we would be, without considering the expectations of society. We seem to be doing perfectly well without . . ." She gestured.

"Without bringing society's notions and demands, or those of anyone else, into our equation?"

"Yes. Precisely." She searched his eyes. "We don't need interference from anyone else. We're working things out between ourselves . . ." She tilted her head, her eyes on his. "Aren't we?"

Ruthlessly suppressing the unease that curled through him whenever he thought of what was evolving between them, of just where his brilliant notion of simply letting what would be, be, was leading them, he nodded. "We are."

She smiled; in contrast to him, she seemed entirely at ease. "Good. So we'll just continue as we have been—and then see where we've got to once we reach Wolverstone." Rising, she headed for the dressing table. "I suppose I'd better make use of that water while it's still warm."

Lips lifting, he waved her on. "Ladies first." As she passed him, and his eyes took in her honey-gold hair, his senses teased by the faint scent he now recognized as hers, he turned, following her with his eyes, and amended, "At least when there's no danger involved."

She laughed and continued to the dressing table.

Inwardly wondering just what would eventually be born of this curious wooing, this courtship of circumstance—perhaps, given they were in Scotland, the whole business might more correctly be viewed as a handfasting?—he sat on the bed to wait his turn.

Dinner was an event that focused their minds. When asked from where they hailed, and where they were headed, Eliza glanced at Jeremy; he stepped in and spun a tale about them living on the outskirts of Edinburgh, having moved there for the work, but having to return to England in a rush to visit Eliza's mother, who was poorly.

But the rabbit pie was excellent, and their fellow lodgers an unthreatening group—two clerks from nearby legal offices, and one of the town's watchmen. The conversation remained general, largely centering around happenings in the town, until Mrs. Wallace removed the last scraps of her apple crumble and shooed them all out of her dining room.

The watchman set out to visit the tavern. The two clerks ducked their heads politely to Eliza and Jeremy and headed for the inn.

Jeremy arched a brow at Eliza.

She met his gaze, then smiled, slid her arm in his, and turned toward the stairs. "We should get as early a start as possible, shouldn't we?"

Climbing the stairs, he smiled. Reaching their door, he opened it and held it for her; he waited until he'd shut it to say, "The earlier in the day that we reach Carter Bar and cross into England, the happier I'll be."

She glanced at him. "I thought you said Scrope wouldn't be at the border itself?"

"I don't think he will be, but . . ." He grimaced as he joined her at the side of the bed. "The damned man has forced us to detour enough to lose a day—we should have been at Wolverstone tonight at the latest."

Her eyes on his, she said, "But there have been consolations."

"Perhaps. Or, more accurately, we've taken advantage of the opportunities"—he watched her step closer, grip his lapels and rise up on her toes—"his actions have presented us with."

From close range, from beneath lids already lowered, she captured his gaze, then breathed, her words a tantalizing waft of heat over his lips, "We're not thinking, remember?"

Then she kissed him, delicately, evocatively, cindering any doubt he might have entertained that she wouldn't be intent on seizing their unexpected extra night together to further advance her understanding.

To further explore the passion that rose so readily to her call.

In him, and in herself.

Eliza was fascinated, utterly enthralled by the appetite she sensed behind his so-contained, so-correct scholarly mien. Last night, she'd been so caught up in the experience, in the sensations and revelations, that she hadn't had any part of her awareness to spare for him. To gain any real idea of how the moment had affected him, whether the satiation, the satisfaction, the simple pleasure that had spread so completely through her had been equally deep, equally pervasive, for him.

She wanted to find out. To use the unexpected opportunity, this unexpected extra night, to explore that, gauge that. To learn the truth of what might be between them, from his perspective as well as hers.

So she had no hesitation in stating her need and inviting him to fulfill it. To let desire rise up through her body, let it spread beneath her skin and resonate with her heartbeat as she pressed her lips to his.

And tempted.

Beckoned and lured.

Then he accepted her invitation, closed his hands about her breasts, and she suddenly had to break from the kiss and let her head fall back on a gasp.

As she rode the crest of rising pleasure.

A pleasure that welled, swelled, and swept her on.

She let it, went with it, ready and eager to see where he would lead her, what he would show her tonight, yet some small sliver of her mind remained attuned to him, watched and catalogued all the little signs.

Like the tension that invested his features, the hard edge rising passion lent the austere planes, the passionate plundering of his lips and tongue as he, button by button, garment by garment, stripped her. Bared her.

To the moonlight spearing through the uncurtained window.

The silvery glow bathed her body in pearlescent light, liming limbs impossibly graceful, gilding her lush curves and erotically shading her hollows; Jeremy could barely breathe, lungs tight, constricted, as with his eyes he drank in her beauty. As with his hands he sculpted and paid homage, as with his lips he traced and savored, and devotion, heavy and real, grew and burgeoned within him.

Anchored him. In the here and now, in the whirling maelstrom of their passions.

His intent was clear in his mind; to give her all she wished, all she wanted—fulfill every desire she had—but to rein himself back and keep himself from falling into the seething cauldron of ravenous desire that surged and swelled between them.

As he hadn't been able to last night.

It wasn't that he imagined she had any real desire to rip his wits away, not even any true conception that she might. His wish to remain wholly captain of his own will tonight was driven more by the need to reassure himself that he could— that he could engage with her, fulfill her hunger, bring her to completion and find his own in her, and still be in control.

As he usually was.

As he always had been with all his previous lovers.

But they had never touched him and made him burn, had never taken him into their arms and made him lose touch with reason.

He was a scholar, a man of rational thought and cautious, intelligent action. Last night, for long moments he'd been beyond the reach of will and mind, suborned by, submerged in, a different reality, but that had to have been because the situation in its entirety had been new to him. Novel and distracting.

Last night, he'd been distracted. Tonight, he intended to

remain fully in command, and that, he reasoned, would set the tone for their future engagements.

And then he'd be safe. All would be well.

That had been his conclusion, but he'd reasoned without her.

Without the sudden boldness with which she, naked and feylike in the silvery moonlight, gripped his jacket and peeled it from him.

Without the sultry demand with which she opened his shirt, then, eyes on his face, spread her hands and devoured.

Devoured by touch, and then by taste.

Razed his control with sensation.

Head falling back, he fought to hold on to some semblance of restraint as she undressed him, freely caressing, exploring, learning . . . every little touch that made him shudder.

Until he stood in the moonlight, as naked as she, while her hands drifted, increasingly bold . . .

Dragging in a breath, desperate to create some mental distance for long enough to find his mind, he grasped her shoulders and tipped, tumbling them both onto the bed.

She laughed and rolled with him, but when he would have rolled her beneath him and filched the reins, she wrestled and insisted, and the lead passed back and forth, with first him, then her, in the ascendancy, madly pushing the other on . . .

Flames erupted and raced over them, until they were panting, skins damp, gasping, grasping, desperate and urgent, and far beyond thought.

She parted her thighs in wordless, mindless, abandoned invitation. With one powerful thrust, he sheathed himself in her—and the conflagration roared.

And vaporized all intentions, cindered all caution, razed all reservations.

Whipped on by unrelenting passion, he rode her hard, and she clung and urged him on. Openly demanding, writhing beneath him.

As if in shedding her youth's attire, she'd converted into a woman in a far deeper sense than simply in appearance.

As if in exchanging breeches for skirts, she'd released, unleashed, a vibrant, sensual woman—one she was determined to let have her way.

To let that sensual wanton infuse her, transform her, conquer her—and willfully conquer him, too.

He couldn't hold against her pull, against the thundering demand to join with her in the madness, the fury, the escalating mind-numbing pleasure of their flat-out, desperate race to completion—because that demand came from within him, not from her.

She was the lure, the potent invitation, but the acceptance came from somewhere deep inside. She connected to him, to some deeply buried essence of him, and effortlessly called it forth.

And he could do nothing but surrender. Linking his fingers with hers, slanting his lips over hers, letting his tongue tangle wildly with hers, whole and complete in a way that rocked him to his soul he danced with her, joined with her as the swirling currents of crystalline passion and searing desire swept them up and on.

Then shattered them. Pierced them, racked them, and broke them, then tossed them into a sea of oblivion where bliss rolled in, enfolded, and soothed them.

Filled them with glowing golden delight, then gently laid them down on some distant shore, satiated, satisfied, beyond replete.

Wrapped in each other's arms.

Far from the crisp, clean sheets he'd been looking forward to stretching out between, the laird found himself settling for the night on a pile of straw.

Scrope, blast the man, hadn't halted in Jedburgh. Or rather he'd stopped for a pint but hadn't stayed. Instead, he'd driven on in the gig he'd confiscated, his horse pacing behind, and stopped for the night in a tiny tavern in the equally tiny hamlet of Camptown.

Roughly midway between Jedburgh and the border, Camptown boasted no other place a traveler might lay his head, and the tavern was far too tiny for there to be any chance of the laird putting up there while avoiding Scrope's notice.

Up until that point he'd been considering simply overhauling Scrope, reading him the riot act and sending him on his way, dallying long enough to see his fleeing pair go safely past in whatever conveyance they managed to arrange. Then he could head directly north for the highlands.

That plan had grown increasingly attractive.

Until Scrope had stopped in Camptown.

Why Camptown?

That was a question McKinsey couldn't answer—to which he couldn't remotely imagine an answer. There were far more comfortable places Scrope could have stopped. Why there? What was the man planning?

Settling deeper into the straw in the hayloft of the barn in the field opposite the tavern, his arms crossed behind his head, his gaze fixed on the dusty rafters above, the laird re-examined the current situation.

His plan of chasing Scrope off had one serious flaw; he'd already done it once, in Edinburgh, and it hadn't worked.

Scrope, it seemed, was fixated on completing his mission despite having been dismissed. To have followed the pair this far—to have followed *him,* his recent employer who had in no uncertain terms dismissed him, in order to pick up the pair's trail—bore witness to Scrope's unbending, unswerving drive to seize his target, regardless of any alteration in circumstance.

If he again attempted to send Scrope packing . . . what was to stop the man from circling around, waiting until Eliza and her gentleman passed by somewhere near the border crossing—as they would at some point have to do—and then following the pair on into England?

He himself couldn't afford the time to follow the fleeing couple and play nursemaid all the way to London.

But once the pair came trotting past . . . if he *then* delayed Scrope and kept him from following them in reasonable time, Scrope would lose their trail.

That was what he needed to do—delay Scrope enough to allow Eliza and her rescuer to race far enough ahead. Far enough to reach some place of safety; he'd seen enough of Eliza's gentleman to be reasonably confident that he would have some place in mind, and make a beeline for it, getting the pair of them off the main roads in the process.

So he would wait until the pair appeared, then collar Scrope and hold him back. An hour or two should see Eliza and her gentleman safely away.

And with any luck, tomorrow would see the job done. Wherever the pair was, St. Boswells, Jedburgh, or anywhere in between, on horse or in a gig, they had a straight and rapid run to the border.

Tomorrow it should be.

And then he would ride north, home, to his castle.

Decision made, his mind shifted to the increasingly urgent arrangements he would need to make as soon as he reached home.

The prospect hung over him like a black cloud, but there was no help for it; he'd been too nice in arranging for others to effect the kidnap of the two elder Cynster girls, telling himself that if he himself hadn't been their kidnapper, he would stand a better chance of persuading them to aid him in return for all and everything he would lavish on them once they married.

The truth was he'd been deeply, fundamentally, rebelliously resistant over being forced by his mother to stoop so low as to kidnap any female. To dirty his hands in such a way. To sully his honor.

Honor above all. The family motto. He hadn't wanted to be the one to bring his name into disrepute.

All very well, but honor wouldn't keep his people safe, and courtesy of the failed attempts to seize Heather and now Eliza, he was left with a stark and unavoidable, last and final chance.

The one option he'd wanted to avoid.

He, personally, would have to kidnap Angelica Cynster.

From the first, he'd set his sights on dealing—treating—with either Heather or Eliza. At twenty-five and twenty-four years old, they were nearer in age to his own thirty-one, were more or less on the shelf marriage-wise, and should therefore, he'd reasoned, have been more amenable to rational discussion and an amicable arrangement.

He'd seen both Heather and Eliza years ago, during the years he'd spent in London before his father's last illness had called him back to the highlands. He could vaguely recall attending balls at which they'd been present, but he'd never sought any closer acquaintance, had never ventured to ask them for a dance; in those days, he'd been looking not for a wife but rather for a good time, and as bright-eyed young ladies, the Cynster princesses had held little interest for him.

Not then. Now . . . he would have infinitely preferred to have been able to deal with Heather, the eldest, or if not her, Eliza.

Angelica, the youngest sister, was an entirely different kettle of female.

He'd never met her—she hadn't been out when he'd been on the town—but he'd learned enough in a very short time to have fixed on her elder sisters as his better options. For a start, Angelica was a bare twenty-one years old; he had little doubt that she would still possess the starry-eyed expectations of a young and very tonnish young lady, especially when it came to the subject of marriage.

Rescripting her expectations . . . would certainly prove a harder task, a higher hurdle, than would have been the case with either of her sisters. But more than that, at twenty-one

Angelica was far from her last prayers; asking her to do what was needed to save his people would feel much less fair than it would have with her sisters.

But he no longer had the luxury of indulging in such nice sentiments—not now he'd stepped back from interfering between Heather and her savior, Breckenridge, and Eliza and her gentleman, whoever he was. He knew why he had; he couldn't—simply could not—stomach the notion of forcing any woman who already loved another to make do with him, to take his hand rather than that of her true knight, her true beloved.

That wasn't romantic but sensible; he needed a woman who would stand by his side and work with him, not a well-born lady who would hate and resent him for the rest of their days.

So Angelica it would now have to be, even if, by all accounts, she was . . . fiery. As fiery as the red and copper glints in her hair. Which, given his own temperament, did not auger well for a calm and well-ordered future—not for him or her.

Of the three sisters, she was the one he hadn't wanted to go near.

Had, from the very inception of his plan, all but crossed off his list.

Fate, it appeared, had had other plans.

The way matters now stood, he had no choice. It was kidnap Angelica Cynster, or lose his home, his lands, and see his people dispossessed and turned out into the world with not much more than the clothes on their backs.

The highland clearances had wreaked havoc with the clans. His own clan, the one he now headed, had largely escaped the turmoil, thanks to the inaccessibility of the glen and his grandfather's political canniness in playing all sides off, each one against the others.

The old man had been an expert juggler; it was his legacy

the laird was now so focused on protecting. His father had done little, either way, other than to make the deal that now hung over his head.

That deal itself wasn't the problem; he had been a witness to it, had considered it a fair and sensible arrangement at the time, and still did.

It was his mother's hijacking of the ancient goblet that stood at the heart of that deal that was the earthquake rocking the ground beneath his feet.

He stared up through the waning moonlight, not truly seeing the roof above his head.

With every step he'd taken, every move he'd made in his plan to reclaim the goblet, he'd questioned his direction, yet each questioning had left him more committed, not less.

Now . . . he didn't even mentally hesitate over the notion of traveling to London, into the lions' den, and kidnapping Angelica.

Because there was no other way.

He would have to do it himself; he couldn't risk anything going awry, not with only her available to place in his mother's scales, to weigh against the goblet.

She, Angelica, was his last chance.

And if he was damned for seizing her, so be it; he would be even more damned if he didn't.

As had been the system since time immemorial, his clan depended on him personally, on the clan lands he held, and the clan business he administered.

If he failed, if he didn't have the goblet to complete the arrangement set in place by his father six months before the old man's death, then there would be no more clan.

He wouldn't lose just the castle, the glen, and the loch; he would lose for everyone the very thing that made them who they were.

Clan had stood at the heart of highland life for centuries untold; it was a spider's web of connections and support that linked everyone who shared his name or blood and held them within its protections.

Clan was the very essence of their life, the beat in their blood, the song in their souls.

Without it, they would die.

He, his countless dependents. The two young boys he now called his own.

Clan was what he stood for, what he represented, and just like his forebears, he would unhesitatingly, without thought or reservation, give his life to protect it, to ensure it lived on.

If not directly through him, then through his heir, the older of those two little boys.

Better he lived; he had no intention of dying. All in all, he did not doubt that his underlying determination would carry him through whatever was to come.

For his clan to survive, he could not fail.

That was all there was to it.

Chapter Fourteen

J eremy and Eliza drove out of Selkirk the following morning, the very picture of a young couple off to visit family. After providing them with a fortifying breakfast, Mrs. Wallace had seen them off from her door, and the ostlers at the inn had had the gig ready and waiting, a neat roan between the shafts. Beside Jeremy, Eliza sat savoring the sunshine as he set the horse trotting along the high street. They passed the church as the town's bell pealed nine o'clock.

The road to Hawick was well surfaced and the scenery pleasant enough. Eliza lifted her face to the light breeze, marveling at the sense of simple happiness that suffused her. She couldn't recall ever experiencing such a sense of inner peace. Of inner calmness and order.

She slanted a glance at Jeremy, managing the ribbons with a ready competency at odds with her scholarly view of him. Her earlier scholarly view of him—that was another aspect that had changed. Dramatically.

Lips lifting, she looked ahead. He might still be a scholar in some ways, but as she'd discovered and had last night confirmed, he was everything she wanted in a man. Some part of her tonnish female self was still faintly astonished by that, but there was no longer any doubt in her mind; regardless of whatever else her strange kidnapping brought about, through it she had found her hero.

She could almost find it in her to thank Scrope and the mysterious laird.

The gig's wheels and the horse's hooves played a repetitive tune as they bowled along. Spring had finally laid its hand on Scotland, setting hedgerows blooming and countless wayside plants springing up along the verges. Thrushes trilled and larks swooped. Shading her eyes, she saw a hawk hovering over a field, searching for prey.

Jeremy didn't speak, but neither did she; their silence wasn't awkward but comfortable. Companionable. Neither were given to pointless conversation, and while with another gentleman she might have felt compelled to fill the silence simply to be polite, with Jeremy she felt no such pressing need.

Another boon allowing her to relax, and, as they'd agreed, simply be.

Be herself. For the first time in her life, she felt she was starting to get a firm sense of who she truly was. Of the woman she could be.

The journey to Hawick was unremarkable, but a little way before the town they were slowed to a walk by a string of farm carts traveling in convoy. By the time they got free of the congestion and trotted into Hawick itself, it was heading toward noon.

Jeremy glanced at Eliza, for an instant watched her face, her serene expression as she looked about the town. She was fleeing a determined kidnapper and an unknown nobleman, yet she appeared . . . content.

He felt the same.

Looking forward, he tooled the gig through the light traffic. Inwardly amazed, yet at the same time very certain. Of what he felt, if not why—why being a word for which scholars had an ineradicable fondness.

Currently, the "why" of his own feelings was beyond him. He'd given up trying to analyze and dissect. He'd wanted to hold back, to confirm his control and observe their interplay from an intellectual perspective last night, and had signally failed.

Yet he didn't feel like a failure; he felt . . . settled. Satiated, admittedly, but the effect went much further, reached much deeper than the mere physical. He felt . . . anchored, assured, far more than he'd ever felt before, as if he'd been a ship on a questing keel and had finally come into port.

Poetic allusion wasn't his strong suit. Inwardly shaking his head, he refocused his mind on the present. On their predicament. On its solution.

He nodded at a good-sized coaching inn coming up on the road just ahead. "It's early, but we may as well halt there for lunch. I don't think there's anything but small villages between here and Wolverstone."

Eliza nodded. "We can eat, check our route, and then"—she met his eyes—"set out on our race for the border."

Slowing the gig for the turn under the inn's arch, he murmured, "With any luck at all, we've lost both the laird and Scrope. There's no reason they might think we would come this way."

"If they're keeping an eye on the Jedburgh Road, they can't be watching here as well."

"True." He still glanced around, was still very much on guard, his instincts alert, but they weren't pricking.

Ostlers came running as he drew the horse to a halt in the inn yard.

Five minutes later, he and Eliza were sitting at a table in the inn's small dining room, their saddlebags at their feet.

"Venison pie, please," Eliza told the serving girl. "And a mug of watered ale."

Jeremy smiled at that, then gave the girl his order. When she bustled away, he reached down and drew the map from his bag. "Let's take a look at the smaller lanes—make sure we've covered not just our options but Scrope's and the laird's as well."

Eliza helped him spread the map. "Do you think the laird's actively following us or simply waiting for Scrope to catch us?"

"We know the laird was on our trail earlier, so we have to assume he's still out there somewhere." The table they'd chosen was in a corner, the bench they were sitting on built out from the wall. A window high above their heads shed adequate light on the map. "Here's Hawick." He put his finger on the mark for the town.

Reaching out with one finger, she traced the route she'd earlier picked out, following the minor lanes from Hawick to Bonchester Bridge, then on via an even smaller lane to hamlets called Cleuch Head, Chesters, and Southdean, to eventually join the highway just before the border at Carter Bar. "That's our route." She glanced sideways at him. "Unless Scrope or the laird picks up our trail and follows us down the lanes, I can't see how they could come up with us—not short of the border."

"I was thinking more in terms of whether there might be anywhere along our route where the lane we'll be on might be visible from the highway, or from some position close by the highway where Scrope or the laird might be waiting, watching, like Scrope was when he ambushed us near St. Boswells . . . but you're right." Satisfied, he sat back. "That lane doesn't run close enough to the highway, not until it angles in to join with it, for us to have to fear our pursuers inadvertently spotting us and mounting an attack."

Meeting her eyes, he grinned. "It looks like we've a clear run to the border, and after that, Wolverstone's not far."

She settled on her elbows. "How far?"

"About thirty miles. Less than three hours. Allowing two hours to get from here to the border, we should reach the castle in time for dinner."

Eliza smiled at the thought of being back within society, within her customary safe circle, then gently shook her head and looked down.

"What?"

She looked up at the question, met Jeremy's eyes. Saw his interest in her answer shining there. She hesitated, searching for her true meaning as well as the words, then said, "I was just thinking . . . despite the trials and tribulations, despite having to run and scramble from Scrope, despite living in fear of being captured by the laird, I've . . . enjoyed isn't the right word, but . . ." She held his gaze. "I can see—I feel—that I've benefited from the last days. I've grown." She straightened her shoulders. "I suppose you might say I've matured—I certainly feel different, more settled, clearer in my mind about . . . a whole host of things. But most importantly, I'm more certain about me." She tilted her head. "And for that I thank you—you've helped me through it all, the rescue, the escape, and you've helped me see things, understand things, too."

His expression had grown serious; he held her gaze, then quietly said, "I feel much the same. While I'll be happy to see Wolverstone, I can't say that I've regretted the last days—quite the opposite. I think in years to come I'll look back upon them fondly."

"Exactly." Reaching out, she closed her hand over one of his, lightly squeezed. "While I'll be happy to know we're safe, as long as Scrope and the laird aren't breathing down our necks I feel no sense of desperation over reaching Wolverstone, over bringing this journey to an end."

Turning his hand, he gripped hers, lightly squeezed in reply.

Approaching footsteps pattered across the floor. They both looked up to see the serving girl hefting a piled tray. Jeremy whipped aside the map. While he refolded it and stowed it away, Eliza helped the girl set out their plates and mugs.

When the girl retreated, leaving them to their luncheon, Jeremy raised his mug to Eliza. "To getting back to our real lives—they won't be the same as they were, but the challenge will lie in making the most of the changes and opportunities this journey has brought us."

"Hear, hear." Clinking her mug to his, Eliza smiled,

sipped, then wrinkled her nose at the taste, making him laugh.

Then they turned their attention to the excellent venison pie.

Half an hour later, they climbed back into the gig. Juggling the reins, Jeremy consulted his fob-watch. "It's not even one o'clock. We should make Wolverstone in good time." He glanced at Eliza. "Ready?"

She waved dramatically. "Onward to the border—and don't spare the horse!"

Grinning, Jeremy flicked the reins, sent the roan trotting out of the inn yard, then turned east, away from the major road they'd followed from Selkirk, which led onward to Carlisle.

With the sun gently warming their backs, they drove out of the town and on down a narrow country lane.

The day remained fine and the lane sufficiently well surfaced for them to make good time.

They rattled through several tiny hamlets. The lane twisted and turned but overall kept them on a southeasterly course. Then a gushing stream swung close on one side, the pale water racing past, tumbling and churning.

The further they drove the darker the sky grew, becoming more overcast, the atmosphere more oppressive and threatening. With every half mile, they saw increasing evidence of recent heavy rains over the Cheviots, the line of moorland hills that marched along the border.

"I just hope we don't run into any quagmires," Jeremy said. Thus far the lane had been well drained, with deep ditches to either side carrying the rainwater away.

Eliza was peering over the gig's side. "These ditches look half full." She glanced ahead to where dark gray clouds hung low, obscuring the horizon. "There must have been a storm."

Jeremy didn't like the look of those clouds. "I just hope our luck holds."

It did, until they reached Bonchester Bridge.

They trotted around a curve and swung into the village, then Jeremy swore and hauled on the reins, drawing the horse to a dead halt.

Several men had come running, waving and shouting for them to stop.

Jeremy and Eliza ignored them, their gazes transfixed by what lay beyond.

Or rather, what didn't.

Staring at the spot where the road simply ended, to start again on the far side of a chasm currently gushing clouds of spray, Jeremy said, "It seems my comment about having a clear run to the border was premature."

Over the following hours, Jeremy evaluated every possible avenue to get them over the border. The Bonchester bridge itself was no more, washed away by a torrent the previous night. The townsfolk were stoic, but the disaster had effectively cut the town in two; the questions Jeremy asked regarding the state of the road further on necessitated a great deal of yelling across the chasm, over the raging tumult below.

Eliza pored over the map and made suggestions, but she seemed more resigned than he, or perhaps she was simply more accepting of fate.

Regardless . . .

"There's no way forward." Grim-faced, he finally slumped into the chair opposite hers in the Bonchester Inn's parlor. Leaning his elbows on his knees, he ran his hands over his face. Looking up, he met Eliza's hazel gaze. "There's no chance of getting across the spate in a rowboat, and even if we did manage to find a way across, there's no gig or similar conveyance available for hire on the other side. Your suggestion of taking that minor lane south and tacking around via Hobkirk won't work, because the bridge at Hobkirk is out, too.

"And although everyone agrees we *might* be able to go east and then around via Abbotrule to pick up our original route at Chesters—mind you, that's assuming the two bridges along that roundabout route are still standing—according to all reports from the other side"—he tipped his head toward the southern half of the town—"there's another bridge just north of Southdean that's been wrecked, too."

Holding her gaze, he shook his head. "We can't get to Carter Bar along that road—the lane we wanted to take."

The one that would have allowed them to avoid any chance of running into Scrope or the laird.

She studied him for a moment, then said, "It's not a disaster. We'll just have to go the other way. We'll get through—we have until now, and we will, somehow."

He looked into her eyes, felt her calm reach into him and soothe him. He sighed, dropped his hands. After a moment, shook his head. "I just can't believe we're stymied again. It's as if all of Scotland is in league with the devil—in this case the laird and his henchman, Scrope."

She smiled. "At least they don't know where we are."

He raised his brows. "There is that. I suppose I should be thankful for small mercies."

"Or not so small." She stirred, sat straighter. "It's too late to go on today—the light's already failing."

He glanced out through the parlor windows; dark clouds had closed in, along with a fine mist.

"I've asked the innkeeper, and there's a room we can hire." Capturing his gaze, Eliza went on, "Given we don't have to worry about Scrope or the laird catching up with us here, we can get a good night's rest, then go on tomorrow morning."

A moment elapsed, then he nodded. "Where's the map?"

She pulled it out from the bags resting beside her.

Once more they spread it out and studied the area. "We've looked at this so often," he murmured, "yet it always seems we're looking for another way."

Silence stretched as they both looked. Both saw.

Eventually, she said, "Except, this time, there isn't another way. Is there?"

Eyes on the map, he slowly shook his head. "We've run out of options. From everything I've learned, the only way we can reach the border from here is to take this lane"—with one finger he traced the route—"heading northwest from here to Langlee, beside the highway south of Jedburgh, and from there we'll have to risk the last stretch of highway to the border. It's about ten miles."

"Hmm." Studying the lane to Langlee, she asked, "Are they sure the lane's passable?"

"There's two bridges along it, but all the locals seem to think they'll still be standing. If they aren't . . . we'll need to tack further north, which means we'll join the highway even closer to Jedburgh."

"And a lot later." Raising her gaze, she met his eyes. "If we head out early tomorrow—at first light—we could be over the border in what? Two hours?"

Leaning back in the chair, he nodded. "About that."

"Then that's what we'll do." She started refolding the map. When he didn't say anything more, she glanced at him, saw him regarding her in the way he occasionally did—as if he was studying her. She arched her brows inquiringly.

His lips twisted. "You don't seem too bothered by having to spend yet another night on the road."

She shrugged. "I'm not. We're in no danger, this inn is comfortable enough, and whether we reach Wolverstone today or tomorrow doesn't change very much, does it?"

"I suppose not."

She pulled one of the bags into her lap and tucked the map away.

"You seem . . . very confident that we'll get through tomorrow."

She glanced briefly his way. "I see no reason not to be."

He captured her gaze, held it. After a moment, he quietly said, "Thank you."

She raised her brows mock-haughtily. "For what? Not dissolving into a panic?" She humphed. "I'm not such a peabrain."

His smile deepened. "No." Reaching out he caught her hand, raised it to his lips and kissed her fingers. "Thank you for being you."

Eliza looked into his eyes, felt absolute conviction lock about her heart. She smiled and handed him the saddlebags. "Come on—we'd better tell the innkeeper we'll take that room."

When true night finally fell, they retired, climbing the inn's stairs to a corner room overlooking, on one side, the front of the inn, and on the other the rushing spate, with the mist-shrouded Cheviots in the background.

Carrying two lighted candlesticks, Eliza led the way.

Following her into the comfortable room with its pleasantly worn furniture—a dressing table and armoire against one wall, a large washstand in the corner between the windows, and a large four-poster bed complete with canopy and brocade curtains—Jeremy closed the door and hesitated.

He watched Eliza circle the bed, place one of the candlesticks on each of the two small bedside tables, then glide toward the window. Moving to the dressing table, he set their bags down, paused, then glanced at her.

She'd closed the curtains over the front window but had halted facing the other; arms raised, hands grasping the curtains, she stood poised to shut out the view of the Cheviots etched in faint moonlight, yet appeared transfixed by the sight.

Or, as he suspected, by the prospect of what lay beyond.

Even as he walked to join her at the window overlooking the raging stream, he wondered at the certainty that had settled in his gut, in his mind.

Halting behind her, without thinking—simply letting that inner certainty take charge and guide him—he slid his hands around her waist and eased her back against him.

On a sigh, she leaned back, her gaze on the dark horizon. "Tomorrow."

She said nothing more, but he knew what she meant and had no insights to offer.

After a moment more of staring into the deepening dark, she straightened, pulled the curtains closed, then turned between his palms.

She studied his face. "But tonight, it's just us. Just you and me."

"Yes." Tonight was their last night in this curious in-between world—this world that was theirs, yet not. Tomorrow, when they reached Wolverstone, they would each return to their customary existence, reassume their usual social persona, and be subject once again to the rules and regulations that pertained on that plane.

"Tonight"—she held his gaze—"can just be for us."

His lips lifted. "There's no one else here." Hands firming about her waist, he urged her closer.

With a gentle, flirting smile, she obliged, pressing nearer; tipping her head back, she stretched up and wound her arms about his neck. "There's no one we need to impress." Her gaze fell to his lips; her lids lowered. "Whose opinion we need to consult."

"No." Slowly, he bent his head, his gaze drifting over her face to fasten, at the last, on her lips. "We can do as we like. As we please." He breathed the last word over her lips.

"Yes."

Together they closed the last fraction of an inch, the last sliver of separation between their lips.

Together they pressed nearer still; mouths melding, tongues seeking and tangling, together they stepped into the waiting flames. Into the welcoming warmth of acknowledged passion, of desire owned and willingly embraced.

Willingly, not just wantonly.

Deliberately, without resistance.

Tonight . . . he wasn't going to even make the attempt

to hold onto control, onto reason—to even pretend that he might, that he could.

A futile effort.

Tonight was fated. A storm, washed-out bridges; clearly fate had decreed they should spend another night together in this in-between place. On this plane divorced from their normal reality.

One more night . . . so that he could bend the knee to the power that lived in their newfound connection.

One more night during which he could accept and embrace his new state. His new reality. So that he could pay due homage to the new and glorious element that had wound about his heart and captured his soul.

He was a scholar; he learned fast.

In this instance, however, she seemed to have come to the correct conclusion faster than he.

Although perhaps by a different route.

She seemed to have no hesitation in, much less resistance to, engaging with that emerging power. In grasping it, working with it, and letting it work on her. Where he had turned wary, gripped by innate caution, she had stepped forward with eager, innocent curiosity, a type of courage he felt forced to not just mimic but also match.

So tonight he would go into their engagement with open eyes and an equally open heart. With acceptance, delight, and no reservations.

He would follow her lead and see where she, and that elemental power, led him.

Where was the harm? They were still far from home, in their land of in-between.

She'd offered her mouth; he tasted her flavors, claimed the slick softness, drank in the promise of her passion. A heady delight.

He took a step back, then waltzed her, circling, spiraling, to the bed.

Breaking from the kiss, she tipped her head back and

laughed, a sultry, giddy, tantalizing sound. Then her eyes met his.

And he saw the wanton there. The woman she became in his arms, the woman she truly was, who, with every night that passed, only grew more confident.

He smiled—he couldn't help it—in anticipation, in welcome.

Reading his eyes, her own gleaming green and gold, she raised a hand to his face, framed one cheek, then stretched up and kissed him.

In blatant, flagrant invitation.

They shed their clothes, garment by garment, first one of hers, then one of his. Hands caressed; fingers stroked, teased.

He shaped her curves, sculpted and possessed, then bent his head to pay homage to her breasts. To feast on their bounty and worship.

Again and again, their gazes met, increasingly heated, smoldering, then flaring, then burning.

Passion steadily mounted.

Breath by breath, caress by caress.

Then ignited.

The pair of candlesticks on the bedside tables shed light enough to see; the warm glow slid over her ivory skin, casting a golden aura over the silken curves he'd bared.

The same glow let her see, let her visually possess the planes of his naked chest before, dropping his shirt, she sent her hands to complete his conquest.

Neither hurried. They had time. In their in-between world they had all night to discover whatever fate had arranged for them to find.

There was no fire burning on the small hearth, but desire kept them warm, with every heated, provocative touch spreading flames beneath their skins.

Until they burned.

Until, naked, they stood beside the bed, achingly, rapaciously hungry for the other's touch, for the other's kiss. For the fiery mating of their mouths, for the evocative, arousing sensation of bare skin imprinting on bare skin—

Desire erupted, broke free. Urgency whipped them; passion drove them on.

Sliding his hands down and around, claiming the globes of her derriere, he gripped and hoisted her against him.

On a gasp, all need and longing, she broke from the kiss; long legs instinctively wrapping about his hips, she clutched his shoulders, panting, eyes burning into his as he positioned her. Lowered her.

Eliza felt the broad head of his erection part her slick folds, let her lids lower as her senses savored, let her head tip back on a moan of greedy relief. Of anticipation and desire and flagrant encouragement.

Yes. Now.

She didn't—thank heaven—have to find breath to say the words. He gripped her hips and ruthlessly drew her inexorably down . . . and thrust up and impaled her.

Delicious shock rippled through her, immediately swamped by ravenous need. By the sensation of him so hard, so thick and long, pressed high within her. By the raging hunger that provoked.

He'd stilled—was holding still—buried deep within her.

Half blind with surging need, she found his lips, brushed a panting kiss to their curves, then nipped the lower. "More."

A near-hoarse demand, but he heard; he was moving even before the word faded.

Drawing back, then thrusting in, gripping her hips so he could plunder.

She tried to shift, tried to ride, but he gave her no leeway, simply held her, and filled her, and made her shudder.

Her climax took her unawares. It erupted, flashed, hard and bright, through her, unraveled her mind, scrambled her senses and dragged a scream from her throat—

Jeremy clamped his lips over hers and drank in the sound.

Savored each evocative whimper of her surrender even as he savored the evocative clutch and release of her slick sheath contracting about his erection.

Eyes closed, jaw clenched, he waited, clinging to the sensations, clinging not to control but to the pleasure of the moment . . .

As it faded he turned to the bed; withdrawing from the snug haven of her body, he toppled her onto the covers.

She sprawled on her back, her richly golden hair spread in mussed glory, her breasts, flushed and swollen, rising and falling, her arms, her hands, lying weak at her sides. He gave himself a moment to enjoy the sight, then, driven by his own brutally aroused need, he grasped her thighs, spread them wide, bent his head and set his mouth to her lush softness.

The scream she uttered was too breathless to carry beyond the room.

He feasted and she writhed. Reaching down, she clutched his head, locked her fingers in his hair.

Sobbed and moaned as he drove her on.

The sounds of her pleasure were as music to his ears; he gloried in all he drew from her. Gloried even more in her abandon; after that moment of initial shock, she gave herself over to the intimate play, surrendered and let him have his way.

Let him love her as he wished. Intimately. Explicitly.

When, with a keening cry, she shattered again, he hesitated for only a heartbeat, then rolled her onto her stomach, climbed onto the bed, gripped and raised her hips. Lifting her to her knees before him, he positioned himself, then thrust hard and deep into her. Into the scalding slickness of her sheath.

Into the pleasured haven of her body.

Into the maelstrom of need and hunger, passion and desire, of a desperate yearning for even greater intimacy that whirled about them, closed around them, and drove them on.

And she strove with him. She pushed back and took him

deeper, braced and urged him on. Her gasps, her sobbing pants, mingled with his own exhalations as, chest heaving, muscles corded and straining, he plundered her body searching for release.

As she claimed him, and held him, pleasured him, and drove him ever on.

His need was a fury, a lashing whip. Desire grew spurs and sank them deep.

Passion rose like a raging sea and swept him on.

And her need was an equally potent force, equally powerful, a sirenlike call of command and demand that wrapped about his senses, that combined with his own wanting to bind him, subdue him, seize, and then consume him.

Passion had its way with them, turned and savaged them, then, on their last desperate gasps, ripped them both from the world.

Tossed them high.

Higher.

Then let them fall.

He collapsed upon her, managed to roll to the side so he didn't crush her.

His limbs no longer functioned, not at all.

He lay there, heart thundering, racked and helpless as he'd never been before, and some part of him marveled at the power, at the pinnacle of glory they'd reached.

At the depth of the satiation that now rolled like a warm sea over him, submerging his senses.

As he lay there, conquered, and surrendered his heart, unable, it seemed, to do anything else.

He felt her hand reaching weakly, blindly. Managed to catch it in one of his. Fingers twining, they lay side by side, trying to find the way back to normal.

Eventually, they stirred, and managed, via inarticulate murmurs and passion-weakened limbs, to wrestle back the covers, climb beneath, and settle themselves in the bed. He reached over her and snuffed out the candle on her side, then slumped back and did the same with the candle nearer him.

The night closed around them, wrapped them in dark arms, yet the rush of water churning and racing outside the window was a reminder of irresistible change, of tomorrow and what it would bring.

Drifting on the cusp of sleep, his mind ranged ahead. There was no question over what their relationship would be once they crossed the Cheviots. Marriage was their only option; he knew that as well as she. Accepted it, too, as she did. Yet the tone of their marriage . . . that still lay in their hands, theirs to determine, theirs to declare.

To decide.

But that was for later. For tomorrow, as she'd said.

For tonight . . . he drew her deeper into his arms. Settled his cheek on her hair and closed his eyes. Sighed, content, as she shifted and sank against him, her pendant trapped between them, over his heart.

In a welter of tangled limbs, they slept.

Chapter Fifteen

They drove out of Bonchester into the rising sun. Eliza was very conscious of the tension afflicting them; she felt as tight as a piano wire and knew without asking that Jeremy felt the same.

Up in the room in the predawn light, they'd discussed whether she should revert to her male disguise, but they'd agreed that the likely instant of confusion when Scrope or the laird—both of whom had last seen her dressed as a youth—first set eyes on her once again in a gown might prove vital.

Might prove the key to them racing past their pursuer or pursuers and getting far enough ahead to elude them. Or at least to cross the border into more friendly territory before said pursuers caught up with them.

Both Jeremy and she were unhappily convinced that somewhere before the border they would encounter either the laird or Scrope. Possibly both. At the same time. Clutching the side of the gig as Jeremy drove the roan as fast as he dared down the lane toward Langlee, she saw no reason not to pray.

The locals had steered them well; both bridges between Bonchester and Langlee were still standing, although at the second they took the precaution of descending from the gig and walking carefully across, Eliza first, with Jeremy leading the horse over the planks.

Reaching the other side, they exchanged a glance, climbed back into the gig, and rattled on.

Just over an hour later, they reached Langlee. The village sprawled to the west of the highway about five miles south of Jedburgh.

Jeremy drew the horse to a halt before the first cottage, where the rest of the village buildings screened them from anyone on the highway. His face grim, he glanced at Eliza. "Once we turn onto the highway, I'm going to drive on hell-for-leather, as fast as I possibly can. The border's about twelve miles on—an hour, perhaps a little more, at our best speed. We can't risk stopping—not intentionally." He held her gaze. "Are you ready?"

She nodded. "Yes. That's our best chance for reaching the border safely, so . . ." She looked at the highway, drew breath, then, chin firming, met his eyes again. "Let's go."

He started to lift the reins, then swore beneath his breath. Transferring the reins to one hand, he turned to her, with his other hand captured her chin, tipped her face to his, and kissed her.

Long, deep. A promise.

A statement.

Hands rising to his cheeks, she kissed him back, equally emphatic. Equally sure.

The horse tossed its head, tugging the reins, jerking the gig.

They broke from the kiss.

Jeremy looked into her eyes, saw her confidence in him, her trust, and her courage, sensed her unwavering support.

He nodded. "Right. Let's go."

Facing forward, he flicked the reins and sent the roan pacing on.

They turned right onto the highway and he dropped his hands. The horse stretched out, legs extending in a racing stride.

There was little traffic that early, and what there was of it was heading the other way. The macadam was wide enough to allow the gig to whisk past coaches without Jeremy having to check its pace.

When they swept past a tiny lane signposted as leading to Bairnkine, a cluster of three cottages in the fields to their right, Eliza raised her voice over the sound of the roan's drumming hooves. "Do you have any idea where the laird or Scrope might think to waylay us?"

She should have thought to ask earlier, but Jeremy shook his head. Without taking his eyes from the road, he called back, "There's not a lot of towns along here, so there's long stretches of road where they can be reasonably sure of staying out of anyone else's sight. The only reason they might hold back is if there's a carriage coming the other way." Lips grim, he added, "I'm hoping the closer we get to the border we'll strike more carriages heading north."

It had to be after nine o'clock, yet there wasn't much traffic on the road. Then again, the Jedburgh Road wasn't the usual route coaches took from England to Edinburgh. Although on the map the road looked reasonably straight, in reality it was straight only for short stretches, frequently curving this way, then that, and always going up and down, dipping and rising, through areas of open fields one moment, through dense fir forests the next.

It was impossible to see very far in any direction.

Maintaining a tight grip on the gig's side, Eliza looked ahead, searching both sides of the road as far forward as she could see, hoping that if Scrope or the laird were lying in wait she might spot them before she and Jeremy reached them.

A line of denser trees winding across the occasional open field to their left suggested a river ran near.

"That'll be the Jed Water," Jeremy said. "It eventually joins the Tweed."

"Do we have to cross it?" she yelled back, the rushing wind of their passage whipping her words away. They hadn't had to cross any river since they'd turned onto the highway.

Jeremy hesitated, then replied, "I'm not sure. Check the map and see."

Reaching down to the bags stowed between their feet,

Eliza found the map. With the rocking of the gig, unfolding it required patience, but she eventually had it open and re-folded to allow her to hold it in one hand and study the right section, while resuming her bracing grip on the gig's side.

"We should pass a turnoff to the right, to a place called Mervinslaw, soon. A little way past that, around a curve, we'll come to a bridge over the river. There's a village on the left just there—it looks to be mostly on the opposite bank, so hopefully there'll be a decent bridge."

Jeremy was frowning. "There must be. I can't remember crossing any fords or even rickety wooden bridges when I drove along this stretch following you to Edinburgh." After a moment, he continued, "In fact, as far as I can recall we shouldn't run into difficulties, even if it's been pouring over the Cheviots."

"Good." Lowering the map to her lap, Eliza looked ahead, searching for a signpost to Mervinslaw. Without a signpost, minor lanes and the driveways to farms set back from the road weren't easy to distinguish.

"There it is." She pointed with the map. "Mervinslaw." Checking the map gave her some idea of how fast they were traveling, of the distance they had to go. "We're almost half-way down the stretch of the highway to the border."

"And we still haven't sighted Scrope or the laird." Jeremy straightened his spine, eased his shoulders, then settled in his seat again. "I'm not sure if that's good or bad."

"We should look on the bright side," Eliza called back.

"Perhaps." It was tempting to join her in her enthusiasm and confidence; at their present rate of travel, another hour would see them over the border and well into England. But he couldn't shake the feeling—more than a premonition, more like a statistical certainty—that they wouldn't get away so easily. That Scrope and the laird wouldn't allow them to.

They rattled on around a wide, rising curve; the dense-ness of the stands of firs bordering both sides of the road made Jeremy nervous. Anyone could be hidden by the thick boughs, watching, and he and Eliza wouldn't know, not until the watcher showed himself.

The tension gripping him racked a notch tighter, but then they crested the rise and the trees fell away, a narrow river valley opening to their left, the line of trees continuing less dense and thick on the right.

"Here's the bridge." It was an arched bridge of brick and stone, carrying the highway across the river, spanning it at a safe height and as wide as the highway itself. He let the horse take the upward rise of the bridge in its still rapid stride, then steadied the roan down the other side.

Crack!

Splinters flew from the side of the gig beside his hip. Jeremy flung himself sideways, across Eliza, even as he looked toward the trees . . . ahead, to the right, he saw light glint off a pistol barrel, then Scrope burst out of hiding, mounted on a heavy gray.

"Halt!" Scrope thundered toward them, waving the pistol.

Jeremy swore. His hands full holding in the plunging roan, he kept his body angled across Eliza's—

He saw the mouth of a narrow lane to the left at the end of the bridge.

Hauling on the reins, he wrestled the panicking roan around, swung the horse's head down the lane, then let the reins run free. "Hang on!"

The roan all but bolted.

Stretching out in a flat gallop, it flew down the lane, the gig bouncing and jouncing behind it.

Still on the road, Scrope cursed.

Jeremy flicked a glance at Eliza, relieved to see she had a white-knuckled grip on the gig's side and on the seat between them. She still held the map, crushed between the fingers gripping the seat. Her gaze was locked on the lane ahead.

It twisted and turned much more frequently than the

highway, going up small hills, then plunging down. They whipped past a thick forest, then the lane curved away from the river and arched over a rise in a wide sweeping turn.

Reining in his own shock, Jeremy worked with the horse until it was pacing again, then took stock. "Scrope will chase us, but that forest back there will slow him down, and this landscape will help hide us from his sight." He grimaced. "But we're on a lane, so if he knows where it leads . . ." He glanced at Eliza. "Where will this lane take us?"

Eliza had already drawn a steadying breath, eased her hold on the seat, and raised the map to look.

She tried to calm her pounding heart enough to function, to subdue her panic enough to think. Jeremy had been driving fast before; even though the horse was pacing again, the gig was now rocketing along. She studied the map, then frowningly looked ahead, comparing what she could see on the map with the countryside. . . .

"There's an intersection coming up ahead—almost a crossroads," Jeremy said. "There's a lane leading south—"

"*Don't* take it." She'd found the spot on the map. "It only goes a little way along, then stops at a village called Falla. There's not even a track that leads on from there."

"Right. Not Falla. So which way? Is there any route that will take us back to the highway?"

She searched the map. "Straight on. Or what passes for that." After a moment, she added, "We're going to have to go around a bit—we'll end up heading north instead of south for a little way, before we can turn and head around down a lane to a place called Swinside. After Swinside, that lane turns south. It'll eventually join up with another lane that will take us back to the highway . . . about five miles from the border."

Grim-faced, Jeremy nodded. "I have no notion what Scrope's thinking, but we have to assume he's going to try to keep us away from the border. I checked before—none of these minor lanes lead into England. The only way for us to cross the border is to get back on the Jedburgh Road, or head much further north to one of the other major roads."

Having confirmed as much from her study of the map, Eliza nodded. "We have to take that lane back to the highway—it's our only reasonable option."

"Pray Scrope is following us rather than using his head and working out where we'll go. If he's chasing us in the hope he'll catch us up—which, all things being equal, he eventually would—we might have a chance."

Eliza looked at the horse. "How's he doing?"

"He's not fresh, but he's strong and willing. He's got a good few miles in him yet, even at this pace." After a moment, Jeremy added, "I'd like to ease back and let him get his wind, but I simply don't dare. We have to get past Swinside and around into the lane back to the highway before Scrope realizes our direction."

He didn't like their chances. Scrope had shown himself to be clever; he would have studied maps ahead of time. He would know the lanes.

But they no longer had a choice over which route to take.

"If we see Scrope again, duck down in front of the seat. It would help if I knew you were as safe as possible so I can concentrate on doing whatever I can to avoid Scrope."

He felt Eliza's gaze touch his face, then she nodded. "All right."

He kept the roan at a racing pace, up hill and down, then they reached the lane to Swinside and slowed for the sharp right turn; once around it, he let the ribbons run free and the horse raced on.

They flashed past the tiny hamlet of Swinside and rocketed on. The lane at last curved fully south once more, following the banks of another uplands stream.

Eliza eyed the stream. "At least it hasn't been raining so hard around here."

"No. We shouldn't have to worry about washed-out bridges in this area."

The lane diverged around another small hill; coming out of its screening shadow, they saw a stretch of dense forest ahead, closing around the lane from either side.

Consulting the map again, Eliza said, "I don't know how far the forest stretches, but the lane we want should be cutting across this one somewhere past that next rise."

They could see that some way into the forest, the lane reached a crest, then disappeared over it.

There was no way to tell what lay beyond, not until they were over the crest and within sight of anyone on the other side.

Jeremy could see no logical reason why he should suddenly feel sure that someone—Scrope or the laird—would indeed be waiting, but his instincts were pricking, sharply, and Trentham and his Bastion Club colleagues had always cautioned him to trust his instincts.

Instincts of this sort he'd never truly felt before, never quite believed he had, but . . .

Before he could ask, Eliza said, "When we reach the intersection with the other lane, we have to turn right, back toward the highway. Left will take us further along the Cheviots, and straight on will come to a dead end just a little way on into the hills."

He nodded. "All right. Just pray Scrope is somewhere behind us, and remember what I said."

They were nearing the crest. From the corner of his eye, he saw her nod, saw her lower the map and take a tighter grip on the gig's seat; she, too, was looking ahead.

The horse crested the rise at speed, and then they were over and flying down the other side. They could hear the burbling of the stream to their right. And sure enough, just ahead, the trees fell back on either side where the lane they wanted to take cut across the lane they were on.

He had to slow the horse to take the turn. Both he and Eliza searched the thinning trees to their right. Then the trees ended and the first hundred or so yards of the other lane came fully into view. They could see a narrow wooden bridge carrying the lane across the stream; thicker bushes crowded the stream's banks and extended back along the lane toward the intersection.

Slowing almost to a walk, Jeremy turned the horse's head.

"*No!*" Eliza pointed down the lane. "There!"

Jeremy didn't even look. The terror in her voice had him hauling hard on the reins and turning the horse . . .

He remembered her warning about the dead end ahead, wrestled and heaved and forced the roan to swing fully the other way.

Crack-ping!

Another shot, one that hit the metal back of the gig's seat.

The horse panicked. Jeremy let the reins flow and let him fly. "Get down!"

Eliza scrambled and crouched down, but a few seconds later she raised her head and peered over the back of the gig's seat.

Jeremy swore at her, but she ignored him. He couldn't spare a hand to push her back down. As he fought to reassert control over the panicked horse, he ground out, "Who was it?"

"Scrope. He was waiting in the bushes nearer the bridge—when he shifted, I saw him." She paused, then added, "If he hadn't moved, I wouldn't have seen him."

"Thankfully, you did." He didn't like the tone of her voice; he couldn't allow her to freeze with shock. "I assume he's following us?"

"After shooting at us, he ran back—I presume to get his horse."

Jeremy cast about in his mind. "Look at the map—which is the best way to go?" He couldn't look himself, but he trusted her to choose as wisely as possible given what little they knew.

"He's not in sight." Easing back onto the seat, she smoothed out the crumpled map and studied it. After a moment, she said, "There's no way back to the Jedburgh Road, not from here. The best we can do now is to keep turning left on this lane. It'll curve north again, and eventually we'll reach another road which will take us over the border . . . but it's a long way out of our way, and even once we cross into England, we'll be much further from Wolverstone than we are now."

Jeremy had never had to assess such weighty options under such pressure, but . . . "We need to get over the border as fast as we can, in whatever way we can. Given Scrope has shot at us twice, we can claim protection from anyone in authority on either side of the border, but in this area the nearest outposts of authority are in England."

Examining the map, Eliza gauged the distances to the nearest major towns, sighed. "Given Scrope is behind us, we can't turn back to Jedburgh, so the nearest town of any size is indeed across the border."

The lane they were now on was similar to the other; if anything, it twisted, turned, dipped, and rose even more dramatically through what was essentially the foothills of the Cheviots.

Jeremy had managed to ease the roan back into its proper pacing stride, but even to her non-horsewoman eyes the beast was tiring.

"What's ahead?" Jeremy asked.

She glanced at the map. "There's a fork just ahead. We need to go left."

They rocketed along a straight, rising stretch. She looked back and frowned. "Scrope hasn't appeared."

"He's probably trying to outflank us." After a moment, Jeremy went on, "If I was him, I'd stay on our right, forcing us to turn away from the border. Once we do, he can come up on either side, but for now keep looking for him on our right."

Gripping the side of the swaying gig, she shifted to look past Jeremy, scanning the trees, bushes, and fields. They burst from a stretch of forest to find a patch of open fields surrounding the fork. Jeremy checked the roan only just enough to take the turn; as they swung onto the left arm, Eliza swiveled and looked back—and saw a horseman, mounted on a heavy gray, charge across the field behind them. "Scrope—but he's not coming directly for us."

Jeremy urged the roan on. "How far away?"

"One hundred and fifty . . . two hundred yards?"

"Damn—what's he doing?" After a moment, Jeremy said, "Look at the map—from the fork to the next place we have to turn, who has the shortest route? Us via the road, or Scrope riding in a direct line?"

"Scrope." A glance at the map confirmed it.

Jeremy's jaw set. "We've got to reach that turn before him. Hang on." Raising the long whip he hadn't until then used, he sent it snaking out over the horse to crack just beside the roan's ear.

If she hadn't been so terrified, Eliza would have spared more of her mind to being impressed. Instead, as the horse responded, she clutched the gig's side and seat and hung on for dear life.

They raced along at a pace far beyond reckless. How Jeremy kept them on the dipping, winding lane she did not know; she prayed they encountered no potholes or unexpected ruts.

"It can't be much further," she yelled over the rattling wheels.

Grim-faced, Jeremy nodded ahead. "There it is."

They flashed into open country again, pushing hard for the crossroads ahead. Another stream crossed their path, another narrow wooden bridge spanning it. "Can you see Scrope?" Jeremy called.

"No—not yet." Eliza raked the country to their right. Scrope had to be coming that way.

The horse's hooves thudded on the wood of the bridge. The gig bumped, rocked . . . then righted as the flagging roan lunged on. The crossroads lay a hundred yards ahead.

Eliza caught a flash of movement through the trees screening the intersecting lane. The roan's next stride drew them to where she could see— "On the lane to the right!" She stared as Scrope came surging on, flogging his gray in a desperate gallop. "My God! He's trying to run us down!"

Time slowed. Jeremy saw the potential outcomes like a kaleidoscope in his mind. He drew the roan in as if slowing for the turn. Eyes on Scrope and the gray, he gauged the distance, the gray's all but uncontrolled speed . . . Scrope saw them and straightened, reaching for the holster in the saddle to his right, then realized the gray wasn't about to halt. Scrope swore and yanked hard on the reins.

The gray reared.

Jeremy dropped his hands, flicked the whip, and sent the roan plunging on.

Straight ahead.

He couldn't have slowed and made the left turn they'd wanted to make; that would have given Scrope their backs, and he hadn't been, still wasn't, prepared to risk that.

As it was, Scrope was fully occupied in controlling the gray, and even if he tried a shot now, Jeremy was between him and Eliza.

White-faced, Eliza glanced back, then looked at him. "This leads to a dead end."

Jeremy's jaw couldn't get any tighter. "I know. We didn't have a choice."

"He's coming after us."

"How far?"

"Three hundred yards or so."

It would have to be enough. The lane—increasingly badly surfaced, but that would slow Scrope as much as the gig— swung around another low hill, temporarily cutting them off from Scrope.

The turmoil in Jeremy's mind cleared; out of all the options they'd had, one remained. "How far before the end of this lane?"

"Not far." Eliza swiveled to look ahead, then pointed. "I think it must end just around that next bend."

"All right." The pieces of a plan fell into place in his mind. "Look at the map. Put one finger on the end of the lane, then look for a place called Windy Gyle—it should be somewhere to our east, in the middle of the Cheviots. It's on the main ridge. Put another finger there, then hold up the map and show me."

Head down, she scoured the map, then gripped it with both hands, held it up so he could see.

He glanced at it, then looked forward again. "What's the distance?"

She looked. "About eight miles."

He nodded. "We're going to take this gig as far as we can—get as deep into the hills as we can. Then we're going to leave it and make a dash for Windy Gyle."

"Why there?"

"Clennell Street, one of the main drover's roads, runs down into England in the shadow of Windy Gyle. And Clennell Street leads more or less straight down to the gates of Wolverstone Castle. I rode up to Windy Gyle with Royce a few weeks ago—it's about ten miles from the castle."

"Can we reach it, do you think, with Scrope mounted and close behind us?"

"I don't know, but it's our best option." He grimaced and urged the poor roan on. "We don't really have any other."

He wasn't sure what he'd expected from her, but her chin went up and she nodded. "Windy Gyle it is, then." She glanced down. "What about our bags?"

"Get out anything you can't leave behind. There's a knife in the bottom of my bag—get it out for me. I don't need anything else in there."

She dragged his bag onto her lap. "I don't need anything at all."

"The water bottles—take them. And your cloak, too."

She didn't waste time answering, just gathered the items,

bundling the water bottles in her cloak and holding his second knife. Then she glanced back. "Scrope just came around that last bend. He's getting closer."

They rounded the next curve; as Eliza had guessed, the lane ended just ahead. Their progress slowed considerably as both horse and lane failed.

Even when the lane petered out, Jeremy kept driving as long as he could, turning upward, into the rising hills. "There's a cottage over there—they'll find the horse." A thin stream of smoke rose into the sky from a distant crofter's hut.

Jeremy finally spotted what they needed, then glanced behind them. Scrope was still out of sight, hidden by the last curve. He hauled on the reins. "Come on. Out and up that sheep track."

Eliza jumped down as the gig rocked to a halt. She raced for the track.

After looping the reins loosely enough to let the horse wander, Jeremy raced after her.

They pelted into the shadows of a cleft between two hills. Ferns grew thickly. Taking the knife and stowing it in his pocket, Jeremy lifted the bundled bottles from Eliza's arms, then urged her on. They started to climb.

To scramble and haul themselves up the increasingly steep sides of the hill.

"He won't be able to ride up this," Eliza said without turning around.

Jeremy grunted. "That's why I chose this way."

They reached the top of the hill, crossed the windswept expanse of the crown at a run, then rushed wildly down into the dip beyond.

And started to climb the next slope.

But Scrope wasn't to be so easily denied.

Twenty minutes of mad scrambling later, they were crossing a wide, almost flat valley between two folds in the hills when they heard the thud of horse's hooves. Looking along the valley, they saw Scrope thundering toward them, pistol in hand, his gaze locked on them as he urged his horse on.

Jeremy swore. "Go!" He pushed Eliza on along the slowly rising sheep track they'd been following. Clumps of gorse surrounded them, thigh-high, occasionally snagging their clothes.

Scrope must have circled and come up to the higher valley by another route. He was racing up along the ribbon of grassy meadowland along the valley floor.

They reached the first rocks and the track became grittier, more stone and rubble as they started on the next steep upward climb. Looking ahead, Jeremy saw another cleft up ahead. If they could make it that far, and rush further into the shadows, Scrope would have to get off his horse to follow . . . could they get far enough ahead to be out of pistol range?

Slowing, starting to feel the effort of so much rushing and running—and if he was, how was Eliza faring?—Jeremy called to her, "Keep going. Fast as you can." He made sure she was climbing and scrambling as best as she could, then he paused, turned, and looked back.

Scrope wasn't far, still in the saddle, arms flapping as he forced the gray through the gorse. He was still out of pistol range but closing.

A knife against a pistol wasn't good odds, but if Scrope missed his shot . . .

Jeremy vacillated—make a stand, or—

The gray jerked, then reared, letting out a low scream.

Taken unawares, Scrope flailed wildly, then toppled from the saddle. The gray bolted.

For an instant, Jeremy stared, then he turned and raced after Eliza.

Only to see that she'd stopped higher up, not that much further on, and turned back to see . . . he waved her on. "Go—go!"

This was their chance to get far enough away from Scrope that he would lose their trail. They reached the cleft and climbed frantically on.

Finally gaining the top of that rise, they both paused and glanced back. Scrope's horse was clearly visible, galloping madly away down the valley. Scrope . . . it took them a few moments to locate him. He was coming on still, wading through the gorse, dogged and determined, the pistol he'd been waving still in his hand.

Jeremy gripped Eliza's elbow. "Come on."

Hauling in a breath, she nodded and they turned to the next rising slope. Jeremy scanned it, then spotted the opening of a narrow valley between two rocky humps. "That way. We need to get out of his sight."

They ran as fast as they could.

As they passed into the narrow valley, Jeremy glanced back. He couldn't see Scrope, but he had no firm conviction that Scrope couldn't see him.

Noon came and went as they climbed. They had to start pacing themselves, walking when they felt sufficiently screened. Their scrambling up shaded clefts grew slower, but they forged on. The next hours passed in tense endurance; they couldn't risk halting, didn't know if Scrope was still on their trail, or if he was close. Close enough to threaten them.

All they could do was labor on.

Eliza had long since forbidden herself to ask even herself the question of whether or not they would ever make it safely over the border; she had to believe they would.

They climbed and climbed, then climbed and walked some more, over a landscape that appeared to have been created by a giant's hand pushing the earth aside so that it crumpled in a series of ever-rising folds, like a tablecloth shoved roughly to one side. She was beyond thankful that of necessity she was still wearing her youth's riding boots beneath her gown. By Jeremy's side, she sloshed through numerous small burns and skirted a narrow lake. The ground was drier up there, possibly because it was rockier. The air was fresh and clear, and carried the tang of the wild, but it grew increasingly cold as slate-gray clouds blew up from the west, roiling and swelling to take over the sky, then rolling steadily toward them.

Even though it was still midafternoon, the light was waning.

The sun had disappeared early in their climb, but enough of its light shone from behind the clouds to guide them. Jeremy had again and again checked their direction and kept them heading steadily east.

Finally they reached the crest of a ridge that appeared nearly as high as the next ridge along, which itself wasn't that far away . . . and beyond that next ridge lay a view over fields and forests that seemed to stretch to infinity.

"England." Jeremy stared at the panorama. "But we can't get down the escarpment except at certain places."

"Like Windy Gyle?"

He nodded. They were both breathing hard.

Eliza was frankly amazed she'd made it this far; walking had never been high on her list of favored activities, but apparently the striding across country she'd been doing with Jeremy over recent days had built up some degree of stamina. She glanced at him, saw him looking along the escarpment, following it further east. "So where is it?"

Raising a hand, he pointed. "There. That peak."

She turned and looked. Moved closer to make sure the rounded peak she could see was the one he was pointing at.

"Clennell Street goes down the escarpment just this side of Windy Gyle."

Measuring the distance, deciding there was still an hour or more walking to go, she blew out a breath. "Well, at least we don't have to go around it."

With that, she looked down and started walking. Trudging along, one foot in front of the other.

Jeremy turned to follow her, but then stopped and turned

back. Retracing the few paces to the edge of the steep slope they'd just climbed, he looked down, back along their track . . . softly swore.

Scrope was still there, still coming on.

Turning, Jeremy joined Eliza, who'd halted a little way along.

"Scrope?"

Jeremy nodded. "But he's quite a way back. With luck, now we're out of his sight he'll lose us completely somewhere along the way."

He waved her on and she turned and went.

Tramping in her wake, he hoped he was right in thinking Scrope was no great tracker. Both he and Eliza were flagging, but from what he could see, so was Scrope. As long as they stayed out of pistol range, they should be safe.

Should be. He would have felt a great deal more confident over their situation had it not been for the question niggling at the back of his mind.

Where is the laird?

Looking ahead, he told himself it was pointless speculating. All they could do was flee as fast as they could and pray they reached one of Royce's holdings before either Scrope, or his employer, caught up with them.

They were mad, the lot of them. "Daft as ale-addled gits."

Then again, they were English, all three of them, Scrope included. Presumably that explained it.

The laird swore and strode on through the gorse as fast as he could. Scrope was between him, and Eliza and her gentleman. Worse, contrary to his every expectation, Scrope was willing to shoot, presumably to kill.

Admittedly, when he'd first seen Scrope waving a pistol while bailing up their fleeing pair north of St. Boswells, he'd had that odd premonition about having to stand by and watch Scrope shoot Eliza's gentleman. Later, however, he'd convinced himself that that thought had been irrationally fanciful—Scrope was a professional; he would know better than to kill a man he hadn't been hired to kill. He'd concluded Scrope had intended merely to use the pistol to intimidate.

But today Scrope had shot at his quarry. Twice. He hadn't shot into the air to frighten; he'd shot directly at them. He'd hit the gig on both occasions, confirming the laird's opinion of Scrope's prowess once outside a town. Shooting a pistol at close quarters in an alley the man might manage, but in the country on horseback he was out of his element.

What worried the laird to the depth of his soul was that on both occasions Scrope could just as well have hit the girl as the man.

Which didn't bear thinking about.

Neither outcome bore thinking about.

He had to catch Scrope and put a permanent end to the man's obsession with Eliza and her gentleman.

And it certainly appeared to be an obsession.

He'd been watching Scrope near the bridge over the Jed Water, waiting to step in if Scrope halted the pair. The pistol itself he'd expected; Scrope's use of it he had not.

Unfortunately, he'd been too far away to immediately intervene, and so he'd found himself chasing Scrope—who proved to have found himself a decent horse.

Hercules was a Trojan, but he wasn't built for speed, and with the laird on his back he was no match for Scrope's gray. Frustrated, furious—and fearing he wouldn't reach Scrope in time to stop the man putting a ball into someone—the laird had ridden as hard as he could after Scrope.

Once they'd hit the hills, however, the terrain had changed, and the laird had steadily closed the distance.

He'd been out of earshot—and he carried no pistol—when he'd seen Scrope riding hard toward Eliza and her gentleman as they'd scrambled on. He'd seen the gentleman send Eliza ahead and turn to face Scrope.

Luckily for the gentleman, the laird had a fine arm and ex-

cellent aim. He'd vaulted from the saddle, scooped up some
flinty gravel, and sent a few sharp shards flying at Scrope's
horse. The stones wouldn't have hurt the horse so much as
stung it, which had proved enough to unseat Scrope.

An outcrop of rock had hidden him from the fleeing pair
as they'd raced on. Scrope, for his part, had stared after his
spooked horse, sworn, then swung around and rushed after
his quarry; he'd never looked back, so he hadn't seen the
laird.

The laird had had to take the time to tether Hercules
before resuming the chase on foot. Now he forged on, pressing on as fast as he could.

He was closing on Scrope, yard by yard, but at the same
time, Scrope was closing on Eliza and her protector.

And the laird was seriously questioning whether, in the
matter of Eliza Cynster and her rescuer, Scrope was entirely
sane.

Under his breath, the laird muttered a prayer that he would
catch Scrope before Scrope caught them.

He couldn't stand by and watch them die.

Jeremy's hand on her back was all that got Eliza to the top
of the next narrow ridge. She stepped away from the edge
and slumped over, hands braced on her knees as she dragged
air into her lungs. Bent over, all but wheezing, she looked
ahead.

Directly in their faces rose a solid wall of rock, too high to
climb. To their left, the ridge ran on, a long fold in the earth's
crust, a sheep track leading along the windswept crest. Further on, the rock wall ended, but she couldn't see what lay
around it.

"Follow the track." Jeremy, also breathing hard, came up
behind her. "It's not that much further."

Thank God! Eliza didn't waste breath saying the words,
but straightened and got her feet moving. At a shambling
run, they followed the narrow track on along the ridge.

They'd reached an elevation where the views back into Scotland were spectacular, but she had no mind left to register the sight. Just how high they were was emphasized when the left side of the ridge fell away in a cliff, increasingly precipitous the further along they went. She slowed and glanced over.

At her shoulder, Jeremy did the same, then urged her on. "Quite a way down."

It had to be hundreds of feet. "Did you see the rocks at the bottom?"

"Yes. Luckily, we're not going that way." Jeremy turned her from the precipice. The rock wall had ended; he pointed across a steep, narrow valley, almost a ravine, to the next ridge. A sheep—or at this height was it a goat?—track zigzagged down, then up the other side. "We have to climb up there, and get through that gap." He pointed to the top of the next ridge, to a narrow cleft between two huge boulders. "Then it's down the other side to Clennell Street."

Windy Gyle towered before them, directly ahead. The ridge that lay before them was the last before they reached the peak itself, hence Clennell Street should lie exactly where Jeremy had said—in the upland valley beyond the next ridge.

With that prospect before her, Eliza drew in a deep breath and set off down the track as fast as she could. She'd kilted her skirts and petticoat some time ago, leaving her booted feet freer, her strides less hampered. Still, she was tired and had to watch her feet.

When she reached the bottom of the dip, she called over her shoulder, "Scrope?"

"Still behind us," came the grim reply.

"Anyone else?"

"Not that I can see, but given our direction, I can't see how the laird might have outflanked us. If he's around, he's at least as far back as Scrope." Who, Jeremy didn't bother mentioning, had put on a burst of speed and was gaining on them.

As they started up the other side of the narrow valley, he glanced back to the ridge they'd left, then, unwelcome premonition prickling once more, looked to the top of the rise they were climbing . . . and inwardly swore. He hadn't noticed earlier how very close the two ridges actually were, but from the bottom of the ravine, the direct distance, or lack thereof, was evident.

Placing a hand on Eliza's back to steady her, he leaned nearer and said, "We need to push hard to get through the gap between the boulders." Hearing the sudden desperation in his voice, and guessing she would too, he added, "Until we do, we'll be within pistol range of the last ridge."

Eliza shot him a glance over her shoulder, looked back and up at the last ridge, then turned and scrambled on faster.

But they could only go so fast. The track, such as it was, was rocky and gravelly; any unwisely placed boot could slip and slide. He was panting, and Eliza was gasping and pressing a hand to her side, when they finally scrambled onto a rocky slope, a reasonably gentle incline that led upward to the twin boulders and the gap between.

Straightening, Eliza took a step and staggered.

Wrapping an arm about her waist, he pulled her up and on.

Their feet seemed heavy as they covered the last yards. "Once we're through and can get going down the other side," he told her, "we should reach Clennell Street and be heading down into England before Scrope—"

"Halt! *Stop*!"

They swung around. On the ridge they'd left, Scrope stood, feet spread wide, swaying a little as he fought to train a pistol on them.

Slowly, Jeremy and Eliza straightened. The options they had left to them flashed across Jeremy's brain.

Surreptitiously, he nudged Eliza. Without taking his eyes from Scrope, he murmured, "Keep edging toward the gap. Slowly."

They stared at Scrope, and Scrope, chest heaving, stared wild-eyed at them.

Sliding her boot sideways, Eliza edged half a step along the incline.

Beside her, Jeremy edged the opposite way; the space between them widened.

Scrope snarled, "Stop! I told you to stop!"

Jeremy took another step away from Eliza, away from the safety of the gap between the boulders.

Scrope swung his pistol back and forth between them. They were near enough to see the burning intent that distorted his features, the maniacal gleam in his eyes. The indecision as he struggled to decide whom to shoot.

Jeremy had assumed the answer would be him. He tensed to spring to his left, further away from Eliza, hoped she would know to run for her life when the pistol discharged—

Scrope's lips lifted in a soundless snarl and he swung the barrel toward Eliza and steadied.

"*No!*" Changing direction, Jeremy flung himself at Eliza.

He hit her as the pistol discharged—felt the rake of hot coals, a searing heat, across the back of his upper left arm—then he and she landed on the rocky ground.

They both lost their breath.

The sudden pain of the wound momentarily stunned him.

"You're hit! You're wounded! Damn it, you're *bleeding*!" Eliza felt close to hysterical, but with a form of fury, rather than fear. Instead of freezing her, it infused and inflamed her, and gave her a strength she hadn't known she possessed.

She wrestled Jeremy back, pushing until she could wriggle from under him and ease him back into a slump on the ground.

He caught her hands before she could examine his wound. "No—we need to run. *Now.*" He started to struggle up.

"Don't be stupid—one pistol, one shot." But his jaw clenched with pain, he insisted on getting to his feet. She found herself helping to haul him up. "Oh, all right. Be my hero, then." Her mouth was running on without her mind; she didn't care. "If it'll keep you happy, we'll go through the gap, down Clennell Street, and on into safety, and *then*—"

"No, you won't."

The undiluted vitriol dripping from Scrope's tones had Eliza turning.

As she'd expected, Scrope had flung his now useless pistol aside, but contrary to her assumptions, he hadn't started after them. He still stood on the other ridge, facing them—with another, smaller, but deadlier-looking pistol in his hand.

"I told you," he snarled, "you won't get away. You can't get away. Victor Scrope doesn't lose his targets."

His arm rose a fraction higher as he took careful aim.

A bloodcurdling roar erupted out of nowhere, all but drowning Jeremy's desperate, "Eliza!"

He grabbed her and pulled her back down to the ground— as on the other ridge a massive figure charged from behind the rock wall directly at Scrope.

The roar had made Scrope hesitate. Seeing the figure rushing toward him, he started to turn to bring the pistol to bear on . . . the laird?

The laird reached Scrope in a furious rush. Grabbing Scrope's pistol hand, he forced it up, pointing the barrel at the sky.

The pistol discharged harmlessly upward, the report ricocheting between the hills.

Eliza resisted Jeremy's efforts to shove her behind him. "No—look!" Eyes glued to the swaying figures grappling on the opposite ridge, she gripped Jeremy's hand. "He—the laird—stopped Scrope from shooting us."

Shifting to sit up—putting her more or less in his lap— Jeremy stared over her shoulder and felt the utter bemusement that had laced her words infect him.

Beyond stunned, they both watched the titanic struggle. Scrope wasn't a small man, but the laird was half a head or more taller. And definitely larger, heavier. The advantage clearly lay with the laird, but he was, transparently, trying to subdue Scrope, while Scrope . . . had transformed into a rabid, raging monster intent only on getting free and coming after his "target."

Locked together, the men wrestled back and forth, boots scuffling on rock and coarse grass. Scrope struck at the laird whenever he could, but the laird merely blocked and caught Scrope's arms again.

To Jeremy, it seemed clear the laird was intent on wearing Scrope out, then securing him. Given the size of the laird's fists, apparent even from Jeremy and Eliza's position, one good blow might crack Scrope's skull. The laird fought like a man very aware of his own strength.

After that first bloodcurdling bellow, the laird had fought in grim silence, but Scrope was increasingly vocal. Finally, literally howling in fury, he broke free far enough to knee the laird—who shifted and caught the blow on his thigh.

In doing so, to keep his balance, the laird swung Scrope toward the edge of the ridge, to the edge of the cliff.

Scrope chose that moment to fling himself back, trying to break the laird's grip.

Scrope succeeded.

On a triumphant bellow, he stepped back.

Off the edge of the cliff into thin air.

The look on his face as he realized was painful to see.

Desperate, he lunged, caught the laird's sleeve, fell—and took the laird with him.

The big man toppled over the cliff and was gone.

"*My God!*" Pressing her hands to her lips, Eliza stared at the empty space where seconds ago both the laird and Scrope had stood.

A wailing scream—a bellow and scream combined—trailed away, then was abruptly cut off.

She wasn't sure if it was her imagination, or if she truly heard the thump of the bodies hitting the jagged rocks far below.

Together with Jeremy she sat and stared as around them the silence of the mountains returned, then darker clouds washed across the waning sun, casting a deeper pall over the opposite ridge and the ravine.

"Come on." Jeremy urged her up.

Slowly, she scrambled to her feet. "I don't understand."

"Neither do I." Jeremy stood, twisting to look over his left shoulder at the gouge the pistol ball had scored across his upper arm. It had bled profusely, but the flow had slowed to sluggish. "But I think we need to get out of the hills to some place of reasonable safety before we stop and try to work it out."

Despite his wish, Eliza insisted on binding up his arm with strips torn from her petticoat. "I always wanted to have a reason to do that," she said, smiling and willing him to let her have her way.

So he did. But as soon as she'd secured her impromptu bandage, he caught her hand, tugged her to him, and kissed her. Ravenous, relieved, and so very thankful.

Overwhelmingly grateful.

And she met him, his roiling feelings mirrored in her kiss, in the barely overcome desperation and the soaring relief that had superseded it.

Drawing back, he rested his forehead on hers. "I thought, for a moment, that I would lose you."

She clung, one hand tracing his cheek. "I . . ." Her voice shook, but she strengthened it and went on, "I felt so angry with you for being shot. I know you did it to save me, but . . ." She shrugged, looked up and met his eyes. "If you hadn't been hurt, I think I would have hit you."

He smiled, then a laugh escaped. He put his good arm around her shoulders, lightly hugged. "Well, we're a pair, it seems, for I wasn't feeling particularly happy with you at one point in the proceedings, either." Glancing at the other ridge, he shook his head. "But we're here, still alive, and they're dead. We survived."

He turned toward the boulders and the gap between.

She hung back, met his gaze when he looked inquiringly at her. She tipped her head at the other ridge. "Should we go and look?"

He held her gaze. "You saw the drop. There's no way any man could survive that fall."

"But . . . we'll never know who he was—the laird—and he did save us at the end."

"True, but that we needed to be saved was his fault in the first place, so . . ." Jeremy blew out a breath. "You could say he just put right what he had originally caused to go wrong. Regardless, we can't dally here. We've only a few hours before it'll get too dark to risk walking on—we need to find safe shelter before then."

Her gaze went to his bandaged arm, and she nodded. "Yes. You're right. They're dead, and there's nothing we can do to help them. And thanks to them both, we need to help ourselves."

Leaving his good arm around her shoulders, she slid her arm around his waist and looked ahead. "Come on, then. On home to England."

They reached the spot beside Windy Gyle where Clennell Street commenced its sharp descent over and down the escarpment. Leaning just a little on Eliza, Jeremy pointed. "The border itself lies just down there, more or less following the base of the escarpment. From here, the hills fall in a series of ridges down to the moorland."

"Just like the ridges we came up."

He drew breath, felt the faintly woozy feeling he'd been fighting for the last hundred yards wreathe through his brain again. Before he could stop himself, he confessed in a rush, "I can't make it down."

Eliza looked at him, concern filling her eyes. "Your wound—"

"It's not so much the wound itself as the blood loss,

I imagine. I can walk on reasonably well for a while, but going down that track . . ." He eyed the descent made for horsemen and cattle, not pedestrians, then shook his head. "Me attempting it would be a recipe for disaster."

She'd been studying his face. She blinked, nodded. Crisply said, "At least you're man enough to say so. Most wouldn't, and then we'd start down, and you'd end up collapsing on me, and then where would we be?"

Lips thinning, he muttered, "Precisely why I mentioned it."

"So"—she looked around—"I suppose we should look for somewhere to spend the night."

He almost grinned. Where had the tonnish young lady who didn't like being out in the countryside gone? She was still there, he suspected, just making the best of things. "We don't have to do that." When she arched a brow at him, he explained, "I told you I rode up here a few weeks ago with Royce."

She nodded, then let him turn her around and start walking up Clennell Street, back into Scotland. "I remember."

"We went to visit his half brother, Hamish O'Loughlin, and his wife, Molly. Their farmhouse isn't far from here." He glanced at the dark clouds rolling ever closer. "Less than an hour should see us there, and I know Hamish will help."

"If he's Royce's half brother, then I'm sure he will."

They found the correct track off Clennell Street and circled Windy Gyle. With no one chasing them, they didn't need to hurry, to look over their shoulders in fear. Contrarily, the lack of pursuit made the going slower; they had time to feel their tiredness, their aches and pains.

Time for Jeremy's wound to start throbbing.

Gritting his teeth against the burning pain, he slogged on, the need to see her to safety strong enough to keep him going.

They circumnavigated the headwaters of a stream, then followed the track down its bank into a shallow upland valley.

Low stone walls appeared, dividing the pastureland into fields. They finally reached the spot where the farmhouse came into view, tucked into a pocket in the hills, snugly protected from the winds and the weather.

Slowing, Jeremy halted and sank back against a low stone wall. "That's it." His tones were clipped, his lips tight with pain.

Head tilting, Eliza looked at him. "I can see it."

Without meeting her gaze, he nodded at the house. "You go on. You can send Hamish back with a horse for me—it'll be easier for me that way."

It sounded so reasonable . . . until she looked back, lifted her eyes, and saw the curtain of misty rain sweeping their way, gradually but steadily blotting out the hills as it came.

"That's all very well, but I'm not leaving you here to get drenched. And don't tell me it's better for me that I don't get wet—I haven't been shot. Allowing someone who has a pistol wound to get drenched and catch a chill on top of it sounds like something my mother would warn me never to do. So!" She looked at him, met his narrowing eyes with blatant obstinacy. "Don't argue. Just get up, lean more on me, and we'll be able to go faster, and then neither of us will get wet at all."

Exhaling through his teeth, Jeremy pushed carefully away from the wall. "If you go on alone, you'll reach the farm before the rain."

"Possibly. And if you'll just shut up and do as I say"—seizing his good arm, she pulled it over her shoulders, keeping hold of his hand—"we might both reach the house before getting drenched. Now come on."

Stifling a sigh, he let her help him along.

A few steps along, she made a rude sound. "I won't collapse if you actually *lean* a little weight on me, you know. Remember, the aim of this exercise is that we both don't get wet, so you might say I have a vested interest in you leaning on me properly."

Lips firming, he did . . . and discovered that together they could go considerably faster. He was tall, but for a woman so was she; tucked under his arm, her arm around his waist, she provided just the right support for his flagging abilities.

They reached the entry to the farm yard just as the first wash of light raindrops pattered over them.

Dogs started barking.

"Don't worry," he murmured, "they're tied up in the stable."

As he'd hoped, the barking brought Hamish to his door.

The big Scot filled the opening, as tall as Royce but significantly wider. The instant he saw who was limping across his yard, Hamish yelled back to Molly, then came striding out to meet them.

"Jeremy, lad—what the deuce are you doing here?"

"He's hurt," Eliza answered. "He's been shot in the arm and it bled dreadfully, and I think he's fainting."

"Nah." Hamish ducked to look into Jeremy's eyes, then grinned. "He's just a trifle weak is all. Here, lass, let me take over."

Eliza reluctantly gave way to Hamish's brute strength; if Jeremy did collapse, better Hamish was there to catch him.

She followed on Jeremy's other side, eyes on his face— and nearly ran into the doorframe.

A gentle hand stopped her. "Here, now."

Turning, Eliza met a pair of bright blue eyes. "You must be Molly."

The small woman with her corona of bright hair smiled. "Aye, that I am. Why don't you come on inside out of the mizzle, and Hamish will bring Jeremy, then we can all sit and have a cup of tea while you tell us what's happened."

Warmth and comfort radiated from the house, from Molly and Hamish. Feeling a weight she hadn't known had settled on her shoulders fall away, Eliza nodded. "Thank you." She smiled weakly. "That sounds heavenly."

Chapter Sixteen

They spent the night cocooned in the warmth of Hamish and Molly's home, enfolded in and succored by the pervading sense of calm, unruffleable family life.

After sitting Jeremy down at her kitchen table, Molly, aided by Eliza, unwrapped the makeshift bandage, pried him from his ruined shirt and coat, then washed, salved, and rebandaged his arm. Hamish helped by providing a glass of whisky, ignoring Molly's admonishing frown.

Jeremy was grateful; the whisky dulled the pain.

He was also grateful for the shirt and jacket Hamish lent him; both were overlarge, but warm and comfortable.

Shortly after, Hamish and Molly's younger children, Dickon and Georgia, twenty-three and twenty years old, respectively, joined them about the table for dinner; after the meal, Hamish and Molly left the cleaning up to the younger ones, ushered Jeremy and Eliza into the parlor, settled them in armchairs, then demanded to be told all.

Between them, Jeremy and Eliza managed a creditably succinct account of all that had happened from the instant Eliza had walked into the back parlor of St. Ives House. They had to backtrack and explain about Heather's kidnapping, of which Molly and Hamish had not yet heard.

Jeremy felt no qualms over disclosing such matters to Hamish and Molly; he knew how close the couple were to Royce and Minerva.

When they reached the end of their tale and described

the unexpected fight they'd witnessed on the edge of the cliff, Hamish exchanged a glance with Molly. "I'll go with Dickon tomorrow at first light and take a look at the bodies."

Molly nodded. "Do."

Then she gathered Eliza and Jeremy and shooed them upstairs to the beds she and Georgia had prepared, instructing them to sleep until they felt like getting up. "I'm sure Hamish will be wanting to go with you to the castle. Once he's seen the body, he might know more of your laird."

Jeremy nodded, exchanged a glance with Eliza, then watched as she thanked Molly for all her help and disappeared into one room, leaving him to do the same and retreat to a room of his own. Alone.

He told himself she was only across the corridor, perfectly safe.

The next morning, he came down to breakfast late. Eliza was at the table, eating a bowl of porridge. Summoning a smile, he aimed it at Molly, standing by the stove. "Sorry—I took your suggestion to heart. Is there any breakfast left?"

There was no one else in the kitchen.

"Of course there is—and I made the suggestion because I meant it." Molly turned back to the stove. "Eliza's just got down herself. Did you sleep well?"

"Well enough." He met Eliza's gaze, noted her eyes were shadowed. Saw the cynical quirk of her brow, as if she knew he was lying.

The truth was he'd found it difficult to slip under sleep's veil. The nagging pain in his shoulder, combined with an underlying disquiet that had had more to do with missing Eliza's warmth beside him—how on earth that had come to be so familiar and in some odd sense required when they'd only shared a bed for five nights he didn't know—had kept him awake long after the house had fallen silent.

He'd slipped into a fitful doze as the sky had been lightening, then he'd slept through the sounds of the busy household waking.

Getting dressed had been a painful chore, but he'd managed it with the same stoicism with which he'd got undressed the night before. The wound was painful and sore, but he had reasonable use of his arm.

Moving it hurt like hell, but . . .

Taking the seat beside Eliza, he thanked Molly as she placed a steaming bowl of porridge liberally laced with honey before him. The aroma reached him. His mouth watered; he picked up his spoon and dug in.

Eliza watched him, satisfied his appetite, at least, was unaffected. Unlike Molly, she knew what he normally looked like in the morning, and the lines bracketing his mouth, etched into his lean cheeks, weren't usually there.

Finishing her own porridge, she exchanged the empty bowl for the cup of tea Molly had ready for her. She seriously doubted Jeremy had slept all that well. She certainly hadn't, too worried over him to find any peace, not until dawn had been streaking the sky.

She'd debated going to check on him, but concern over waking him if he had managed to fall asleep had kept her in her own little bed. Tossing and turning, then later dreaming that he'd started a fever, but his color this morning was normal, not flushed, so it seemed that it had indeed only been a dream. The beginning of a nightmare.

She sipped her tea and nearly sighed. She smiled at Molly. "Lovely."

Sounds at the front of the house grew louder, then resolved into Hamish and Dickon returning. Both came into the kitchen. While Hamish went to drop a kiss on Molly's curly head, Dickon nodded to Jeremy and Eliza, then looked at Hamish. "I'll go rub the horses down."

Hamish nodded and took a seat opposite Jeremy. "Aye—I can tell this lot all that's needful, but no doubt you'd best be ready to ride down with the three of us—your Uncle Ro'll want to question you as well as me, to make sure you didn't spot something I missed."

Dickon grinned, ducked his head, and went.

Hamish smiled fondly at Dickon's back. "Idolizes his uncle Ro, he does."

Jeremy arched his brows. "He could do a lot worse."

"Verra true." Hamish folded his hands and leveled his gaze on them. "The bodies, sadly, were gone by the time we reached the spot."

"Gone?" Jeremy pushed his empty bowl away. "How?"

"I'm thinking it'll be one of the droving crews coming past—there were signs riders had been at the spot, milling about for a time before riding on north. It's the way around here—we find a body, we take it to the magistrate in the nearest town. He'll report the death and arrange for burial." Hamish grimaced. "Trouble is, the nearest town depends on the route the riders were taking. That said, however, there's no doubt whatever that your men fell to their deaths on the rocks." He grimaced again, this time plainly in distaste. "Plenty of evidence to attest to that."

Jeremy digested that, then asked, "How do we go about finding where the bodies were taken?"

Hamish met his gaze. "I'm thinking that you'll have enough on your plate just now, what with Eliza here having gone missing more'n a week ago, and everyone who knows you both waiting and expecting you to reach Wolverstone days since. Best you leave locating the bodies—and learning what we can from the laird's—to me and Royce. Once I track the bodies down, he'll be able to pull his usual strings and learn all we need."

After a moment, Jeremy inclined his head. "Thank you—that would almost certainly be the best way forward. However"—he glanced at Eliza—"it might be wise not to inquire too openly. We don't want anyone asking why we're so interested in learning the laird's identity, and as for Scrope, I'd be surprised if he isn't known in certain circles as the villain he was. Again, we don't want to allow any connection to be drawn between Eliza and Scrope."

"No." Hamish was nodding. "Or between you and Scrope, come to that. Leave it to Royce and me—we'll get the information without anyone the wiser." Hamish grinned. "If necessary, we'll lie. Royce always was good at weaving stories."

Jeremy grinned back. "I imagine that would have been a required talent in his previous life." Over the years of the wars with France, Royce had been England's spymaster in charge of all covert English agents on the Continent.

"So." Hamish looked from Jeremy to Eliza. "Are you ready to start out again? It'll take us an hour, a bit more, to reach the castle."

Eliza looked at the clock on the dresser. "It's just eleven o'clock—if we leave now, we should reach there before they sit down to luncheon."

"Aye—so I'm thinking," Hamish said.

Jeremy caught Eliza's gaze. "The track's too steep for a gig—we'll have to go on horseback."

"Oh." Her face fell.

Hamish frowned. "We've plenty of horses."

Eliza grimaced. "It's not that. I'm . . . not a very confident horsewoman."

Both Hamish and Molly blinked; an instant of silence ensued.

Molly broke it. "Well, then." She spoke to her husband. "Give Jeremy Old Martin, and he can take Eliza up before him."

"Good idea." Nodding, Hamish rose. He looked at Jeremy and Eliza. "If you've finished here, we might as well get going."

Jeremy and Eliza thanked Molly, sincerely grateful for her cosseting. Molly beamed, pressed their hands, and wished them well, then they followed Hamish out to the stable.

Dickon was there; between them, the three men saddled three horses.

Jeremy insisted on saddling Old Martin, a placid older gelding. "Moving my arm helps."

It also hurt, but he had a suspicion that if he didn't use the arm normally, it wouldn't heal as well as it might.

While he buckled the saddle girth, he finally put his finger on what it was that seemed so different between now and when he'd visited Hamish and Molly with Royce two weeks ago. *He* was the only thing to have changed.

And he had changed—dramatically.

He felt older, more mature. More tried and tested. He'd been through the fire and had survived and emerged on the other side; he now knew his own mettle.

He also had a much clearer vision of how he wanted his life henceforth to be.

Girth tightened, he flipped the stirrup down, then turned to Eliza.

Looked at her, met her hazel eyes . . . and felt his heart expand and his awareness lock on her. She was the essential central foundation he needed for his future, the future he now wanted—his future with her.

She smiled a trifle tentatively, unsure of his thoughts.

He returned the smile fleetingly; now was not the time for the discussion they would have to have, the discussion they wouldn't be able to avoid once they reached Wolverstone and returned to their normal lives. He held the horse steady. "Would you rather ride before, or behind?"

She glanced up at the horse's back; Old Martin was a good seventeen hands tall. "Before, if you don't mind."

"I don't. Here—take my hand." He helped her up, then swung up behind her.

Hamish and Dickon were already mounted and waiting in the yard.

After making sure Eliza was comfortably and safely settled before him, Jeremy walked Old Martin out, appreciating the gelding's steady, unhurried gait and broad back—appreciating why Molly had suggested him as a mount. There was no chance Old Martin would bolt even if Jeremy dropped the reins.

"Right then." Hamish nodded. "Let's away."

Hamish led the way out, Jeremy followed, and Dickon brought up the rear. In line, they trotted up the track, back to Clennell Street, then turned south, to England and Wolverstone Castle.

When their party passed through the wrought-iron gates that marked the entrance to Wolverstone Castle and came within sight of the castle's front steps, Eliza could barely believe her eyes. "Where the devil did they all come from?"

From behind her, apparently equally transfixed by the crowd waiting to greet them, Jeremy murmured, "And why?"

"My parents," she whispered, "I'd expected, and Royce and Minerva, of course, and Hugo and Cobby and even Meggin—we knew they might be here. But my sisters, and Breckenridge, and Gabriel and Alathea, and Devil and Honoria and Aunt Helena?"

"Leonora and Trentham I thought might come, but Christian and Letitia, and Delborough and Deliah, and, to cap it all, Lady Osbaldestone?"

Before Eliza could do more than make a disbelieving sound, they drew close enough to have to plaster on reassuring smiles.

They halted in the forecourt. As Jeremy dismounted, with beaming smiles and cries of welcome their watchers broke ranks and flooded down the steps. By the time he lifted Eliza down, a small tide of females had reached them, and then they were swamped.

Caught up in her mother's scented and transparently hugely relieved embrace, Eliza barely had time to assure Celia that she was all right before her father pulled her into a crushing hug, then passed her to Heather, then Angelica, and Gabriel, and Alathea . . .

The sound of a dozen voices rolled over them, all exclaiming and asking questions, which Hamish—bless him—

fielded as best he could. After days of relative isolation, with just Jeremy for company, Eliza felt like she was drowning.

Not just in the noise and the physical crowd, but in the emotions swirling around her; happy though they were in general, an undercurrent of worry, of concern, remained.

On her parents' part, she knew that worry would persist until she and Jeremy had told their tale and then sorted out their . . . consequences.

She wasn't ready to think of those yet.

Catching his gaze, seeing in his brown eyes the same sense of being overwhelmed, she smiled, a small private smile that he returned before they were both drawn once more to attend to those who stood all around them.

Eliza finally reached Meggin and embraced her warmly. "You were right—we didn't come close to making it in a day. The food came in useful."

Meggin laughed and drew back to hold Eliza at arm's length. "I'm just so glad—we're all so glad—you made it through. We were so worried when you didn't make it by the second, or even the third, day."

"After that, we lost count and just worried." Cobby pushed through to hug Eliza. "Sadly, our wonderful decoy didn't work as well as, or for as long as, we'd hoped. Did you have Scrope and his crew on your tail all the way?"

"No—we didn't see Genevieve or Taylor after we left. Only Scrope and laird."

"The laird?" Devil turned from speaking with Jeremy. "I'll be interested in anything more you learned of him."

Eliza opened her mouth, but a sharp clap drew all attention to Minerva, Duchess of Wolverstone, who had gone inside but now stood at the top of the steps.

"If you want to know all, then I suggest you let poor Jeremy and Eliza gather their wits. If you will all come inside, luncheon is on the table, and after we've refreshed ourselves, we can gather in the drawing room and all hear the entire story at once." Minerva swept the gathering with a sharp hazel gaze. "So no more questions, not until we're settled in the drawing room."

Devil turned back to Eliza, but, lips now firmly shut, she just smiled at him. When he frowned back, trying for intimidation, she laughed. "You heard what our hostess decreed. You'll just have to wait like everyone else."

Which suited the powerful Duke of St. Ives not at all, but even he wasn't immune to Minerva's power. Especially given his own duchess had now fixed her eagle eye on him; with a grunt, he waved Eliza, Meggin, and Cobby on, then crossed to give Honoria his arm.

With Angelica, also keen to hear more, on her other side, Eliza climbed the steps. Looking across, she saw Jeremy flanked by his sister, Leonora, Viscountess Trentham, and his brother-in-law, Tristan, Viscount Trentham. Christian Allardyce, Marquess of Dearne, and his wife, Letitia, flanked Trentham and Leonora respectively.

Eliza's aunt Helena, Dowager Duchess of St. Ives, and Lady Osbaldestone had gone ahead, each claiming one of Hugo's arms—and, Eliza had not a doubt, subtly interrogating him; the two grandes dames were the only ones present who would dare defy Minerva's decree.

They all walked into the cool shadows of the great hall, and Eliza felt the web of her connections—familial, social—click into place once more. As if she'd stepped back into some preordained spot, some already carved niche labeled with her name. And the shape of that niche defined who and what she was. . . . she wriggled her shoulders, sloughed off the thought, smiled at Angelica, who had looked at her quizzically, and walked on.

She wasn't the same person she had been, but she didn't yet know exactly who she now was. She would have to learn the answer, soon, but . . .

With Minerva in her carver at the end of the table monitoring all conversations, the company restrained themselves, and luncheon passed off quickly and smoothly.

Feeling considerably more refreshed, fortified for what was to come, Eliza took the armchair Royce waved her to in the drawing room, one of a pair he'd set flanking the huge fireplace and facing the long, elegantly comfortable room. The rest of the company disposed themselves on the various sofas, chaises, and chairs, the men spread around the room behind their wives.

All except Royce, who remained between the two armchairs, his back to the fireplace. As Jeremy sat in the other armchair, Royce turned to Eliza and smiled encouragingly. "Why don't you start with what happened when you left the ballroom in St. Ives House?"

She nodded and began, "I received a note, passed on by one of our footmen."

Eliza told of her kidnapping, at Royce's request describing Scrope, Genevieve, and Taylor, then detailing all that had happened from her perspective until Jeremy, Hugo, and Cobby had arrived to rescue her from the basement of the Edinburgh town house.

Royce turned to Jeremy. "How did you learn where she was? Start from when you saw Eliza being whisked past in a carriage up the Jedburgh Road."

Jeremy nodded and took over the tale, filling in what he'd done while Eliza had been taken to Edinburgh and held at the town house. After outlining how he, Cobby, and Hugo had arranged and executed Eliza's rescue, he smoothly continued with their journey out of Edinburgh, avoiding all mention of Eliza's problem with riding, simply stating that soon after leaving Edinburgh they were forced to go on in farm carts, those being the only conveyances available.

When he reached the point of spotting the laird on their trail from the church tower in Currie, he looked at Cobby and Hugo. "I'm assuming your decoy drew Scrope off—we didn't see him until much later."

Cobby cleared his throat. "As to that . . ." He explained what had happened, culminating in his and Hugo's return to

Edinburgh. "But we checked at the stables in the Grassmarket, and they said you'd ridden out, and although a laird—the stableman called him that—had asked after two people who had set out that morning, the stableman didn't think he was interested in you two—he'd asked after an English young lady and a gentleman."

Jeremy frowned, then shrugged. "However he did it, he realized we were on that road and came after us."

"Just the laird?" Devil asked.

Jeremy nodded. "We didn't see Scrope until later the next day, outside Penicuik. But that's getting ahead." He returned to them racing into the Pentland Hills to avoid the laird. He continued in simple, declarative vein, reciting the facts but nothing more. None of the emotions, none of their fears, much less their evolving passions.

Eliza seemed content to let him continue; when he glanced her way, she nodded. When he described their escape from a pistol-waving Scrope in St. Boswells, exclamations abounded. Smoothly, he went on, outlining their subsequent journey, the hurdles of the washed-out bridges, then their last wild race for the border.

His audience sat in absolute, unmoving silence as he recounted their flight from Scrope—no longer merely waving a pistol but actively shooting—culminating in that moment high on the ridge in the Cheviots, and the final, definitive appearance of the laird.

"He's *dead*?" Devil sounded incredulous.

"We couldn't afford the time to stop and look—the weather was closing in. As it was, we made it to Hamish's farmhouse just as the rain came down." Jeremy nodded at Hamish. "But Hamish and Dickon went back at first light."

All attention swung to Hamish as he told what he and his son had seen. As Hamish had predicted, Royce questioned both Hamish and Dickon closely.

Under the cover of the interrogation, Jeremy glanced at Eliza. Their gazes met, held, but he couldn't tell what she was thinking, how she was feeling, how she now felt about their adventure, about their journey. About what came next.

The sensational end to their flight resulted in considerable discussion over whether the laird was truly dead, and if so, what did that mean? Would they ever learn what the kidnappings had been about—what he'd sought to accomplish through them?

All unanswerable questions, and largely redundant as far as Jeremy was concerned.

But the presence of all the others kept him in the armchair, an effective constraint stopping him from rising and going to Eliza, taking her hand, and slipping away . . .

Meggin, bless her, noticed that Eliza was tiring; she rose from the chaise nearby, had a whispered conference with Minerva, who nodded, then Meggin went to Eliza and suggested she might like to retire to refresh herself and rest before dinner.

Eliza glanced once at Jeremy, then fell on the offer with an alacrity he shared. Would that he could escape so easily, but he managed an easy, encouraging smile as Eliza's eyes again met his, then she turned and, with Meggin, left the room.

When Meggin closed the drawing room door behind them, Eliza almost sagged with relief. "Thank you! I've never before noticed how noisy such gatherings are—I must be out of practice."

Meggin grinned. "I have to admit to being a bit overwhelmed myself, but everyone's been very kind."

They started toward the wide staircase. "I can't thank you enough for coming," Eliza said. "Your children—will they be all right without you?"

"We left them with my sister and her husband—they live a little way out of Dalkeith—so my brood will be enjoying themselves hugely with their cousins, I imagine." Meggin met her gaze as they climbed. "But as Cobby and Hugo were in such a state over not having kept their decoy-disguise for long enough, and were fixed on coming here as they'd intended and confessing all, I decided I needed to be here to support them."

Eliza smiled. "I'm very glad you came." It was odd, but she now felt closer—more of a mind, with more shared connection—to Meggin than she did to her own cousins. As if the new her, the her that had been molded and forged through the kidnapping, her rescue, and their flight, had already shifted from the exclusive circles of the London haut ton to . . . if not the Edinburgh ton, then to some other social sphere.

Some esoteric scholarly social circle where both she and Jeremy could be themselves. Their true selves.

Pondering that insight, she followed Meggin to the room Minerva had had prepared for her.

To find a bath waiting, a footman tipping in the last pail of hot water.

"Oh, joy!" Eliza sighed. "I don't want to think of how long it is since last I bathed."

A little maid was waiting with towels and scented soap to assist her out of her gown and help her wash her hair.

Meggin offered to follow the footman out, but Eliza begged her to stay.

They chatted about this and that, a conversation about inconsequential, ordinary, day-to-day things that required no great ingenuity, or subtlety, to maintain.

Then Meggin saw the clock on the mantelpiece, exclaimed at the time, and left to check on Cobby and Hugo.

When Eliza finally rose from the tub and, wrapped in a robe, toweled her hair dry, she felt . . . like her old self, but not.

She was increasingly certain she could never go back to that earlier self, her previous incarnation. Whatever changes the last week had wrought, they were irreversible.

Her parents had brought a trunk of her clothes; she had the little maid, Milly, lay out one of her own dinner gowns.

"That will be all for the moment, Milly."

"Yes, miss. Would you like me to come and help you dress, and put up your hair, later?"

"Please." Eliza smiled as she sank onto the dressing stool and picked up her comb. "I'll need help to make it presentable. I'm just going to comb it out, then take a nap."

Milly bobbed. "I'll be back at the first bell."

The door had barely shut behind the little maid when it opened again and Heather, followed by Angelica, walked in.

Meeting her sisters' eyes in the mirror, Eliza immediately knew what they wanted. The truth, the whole truth, and nothing but the truth.

Heather dragged up a chair to one side of the dressing stool; Angelica perched on the end of the stool itself, nudging Eliza with her hip to make room.

"Now," Angelica said, "tell all. All the stuff you left out downstairs."

"Did you really walk through Edinburgh dressed in breeches?" Heather pretended to be scandalized, but her eyes gleamed. "I would have given anything not to have to trudge for miles and miles in skirts."

Eliza nodded and kept combing. "Breeches are much better." With the comb, she pointed to the riding boots she'd been wearing, set neatly by one wall. "And those helped even more. Riding boots are much better than half boots for walking, even under skirts."

"When did you stop wearing the breeches?" Angelica looked around. "Have you got them here?"

Eliza explained, knowing full well that her sisters were merely biding their time until they could lead her to the topic they most wanted to discuss.

Eventually, Heather broached it. "Both Jeremy and you seem altogether calm and settled. So what have you decided, you and him?"

Eliza drew a deeper breath, tipped up her chin. "We decided, shortly after we set out from Edinburgh, once we knew we'd be spending days, and nights, alone, that we weren't going to dwell on the outcome, weren't going to think or discuss it, not until we'd reached safety."

Heather frowned. "Why on earth not?"

"I suppose you might say so that we didn't . . . prejudice what might evolve, all on its own, between us. We just wanted to let ourselves get to know each other, without preconceived results."

Heather looked uncertain, but Angelica slowly nodded. "All right. I can understand that. But what about now?"

"Now," Eliza said, laying down her comb, "he and I need to discuss what we feel, and what we want and how to go about things . . . but clearly we can't do that until we get a chance to speak privately, without the entire gaggle of our families looking on."

"That," Angelica said, head tilting, "is very true." In the mirror, she met Eliza's eyes. "Do you want us to"—Angelica wriggled her fingers, moving them through the air in mimicry of lots of horses—"help matters along?"

Eliza looked into Angelica's eyes, took in her younger sister's expression, then looked at Heather, saw the same support in her elder sister's eyes. "If you can, I'll be eternally grateful."

"Consider it done," Heather said. "I'm sure a word—the right word—in Minerva's ear, and Honoria's, will do the trick."

"Nothing like duchesses to get people moving," Angelica averred.

Heather tilted her head, her gaze still searching Eliza's face. "You've changed," she said. "I don't know exactly how, but . . ."

Angelica humphed. "Of course she's changed. She's found her hero, and if I'm any judge, she's his heroine." Rising, Angelica caught Eliza's eyes in the mirror and grinned. "Which means we should leave so she can get some rest, because she'll need her strength for tonight."

Eliza blushed.

Heather saw; her brows rose, but she contented herself with a knowing smile and got to her feet. "Angelica's right—we'll leave you. Just promise you'll call on us if you need any help."

Eliza felt her smile wobble as she stood. Turning to her sisters, she flung an arm around each of them and hugged. "Thank you."

They hugged her back, then drew away.

Heather wagged a finger as she turned to the door. "Just remember—you have to send word to us first once you and Jeremy finalize your discussions."

"Yes, indeed." At the door, Angelica turned. "No letting Lady O find out about anything first."

Eliza laughed. "Heaven forbid!"

With a smile, she watched her sisters leave. The smile, and the warmth imparted by her sisters' tacit approbation of Jeremy, lingered as she walked to the bed, lay down on the counterpane, and closed her eyes.

She wasn't the same person she had been, but she didn't yet know exactly who she now was. Perhaps, but she was getting a clearer view of herself with every passing minute.

She's found her hero, and . . . she's his heroine. Angelica had a habit of putting her delicate finger squarely on the heart of things.

Eliza had been searching for her hero for years, and she knew, to her heart, to her soul, that she'd found him in Jeremy Carling.

Totally unexpectedly, but incontrovertibly.

He was hers, and she was his, and in subtle ways that she couldn't explain yet was nonetheless conscious of, that had changed her. It had changed her view of herself; it had changed how she felt about herself. Their flight, and the way he interacted with her—all the ways in which they connected, shared, and exchanged bits and pieces of themselves—had altered and molded and re-formed her into a lady who was . . . much stronger and more confident than the young lady she'd been.

As there was no going back, she could only go forward. Forward into their joint future. A future society would demand and insist they share . . . but there was no reason they needed to allow society to dictate the tenor, the type, of their union.

It had been his farsightedness in suggesting they leave the details of their "outcome" until later, until now, that had allowed them to see what might be, but she was increasingly sure she would need her newfound courage to secure the future as she now imagined it and wanted it to be.

She knew what she wanted with a certainty that previously had never been hers. She'd rarely, if ever, felt so immovably determined.

She'd rarely felt so arrogantly Cynsterish, truth be told.

There was, now she'd looked, no doubt whatever in her mind. She wanted to translate the relationship, the partnership that had evolved between her and Jeremy during their mad flight through a world not their own, onto this plane. She wanted to bring that same closeness, that sharing, that reciprocal reliance, into this, their normal world, and embed it, enshrine it, in their union.

That was what she wanted—the style of marriage she knew they could have, and was absolutely determined they would indeed have.

The only questions remaining were, first, how?

How was she to effect the translation from a life lived under pursuit, to a life lived among the ton?

And lastly, the even more vital question: When all was said and done, now they were back in society's fold and the ton had once again laid its hands upon them, would he be willing to go along? More, was he, as she was, willing to fight to hold on to the relationship they'd discovered they could share?

Those two questions circled in her brain, around and around, until sleep stepped in and dragged her down.

"What was the damned man looking to achieve?" Devil appealed to the room at large—Royce's library, to which all the males had escaped and where they now reposed in various chairs, or propped their shoulders against shelves, or, in Royce's case, prowled restlessly before the long windows—but no one answered.

The "damned man" to whom Devil referred was, of course, the late laird.

Eventually, Royce said, "Once we learn his identity, we might gain some insight. You can leave that to Hamish and me. He'll track the riders and learn where they left the body. I'll follow up, without revealing why I'm interested. The bodies were found near enough to my lands, so my questions won't seem too remarkable. If the man truly was a highland nobleman, then there's certain to be talk. There's no way the death of such a man could pass unremarked. One way or another, we'll follow his trail back."

"What I don't understand," Lord Martin Cynster, Eliza's father, said, "is why he, the laird, fought with Scrope, who, by all accounts, was his henchman, and who at the time had Jeremy and Eliza bailed up." Lord Martin spread his hands. "Why arrange a kidnapping, only to let Eliza escape? More, to *ensure* she escaped? It makes no sense."

Jeremy had let the arguments run. Now he shifted and said, "I've been thinking about that. His actions would, presumably, make perfect sense if we knew his motives. Let's say he—for some reason we don't know—needs an unmarried, unattached, Cynster girl. So he arranged for Heather's kidnapping, but as soon as that went awry"—Jeremy looked at Breckenridge, seated across the room—"correct me if I'm wrong, he dismissed his hirelings."

Breckenridge nodded. "Yes, that's right. Go on."

"So . . . Fletcher and Cobbins, wasn't it? They would have

described you to the laird. You pulled the wool over their eyes, but what if the laird saw enough to be suspicious, at least to some degree, of your station? You said he followed you, but when he caught up with you—in open country with no one else about, him on horseback, very possibly with a weapon, and you on foot, almost certainly unarmed and with Heather to protect—what did he do?"

"He watched," Breckenridge replied.

"Did you . . ." Jeremy gestured. "Sense any menace from him?"

Breckenridge hesitated, then replied, "No. I remarked on it at the time. He watched *assessingly*. He made no friendly overtures, but neither did he make any threatening moves."

Jeremy nodded. "Exactly. And then once you'd walked on, he checked at a local tavern and learned you'd taken Heather to a manor owned by her family."

"And then he left the area," Breckenridge said. His eyes on Jeremy's, he added, "Because he knew Heather was safe?"

Jeremy nodded again. "That's what I surmise. Once he gauged what sort of man you were, and that you were protecting Heather, and I don't know but would guess that he'd seen you and her together?"

Breckenridge nodded curtly.

"Well," Jeremy blew out a breath. "Let's remember we're dealing with a highlander, a nobleman. Let's assume he hunts—"

"And he's used to commanding men," Royce cut in, "used to reading men, and he trusts his instincts." He'd stopped pacing and was looking at Jeremy. "Your hypothesis is starting to make sense. How does it fit with what happened with Eliza?"

"She's the next Cynster girl—the next Cynster sister. So this time the laird sends a henchman who's both more determined and more experienced than Fletcher and Cobbins. Fletcher and Cobbins were effective enough, but Scrope was more so, more ruthless, and also more accustomed to dealing with the ton. Eliza's kidnapping was neat and efficient, and Scrope struck in the one place he could be certain Eliza would be, relatively speaking, unwatched."

"True," Devil said, his tone terse.

"Scrope's use of laudanum to keep Eliza subdued through the journey, rapid though it was, again suggests Scrope was of a different caliber to Fletcher and Cobbins. But, again, once Scrope lost Eliza"—Jeremy looked at Royce—"I think the laird dismissed Scrope and came after Eliza and me himself.

"I originally thought Scrope and the laird were working together, chasing us. But"—Jeremy nodded at Cobby and Hugo—"as Cobby reminded me, if that had been so, then we should have seen Taylor, one of Scrope's crew, helping. I can understand that the nurse, Genevieve, wouldn't have been all that much use in the chase, but Taylor? He wasn't a mindless thug—he tracked down Cobby and Hugo faster than we'd expected."

Pausing, Jeremy glanced around the circle. "The only reason I can think of for Scrope *not* to have Taylor helping search for us is if Scrope had been dismissed, so let Taylor and Genevieve go, but then Scrope decided to disobey the laird's orders and go after Eliza on his own."

"By all accounts," Gabriel said, "the laird, whoever he was, was not a man most people would gainsay."

Jeremy grimaced. "Just from what I saw of him—always at a distance—I would have to agree. He cut an impressive and intimidating figure. Just watching him walk was warning enough. But from what Eliza has said, Scrope wasn't your average kidnapper, either. He may not have been a gentleman, but he wasn't far from it." Drawing in a breath, Jeremy paused, then went on, "And from what we saw of Scrope over the last days, especially from how he spoke just before the laird intervened . . . well, he didn't sound all that sane. It was as if the notion of Eliza escaping was, to him, simply *insupportable*. I think it's telling that, at the last, it was Eliza he aimed at, not me."

Various mutterings greeted that, but Royce was nodding. "Let's concede the notion that losing Eliza caused Scrope to fixate on getting her back, regardless of how he did it. Given that scenario, could the laird have been following you with the same purpose as you've hypothesized he had in following Heather and Breckenridge—that he was seeking not to recapture Eliza but to consider you, her rescuer, and, if you passed his standards and protected Eliza and got her to safety, then he would let her, and you, go?"

Jeremy nodded. "I've thought back over all that we saw of him, and, yes, that hypothesis could fit. If he wasn't desperate over *which* Cynster girl he took, then he could afford to be lenient, adjust his plans, and go after the next. He didn't need Eliza *per se* any more than he'd needed Heather specifically—he just needs, needed, a Cynster sister."

"So you're saying he—who had originally hired Scrope—attacked Scrope because Scrope was acting in a way that would endanger Eliza?" Christian looked skeptical.

But Jeremy nodded again. "As far as I can see, that's the only explanation that fits all the evidence." He waved at Breckenridge. "All that we've seen."

Breckenridge, too, nodded. "We shouldn't forget that the laird's instructions to Fletcher and Cobbins made it very clear that Heather was not, under any circumstances, to be harmed. 'Not a hair on her head' were, I believe, Fletcher's words."

Silence fell while all present digested that and absorbed the implications of Jeremy's hypothesis.

Eventually, Lord Martin stirred. "I suppose, given he is a nobleman, then we have to allow that he might have some allegiance to honor."

"I think," Royce said, "that we might need to allow that. Regardless, the man's now dead. We still don't know what motive drove him to seek to kidnap one of the Cynster girls, but once we learn his identity, no doubt that, too, will become clear."

"But as he's dead," Lord Martin said, "then presumably there is no further threat to the girls."

"Thank God!" Gabriel's exclamation was echoed by Devil. "If I had to put up with much more harping from Angelica on the subject of my overprotective tendencies, I'd be inclined to wring her neck myself." He shook his head at the others. "She has a tongue that's sharper than any sword. I pity the poor sod she decides is going to be honored by having her to wife."

The laughter of all the others was cut short by the resonant *bong* of the bell, warning them that it was time to dress for dinner.

They all rose, stretched, then filed out of the library.

Royce, at the rear, following Jeremy, clapped him on the back. "Good work. Thanks to you, tonight is going to be a festive occasion."

Lips lifting, Jeremy inclined his head. "You should thank Eliza—she did her part, too."

Royce smiled and nodded. "I will."

Later that night, Jeremy lay on his back in the very real comfort of a bed long enough to accommodate his length and wondered, rather woozily—courtesy of the draft the doctor, summoned by an insistent Minerva, had given him—whether Morpheus would oblige and allow him some rest.

His arm still throbbed dully, distantly, although the draft had indeed deadened the pain.

His brain seemed determined to keep going round and round, not quite focusing on anything in particular, but equally unable to stop.

And beneath his whirling thoughts lay a disturbing, disquietening sense of something not being right.

The castle gradually settled, and silence fell. He'd almost resigned himself to not getting any sleep when the door to his room opened. Just a crack at first, then it swung fully open and Eliza whisked in and shut the door behind her.

He blinked, concluded, as she glided to the bed, peered at him through the dimness, then whispered, "You're not asleep, are you?" that she wasn't an apparition, a figment of his neediness.

"No." After a second's consideration, he inquired, mildly, "What are you doing here?" The words came out a trifle slurred.

She was already shrugging out of her robe. "Ssh—no need to talk. I just wanted to be with you, to make sure that you're all right."

Beneath the robe, her long, slender body was sheathed in a fine cotton nightgown.

Lifting the covers, she slid into the bed on his uninjured side. She snuggled against him as she normally did, or more correctly as she had done for five of the six nights past. Obligingly, he raised his good arm and she snuggled closer yet.

Her warmth spread like a balm over his uninjured side, then sank beneath his skin and spread further. Reached deeper.

She sighed and settled her cheek on his chest. "Just sleep."

Part order, part instruction—all in all, an excellent suggestion. His lips had curved; his smile deepened as he squinted at her bright head. Then he did as ordered and relaxed; letting his head sink back into the pillow, he closed his eyes.

It was strange; just having her there calmed his whirling thoughts.

Her appearance in his room, her presence in his bed, didn't, he knew, resolve any of the issues, answer any of the questions, revolving in his brain. Those issues, those oh-so-pertinent questions, lay before them, but that was for tomorrow.

For tonight . . . everything was now right, as it should be.

Now he could fall asleep.

And he did.

Chapter Seventeen

wo mornings later, Jeremy stood amid a chaos of carriages, horses, footmen, and grooms, with friends and close acquaintances clapping him on the back and wishing him well, and scented ladies he'd known and largely avoided for years patting him on the cheek and stating their expectation of seeing him soon in London, as the bulk of those who'd gathered at Wolverstone prepared to depart.

He didn't know which deity to thank for prompting the general exodus, but he was immeasurably grateful.

Hugo, Cobby, and Meggin were the first to actually leave; they would drive back to Edinburgh in Hugo's curricle. Cobby had driven Jeremy's curricle down, and Jasper was now eating his head off in Royce's stable.

"I say," Cobby said. "I took a quick gander at your notes on Wolverstone's Sumerian tome. Fabulously exciting! Don't forget to send me a copy of the paper when you present it to The Royal Society."

When Jeremy looked blank, Cobby frowned. "You are going to present your findings, aren't you?"

Jeremy blinked. "Ah, yes." It had taken long minutes to remember the fantastic find he'd uncovered. "Of course—I'll send you a copy once it's done." Eventually.

The realization that, from the moment he'd turned his curricle north in pursuit of Eliza, he hadn't once thought of the critical text he'd discovered struck him as epitomizing how much he'd changed. Even now, while matters between him and Eliza remained unresolved, he felt no inclination to spare time for his notes.

Hiding that frankly shocking discovery behind an easy smile, he shook hands with Cobby, clapped his friend on the back, then let him go and turned to farewell Meggin.

"Take care." Meggin stretched up to kiss his cheek. Drawing back, she searched his eyes. "And be sure to bring Eliza up for a visit when this is all over."

That "this" hovered over him, and over Eliza, too. He nodded. "I will."

Eliza chose that moment to join them. Meggin turned, and she and Eliza embraced warmly.

"Thank you so much for all your help," Eliza said.

Meggin laughed and repeated her invitation.

Eliza's face lit. "Of course we'll come." Then she turned to Cobby and Hugo, wishing them well and laughing at something Hugo said.

Jeremy watched her. Her acceptance of Meggin's invitation had been genuine, sincere; her interaction with his friends pleased and reassured him.

Although she'd spent the last two nights sleeping alongside him, ensuring he, too, got a good night's rest, on both mornings when he'd woken, she'd already gone. And courtesy of the small army that until now had inhabited the castle, he and she had had not a moment alone in which to exchange opinions on anything. Consequently, he had no idea what she now thought, was thinking, about him, about them, about their necessarily joint future, not now that they'd returned to their customary world.

What he was in no doubt about was how all those present, barring only Cobby, Hugo, and Meggin—climbing into Hugo's curricle even as he pondered—saw him. And therefore how they saw the looming connection-that-had-to-be between him and Eliza.

Her elder brother, Gabriel, was only the latest to reinforce that view.

After standing beside Jeremy and waving Hugo, Cobby, and Meggin away, Eliza was hailed by Breckenridge; she hurried off to speak with her sisters, whom Breckenridge was escorting back to town. Leaving the space at Jeremy's shoulder to be filled by her brother.

"I wanted to thank you for saving her." There was no doubting the sincerity in Gabriel's deep voice. "Your plan to get her back here within one day was a good one, and with either Heather or Angelica it would have worked, but I know it was Eliza's lack of riding skills that skittled the plan. It wasn't your fault you and she spent days getting to safety. Indeed"—Gabriel's lean lips curved—"for someone who spends his days with his nose buried in dusty books, you did exceedingly well avoiding all the dangers and getting past the hurdles to get her safely here. But the wider outcome wasn't any part of your plan, and no fault of yours, yet you've made it plain enough you're willing to accept it, and for that I—and the rest of us, too—honor you."

Jeremy didn't want them to honor him in that way, yet he could hardly protest that there was no need, that his willingness to save Eliza in the wider sense wasn't primarily driven by any sense of obligation, not when he didn't know what Eliza was now thinking. Whether, now they were back in society's fold, she wished to cast their upcoming union in an obligatory light. His gaze on her as she chatted with Heather and Angelica, he replied, "I . . ." Sliding his hands into his pockets, he lightly shrugged. "It's the right thing to do, for both of us."

That, at least, was true.

Gabriel inclined his head. "Regardless." He held out his hand. "Call on us for anything you need."

"Thank you." Jeremy shook Gabriel's hand, then smiled at Alathea as she joined them.

The farewells continued. Jeremy had much the same conversation with Devil as he'd had with Gabriel, with much the same result. Having to skirt the question of just what the true relationship between him and Eliza was—having to let Devil, Honoria, Helena, Lady Osbaldestone, and all the rest leave with the clear impression that the union everyone had been careful not to directly mention would be one based on honor and driven by a need to preserve Eliza's reputation . . . allowing that view to remain unchallenged literally grated on his nerves.

They felt rubbed raw by the time he'd waved away the carriage conveying Christian, Letitia, Delborough, and Deliah back to Lincolnshire.

Yet he had to admit to feeling grateful that so many had come in support of him as well as Eliza. On receiving the message he'd sent from Edinburgh, Royce had sent riders to Leonora and Tristan in Surrey, and to Eliza's parents in London. Gabriel and Alathea had come north with Lord Martin and Lady Celia. Devil and Honoria had driven up, too; as Helena had been staying with them at the time, she, too, had come. Leonora and Tristan had broken the long journey north at Dearne Abbey, and found Delborough and Deliah visiting there, along with Lady Osbaldestone. Not knowing what the state of affairs might be north of the border, Christian and Letitia and Delborough and Deliah had joined Tristan and Leonora, and Lady Osbaldestone had, of course, come too.

Lady Osbaldestone had elected to return to London with Helena in Devil and Honoria's carriage; it followed Christian's down the drive. Gabriel and Alathea had already set out for London.

On the other side of the forecourt, Eliza had had more than enough of being lectured by her sisters. She hugged Heather, who then allowed Breckenridge to hand her up the carriage steps. On the top step, Heather turned and fixed Eliza with an admonitory look. "Remember, hold firm. You know what you want—so make sure you get it."

Beside the carriage, Breckenridge rolled his eyes and feigned deafness.

Eliza rolled her eyes, too. "Stop fussing. I know what I'm doing."

"Yes," Angelica said, preparing to follow Heather, "but will you stick to it? We all know you're softer, more malleable, than Heather or me. If you lose heart on this, if you allow yourself to be persuaded to settle for anything less than your dreams, we'll . . ." On the top step, Angelica narrowed her eyes to green shards. "Well, I don't know what we'll do, but I do know we won't stand for it. So don't backslide."

With that, Eliza's irritating younger sister turned and disappeared into the carriage.

Leaving Breckenridge to follow.

He grinned ruefully and gave Eliza a light hug. "As your soon-to-be brother-in-law, I would merely add . . ." He paused, then sighed. "He's a good man, Eliza. Whatever you work out between yourselves, don't forget that—or all that he did, all he's given, to keep you safe."

She blinked. Carefully hugged Breckenridge back; he was still recovering from the life-threatening wound he'd received while saving Heather. "I know what sort of man he is. I'm not likely to forget."

He was her hero in more ways than anyone seemed to realize. That not even her sisters seemed to actually understand that felt very like her last straw, but now that the causes of her irritation had largely left, she could draw breath—and rein in her temper before it actually broke loose.

Lady Osbaldestone and her aunt Helena had gone so far as to assure her that being married to a man known for his propensity to bury himself for weeks at a time in his library wouldn't be that bad; they'd patted her hand and told her she would find plenty of other interests to fill her time.

All of them—all—had behaved, and had alluded to Jeremy, as if he was somehow second-rate. As if their marriage would be a second-best, a not-best outcome, for them both. At least Heather and Angelica had acknowledged the possibility of another outcome, although neither seemed to have all that much faith that better outcome would come to be. Not if the matter was left in Eliza's and Jeremy's hands.

At that moment, Jeremy strolled up. He shook Breckenridge's hand, squeezed the hands Heather and Angelica held out of the carriage windows. Then Eliza's parents came up, along with Royce and Minerva. Breckenridge climbed into the carriage; shutting the door after him, Royce signalled the coachman.

With waves and farewells all around, the carriage rumbled off.

And, finally, they were alone.

Or at least surrounded only by those who had a real reason to be there: Eliza's parents, Leonora and Tristan, and their hosts, Royce and Minerva.

Chatting among themselves, those others all ambled back to the steps, clearly intending to return indoors.

After considering the general retreat, Jeremy glanced at Eliza, still beside him. "Would you like to go for a walk?"

Relief shone in her eyes. "Yes, please. I definitely don't want to go inside and sit."

A feeling for which he had a great deal of sympathy. "We can walk to the stream and take the path around the lake."

She nodded and they headed across the front of the castle, leaving the drive for a well-tended path that led through beds and down the edge of a lawn to the stream.

Taking her hand, he steadied her across the planks of a wooden bridge that arched over the burbling stream. "I'm almost grateful to Scrope for shooting me, given he didn't do too much damage." Meeting her eyes as, surprised, she glanced at him, he grinned ruefully. "Thanks to the wound, we've been able to claim at least a few days' grace before making our expected appearance in London."

Before declaring their engagement and making the necessary plans to wed.

She grimaced. "That's true."

"But as they have all consented to give us the time . . . perhaps we should use it."

Stepping onto the path that ran along the other side of the stream, she arched her brows. "What did you have in mind?"

He hesitated, then said, "Tell me your favorites—colors, flowers, music—anything on which you have an opinion."

She laughed, and did, then demanded the same of him.

They traded likes, dislikes, opinions, and views as they strolled toward the lake. Jeremy found the questions, and his answers to hers, coming more easily to his tongue than he'd expected; talking to young ladies had never been his forte, but in this case . . . this was the lady with whom he would be sharing the remainder of his life; there was no real need to censor his tongue.

What he did need was to learn more about her, even though, to his mind, he already knew the most important things. He knew he liked her laugh, knew that a certain private little smile of hers made him feel like a king. But he paid attention to the answers she gave, his attention wholly locked on her . . .

Wooing her.

With an odd little start, he realized that was what he was doing. More, that he was doing it deliberately, with intent and passion . . . because some part of him, that newfound part of him that had emerged over recent days, drawn out from some recess of his soul by the demands of their flight, believed she deserved it. That she deserved so much more than a preordained union.

Once he realized, somewhat to his surprise, he didn't draw back, but instead went further, set himself to charm and amuse and draw her out. And found he could.

Eyes laughing, she responded openly, without guile. They reached the lake and continued strolling beneath the trailing branches of the willows, taking the path that led away from the house, slowly circumnavigating the lake.

Eliza found herself captivated, her heart captured all over again. Sliding her arm into his, she walked by his side and asked after his uncle Humphrey, asked him to describe the house at Number 14, Montrose Place, where he and his uncle lived. He duly described the house and gardens with the degree of detail she expected from him, but even she detected the one glaring omission. She arched a brow at him. "What about the library?"

He pulled a face, almost a wince. "Actually, it's libraries. There are two. I converted what used to be the conservatory into a drawing room, and then took over the original drawing room for my own."

Before he could do violence to his feelings and offer to reverse the conversion—as his somewhat stricken expression suggested he was about to do—she leapt in to ask, "So the new drawing room overlooks the back garden?"

Somewhat warily, he nodded.

She smiled and pressed her shoulder to his. "That's all the rage these days, you know."

"It is?" He looked at her cynically. "You're making that up."

She laughed and shook her head. "No, truly. It was in all the lady's journals these months past—the latest trend."

"Ah." He nodded. His face cleared. "Well, then, it appears we're ahead of the times. I must remember to tell Humphrey."

"He sounds like he would appreciate the cachet."

"Indeed, he will."

The light banter continued, yet beneath the airy comments there was a thread, a direction, she hadn't missed. He was, in his own way, telling her about his life, his home, the sort of life he led—and asking after hers.

Showing her, revealing to her, the information they hadn't had time to share before ending up engaged-by-default, courtesy of Scrope and the laird.

He didn't have to do it, to extend himself in this way, to let her see the little things, the minutiae of his life that were important to him, that meant something to him.

And he didn't have to be interested in her. Yet he was;

there was nothing the least fabricated in his attention, his interest. Indeed, being the focal point of his undivided attention gave her a definite thrill; as a scholar, his concentration was truly impressive and having that concentration trained on her was in itself riveting.

Knowing him for the scholar he was, largely divorced from the social scene, she hadn't expected him to court her like this. That he had, that he was, made her lose her heart again.

They'd rounded the lake and turned toward the castle. Looking up at the turreted keep, he sighed. "I have to confess I know nothing about betrothals, about what we need to do, publicly or privately." He slanted a glance at her. "I'm assuming you do?"

She held his gaze for a moment, then nodded. The segue had been so seamless, so smooth, but he'd shifted from the theoretical to the practical, to the issues with which they now had to deal. "First comes a notice in the *Gazette*. There's a fairly standard wording."

"And then?"

She drew in a breath, her lungs suddenly tight, let it out with, "That depends very much on us. On what we decide. On our . . . direction."

When he frowned, clearly not comprehending, she explained, "What we do after the notice of our betrothal is posted will signal to the ton, to society at large, what the . . . for want of a better term, basis of our marriage is to be." She fought and succeeded in keeping her tone direct and matter-of-fact. "In circumstances such as ours, there's an expectation that, following the notice in the *Gazette*, matters will be organized quietly, and our wedding will be a subdued, family and close connections only, affair."

"Ah." Raising his head, he looked toward the battlements.

She couldn't see his features, his eyes, couldn't get any real sense of what he was thinking. But she needed to know. This was the crux, the point to which his earlier tack that they not think about society's expectations but simply let what might be between them evolve had brought them to.

Were they to marry for love—were they to grasp the chance for the ultimate happiness she felt sure was within their grasp? Or were they to step back to the safety of a conventional, socially dictated union, one which left them both, at least theoretically, free to step back from love.

Free to remain uncommitted to love.

"We have to make a decision, you see—a choice, one way or the other." She tried to catch his eye, but he didn't look her way.

"Yes. I see."

From what she could glimpse of his face he appeared to be frowning in a rather scholarly way, as if the question of what lay between them was a matter for analysis.

A matter yet in question.

She was tempted to press, yet . . . it was possible he hadn't thought through his feelings yet. Hadn't yet decided on his direction. Men, as her brothers' and cousins' wives frequently pointed out, were often reluctant to engage in such emotional decision making, and while Jeremy might be a scholar, he was also undeniably a man.

Perhaps she should give him time to think, to reach his own conclusion before she advanced hers.

Angelica's words rang in her mind, but she pushed them away. She wasn't backsliding. She knew what she wanted, and she wasn't turning aside from her goal in the least, but she couldn't have what she wanted, couldn't attain her ultimate goal, if he didn't want it, too.

They'd reached the house.

Jeremy held the side door for her, then followed her into the corridor. "Tell me—what's the most unusual, unconventional wording you've ever come across for a betrothal notice?"

The question took her by surprise. "Unusual?" She racked her brain, then shook her head. "I don't think I've ever seen anything but the norm."

"No 'Lord and Lady Higginbotham are hugely relieved to announce the betrothal of their fifth daughter Priscilla to Mr. Courtney'? 'Mr. and Mrs. Foxglove are ecstatic in declaring their eldest daughter Millicent is to be wed to Viscount Snaring'?"

She laughed. "No mention of relief, no matter how real, much less ecstasy."

He humphed. "I think we should make an effort to be original—at least to assess our every option."

She was struck by the reminder of the way his mind worked. "Like we did during our flight?"

They'd reached the large front hall. Halting, lifting her hand from his sleeve, he turned to face her; his fingers lightly clasping hers, he met her eyes. "Yes. Just like that."

Her heart skipped a beat; she searched his eyes. Did he mean—

The gong for lunch cut across their senses, fracturing the moment.

Multiple female voices approached the top of the stairs; the rumble of male voices came from the direction of the library.

Their gazes returned to each other, met, held.

Jeremy's lips twisted. He offered his arm. "Shall we?"

Stifling a sigh, telling herself they would have plenty of time later to pursue their discussion, Eliza set her hand on his sleeve and walked beside him to the dining room.

If Jeremy had harbored any doubt as to what Leonora and Tristan, Royce and Minerva, and Eliza's parents imagined the "basis" of his and Eliza's union would be, the fact that not one word on the subject, not even an allusion to it, was uttered throughout the meal would have set him straight.

The delicate avoidance, the implied awkwardness in even alluding to it, was smotheringly pervasive. No one wanted to raise the issue of the social compulsion to which they all—patently—believed he'd bowed.

He had surrendered to a compulsion, but not that one.

What their attitude implied about Eliza set his teeth on edge.

Admittedly, neither he nor she had made any statement, any declaration, yet he couldn't comprehend how Leonora, and even Tristan and Royce, who had both known him for over a decade, could be so blind to the truth.

A truth he felt in every sinew, that had sunk to his very bones.

He was different; he'd changed. And it wasn't simply their flight from danger that had brought about the transformation.

"We've had a good year thus far in Somerset," Lord Martin replied to Royce's query. "The planting went well and, barring disaster, the yields should be excellent."

The male conversations revolved about cattle, sheep, and crops. How the ladies managed to restrain themselves Jeremy didn't know, but not once was society in any of its many guises so much as mentioned.

On his right, seated opposite Celia, Leonora said, "I'll have to exert myself and find a new governess. Or perhaps an extra governess—our girls have been protesting that they want to learn Latin, and more arithmetic and geography, if you can imagine."

"Oh, I can," Minerva replied. "Ours, sadly, are tomboys, and, of course, Royce is no help in reining them in, but they seem much more inclined to . . . shall we say more *esoteric* pursuits than embroidery, music, or painting."

Their nearest and dearest were tiptoeing around them, and even more around the subject of their marriage.

Halfway through the meal, he exchanged a glance with Eliza. From the set of her lips, she, too, was finding said tiptoeing trying.

He toyed with putting his question about interesting ways to couch a betrothal notice to the table at large, but as he and Eliza hadn't yet discussed and agreed on anything, he refrained.

That last thought kept him quiet through the rest of the meal. He often was silent at the table, but this time it wasn't Mesopotamian hieroglyphics with which he was wrestling.

Eliza hadn't actually *said* anything about what type of marriage she wanted. Had she? He wasn't the most observant sort, not when it came to people, females in particular, but although she'd come to his bed for the past two nights, although she'd responded quite gratifyingly to his attempt to woo her, she hadn't actually stated what she wanted.

He thought he knew; he hoped he was right, but . . . she hadn't actually *uttered* any words on which he could pin his future.

Indeed, the more he thought of it, the more he analyzed, as was his wont, the more he grew unsettlingly aware that his assumptions about them and their future, about what she wanted their marriage to be, were, thus far, based solely on his interpretations of her actions, necessarily viewed through the prism of his own hopes and fears. His needs, his wants.

The reality of hers could conceivably be quite different.

He could, very easily, be wrong.

And all those sitting around him could equally easily be right.

What if they were?

He glanced across the table. Like him, she was silently eating, and paying scant attention to the conversations around her. He tried to view her—her behavior, her expressions, the words they'd exchanged—objectively, dispassionately. Asked himself if what he'd seen might fit equally well if not better with the notion that, having returned to her customary world, she was now happy to slide into the niche that her parents, his family, and their friends had waiting for her—and him—a niche based on preconceptions and on what they believed was preordained.

Sliding into that niche would certainly be easier.

On them both.

Easier to simply surrender the reins, sit back, and follow

the prescribed pattern—starting with a conventionally worded notice in the *Gazette*.

All he had to do was ask her to marry him and then let matters take their course.

He wouldn't have to wrestle with what he felt, what she felt, wouldn't have to make any real adjustments to how he lived his life. Not if he settled for a socially dictated marriage based on obligation and mere affection.

If that was what he wanted, it would be easy to make happen.

But was that what he wanted?

By the time the meal ended and they all rose from the table, he was no longer sure—not of him, not of her, not of what they both wanted, let alone might have, for their future.

Jeremy took himself off for a longer walk. This time alone. He needed to think things through, to get clear in his mind what he wanted—and then devise some clever way to learn what Eliza wanted before he made a fool of himself by making a bid for an option she didn't want.

It might have been easier if he'd been able to speak with her in private, without any of the expectations that—as he'd feared—now all but literally pressed down upon them, but as they'd left the dining room her mother had claimed her attention; engrossed in conversation, Eliza had started up the stairs with the other ladies, presumably heading to Minerva's sitting room, the duchess's favored retreat.

He'd glanced at Eliza's back, then, conscious of the three men following at his heels, he'd walked on down the corridor, not to the library but past it, to a side door that gave access to the gardens.

Stepping out of the house, he closed the door and set out along the gravel path, and felt an oppressive weight ease from his shoulders. From his mind.

This was what he needed, space and silence in which to think.

Sliding his hands into his trouser pockets, he fixed his gaze on the path and walked. He would have preferred to have ridden, or driven, but his wound still rendered either activity unwise.

His mind worked on logical lines; logic was the natural perspective from which he approached any subject he needed to understand.

He needed to understand this.

Comparing himself in this situation with what he knew of other men seemed a sensible place to start. He had always, to himself and all others, been a scholar, not a warrior. Yet most of the men he knew outside of academe were unquestionably warriors—Tristan, all the other members of the Bastion Club, Royce, all the Cynsters; he was well acquainted with the characteristics of the breed.

He might always have been a scholar, but having to rescue Eliza from Scrope and the laird had brought another, underlying, perhaps latent side of him to the fore—a side instantly recognizable as a warrior persona—and as the freely acknowledged approval and approbation of Gabriel, Devil, Royce, and all the others had proved, they, too, had seen his actions and reactions as those not of a scholar but of a warrior like them.

So . . . he was a mixture. A scholar-warrior, or a warrior-scholar, it didn't matter which. What mattered was that, underneath all, he was subject to the same impulses and compulsions as all the other warriors he knew, but in his case those impulses and compulsions were influenced and tempered by his scholarly side.

He wasn't sure if that made him more cold-blooded than them, or simply more clearheaded.

Regardless, the pertinent issues surrounding marriage were ones he'd seen all those others face; he knew how they'd responded. Had any of them been in his shoes . . . he snorted, muttered, "They would seize the chance of getting what I want—Eliza as my wife—without having to speak of love, without having to expose my heart, or acknowledge any of the concomitant vulnerabilities."

He was very aware of those vulnerabilities, yet . . . perhaps it was the scholar in him, but he'd never seen the point in fearing them, or fighting them, at least not to the extent of forgoing what was offered in return. He'd never seen the point in allowing a dislike of one aspect of a desirable coin to prevent him from seizing the coin altogether. "But they would try their damnedest to conceal their true feelings. If I asked, they'd tell me to seize the chance, and allow the assumption that the union between me and Eliza will not be a love-match to stand."

For every gentleman-warrior he knew, marrying the lady they'd loved without having to declare or in any way expose their feelings had been a holy grail. Not one of them had succeeded in attaining it, yet that goal was now before him, placed by circumstance all but in his grasp, his for the seizing.

And he didn't want it.

He knew they'd think him mad . . . or at least they would have before they'd all married. Now . . .

Now, they might just understand.

Each of them, ultimately, had made that other choice. The choice he wanted to, felt driven to, make.

He saw no reason to deny love—its joys, its challenges, its sorrows, all that it encompassed—just because everyone had assumed that he, simple scholar that he'd appeared to be, wouldn't want it. That he wouldn't want to wrestle with such a powerful emotion, to invite its distractions and upheavals into his well-ordered life—but he did.

He didn't need to consider his own feelings further. He *knew* what he wanted.

All he needed was to discover whether Eliza wanted that, too.

Then they could move on.

Into the future that was right for them, rather than the bland and boring future everyone envisaged for them.

A footstep behind him had him glancing back. He wasn't terribly surprised to see Tristan striding along with the clear intention of catching him up.

Stifling a sigh—long-suffering, but resigned—he halted and, schooling his features into a polite but uninformative expression, waited for his brother-in-law.

Tristan met his gaze, tried, unsuccessfully, to see past his mask, then, with an easy gesture, waved them both on. "I imagine you're trying to see your way through all of this."

Jeremy nodded curtly. "Indeed." He was trying to see how to get Eliza to tell him what she felt.

"Obviously," Tristan continued, pacing alongside him, "not in any way foreseeing, or having any experience of, such a situation, you must be wondering about the ins and outs—the details, the requirements, the social commitments."

"Hmm." Jeremy was wondering if it would be fair to simply tell Eliza how he felt, or whether, if he did, she might feel obliged to pretend to feel the same for him—or, potentially even worse, to be terribly kind about it all. Ugh.

Beside him, Tristan went on, "The truth is, all you need to do is ask her to be your wife—you don't need to pretend to any deeper emotion. No one expects you or she to pretend yours will be a love-match."

But what if it was? What if they didn't need to pretend?

It was on the tip of his tongue to voice those questions—and upset Tristan's apple cart entirely—when his brother-in-law continued, "Everyone knows that Eliza isn't the wife you would have chosen, any more than she would have seen you as the man of her dreams, but as neither of you is in any way attached to any other, and as in all other respects the match is perfectly acceptable, then the ton can be counted on to nod and smile and give your marriage its blessing."

The ton could go hang—

Jeremy literally bit his tongue to hold back the words that scalded it. Apparently along with all else, his warrior self had a much hotter temper than the milder scholar possessed; the suggestion that Eliza didn't really want him, or that he didn't truly want her, had been enough to send it soaring. Keeping his eyes on the path so that Tristan wouldn't glimpse his fury, tamping down the urge to rip his brother-in-law's head from his shoulders, verbally at least—reminding himself that he *liked* Tristan, and that Leonora liked him even more—he swallowed the sudden surge of rage and managed a grunt.

Tristan, of course, took it as agreement. He clapped him on the shoulder. "Right then—all you need do to set the ball rolling is ask her for her hand. No need in the circumstances to seek Martin's approval—of course you have it, you may take that as read."

Lord Martin would need to find his sword if he wanted to get in Jeremy's way.

"Once you've asked and she's accepted—which of course she will—then all of us here stand ready to help you both in organizing all the rest." After a moment, Tristan ducked his head, trying to read Jeremy's expression, his reaction to the advice.

By then Jeremy had his features under complete control again, but he wasn't about to trust his tongue. His face set in uncompromising lines, he nodded once and gave another grunt.

From the corner of his eye, he saw Tristan smile, apparently relieved. "No great rush, of course," Tristan said, "but the announcement will probably need to go out within the week."

Another grunt appeared to satisfy. If Jeremy hadn't discovered Eliza's true feelings within a week, he'd go mad.

The path they'd followed had circled the house, leading them to a door in another wing.

"How's the wound?" Tristan asked as he held the door open.

His arm was the least of his concerns. Stepping over the threshold, Jeremy growled, "Still sore."

Leaving Tristan to follow, he stalked on and headed for the library.

None of the others would bother him if he buried his nose in one of Royce's ancient tomes; there were some benefits to being a renowned scholar. All he'd have to do was turn a page now and then, and they would imagine he was reading. Perfect cover for what he really needed and intended to do—to work out a way to learn if Eliza returned his regard.

To discover if she loved him as he loved her.

Eliza's afternoon degenerated from the tryingly bizarre to the bizarrely trying.

She couldn't believe—could barely comprehend—the lack of perception that three ladies she'd previously considered to be among the more intelligent of their class were intent on displaying over her, Jeremy, and their upcoming marriage.

No one questioned that the marriage would occur, but in all other respects, reality and the ladies' expectations dramatically, if not diametrically, diverged.

Her mother had waylaid her in the front hall with a question over the timing of Heather and Breckenridge's wedding. The date had not yet been set because of Breckenridge's near-fatal injury and his subsequent convalescence, but now that their engagement ball was successfully past, thoughts had turned to the wedding.

Eliza hadn't understood her mother's reasoning in asking her, until, having steered her through the doorway into Minerva's sitting room upstairs, Celia had declared, "With your own wedding now in the offing, we'll need to consider just how to balance the two."

Eliza had frowned, then had sat on the sofa beside her mother. "Balance in what way?"

"Well, dear, with Heather and Breckenridge's marriage being a love-match, everyone will expect all the romantic trappings." Celia had met Eliza's eyes, her hazel gaze compassionate, her lips curving in a sympathetic, almost commiserating smile. "With you and Jeremy . . . well, no one would want to put you both through that."

Eliza had been so stunned that she'd simply stared. She hadn't known what to say.

Which, of course, had led her mother to pat her hand consolingly and turn to Minerva and Leonora to ask their advice on, firstly, what they thought society would deem an acceptable betrothal period for Eliza and Jeremy—no longer than necessary seemed to be the consensus—and in light of that, what length of time could be reasonably allowed between Heather and Breckenridge's matrimonial extravaganza, and Eliza and Jeremy's quieter, more reserved nuptials.

Her mind reeling, Eliza tried to formulate some way— some acceptable words—with which to correct the clearly prevalent misconceptions, but every time she assembled appropriately temperate phrases and sentences, one of the other three would make another, even more outrageously erroneous comment, leaving her blinking, knocked off-balance, and speechless again.

More than once she was on the brink of leaping to her feet and stating, forcefully, *You have it all wrong.*

But then Minerva, Leonora, and Celia started talking about house, home, family, and children, and Eliza shut up and listened.

Listened because they didn't speak of her and Jeremy but, instead, of their own experiences, occasionally referring to their expectations of Heather and Breckenridge, but in the main speaking about, describing, the sort of married life Eliza had, for all her life, imagined would be hers.

What they spoke of made the distinction between what a lady could expect from a love-match versus a socially dictated match crystal clear.

That clarity focused Eliza on the critical question she had until then allowed to remain unanswered, even in her mind.

Did Jeremy love her?

She wasn't in any doubt of the nature of her regard for him.

A fortnight before, she would have scoffed at the notion that she might fall in love with Jeremy Carling; she now knew better. And the way she'd felt on the ridge, when he'd flung himself across her and knocked her down, and so saved her from being shot at the expense of being shot himself, left absolutely no room for doubt.

She was head over ears, irredeemably in love with a sometimes absentminded scholar who, when the need arose, could transform into a male every bit as protective as her brothers or cousins.

Not the slightest hint of wavering or uncertainty remained in her breast—not over her feelings for him.

His feelings for her . . . of those she was less certain, but as she'd assured her sisters, she wasn't so weak that she would step back from the challenge of seeing their feelings made clear, openly and directly acknowledged between them.

A risk, perhaps, yet . . . the more she thought of the way he'd cared for her, the way he and she interacted, even now, the way he'd held her and made love to her . . . the way he'd unhesitatingly risked his life to save her.

In her heart of hearts, where she didn't need facts or evidence to justify her conclusions, she knew. Knew that he loved her.

Yes, they might have to, as so many couples did, dance around the subject until he felt comfortable enough to say the words, but having seen that dance performed often and knowing that the end was always the same, she had no real worries on that score.

Between the two of them, they would get to the point they wanted to reach—just as they had during their flight from Edinburgh. There would be hurdles and setbacks, but she had no doubt of their abilities to somehow, together, overcome them.

They would, at a time of their own choosing, reach the point where they would say to each other: I love you.

And when they did, they would know the other meant each of those three little words.

All that, to her mind, was a certainty. She didn't know their timetable, but their destination shone clear and bright in her mind.

The step after that, however, looked decidedly murky.

If theirs was truly to be a love-match, as she was sure it would be, yet everyone—their families included—deemed it a marriage forced upon them by circumstance . . . would it matter?

Would it change how they went on, how they lived their married lives?

She honestly wasn't sure.

For herself, she didn't care what society at large thought of them, and she suspected Jeremy would be even less sensitive to social stigma, but given her intemperate reaction to her mother's, his sister's, and Minerva's comments . . . how would they respond to a lifetime of such well-intentioned, but so wildly erroneous, and therefore rather insulting, remarks?

Returning to the conversation that had been carrying on without her, as if in illustration she heard Minerva say, "Of course, there's always the question of other interests—with Royce, it's the estate, but thankfully, after that last foray with Delborough and company, he hasn't become involved in any other governmental-type missions, much to my delight."

"Tristan," Leonora said, "has his hands full with his aunts, cousins, and the other old dears. On top of the estate, they're more than enough to keep him busy."

Celia laughed. "In my day, anything that kept a man absorbed and away from temptation was to be applauded." She paused, then added, "I must remember to tell Heather to encourage Breckenridge to develop some hobby that will keep him away from town."

Minerva arched a brow. "And all the ladies?"

Celia nodded. "I'm quite sure where *his* interest lies, but I wouldn't discount some ladies believing they might prove a worthy distraction."

"Very true," Minerva said.

Leonora looked at Eliza and smiled reassuringly. "At least that's something you won't have to contend with. The only distraction you'll ever have to compete against will be ancient, dead, and either leather-bound or engraved in stone."

Minerva chuckled.

Celia started to, then her expression changed to a frown. "Well, yes, but that does bring up another consideration." She looked at Eliza. "You'll need to have some absorbing interests of your own, my dear. You won't want to make too many demands on Jeremy's time."

"I hate to say it, but he's dreadfully absentminded when he has his nose in a tome," Leonora said. "You'll need to make allowances, I fear."

Eliza felt herself grow warm, not with embarrassment but with anger. Rising abruptly, she managed to state, "Please excuse me. I believe I need some air."

Bobbing a curtsy, she strode for the door, not caring in the least that she left them blinking in surprise.

Of course, they thought of her as the quiet one, the reserved one, the one with no real temper to speak of.

But she'd changed.

So had Jeremy.

And she was perfectly certain that neither of them was going to change back, no matter what anyone thought.

Reaching the door, she opened it, stepped into the corridor, closed the door behind her, then exhaled through her teeth, her frustration escaping in a long hiss.

She'd had to leave—before she'd told them exactly what she thought of having to compete with some musty old tome for Jeremy's attention. "Huh!" Head lowering, brows drawn down in a distinctly black frown, she stalked off.

If she recalled aright, there was a way up to the battlements; she would find it and sit down in the breeze until she calmed down.

Then she would take a leaf out of Jeremy's book, consider her options, and make a plan.

It was their new selves, their changed selves, that fit so well together.

That night, after they'd all retired to their rooms and the castle had quieted beneath the blanket of the night, Eliza stood before an open window looking out at the dark panorama of the Cheviots, and, once again, retrod the line of logic that held her there—looking out at the night, the fingers of one hand locked around the rose quartz pendant lying between her breasts, her white poplin nightgown ruffling gently in the breeze, with her feet firmly planted.

She wasn't going to go to Jeremy's room tonight.

She couldn't.

Because she couldn't push.

Because, courtesy of the revelation that had come to her on the battlements that afternoon, she'd realized that she had to wait for him to make up his own mind.

She'd fallen in love not with the scholar but with the man he'd shown himself to be during their flight through the lowlands. That was the man who had captured her heart, and she was perfectly certain that the she he'd come to love enough to protect with his life was the lady who'd sat beside him in the gig as they'd rocketed along the lanes on the other side of the Cheviots.

He had to decide whether or not he intended to remain the man he'd become through their reckless flight, or whether he wished to revert to his earlier self, the scholar and nothing more.

For herself, she'd already made her decision. The life she could live as her new self, in her new incarnation, was so much more enthralling and exhilarating than the life she would have lived as her previous self. She would embrace her new self, her new life, her new purpose, and accept whatever risks might come.

But she couldn't make that decision for Jeremy any more than he could have made the decision for her.

And them seizing their love with both hands was, would be, the equivalent of seizing and holding on to their altered selves, because it was those newfound selves who had fallen in love.

The pressure of the others' views, of their lack of comprehension, was pushing them back to their old selves, to being the lesser people they'd previously been. But their new selves were so much more, promised so much more.

So she had to give Jeremy time.

Impatience pricked, a spur sharpened by a hunger she'd felt for no other man, but caring for a man came in many guises, and in this instance keeping her distance was the right thing to do. She'd considered her options and made her plan—a simple, direct, effective plan. Having made her decision, she now stood poised to put it into action.

The instant he made a move—any move that told her clearly that he wanted to go forward, hand in hand with her, and claim the love they already shared—then she would step up to stand beside him so they could take the next step together.

She didn't need to think any further than that. All she had to do now was wait.

Wait for him to realize that her heart was his, already his, now and forever more.

And that in the same vein, his was hers.

Chapter Eighteen

With the curtains drawn against the night, Jeremy, still fully clothed, paced back and forth before the empty hearth in his room. Rehearsing his arguments, reaffirming his facts, his conclusions.

That nothing had occurred to jolt the others—Martin, Celia, Tristan, Leonora, Royce, and Minerva—from the apparently universal view of his and Eliza's pending relationship had been amply demonstrated over dinner and the two hours following; he'd spent most of the latter in the billiard room, trying to keep the conversation away from that subject so he wouldn't react, wouldn't lose his temper and make rash statements—statements he had yet to verify with Eliza.

But they were going to get to the bedrock of it, him and her, together, tonight, just as soon as she arrived in his room.

He'd seen enough, sensed enough of her reaction to the others' blindness, to feel reasonably confident that her view of him and her closely aligned with his own. He hadn't missed her reaction on the ridge when he'd been shot, either, nor had he forgotten her refusal to let him push her behind him when Scrope had leveled the second pistol on them.

From experience with Leonora, he knew females could be every bit as protective of males they cared for as those males might be of them. Protectiveness was one instinct that had no gender restriction.

Of course, there was a significant difference between "caring for" and "loving," which was the single point he needed to clarify.

How? was the question that had him pacing.

One thing was certain: the time for beating about the bush was past. They needed to decide, tonight, just what sort of future they wanted together, and then tomorrow they needed to set everyone else straight.

So . . . how to learn the answer to his one crucial question?

Sadly, there seemed no easy, let alone subtle, way forward. He was going to have to simply ask. But *Do you love me?* sounded rather abrupt. Not to mention desperate.

Halting, he ran both hands through his hair. "If there's a standard wording for a betrothal notice, why isn't there some well-worn, equally well-established phrase for inquiring if a lady loves you?"

No answer came. Instead, the clocks throughout the huge house pealed the hour—twelve bongs, tings, chimes. . . .

"Twelve?" Startled, he swung to the door. "She's usually here by now."

On the past two nights, Eliza had arrived well before midnight. .

He narrowed his eyes. Set his jaw. "No." He stalked to the door. "No. No. And no. We are not enduring another day in this unresolved state."

Flinging open the door, he stepped into the corridor, caught the door, and pulled it shut behind him. After a moment mentally orienting himself and recalling which corridor led to Eliza's room—she'd mentioned its location when she'd rushed into his room last night—he stalked off.

To have the discussion they had to have. Now. Tonight.

People thought scholars were patient souls, and with respect to their studies they usually were. On all other matters, particularly over anything that got in their way, they tended to be not just impatient but also irascible, testy, and distinctly intolerant. Such were the traits of a scholar.

He was a scholar to his soul, and the state of unknowing, of uncertainty, of not having everything settled and decided was driving him insane.

As he crossed the shadowed gallery and started down the corridor to Eliza's room, the question of why she hadn't come to his room rose in his mind. . . .

He swatted it aside. If there was a reason, she would tell him. Most likely the others' foolishness had made her wonder . . . something like that.

Reaching her door, he tapped. Without waiting for any answer, he turned the knob and stepped inside.

No candle burned, but his eyes had already adjusted to the night; he saw the mound in the bed shift, then Eliza sat bolt upright, peering across the room. "Jeremy?"

He shut the door and advanced on the bed. "We need to talk."

She nodded; although the light was poor, he thought she nodded eagerly. "Yes. We do." Curling her legs beneath the covers, she looked up at him.

Plainly encouraging.

Just to check, and because some semblance of manners was pricking at him, halting beside the bed, he asked, "You don't mind?"

"No." After an instant's pause, she added, "I'm glad you came."

Swinging up to kneel, she walked on her knees to the edge of the bed, reached out, gripped his lapels, and drew him nearer, until his legs hit the side of the bed.

Curling his hands about hers, he said, "We need to talk about you and me." He looked down at her, at the delicate face turned up to his. "About us, and the life we'll have together—about what we want it to be like."

She'd left the curtains open; silver moonlight washed through the room, providing enough light to, at close quarters, see each other's features, to see the directness and feel the warmth in each other's gazes.

He hadn't thought of exactly what to say—hadn't stumbled on any neat phrase that would lead her to reveal what he wanted to know. Looking into her face, searching, hunting for inspiration, he reached deep within and found the words waiting.

He'd wanted to ask, *Do you love me?*

Instead, he said, "I love you." His hands tightened on hers. He'd sunk so deeply into her eyes he felt like he was drowning. But the scholar in him was still there. "At least . . . I think I do. I've never felt this way for any other woman." He felt his lips curve even though he didn't feel like smiling. "It's as if, to me, to my senses, you are the personification of the most fabulous hieroglyphic manuscript ever created—you hold my attention, my interest . . . I want to know every little thing about you, every curlicue, every quirk, every subtle nuance. I value and revere every little thing that makes you you, and I feel a burning need to treat you as my most precious treasure, to behave in every way as if you are."

Raising one of her hands to his lips, his eyes locked with hers, he kissed her fingers. "So I think, yes, that it must be love—that I love you. What else could this enthralling, compulsive fascination be?"

She searched his eyes, her own now alight, her face already rapturously glowing, then she laughed, lightly, gloriously, and the joyous sound shook him to his soul.

"Only you could describe it so clearly." Head tilting, her eyes on his face, locking again with his, she said, clearly, straightforwardly, simply, "Which is one of the reasons why I love you." Sliding one hand from beneath his, she laid her palm to his cheek. "And I'm very sure that it is love I feel, because I've been searching for you, hunting high and low, for what seems like forever. All through the ton, but I never met you there . . . or, at least . . ."

"You never met the me I now am there. You only met the absentminded scholar." He paused, then went on, "I've changed. This journey—your abduction, the rescue, and our flight—has changed me."

"And it's changed me—I feel like a different woman.

I know myself now, and feel confident in so many ways I never did before."

"Before, we met as the people we were. Now . . . we're the people we were meant to be, that we always had it in us to be."

"You feel that, too? That it's the people we now are who've fallen in love?"

"Yes." He grimaced. "But sadly no one else seems to see the changes."

She gestured dismissively. "They don't matter. In this, only we do. This is our truth, our reality. It's who we really are, and who we want to be. It's how we want to live from now on—and that's all that truly matters."

For a moment, he held her gaze, then he released her hands and reached for her. "I'm glad you feel that way. Together we can be the people we wish to be, and what the rest of our world thinks will be irrelevant."

His hands slid about her waist; feeling them firm and urge her to him, Eliza went gladly, shifting forward to lean into him. Raising her arms, she wrapped them about his neck. Locked in, willingly captured by, his tawny caramel gaze, she felt her heart soar, buoyed by an effervescent joy beyond anything she'd ever known. At the same time, she felt anchored by certainty. By the firm grasp of his hands, by the directness of his gaze. By their mutual determination, and the implied assurance that this was how they would always be—straightforward, direct.

And true.

She tipped up her face, brought her lips to his. "I'm glad you agree, too."

They kissed. Impossible to tell who kissed whom, for they acted together. In concert. By mutual accord.

The caress deepened in the same way. Step by step, but who led and who followed constantly changed; both knew what they wanted and where they were going.

Both knew the way.

Into passion.

Into those moments when their hearts beat harder, heavier, when their breaths became increasingly ragged.

Into an exchange where senses blossomed and sensation became a means of communication, him to her, her to him, messages of love, of devotion and commitment, of worship and desire carried by increasingly heated kisses, by intense, lingering touches, by strokes and caresses that became ever more demanding, more commanding, ever more explicit.

Ever more arousing and needy.

Hungry and greedy.

Effortlessly together, hand in hand, they walked onto that plane where the world fell away and there was only them.

Their hearts, their needs, their wants and desires.

Their commitment.

Jeremy drew away, in one sweeping movement drew her nightgown off over her head; she helped, untangling her arms from the sleeves.

Taking another step back, the garment falling, forgotten, from his fingers, he let his gaze openly rove her body, naked and delectable as she balanced on the bed on her knees. The moonlight had strengthened, etching the scene in silver, bathing her limbs with a pearlescent wash that heightened his perception of her as a treasure beyond price.

"You are . . . indescribably beautiful." His features were too passion-set to smile; he met her gaze, trusting she would see his feelings in his eyes, not caring in the least that she did. "You truly are beyond compare."

He stepped closer, his gaze falling to the mounds of her breasts, to the rose quartz crystal that dangled between, suspended on its link-and-bead chain. To the tight, rosy peaks of her breasts, to the soft flush of desire that had already spread so evocatively beneath her skin.

His gaze swept lower, over the indentation of her waist, the flat plane of her belly, over the flare of her hips, down the taut length of her thighs, over the thatch of downy blond curls at their apex.

Drawing breath past the constriction banding his lungs, he forced his gaze upward; slowly drinking in the wondrous sight, he could almost hear the warrior within whisper: *Mine.*

Eliza could barely breathe. The long burning perusal was nothing less than a stamp of possession, a brand seared into her senses, into her psyche. She felt it, knew it. The night air caressed her skin with cool fingers, yet still she burned— burned for him.

She didn't tremble or shake but held out her arms; boldly, brazenly, a siren's smile on her lips, with her hands she beckoned him nearer.

He saw, read the invitation, instinctively moved to respond, then reined himself back. Halting with their bodies mere inches apart, he reached out with one hand and twined his fingers with hers. Raising his gaze, meeting her eyes, he said, his voice pure gravel, "I suspect I should formally propose."

Smile widening, she reached for his nape, drew him to her, and kissed him—hard, fast. Hungrily . . .

The lancing sensation of his coat brushing her already tightly furled, achingly sensitive nipples made her shudder. Forced to break the kiss, she gasped, "Later. Tomorrow." Grasping his coat with both hands, she hauled the sides wide. "For tonight, for now . . ."

She didn't bother finishing the sentence, deeming the urgent energy she focused on undressing him statement enough. She succeeded in wrestling the coat back over his shoulders; he obliged and shrugged free of it—and winced.

She saw. "Is your wound still painful?"

He grimaced. "More that it limits my movements—forget about it."

"Huh!" Stepping from the bed, brushing his hands, more intent on roaming her naked curves than undressing himself, aside, she insisted on assisting him, unknotting and un-winding his cravat, unbuttoning his waistcoat, then his shirt. Pressing close, her hands sliding over his naked chest, she smiled into his eyes. "Consider me your valet for the night."

The scoffing sound he made suggested that was utterly impossible, but he surrendered and followed her lead, toeing off his shoes, undoing the buttons at his waist.

And then, finally, he was as naked as she. Delighted, she wound her arms about his neck and went into his embrace with a bliss-filled sigh, one that hitched, quavered, under the sudden onslaught of the deliciously pleasurable, intensely erotic sensations that sparked as their bodies met, skin to skin, hardness to softness, and her senses swam.

Despite the passionate desire smoldering hot and urgent in his eyes—despite the telltale tension she now recognized, rejoiced in, that held him—despite the heated desperation in his grip, he captured her gaze, murmured, even as his gaze drifted to her lips, "We'll need to talk about our betrothal, and our wedding."

The words were rough, passion edged, only just decipher-able.

It was a challenge to focus her mind enough to answer, but if he could find wit enough to ask, she would match him even in that. "I believe," she breathed back, lids lowering, her senses reeling as his hands shifted, evocatively rising over the planes of her back, "that we've reached what the grandes dames would term an understanding. Given that we have"—his hands firmed possessively and he drew her nearer, her breasts pressing against the muscled planes of his chest, the crisp hairs abrading her sensitized skin; it took effort to find breath to conclude—"we can leave such details for tomorrow. For now—"

Reaching up, she drew his head down the last inch and pressed her lips to his. Kissed him with all the passion and desire that had been building, building, between them.

He kissed her back, took control, ravished her mouth,

claiming with a blatantly ravenous passion, and the volcano of their need erupted.

Wants and hungers collided, geysered.

Their hands spread, clutched, raced and traced.

Their pulses thundered.

Then he lifted her, laid her on the bed, and followed her down.

Winced again.

"Your arm." Despite the raging fever in her blood, she had no difficulty focusing on his hurt. Holding him back, she struggled up onto one arm. "We can't do anything that might open the wound again."

She'd forgotten; they hadn't made love since he'd been shot.

He hesitated, flexing his left arm. He met her gaze, then his lips curved in a slow, distinctly wicked smile. "So we'll dance in a different way—one that won't put undue strain on my arm."

"Oh?" She arched her brows. "How?" Both a blatant command and a haughty demand.

His smile widened in appreciation. Gripping her waist, he rolled onto his back, lifting her over him as he did. "Like this." He settled her astride him, her knees to either side of his waist, then he eased her back.

She needed no further directions.

She laughed; placing her hands on his shoulders, she leaned forward and kissed him—made the wild, wanton caress into a promise.

One of his hands pressed between her shoulder blades, holding her to the kiss; his tongue dueled and tangled hotly with hers, while his other hand glided, reverently tracing her curves, before slipping between her thighs to cup her, then to stroke and caress her soft flesh until the folds were swollen and slick.

Then first one, then two, long fingers slid into her body; he worked them deep, then repetitively stroked, his thumb circling the tight nubbin of nerves just behind her curls.

Until she was gasping, panting, flooded with need and want, and an urgency too sharp and desperate to deny.

She broke from the kiss; too breathless for words, her senses aflame, her body aching for just one thing, she followed the guiding prompting of his hands until she felt the broad head of his erection nudge at her entrance, then eased back and took him in.

Eyes closing, nerves taut and quivering, she caught her breath at the feel of the heavy rod of his erection inch by inch impaling her. Filling her. Possessing her. The sensations, so different in this position, washed through her; they merged with her rising emotions, forming a sea of passion and desire, of surrender and love that flooded her and swept her on.

Slowly, achingly slowly, she sheathed him fully in her body. Enshrined him in her heart.

Reached for him with her soul.

Jeremy drank in the glory suffusing her face and decided this was heaven. His, at least—his heaven on earth. She moved upon him, instinctive and sure, increasingly confident in and abandoned to her pleasure. And his. He closed his eyes and let her loving roll over him. The sensations of her silken limbs shifting, sliding, smoothly over his, caressing, stroking, artfully inciting, the wonder of the heated clasp of her tight sheath, the joy of her breasts teasingly swaying over his chest, sometimes brushing as she shifted as she rode him, all contributed to a state bordering on ecstasy.

She adjusted, and took him deep, then deeper. Wrapped him in her bounty, then ripped his wits away. Razed them, wantonly cindering his control, then brazenly she set herself to stoke the conflagration that, as ever, already blazed between them.

That licked over their skins with searing flame, that beat through their veins like elemental thunder.

His hands roamed her hips, the long lines of her flexing thighs, then swept up to capture her breasts and worship.

Rearing up, eyes closed, head high, she gasped and rode

him ever harder; her hair dancing about her shoulders in golden disarray, she whipped the storm of their passions to new and dizzying heights.

Until need and want and passion coalesced into one driving desire.

One aching, ravenous hunger.

One powerful, overwhelming, impossible to deny urge.

On a growl, he came up on his good arm, propped on that elbow, and with his left hand captured one breast and brought the tightly furled nipple to his mouth. Licked, laved, then drew the tight bud into his mouth and suckled.

She uttered a smothered scream, found his head with her hands, locked her fingers in his hair and held him to her as she rose and fell and drove them both on.

Then she tightened about him.

Releasing her breast, he palmed her nape, braced his arm and rose higher to claim her mouth, deliberately shifting the angle of their joining.

Driving her inexorably to that indefinable edge.

And over it.

She went. On a scream he drank, she soared high, higher, then she broke, shattered, and fell.

And took him with her.

Unable to resist, on a grating groan he thrust hard, high, and felt the powerful contractions of her sheath clamp about him. Felt her body claim and receive him.

He shuddered as he sensed the reality of that other side of him so close to his surface, just beneath his skin, that other side of him that she and only she connected with, that she so effortlessly drew forth. A primal, primitive, wildly possessive side, it drove him to take her, to claim and chain her, his forever more.

With that other side in the ascendancy, he could accept nothing less.

But possession worked both ways.

Their bodies clinging, with him sunk deep within her and

their hearts thundering to a single beat, he knew that to his soul, and accepted it as right. As inevitable. Unavoidable. Irretrievable and irrevocable.

As the way he and she would always be.

Each other's.

Joined by that power the poets called love.

On the heels of that acceptance, simple and soul-deep, completion rolled over him, through him, not simply physical satiation but an elemental completeness in so many ways, on so many planes. She brought him the part of himself he'd been missing for so long, and made him whole.

Spent, exhausted, he slumped back to the pillows and she collapsed on top of him. He closed his arms around her. Felt her drag in a breath, then let it go. Her limbs sank against his in total surrender.

Not to him but to what had raged between them.

To what, acknowledged, now lived between them, their new reality built on their new, changed selves.

The harshness of their breathing eased; the night's silence returned along with his hearing. Aware of the tug of the tide of ecstasy, the growing temptation to let go and let bliss carry him away on that golden sea, he lifted her from him, settled her, boneless, back in his arms, then he shifted his head and pressed a kiss to her forehead. "This is the truth of us—how we're meant to be."

She pillowed her head just beneath his shoulder, then dropped a warm kiss on his chest. "This is how we are, and how we will be."

The words rang with her commitment, one to match his.

Eyes closing, he blindly groped, found the covers, flicked them over their cooling bodies, then he closed his arms about her, lay back, and surrendered to the bliss they'd wrought.

Chapter Nineteen

J eremy departed from Eliza's room only just in time
to avoid the maids, leaving Eliza with strict instructions to get dressed and meet him as soon as possible.
Enthused and determined, she rushed through her
ablutions, hurried into her clothes, and brushed and coiled
her hair.

Finally presentable, she walked briskly from the room.
She had no clear idea what Jeremy intended, but she recalled
well enough that they had issues to discuss.

Not that she was all that bothered with the details, not
after the night had clarified the one, truly important issue in
such a definitive way.

Love. She was still trying to absorb it. Yes, she'd known
she loved him, and yes, she'd hoped and suspected that he
might love her in return.

But now she knew.

Not only knew but . . . somehow last night had been different, with every caress in some intangible way emphasizing
their new truth. Crystallizing and anchoring their love.

Last night had been a demonstration of love, of love in
the flesh.

Smiling, feeling as if her face might crack so great was
her happiness, she reached the end of the corridor. Stepping
into the gallery, she saw Jeremy loitering before one of the
long windows, pretending to look out.

Seeing her, he turned and, long legs eating the distance,
joined her.

"Good." His gaze roved her face, the caress almost a kiss. Taking her hand, he raised it, briefly brushed her fingers with his lips, then said, "Come on. I know where we can talk without being interrupted."

He led her downstairs, then down the long corridor to the library.

Ushering her inside, he closed the door and locked it.

She glanced around, then, eschewing the large desk, walked down the room to where a sofa sat facing the vista visible through a pair of long windows.

Jeremy followed. They rounded the sofa, but before she could sit, he caught her hand. Drawing her to face him, he trapped her other hand, too, held each in one of his.

He looked into her eyes and simply said, "Dearest Eliza . . ." He paused, then went on, "I hadn't seriously looked about me for a wife, but if I had, I would never have imagined that my eye would settle on you, let alone that my heart would. That I might fall in love never truly crossed my mind, yet here I stand, irresistibly and irrevocably in love with you." That was more than he'd intended to say. Drawing breath, he continued, "But as I am so deeply in love with you that I cannot imagine living without you, will you please do me the inestimable honor of consenting to be my wife?"

The slow smile that broke across her face dazzled him.

Eliza took a moment to assemble the right words. Searching his eyes, her heart in hers, she drew breath, and replied, "Dearest Jeremy, I've been looking, searching, everywhere for my hero, for the one man who could sweep me off my feet and into wedded bliss. Had we remained in London, I would never have found him, for I would never have realized"—raising one hand, she placed her palm to his chest—"that my hero's heart beat beneath this particular chest. But the trials of the last weeks have shown me the truth—your truth, and our truth. So as I'm so much in love with you that I can't imagine life other than by your side, yes, I will indeed marry you."

The smile that filled his eyes warmed her, wrapped around her. He again kissed her fingers, first one hand, then the other. "Excellent." His smile turned wryly teasing. "Now that we've got that detail dealt with, we need to make plans."

She nodded and sat, drawing him down to sit beside her. "Are we going to make a stand?"

"Oh, I think so—don't you?"

Chin firming, she nodded. "So—how are we going to open everyone's eyes?"

There was, of course, only one way. A way most members of the haut ton would shudder to even contemplate.

They had no such qualms.

Breakfast was no use to them as Celia habitually did not join the company, preferring a tray in her room. Given they did not wish to encounter any of their supposed mentors, not until they could speak with them all at once, they slipped into the breakfast parlor and hurriedly broke their fast as the dishes were being set out, then escaped from the house before even Royce appeared.

They went out to the stable to check on Jasper. The young black was restive, pining for a run. With Jeremy unable to risk his wound reopening, Eliza suggested, and, somewhat warily, Jeremy agreed, that she should drive them in the gig, Jasper between the shafts, into Alwinton, the nearest village.

Despite a few minor scares, Eliza managed well enough. They tooled around the village and along several lanes, then returned to the castle just as the rest of the company were sitting down to luncheon.

"Our timing, thus far, is perfect." Her arm through Jeremy's, Eliza walked toward the family dining room.

Jeremy looked into her face, glowing, luminous, and not just from their drive, and smiled. "Remember what we planned. No second thoughts?"

She shook her head decisively. "None."

They swept into the dining room, and the others all looked up.

Beaming, letting his happiness overflow for all to see, Jeremy halted Eliza at the side of the table on which the pair of them usually sat, let his gaze rest briefly on each of the six faces turned to them in surprise, then announced, "Eliza has done me the honor of agreeing to be my wife. *However*, we wish to make it clear to all, to you and subsequently to the rest of the world, that we are not marrying because we in any way feel we must, not because of any ton expectation or social dictate."

He paused, once again letting his gaze circle the faces, now looking even more taken aback, then he looked at Eliza, saw the same truth he was projecting shining like a beacon in her eyes and joyously lighting her expression. Lifting her hand from his sleeve, his eyes on hers, he raised her fingers to his lips. Kissed. Then he turned to the others and declared, "We're going to marry because we're in love. Because we found love, or it found us, somewhere in Scotland. And we're not going to pretend that it didn't happen—we don't want to take the coward's way out and not acknowledge our truth, our reality."

Every last implement had been laid back on the table; a stunned but expectant silence prevailed.

Jeremy smiled. "So," he concluded, "we wish to marry, and we wish the occasion to be puffed off to the very top of everyone's bent. We intend to place a highly unconventional notice in the *Gazette,* and we wish that to be followed by a major engagement ball. As for our wedding, we want that to be a spectacular celebration. We want our love to be publicly acknowledged, to be known and understood by all—to, figuratively speaking, shout the fact from the rooftops."

Glancing around the table again, he took in the dawning understanding breaking across all the faces and let his smile widen. "In short, we want everyone to know that we are"—

he looked at Eliza, and, eyes misty but smiling beatifically, she responded, saying the words with him—"beyond lost in love."

Silence reigned for half a second, then Eliza dragged her gaze from Jeremy's eyes and looked at her mother.

Celia rose from the table; tears streaming down her cheeks, she held out her arms. "Oh, my darling children!"

Eliza went into her arms and held her mother as Celia dissolved into happy tears.

Then Minerva was there, laughing, smiling, hugging Eliza and Celia both, then passing them to Leonora so Minerva could envelop Jeremy in a scented embrace.

Moments later, Celia, openly laughing and crying at the same time, displaced her "I am so thrilled!" She kissed Jeremy's cheek, then drew back to beam up at him. "You did that just right."

After bestowing another surprisingly strong hug, Celia passed him on to Martin.

Who was simply delighted and said so.

Among the men, backs were thumped and hands wrung. Exclamations abounded. Explanations were requested and made, as far as they could make them.

Royce shook his head. "I didn't see that coming, but in retrospect I should have." He met Jeremy's eyes. "Fate has a way of catching up with one when one least expects it."

Jeremy grinned. "I was and am happy to be caught."

Royce's lips quirked, his gaze going to his duchess. "In the end, aren't we all?"

The meal for the moment forgotten, they stood and laughed and talked. Jeremy caught Eliza's eye, and she smiled and nodded. The sincerity of the others' pleasure and joy at their news, their unreserved acceptance of it, was transparent and could not be doubted.

They'd succeeded thus far. They'd shattered the perception of their union that had prevailed among this group.

"Next, we take on the ton," Eliza murmured.

Jeremy smiled. "And we'll triumph there, too."

But it was Leonora who gave him most hope that convincing the ton wouldn't be difficult. "We had wondered, of course, but neither of you are all that easy to read—you're both quieter, more reserved—so until you said it, we couldn't presume." Her eyes on his, she smiled a touch mistily. "Love is not something you can impute to another, but, darling Jeremy, I am so very happy for you both—and Humphrey will be utterly delighted." Glancing at Eliza, then looking at Tristan, Leonora went on, "Trust me—the words might be hard to say the first time, but they get easier with the years, and you'll never regret saying them, now or in the future."

Turning back to him, stretching up, Leonora kissed his cheek, then patted his arm and left him to move to Tristan's side.

Jeremy watched his sister and brother-in-law, saw the affection that so effortlessly flowed between them. Knew he and Eliza would from now on share a similar unremarked yet remarkable connection.

To his left, Martin, beaming widely, pumped Royce's hand, while Minerva stood alongside Royce, her arm in his, her lips curved and her eyes shining.

Their grand denouement had got them over the first and highest hurdle; the rest, as Leonora had said, would come more easily.

Jeremy glanced at Eliza, to his right.

She met his gaze, a fleeting moment laden with that recognition that only, he now realized, came with love, then she turned to Celia as her mother returned to wrap her once more in a warm embrace.

Eliza returned the hug, wondering.

Only to hear Celia whisper softly, "My darling girl—welcome to the club!"

* * *

Notice appearing in the Gazette, *May 15th, 1829*

Lord Martin and Lady Celia Cynster of Dover Street and Casleigh, Somerset, are thrilled to announce the betrothal of their daughter, Elizabeth Marguerite, to Jeremy William Carling, of Montrose Place, brother of Leonora, Viscountess Trentham, and nephew of Sir Humphrey Carling. An Engagement Ball will be held in two weeks' time at St. Ives House, in celebration of the happy couple's declaration that they are utterly and irredeemably lost in love.

Epilogue

H appy?" Jeremy asked, entirely redundantly as he waltzed Eliza around the massive ballroom.

Eliza's face glowed; she was radiant, in his eyes beyond compare. "I'm the happiest lady here tonight, bar none."

Around them, the crème de la crème of the ton, summoned to bear witness to their engagement, circled and swayed, smiled and chatted. The event, and the select dinner that had preceded it, had been an unqualified success, and none was more grateful for, and more satisfied with that, than Jeremy. He had secured the wife he needed, in the way they both needed, and he was utterly content.

"If you are the happiest lady, then I am, without doubt, the proudest and luckiest man." He smiled into her eyes as he whirled her. "You take my breath away."

Eliza laughed back, gratifyingly breathless, too.

Martin and Celia, also waltzing, passed by them as they negotiated a tight turn. When he and Eliza were once more precessing back up the long room, Jeremy murmured, "I think the second happiest lady in the room must be your mother. She's settled her eldest two daughters creditably and, judging by all the usual signs, the ton wildly approves of both matches." He paused, then added, "I wasn't sure they would. Heather and Breckenridge, yes, but you could have reached much higher, as the grandes dames would phrase it."

Smiling fondly, Eliza shook her head. "No, I couldn't have—or rather, wouldn't have. And all the grandes dames and the gossipmongers know that. So they are, naturally, in alt, all quite delighted that you've come along and claimed my heart and my hand."

"I must admit, I don't quite understand that. I'm a scholar, not an earl."

"You forget—Heather's twenty-five, so was at her last prayers, and I'm twenty-four, not much younger. The notion of two Cynster girls languishing on the shelf made all the social mavens uncomfortable—if we held out that long, and potentially even longer, for our heroes and refused to marry any other men, just think of the precedent, the example to other young ladies that would set." Tilting her head, Eliza looked into his eyes and smiled that private smile that never failed to touch him in some indefinable way. "But Heather found her hero, and so did I, so all's well once more within the ton."

"Ah." He nodded sagely. "Now I understand." Through the throng filling the dance floor, he glimpsed Heather and Breckenridge, also dancing. No one, seeing the light in their eyes as they revolved, completely absorbed in each other, could doubt the nature of their connection. "I think Heather must qualify as the third happiest lady present."

"Very likely. She may even be happier than Mama, who has divided loyalties, so to speak."

"And next . . ." Scanning the dancers, then, able to see over most heads, looking further, Jeremy murmured, "Would it be your aunt Helena, your aunt Horatia, or Lady Osbaldestone?" He glanced down at Eliza. "Which do you think?"

But Eliza shook her head. "Oh, no—none of them. You've missed the lady who, now I think of it, is almost certainly the *second* happiest lady here tonight. Indeed, the more I think of it, that must be true. She, of all others, has the most cause to be thrilled."

Jeremy racked his brains.

Knowing he liked puzzles, Eliza waited.

But after two more revolutions, he shook his head. "No. I can't fathom it. So who, my darling, is the second happiest lady here tonight?"

Eliza laughed. "Angelica, of course." She tipped her head to the side of the dance floor.

Glancing that way, Jeremy saw Eliza's younger sister standing by the side of the room.

"Just look at her face—at her smile, at her eyes," Eliza said.

Jeremy had to admit that, even from a distance, Angelica's delight was plain to see. "But"—he looked at Eliza, let her see the puzzled frown in his eyes—"why? Why should she be especially thrilled?"

"Because not only are both Heather and I engaged, very happily to our heroes, who happen to be gentlemen of whom the ton at large and our family in particular approve— proving that waiting for the right gentleman is the sensible course for Angelica, too—but the laird is now dead."

"What's he got to do with it? With Angelica?"

"Because had he lived, a continuing threat to 'Cynster sisters,' then Angelica, Henrietta, and Mary would have been kept under the closest imaginable guard. Our brothers and cousins had already become unbearably autocratic and obsessively protective before Scrope whisked me away— can you imagine what they would have been like after that? According to Angelica, she was forbidden to set foot outside the house in Dover Street without at least one of them at her elbow, and both Rupert and Alasdair came up to town and took up residence at home, so there was always one of them in the house, on hand. Or, as Angelica put it, underfoot. She, in particular, had no peace, and, even more importantly, no opportunity at all to hunt for her own hero, which, of course, she's now even more set on doing than she was before."

"But she's only . . ." Jeremy ransacked his memory. "Twenty-one, isn't she? She's years younger than you—she has plenty of time."

"Yes, but you have to remember that she's grown up together with Heather and me. She's the youngest, but she discounts the three years between me and her. To her mind, now Heather's engaged to Breckenridge, and I'm engaged to you, it's her turn next. And for Angelica, next means now. You may be absolutely certain that she'll set out to search for her hero in earnest tomorrow. Or, as the case may be, tomorrow evening. I'm quite sure she'll have already assessed all those attending tonight."

The music ended. The dancers swirled to a halt; the gentlemen bowed and the ladies curtsied. Rising, Eliza set her hand on Jeremy's proffered sleeve, then glanced at where Angelica had been, but the crowds blocked her view. Turning back to Jeremy, she smiled, eyes dancing. "Knowing Angelica, her search for her hero is bound to be, at the very least, highly entertaining."

Jeremy met her eyes. "I shudder to ask, but why?"

Eliza hesitated, then said, "Take every strong female trait Heather and I have, put them together, then double them, and you'll have some notion of what Angelica is like. Of the three of us, she's the most stubborn, the most decisive, the cleverest by far, the most determined, and she's very good at manipulating people—exceptionally good at getting what she wants. Angelica might be the youngest, the shortest, the smallest of the three of us, but she's also the boldest, the strongest, and she's the one with a fiery temper, too."

"Well, her hair is reddish, after all," Jeremy said. "But I still don't understand why her romance should be especially entertaining."

"Because whoever Angelica sets her heart on, you can be absolutely certain there'll be fireworks."

"Ah." Placing his hand over hers on his sleeve, Jeremy gently squeezed her fingers. "Have I mentioned how very grateful I am that we've managed to reach this point without any fireworks?"

Eliza laughed, then nodded toward a door. "That's where all this started." She looked up and met Jeremy's eyes. "That's where I was standing when the footman brought me the note that took me to the back parlor and Scrope." She searched Jeremy's eyes. "I was so desperate to find my hero that I went—and that's how I came to be in that coach heading north toward Jedburgh, calling to you for help."

Jeremy's lips quirked in an understanding smile. "So you've come full circle—back to where you started, but with me by your side."

"With my hero, my fiancé, and my husband-to-be." Eliza's gaze grew misty. "Fate was kind."

"More than you know." Jeremy held her gaze. "I left Wolverstone that day wondering how to find the bride I had finally come to accept that I needed—and fate stepped in and set me the task of rescuing you." He raised her hand to his lips, kissed her fingertips. "And so here I now stand, with the lady who will be the perfect wife for me on my arm." He smiled. "Fate has, indeed, blessed us."

"To our credit," Eliza said, "we were up to the challenges she threw our way."

"True. Fate dealt the cards, but it was you and I who played the hand."

"And won."

"Yes—we won. Everything we wanted, all that we desired."

"And now"—she glanced about them, at their families, connections, and friends all gathered to wish them well—"now that we've claimed our just reward, our future looks rosy." Looking up, she smiled into Jeremy's eyes. "I can't wait for it to start."

* * *

Watching Eliza smile at Jeremy, watching Jeremy set Eliza's hand on his sleeve, and, head bent to hear what Eliza was now saying, stroll on down the room, Angelica Cynster sighed. Relieved, content, happy, and delighted.

All was once again well in her world, just as it ought to be.

Glancing to where Heather and Breckenridge stood chatting with Great-aunt Clara, Angelica smiled; she thoroughly approved of her sisters' choices. They had searched for and found their heroes, and all was well with them.

Which meant she could now turn her full and complete attention to her own search, to locating and snaring her own hero.

Wherever the damned man was.

Sending a brief glance skating over the shoulders around her, she muttered, "He's not here, that's clear. So where should I look next?"

Fingers rising to close about the rose quartz pendant depending from the strange old chain comprised of gold links interspersed with amethyst beads that she now wore, she waited for inspiration to strike. The necklace was now hers—her talisman just as it had been Heather's, and then Eliza's. And, apparently, Catriona's, too, so many years ago. Eliza had passed it on to Angelica on the day Eliza and Jeremy, along with Celia and Martin, had returned from Wolverstone. Eliza had explained Catriona's or possibly her Lady's—directive that the necklace was to be passed down among the Cynster girls as each found their hero, their fated husband. Angelica wasn't sure she believed in fate, but she was happy to accept whatever help came her way with respect to locating her hero. She'd already combed the ton for him, or at least all of the ton she was allowed to explore, the tonnish entertainments deemed suitable for a well-bred young lady of her age.

"Clearly, I need to cast my net wider." Clinging to the shadows along the wall beneath the overhang of the gallery, she considered what alternatives she might have, what wider fields she might wander. Most of the gentlemen present were either related or connected in some way, so all knew better than to disturb her seclusion, and for the same reason the grandes dames, who would otherwise ensure she was introduced to every potentially eligible gentleman in the room, had tonight no reason to turn their beady gazes her way, leaving her free to think.

To set her mind to defining her way forward.

Tomorrow, she felt sure, was the time to start—to strike out on her own now that her brothers and cousins had relaxed their vigilance after learning that the laird had died, and his threat against "Cynster sisters" along with him. Their obsessive protectiveness had subsided to its usual irritating, but manageable, level, but there'd been so much to do with preparing for this ball that she'd set aside her concerns to help Eliza and Celia.

But now the ball was nearly at an end, and it was time to reinstitute her search—indeed, to intensify it given she now wore the necklace and was therefore marked by The Lady as next in line to find her true love. Even more pertinently, she should make a start before her brothers and cousins realized, and remembered that the laird was not the only dangerous male inhabiting the wider ton.

The whole question of the laird's intentions as yet remained a mystery; Royce, Duke of Wolverstone, had volunteered to discover the man's identity, but yesterday word had arrived that Royce and his half brother Hamish had still not located the band of drovers who had removed the laird's body and that of his henchman Scrope from the bottom of the cliff over which they'd fallen. Regardless, there was no question that the man had died, and eventually, as always, Royce would prevail, and then they'd know the whys and wherefores, but the laird's motivations no longer concerned her . . . or at least they wouldn't, not unless some other member of his family took up the vendetta . . . no—she wasn't going to entertain that thought.

Glancing at her eldest brother, Rupert, standing chatting with others nearby, she fervently prayed the possibility of a family vendetta continuing did not occur to him. Or to Alasdair, or Devil, or any of the others. If it did . . . they were quite capable of making her life a misery, regardless of whether there was any real threat or not.

Narrowing her eyes on Rupert, she murmured, "Best to start as I mean to go on, and best to start immediately—tomorrow it shall be."

Pushing away from the wall, she moved into the crowd, smiling, nodding, exchanging comments here and there as she made her way toward the exit. Catching sight of her mother, she detoured to explain that she had an incipient headache and would take the carriage home, then send it back the short distance for Celia, Martin, and Eliza, who wouldn't be free to leave until the last stragglers had departed.

Having received her mother's blessing, Angelica continued to the door, then descended the stairs to the front hall. Devil's majordomo, Sligo, on watch, popped up with her cloak and to inquire if she needed assistance. She let him summon the carriage and help her into it.

With the door shut, Angelica leaned back against the squabs. Alone in the comfortable dark as the carriage rattled over the cobbles toward Dover Street, she focused on what lay ahead.

Her hero. Wherever he was, she intended to hunt him down.

And then . . . love, she fully expected, would take care of the rest.

But finding him was her test, the challenge she faced, the hurdle she had to overcome to prove she was worthy; she seriously doubted that he would find her. Regardless, she fully intended to enjoy herself while she searched. Who knew? She might not stumble on her hero for a year or more . . .

She frowned. That might not be how matters came to

pass. Henrietta—to whom Angelica was supposed to pass the necklace after she'd found her hero—was only a few months younger than Angelica.

Henrietta was just a few steps behind Angelica in the hero-hunt. So . . .

"Hmm . . . I might not have as much time as I'd thought."

Frowning more definitely, she refocused on her purpose and mentally reaffirmed the specifics of her hero. Tall, handsome, and well set-up went without saying, and she had a distinct preference for dark hair, but she was willing to compromise on that. What was far more important was the requirement that, once he'd realized and had had it made clear to him the role he was to play in her life, her hero should look at her in exactly the same intelligent and knowing, yet no longer caring how he might look to others, besotted way that Jeremy looked at Eliza.

The same way Breckenridge looked at Heather.

The exact same way her father still looked at her mother, even after all these years.

That look was the key.

Relaxing against the seat, frown evaporating, replaced by an inflexibly determined expression, Angelica nodded. "That's what I want, and that's what I will have. Or my name isn't Angelica Cynster."

Coming February 2012 from

Stephanie Laurens

and

Avon Books

The Capture of the Earl of Glencrae

Turn the page
for an excerpt from

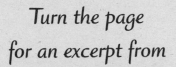

Viscount Breckenridge
to the Rescue

Available now from

Stephanie Laurens

and

Avon Books

eather Cynster knew her latest plan to find a suitable husband was doomed the instant she set foot in Lady Herford's salon.

In a distant corner, a dark head, perfectly coiffed in the latest rakish style, rose. A pair of sharp hazel eyes pinned her where she stood.

"Damn!" Keeping a smile firmly fixed over her involuntarily clenching teeth, as if she hadn't noticed the most startlingly handsome man in the room staring so intently at her, she let her gaze drift on.

Breckenridge was hemmed in by not one but three dashing ladies, all patently vying for his attention. She sincerely wished them every success and prayed he'd take the sensible course and pretend he hadn't seen her.

She was certainly going to pretend that she hadn't seen him.

Refocusing on the surprisingly large crowd Lady Herford had enticed to her soiree, Heather determinedly banished Breckenridge from her mind and considered her prospects.

Most of the guests were older than she—all the ladies at least. Some she recognized, others she did not, but it would be surprising if any other lady present wasn't married. Or widowed. Or more definitively on the shelf than Heather. Soirees of the style of Lady Herford's were primarily the province of the well-bred but bored matrons, those in search of more convivial company than that provided by their usually much older, more sedate husbands. Such ladies might not be precisely fast, yet neither were they innocent. However, as by common accord said ladies had already presented their husbands with an heir, if not two, the majority had more years in their dish than Heather's twenty-five.

From her brief, initial, assessing sweep, she concluded that most of the gentlemen present were, encouragingly, older than she. Most were in their thirties, and by their style—fashionable, well-turned out, expensively garbed, and thoroughly polished—she'd chosen well in making Lady Herford's soiree her first port of call on this, her first expedition outside the rarefied confines of the ballrooms, drawing rooms, and dining rooms of the upper echelon of the ton.

For years she'd searched through those more refined reception rooms for her hero—the man who would sweep her off her feet and into wedded bliss—only to conclude that he didn't move in such circles. Many gentlemen of the ton, although perfectly eligible in every way, preferred to steer well clear of all the sweet young things, the young ladies paraded on the marriage mart. Instead, they spent their evenings at events such as Lady Herford's, and their nights in various pursuits—gaming and womanizing to name but two.

Her hero—she had to believe he existed somewhere— was most likely a member of that more elusive group of males. Given he was therefore unlikely to come to her, she'd decided—after lengthy and animated discussions with her sisters, Elizabeth and Angelica—that it behooved her to come to him.

To locate him and, if necessary, hunt him down.

Smiling amiably, she descended the shallow steps to the floor of the salon. Lady Herford's villa was a recently built, quite luxurious dwelling located to the north of Primrose Hill—close enough to Mayfair to be easily reached by carriage, a pertinent consideration given Heather had had to come alone. She would have preferred to attend with someone to bear her company, but her sister Eliza, just a year younger and similarly disgusted with the lack of hero-material within their restricted circle, was her most likely coconspirator and they couldn't both develop a headache on the same evening without their mama seeing through the ploy. Eliza, therefore, was presently gracing Lady Montague's ballroom, while Heather was supposedly laid upon her bed, safe and snug in Dover Street.

Giving every appearance of calm confidence, she glided into the crowd. She'd attracted considerable attention; although she pretended obliviousness, she could feel the assessing glances dwelling on the sleek, amber silk gown that clung lovingly to her curves. This particular creation sported a sweetheart neckline and tiny puffed sleeves; as the evening was unseasonably mild and her carriage stood outside, she'd elected to carry only a fine topaz-and-amber Norwich silk shawl, its fringe draping over her bare arms and flirting over the silk of the gown. Her advanced age allowed her greater freedom to wear gowns that, while definitely not as revealing as some others she could see, nevertheless drew male eyes.

One gentleman, suitably drawn and a touch bolder than his fellows, broke from the circle surrounding two ladies and languidly stepped into her path.

Halting, she haughtily arched a brow.

He smiled and bowed, fluidly graceful. "Miss Cynster, I believe?"

"Indeed, sir. And you are?"

"Miles Furlough, my dear." His eyes met hers as he straightened. "Is this your first time here?"

"Yes." She glanced around, determinedly projecting confident assurance. She intended to pick her man, not allow him or any other to pick her. "The company appears quite animated." The noise of untold conversations was steadily rising. Returning her gaze to Miles Furlough, she asked, "Are her ladyship's gatherings customarily so lively?"

Furlough's lips curved in a smile Heather wasn't sure she liked.

"I think you'll discover—" Furlough broke off, his gaze going past her.

She had an instant's warning—a primitive prickling over her nape—then long, steely fingers closed about her elbow.

Heat washed over her, emanating from the contact, supplanted almost instantly by a disorientating giddiness. She caught her breath. She didn't need to look to know that Timothy Danvers, Viscount Breckenridge—her nemesis—had elected not to be sensible.

"Furlough." The deep voice issuing from above her head and to the side had its usual disconcerting effect.

Ignoring the frisson of awareness streaking down her spine—a susceptibility she positively despised—she slowly turned her head and directed a reined glare at its cause. "Breckenridge."

There was nothing in her tone to suggest she welcomed his arrival—quite the opposite.

He ignored her attempt to depress his pretensions; indeed, she wasn't even sure he registered it. His gaze hadn't shifted from Furlough.

"If you'll excuse us, old man, there's a matter I need to discuss with Miss Cynster." Breckenridge held Furlough's gaze. "I'm sure you understand."

Furlough's expression suggested that he did yet wished he didn't feel obliged to give way. But in this milieu, Breckenridge—the hostesses' and the ladies' darling— was well nigh impossible to gainsay. Reluctantly, Furlough inclined his head. "Of course."

Shifting his gaze to Heather, Furlough smiled—more sincerely, a tad ruefully. "Miss Cynster. Would we had met in less crowded surrounds. Perhaps next time." With a parting nod, he sauntered off into the crowd.

Heather let free an exasperated huff. But before she could even gather her arguments and turn them on Breckenridge, he tightened his grip on her elbow and started propelling her through the crowd.

Startled, she tried to halt. "What—"

"If you have the slightest sense of self-preservation you will walk to the front door without any fuss."

He was steering her, surreptitiously pushing her, in that direction, and it wasn't all that far. "Let. Me. Go." She uttered the command, low and delivered with considerable feeling, through clenched teeth.

He urged her up the salon steps. Used the moment when she was on the step above him to bend his head and breathe in her ear, *"What the devil are you doing here?"*

His clenched teeth trumped her clenched teeth. The words, his tone, slid through her, evoking—as he'd no doubt intended—a nebulous, purely instinctive fear.

By the time she shook free of it, he was smoothly, apparently unhurriedly, steering her through the guests thronging the foyer.

"No—don't bother answering." He didn't look down; he had the open front door in his sights. "I don't care what ninnyhammerish notion you've taken into your head. You're leaving. Now."

Hale, whole, virgin intacta. Breckenridge only just bit back the words.

"There is no reason whatever for you to interfere." Her voice vibrated with barely suppressed fury.

He recognized her mood well enough—her customary one whenever he was near. Normally he would respond by giving her a wide berth, but here and now he had no choice. "Do you have any idea what your cousins would do to me— let alone your brothers—if they discovered I'd seen you in this den of iniquity and turned a blind eye?"

She snorted and tried, surreptitiously but unsuccessfully, to free her elbow. "You're as large as any of them—and demonstrably just as much of a bully. You could see them off."

"One, perhaps, but all six? I think not. Let alone Luc and

Martin, and Gyles Chillingworth—and what about Michael? No, wait—what about Caro, and your aunts, and . . . the list goes on. Flaying would be preferable—much less pain."

"You're overreacting. Lady Herford's house hardly qualifies as a den of iniquity." She glanced back. "There's nothing the least objectionable going on in that salon."

"Not in the salon, perhaps—at least, not yet. But you didn't go further into the house—trust me, a den of iniquity it most definitely is."

"But—"

"No." Reaching the front porch—thankfully deserted—he halted, released her, and finally let himself look down at her. Let himself look into her face, a perfect oval hosting delicate features and a pair of stormy gray-blue eyes lushly fringed with dark brown lashes. Despite those eyes having turned hard and flinty, even though her luscious lips were presently compressed into a thin line, that face was the sort that had launched armadas and incited wars since the dawn of time. It was a face full of life. Full of sensual promise and barely restrained vitality.

And that was before adding the effect of a slender figure, sleek rather than curvaceous, yet invested with such fluid grace that her every movement evoked thoughts that, at least in his case, were better left unexplored.

The only reason she hadn't been mobbed in the salon was because none but Furlough had shaken free of the arrestation the first sight of her generally caused quickly enough to get to her before he had.

He felt his face harden, fought not to clench his fists and tower over her in a sure-to-be-vain attempt to intimidate her. "You're going home, and that's all there is to it."

Her eyes narrowed to shards. "If you try to force me, I'll scream."

He lost the battle; his fists clenched at his sides. Holding her gaze, he evenly stated, "If you do, I'll tap you under that pretty little chin, knock you unconscious, tell everyone you fainted, toss you in a carriage, and send you home."

Her eyes widened. She considered him but didn't back down. "You wouldn't."

He didn't blink. "Try me."

Heather inwardly dithered. This was the trouble with Breckenridge—one simply couldn't tell what he was thinking. His face, that of a Greek god, all clean planes and sharp angles, lean cheeks below high cheekbones and a strong, square jaw, remained aristocratically impassive and utterly unreadable no matter what was going through his mind. Not even his heavy-lidded hazel eyes gave any clue; his expression was perennially that of an elegantly rakish gentleman who cared for little beyond his immediate pleasure.

Every element of his appearance, from his exquisitely understated attire, the severe cut of his clothes making the lean strength they concealed only more apparent, to the languid drawl he habitually affected, supported that image—one she was fairly certain was a comprehensive façade.

She searched his eyes—and detected not the smallest sign that he wouldn't do precisely as he said. Which would be simply too embarrassing.

"How did you get here?"

Reluctantly, she waved at the line of carriages stretching along the curving pavement of Wadham Gardens as far as they could see. "My parents' carriage—and before you lecture me on the impropriety of traveling across London alone at night, both the coachman and groom have been with my family for decades."

Tight-lipped, he nodded. "I'll walk you to it."

He reached for her elbow again.

She whisked back. "Don't bother." Frustration erupted; she felt sure he would inform her brothers that he'd found her at Lady Herford's, which would spell an end to her plan—one which, until he'd interfered, had held real promise. She gave vent to her temper with an infuriated glare. "I can walk twenty yards by myself."

Even to her ears her words sounded petulant. In reaction, she capped them with, "Just leave me alone!"

Lifting her chin, she swung on her heel and marched down the steps. Head determinedly high, she turned right along the pavement toward where her parents' town carriage waited in the line.

Inside she was shaking. She felt childish and furious—and helpless. Just as she always felt when she and Breckenridge crossed swords.

Blinking back tears of stifled rage, knowing he was watching, she stiffened her spine and marched steadily on.

From the shadows of Lady Herford's front porch, Breckenridge watched the bane of his life stalk back to safety. Why of all the ladies in the ton it had to be Heather Cynster who so tied him in knots he didn't know; what he did know was that there wasn't a damned thing he could do about it. She was twenty-five, and he was ten years and a million nights older; he was certain she viewed him at best as an interfering much older cousin, at worst as an interfering uncle.

"Wonderful," he muttered as he watched her stride fearlessly along. Once he saw her safely away . . . he was going to walk home. The night air might clear his head of the distraction, of the unsettled, restless feeling dealing with her always left him prey to—a sense of loneliness, and emptiness, and time slipping away.

Of life—his life—being somehow worthless, or rather, worth less—less than it should.

He didn't, truly didn't, want to think about her. There were ladies among the crowd inside who would fight to provide him with diversion, but he'd long ago learned the value of their smiles, their pleasured sighs.

Fleeting, meaningless, illusory connections.

Increasingly they left him feeling cheapened, used. Unfulfilled.

He watched the moonlight glint in Heather's wheat gold hair. He'd first met her four years ago at the wedding of his biological stepmother, Caroline, to Michael Anstruther-Wetherby, brother of Honoria, Duchess of St. Ives and queen of the Cynster clan. Honoria's husband, Devil Cynster, was Heather's oldest cousin.

Although Breckenridge had first met Heather on that day in sunny Hampshire, he'd known the male Cynster cousins for more than a decade—they moved in the same circles, and before the cousins had married, had shared much the same interests.

A carriage to the left of the house pulled out of the line. Breckenridge glanced that way, saw the coachman set his horses plodding, then looked right again to where Heather was still gliding along.

"Twenty yards, my arse." More like fifty. "Where the damn hell is her carriage?"

The words had barely left his lips when the other carriage, a traveling coach, drew level with Heather.

And slowed.

The coach's door swung open and a man shot out. Another leapt down from beside the driver.

Before Breckenridge could haul in a breath, the pair had slipped past the carriages lining the pavement and grabbed Heather. Smothering her shocked cry, they hoisted her up, carried her to the coach, and bundled her inside.

"Hey!" Breckenridge's shout was echoed by a coachman a few carriages down the line.

But the men were already tumbling through the coach door as the coachman whipped up his horses.

Breckenridge was down the steps and racing along the pavement before he'd even formed the thought of giving chase.

The traveling coach disappeared around the curve of the crescent that was Wadham Gardens. From the rattle of the wheels, the coach turned right up the first connecting street.

Reaching the carriage where the coachman who'd yelled now sat stunned and staring after the kidnappers' coach, Breckenridge climbed up and grabbed the reins. "Let me. I'm a friend of the family. We're going after her."

The coachman swallowed his surprise and released the reins.

Breckenridge swiftly tacked and, cursing at the tightness, swung the town carriage into the road. The instant the conveyance was free of the line, he whipped up the horses. "Keep your eyes peeled—I have no idea which way they might go."

"Aye, sir—my lord. . . ."

Briefly meeting the coachman's sideways glance, Breckenridge stated, "Viscount Breckenridge. I know Devil and Gabriel." And the others, but those names would do.

The coachman nodded. "Aye, my lord." Turning, he called back to the groom, hanging on behind. "James—you watch left and I'll watch right. If we miss seeing them, you'll need to hop down at the next corner and look."

Breckenridge concentrated on the horses. Luckily there was little other traffic. He made the turn into the same street the coach had taken. All three of them immediately looked ahead. Light from numerous street flares garishly illuminated an odd-angled four-way intersection ahead.

"There!" came a call from behind. "That's them—turning left into the bigger street."

Breckenridge gave thanks for James's sharp eyes; he'd only just glimpsed the back of the coach himself. Urging the horses on as quickly as he dared, they reached the intersection and made the turn—just in time to see the coach turn right at the next intersection.

"Oh," the coachman said.

Breckenridge flicked a glance his way. "What?"

"That's Avenue Road they've just turned into—it merges into Finchley Road just a bit along."

And Finchley Road became the Great North Road, and

the coach was heading north. "They might be heading for some house out that way." Breckenridge told himself that could be the case . . . but they were following a traveling coach, not a town carriage.

He steered the pair of blacks he was managing into Avenue Road. Both the coachman and James peered ahead.

"Yep—that's them," the coachman said. "But they're a way ahead of us now."

Given the blacks were Cynster horses, Breckenridge wasn't worried about how far ahead their quarry got. "Just as long as we keep them in sight."

As it transpired, that was easier said than done. It wasn't the blacks that slowed them but the plodding beasts drawing the seven conveyances that got between them and the traveling coach. While rolling along the narrow carriageways through the outskirts of the sprawling metropolis, past Cricklewood through to Golders Green there was nowhere Breckenridge could pass. They managed to keep the coach in sight long enough to feel certain that it was, indeed, heading up the Great North Road, but by the time they reached High Barnet with the long stretch of Barnet Hill beyond, they'd lost sight of it.

Inwardly cursing, Breckenridge turned into the yard of the Barnet Arms, a major posting inn and one at which he was well known. Halting the carriage, to the coachman and James he said, "Ask up and down the road—see if you can find anyone who saw the coach, if they changed horses, any information."

Both men scrambled down and went. Breckenridge turned to the ostlers who'd come hurrying to hold the horses' heads. "I need a curricle and your best pair—where's your master?"

Half an hour later, he parted from the coachman and James. They'd found several people who'd seen the coach, which had stopped briefly to change horses at the Scepter and Crown. The coach had continued north along the highway.

"Here." Breckenridge handed the coachman a note he'd

scribbled while he'd waited for them to return. "Give that to Lord Martin as soon as you can." Lord Martin Cynster was Heather's father. "If for any reason he's not available, get it to one of Miss Cynster's brothers, or, failing them, to St. Ives." Breckenridge knew Devil was in town, but he was less certain of the others' whereabouts.

"Aye, my lord." The coachman took the note, raised a hand in salute. "And good luck to you, sir. Hope you catch up with those blackguards right quick."

Breckenridge hoped so, too. He watched the pair climb up to the box seat of the town carriage. The instant they'd turned it out of the yard, heading back to London, he strode to the sleek phaeton waiting to one side. A pair of grays the innkeeper rarely allowed to be hired by anyone danced between the shafts. Two nervous ostlers held the horses' heads.

"Right frisky, they are, m'lord." The head ostler followed him over. "They haven't been out in an age. Keep telling the boss he'd be better off letting them out for a run now and then."

"I'll manage." Breckenridge swung up to the phaeton's high box seat. He needed speed, and the combination of phaeton and high-bred horses promised that. Taking the reins, he tensioned them, tested the horses' mouths, then nodded to the ostlers. "Let 'em go."

The ostlers did, leaping back as the horses surged.

Breckenridge reined the pair in only enough to take the turn out of the yard, then he let them have their heads up Barnet Hill and on along the Great North Road.

For a while, managing the horses absorbed all of his attention, but once they'd settled and were bowling along, the steady rhythm of their hooves eating the miles with little other traffic to get in their way, he could spare sufficient attention to think.

To give thanks the night wasn't freezing given he was still in his evening clothes.

To grapple with the realization that if he hadn't insisted

Heather leave Lady Herford's villa—hadn't allowed her to walk the twenty-cum-fifty yards along the pavement to her carriage alone—she wouldn't have been in the hands of unknown assailants, wouldn't have been subjected to whatever indignities they'd already visited on her.

They would pay, of course; he'd ensure that. But that in no way mitigated the sense of horror and overwhelming guilt that it was due to his actions that she was now in danger.

He'd intended to protect her. Instead . . .

Jaw clenched, teeth gritted, he kept his eyes on the road and raced on.